War with Kandrok

War with Kandrok

Death Bringer
Book III
Part I

Zodiac Universum

Adrianna Biełowiec

WAR WITH KANDROK

By Adrianna Biełowiec

***

All material contained herein is Copyright
Copyright © Adrianna Biełowiec, 2022

***

Originally published in Polish as Wojna z Kandrok
Translated and published in English with permission.

***

Paperback ISBN: 979-8-9869299-8-9
ePub ISBN: 979-8-2151853-0-8

***

Written by Adrianna Biełowiec
Published by Royal Hawaiian Press
Cover art by Tyrone Roshantha
Translated by Szymon Nowak
Publishing Assistance by Dorota Reszke

***

For more works by this author, please visit:
WWW.ROYALHAWAIIANPRESS.COM

***

Table of Contents

About 30,000 B.C.

"Object number two thousand and twelve," Tepew, bored, muttered under his breath. He glanced at a gold platform next to a test space, on which a virion-shaped device recording the course of an experiment was working. "Dead man."

Nimja set about inspecting the still-warm body of the humanoid jaguar, pinned with rims and chains to a couch. Extreme terror still smoldered in the eyes getting blurry, jaws flung open in postmortem contraction. In the bright laboratory light, the aftermath of a thousandfold accelerated transmutation that the body couldn't withstand was clearly visible: the cat's tail reduced almost to a tailbone, the mottled fur almost transformed into human skin, the claws embedded in the fingers, the muzzle contracted into a caricature of a face, additional lopsided joints of the hind paws ... legs? Again, that damned "almost" dominated. Tepew wanted to see absolute perfection in front of him, so that not even an Onkalot hair remained on the perfectly human body.

"Take him." He waved his hand towards the carcass.

Two slaves standing by the door, invading Tepew's privacy as much as the ceiling above his head, moved to the center of the room. They unhooked the body, grabbed it from both sides and began carrying it to a bio-integration chamber connected by an isthmus to the laboratory. The Nimja member watched them indifferently as they passed. He could easily dispose of the corpse by himself, for example breaking it telekinetically into atoms, but he loved the feeling when he was served, and moreover it took a lot of energy to use the faculties of his mind. By manipulating their genes, he had created many varieties of slaves in his image, giving them the form of a humanoid dog-like appearance; they could even interbreed. They had pointed ears like his sticking out on top of their heads, short mouths, feet and hands with vestigial claws, and large tails. Furs of various colors and lengths, but not black. This coat color was reserved exclusively for Nimja, it occurred naturally rarely anyway, dominated by the variations of gray that also fell to his assistant, the Bone Crusher, as Nacxit had been named by Onkalots. Tepew, in turn, had been called by this simple feline people of Chulimal the Off-kilter Fang. It came from the upper left tooth, which was broken in the middle. Tepew could regenerate him instantly in many ways, such as with a molecular glue with the properties of stem cells, but he left this one shortcoming in himself to remind him of how much he hated Nanawak who had once disfigured him. Coming back to the color of the coat: he was proud that a few million years earlier he had been born black and rare. That he didn't have to change anything in himself. Flowing, inwrought robes, diadems, and staves of power also belonged exclusively to the kind of gods. Made for physical labor and obeying orders, slaves might have been more muscular and taller than Nimja members, having some of their genetic material, but they would never catch up with their creators in intelligence. Their clothes also had to be simple, usually they wore furs, tunics, armor or just hip covers.

"Give me another one."

Tepew walked to the window and glanced at the landscape of Tamasul: three moons visible at this time, columnar mountains tens of kilometers high, crystal clear bodies of water, lush flora, and a mass of multicolored precipitated crystals protruding from the red soil like splayed hand bones. There were over a hundred Nimja members on the planet, and they all experimented at one research center, which seemed to be as rare as the natural presence of life in space. Once upon a time, a harmonious nation of travelers and creators had gradually transformed into a society of loners, offensive to each other, each preferred to live in isolation, surrounded by inventions, slaves and the growing madness of bored beings who had achieved immortality and had probably seen everything already. Developing mind-related technology had made them introverts. But it seemed like a cosmic constant - the fruits of civilization destroyed the bonds between beings everywhere.

Nimja evolved from a being called resib, which through biological convergence formed on their home planet. It resembled an Earth jackal except that it was more barrel-shaped, coarse, and muscular. When Nimja learned to reach the stars, they discovered that the universe was not one, but that there were infinitely many of them in the cosmos - they couldn't determine it definitively, because they had never personally, measuredly, or with the help of psionic probing of the Observers, to which belonged Nanawak, found the Ultimate Boundary. They also hadn't found intelligence in space. They were terrified to find themselves alone among dense animals, sometimes discovered in worlds with suitable living conditions. Only some of them showed pathetic scraps of higher intellect. Nimja members realized that since they were alone and had knowledge, maybe such was a cosmic plan - they had been formed to create. So, they found the right organisms and by rummaging in their genetic material, often adding their own or artificially creating them from scratch, they formed intelligent species. For example, from monkeys and pigs with soft, pink skin, they created delicate, tailless people, the same genetic material, slightly changed, was used to create Kandrok, while jaguars were used to create the wild nation of Onkalots. Fauna, flora, cultural elements and languages jumped from planet to planet, distributed by Nimja, evolving locally. Initially, the creators had perspectives, but over time they treated creationism as pure entertainment and an experimental field. They created because they could. They placed species on different globes, favoring some more over others, and for tens of thousands of years they watched what happened.

Once it occurred to them that it would be interesting if their creations ever started to fight with each other.

Tepew liked the evil, aggressive nation Kandrok from the planet Asephor 'Cerotis, which had already invented nuclear weapons, while Earthlings still wallowed and it looked like they would not invent the wheel for millennia. Perhaps they would need to be helped, because what kind of entertainment would it be when Kandrok found and attacked them one day, and people would throw stones at their spaceships? Therefore, Nimja gathered at Tamasul to jointly improve or degrade the quality of their organic products, they could conduct other experiments along the way. Usually, men and women met every few centuries for procreation purposes (despite many ways to obtain offspring, it was decided to keep the pleasant act of copulation), and less willingly to cooperate. Tepew hoped there would be no conflict between them like the last time, which had resulted in a battle and turning another fertile planet into a barren desert.

After a long time, not two guards entered the laboratory, but three, holding the struggling and thundering Onkalot. Tepew, who kept cold indifference sprinkled with boredom, was somewhat surprised by this symptom of energy and bravado in the experimental subject. The beings of Chulimal were, as a rule, quiet and indifferent to their fate. The imported humanoid jaguar, however, wanted to fight. Despite the chains on his paws, he tore the guard's mouth with his claws, and the latter punched him in retaliation. "Evidently there are changes in certain tribes of humanoid jaguars," the Nimja member thought.

"Enough."

Telekinetically, he inflicted pain on the Onkalot and sent him to the ground. Gasping, curled up, he was moved by the guards onto a couch. They attached the chains to grapples and rings, connected apparatus. Tepew would have dealt with the object using mind control or just a touch of telekinesis, but the cutting-edge experiments performed may have proved to have unpredictable results.

He turned on the virion recorder so that he didn't miss even the slightest change in the humanoid jaguar's body. If the experiment eventually succeeded, Tepew would have a complete set of detailed records at his disposal.

"Object number two thousand and thirteen. The injection didn't work the last time, so let's try a new artifact now. Maybe this version will do something."

Sweeping the shining, clean floor with a flowing robe, he walked over to a nearby terrarium; along with Tepew moved spherical robots sending convenient lighting from above. With caution and considerable apprehension, he took out a golden mouse. It was not an ordinary animal, but the progenitor of innovative technology - a living artifact encrusted with gold, which distorted, transformed and directed cosmic energies. By pairing the mind with it, it was possible to change one organism into another, or to influence the environment by means of thoughts. Nobody could say who the creator of the artifact was and where it came from, rumor had it that it was created by someone much more powerful than Nimja, perhaps even theoretically existing Kzan Mukata themselves. Tepew thought this was utter nonsense, but nevertheless decided to try the new method in his fruitless experiments.

The dizzy Onkalot had trouble focusing his eyesight, but managed to register Tepew putting the small rodent in a container next to the couch. He recognized it was the mouse. What was it for? Was this a reward snack for working with this monster? Once he regained his normal vision, he tilted his head back and stared at the animal with his green eyes. There was something about it that attracted attention and disturbed at the same time, but it was not about the specific color of the gods' ore. The fear appeared unexpectedly, as if it had come from an extra-mental source. The Onkalot felt his whole body find itself in the range of this terrible force that he didn't comprehend, so he couldn't defend himself against it. There was not much he could do anyway, pinned to the couch. He glanced at the Nimja member, looking for an explanation on his face, at least a hint of sympathy, but saw only satisfaction and a growing contentment manifested by a gleam in his eyes, raising his lips, and exposing his fangs.

The humanoid jaguar jerked himself in a violent paroxysm of pain. He roared. Muscles involuntarily arched the body as far as they could. If it hadn't been for yokes, he would have broken his spine. He watched in extreme horror as his torso changed, and there was no way he could stop this blasphemous process. Tepew could - but satisfied, the Nimja member preferred to observe the torment of his research object. The slaves handed him something orange through the cannulas, and the pain eased a little, but still caused unbelievable suffering.

His tail began to contract and languish like a dead snake lying in full sun for days, until ... it dropped off! He lost all claws similarly. Off the beautiful, mottled fur was falling hair until the critical point, till no hair could hold onto the root, revealing smooth skin. Then it got even worse - something started to happen to the bones that began to transform and move.

The screaming Onkalot gurgled as he vomited blood and bile; the organic liquids flowed out also of the remaining orifices of the body. In addition, there were also skips like in a person dying from a neurotoxin.

He was so exhausted that he finally ceased to care. It didn't matter if he died or lived, because that life didn't belong to him anyway.

Metal rang - the slaves took the safeguards off him and those nasty tubes sticking out of his body like giant leeches. To his own disbelief, he realized that he was no longer tormented by agony. Under natural conditions, such excruciating pain didn't subside from breath to breath. Focused on the mice, he glanced at his body with fear and his heart beating madly. He no longer had the strength to scream as he examined the naked pinkish skin, nails instead of claws, hands instead of paws. And his teeth? What happened to his teeth?! Now he had small, fragile rectangles!

Tepew wasn't grinning in savage satisfaction as he looked at the human after the accelerated transmutation, though that should have been the reaction to his success achieved at last, he was concerned. Everything had happened too fast; no one knew anything about this damned artifact.

"Object number two thousand and thirteen," he dictated to the recorder, "completely changed. Visually, no errors are visible. The unidentified artifact called q'umaraq turned out to be appropriately modified. I am committing it for further research to rule out random effects. Bone Crusher, come here!"

No answer came. Tepew looked into a short corridor connected to an adjacent laboratory separated by a membrane.

"Bone Crusher, come here! It worked!" He sent the message telepathically. Certain things were not appropriate to be discussed at a distance.

The assistant, whom Tepew liked to call by the nickname given to him by the savages, sat surrounded by a group of Onkalots, explaining to them how to build a pyramid with appropriately arranged rock blocks. It was a favorite species of the Crusher, therefore, wanting them to feel more comfortable with him and to better assimilate the lessons of the 'god of the stars', he transferred the atole from the natural body to the artificially created one. He took the form of a similar anthropomorph, covered with very short fur, almost like brick-colored skin, had a cat's head and tail, retained small claws on his limbs, while his back was decorated with black stripes. Changing the evolutionary body was not uncommon among Nimja members, though the conservative majority saw it as an insult to the species. Having caught the transmission, the Crusher got up and walked into the next room, deactivating for a moment the membrane separating the environments. In Tepew's transmutation lab also appeared gray Nanawak with heterochromatic eyes - one yellow and other green. He worked in the next room with Kandrok's scientist, to whom he explained the principles of an ion drive.

"You should help me, not do stupid things," Tepew said to the Crusher.

"In fact, I'm done. My Onkalots can now be released on Chulimal. They will build pyramids."

"If they learn something from your lessons." Tepew presented the broken tooth in a mocking smile. "Have you forgotten? We designed them so that they stop developing soon."

The Crusher didn't like this directive from the time when new intelligent species had been created, but as an assistant and low in the hierarchy, the young Nimja member didn't have much to say. He could at most mumble his grievances in solitude.

Looking at the man watching his body in amazement, Nanawak pursed his lips contemptuously.

"I bet that accelerated transmutation wasn't going well, so you substituted the man when no one was looking, and only then you called us." As an Observer, he knew that it wasn't true, but he couldn't let go of his irony at Tepev, who would now start to strut in front of everyone because of his success.

"Then see the recording," Tepew replied calmly, not letting himself to be provoked. The Crusher began to walk around and eye the man up, which ended up with one staring into the eyes of the other - the Nimja member in appreciation of Tepew's genius, and the man in horror, aware of the power of these damned gods. "I used q'umaraq."

"Risky. We don't know what this artifact is." Nanawak crossed his arms over his chest. "Okay, the experiment was successful, congratulations. But how are you going to use this phenomenon?"

"Put him back in the observation room and secure him." Tepew gestured to the human guards, then replied, "I don't know yet."

"You have to take into account the fact that your success may have been a one-off." The Nimja member made a point of fanning the flame of their silent rivalry.

"You'll see that we'll soon have more animal gold artifacts at our disposal."

"We can give them to Onkalots, they are the weakest after all," suggested the Crusher shyly. "I don't think upgrading them with psionic abilities is a bad idea either."

Nanawak began to wander around the room, looking at small animals in terrariums brought from different planets. He stopped in front of a badger.

"Let Onkalots get psionic abilities, but adding artifacts to that would be an exaggeration. Q'umaraq will be just for us. Kandrok to Asephor 'Cerotis will carry cybernetics. On those people which we made from scratch, unrelated to Earthlings, we will impose a civilization focused on the development of mechanics. What about Earthlings then? The string technology, digital, crystal? Maybe raminator one?"

He stuck his finger out, the badger straightened and started to sniff it through the slits in the lid of the container.

Tepew shot Nanawak's back a dry look. He didn't like that the Observer bossed around like that.

"I'll think about it later, but digital civilization sounds best. The raminator one, based on the energy streams of pulsars and black holes, would push Earthlings forward too quickly, and then we would have to destroy them or weaken their genomes. We have to consult everything with the rest of Nimja. Our project promises to be interesting."

"It will be interesting only in a few, maybe tens of thousands of years." Nanawak smiled cruelly. He moved and this time he pulled a terrified mouse out of a terrarium. He made a cage of the clawed hand, curving his fingers into bows, and watched in amusement as the squeaking animal tried in vain to squeeze through the small slits.

Pretending to be always submissive, the Crusher looked at his neighbors with mock, silent indifference. He knew he had to do something about q'umaraq, which was only a neutral tool in itself. In him as a poor Nimja member, no one would be interested, so he should have easily stolen the artifact, reached Chulimal alone and released it somewhere in dark jungles of the planet, so that other Nimja members couldn't duplicate this mysterious technology. In turn Onkalots would gain the valuable defensive weapon; there would probably be no one among them who wanted to use the artifact with malicious intent. After all, the restraining genes of humanoid jaguars couldn't have caused them to become monsters like Kandrok.

Genetics was not, however, one of the Crusher's strengths. He also didn't witness the aggression of some isolated experimental objects, whose distant descendants one day would create the Jun Kame tribe.

1. Hunt for human game

For General Kiret Biffter, phobic delusions began to mix with reality as space sickness took its toll on him. It was experienced by those who were stuck in a machine burdened with speed and radiation, which didn't properly protect the bodies of the crew.

The fact turned out to be the first explosion, when Kandrok damaged the stern of the naval craft Perfarius, which was preparing to jump with the elevator's propulsion. Then there was an acceleration, and the great unknown whether the sensations accompanying the journey were real, or the anoxic, shaken brain produced fictional images. "The hallucinations in space didn't seem to be so real, and didn't last that long," the former emperor contemplated. "Are they also felt organoleptically? If you see a destroyed planet on a holograph, can you hear the thunder of an explosion coming from it, and smell the stench of burning while you are still above the atmosphere?" To Necron, who had never been drunk silly, these matters were alien (but the road to it didn't seem very long, as he had drunk more and more recently). He also didn't experience any major irregularities in the operation of the equipment during spatial flights.

He had time to think of Lieutenant Tsar Seymour who would have a lot to say about the vision, when another explosion occurred along with a shock. Life support systems gave Kiret a decent boost - a designer drug injection, an electrical impulse and a charge of cold compressed air brought him back to full consciousness. He felt as if he had been stripped and tortured by a group of thugs, and then on his bloody body had been put acid-drenched armor.

Jenny Sandstorm was sitting beside and screaming, staring at the cover in front of her. It is possible that it was her screams that brought Necron back to functionality condition.

He was totally confused!

Now they were really breaking, in a spiral of fire, through the atmosphere of some planet, and well-terraformed. It certainly wasn't CD4G5 named Ghost Planet - the original destination of their journey, where Necron had intended to hide Jenny from Kandrok. The local sky sparkled with a perfect blue, the vegetation had gotten solidly wanton, the air gloated over cleanness - at least visually, because Kiret couldn't determine its composition - and the river to which they were approaching in diving flight ... There were no rivers on CD4G5, only artificial lakes, where water molecules had formed as a result of the breakdown of local compounds and the synthesis of precipitated elements.

"We will die!" Sobbed Sandstorm, effectively interrupting the general's thoughts senseless at such a dramatic moment.

Kiret felt a momentary dread when it turned out that the AI was not working, which prevented 'Perfarius' from autonomously aligning the flight. However, the damaged ship could be steered manually, although to a limited extent - the fins unnecessary in space were being blocked by something. Kiret tried to find out where they were. Few instruments functioned, all armament was out of service, interplanetary and interstellar navigation too. Fuel had evaporated or leaked, and the main batteries were fried. Yellow acrid fumes from the board lining began to build up in the cockpit. Out of the drives remained anti-gravity one, but it had enough power to, at best, plow the ground, as in the antediluvian landing method. Behind the ship stretched a long tail of black smoke emerging from the crown of fire. However, puffs presented themselves worse in the place they had pierced - they looked like a circular gate to hell. Or the radioactive throat of a pulsar bringing death to all that existed, where lightnings of unnatural origin banged.

Kiret realized that he was seeing the effect of using the elevator drive too close to the planet.

So, the node was created nearby, though theoretically it shouldn't, because it was materio-phobic, on which Captain Victor Shane had once discoursed. Necron didn't rule out that there had been some physical reaction during Kandrok's fire. After all, what did Kiritians know about enemy weapons and nodes? Judging by the state of the clouds, Perfarius must have been thrown after the leap perhaps two hundred thousand kilometers from the thermosphere, because if it had found itself in the atmosphere, the conveyor energy wave would have swept away half a continent.

"Atla," Biffter voiced his guess. "It must be Atla. Something didn't work and we were thrown onto Atla." He placed comfortingly a hand on the teenager's trembling shoulder for a moment. "It's okay, Jenny. It's over. We escaped from Kandrok. Report," he said instinctively, and immediately corrected himself, "Did something happen to you? How are you feeling?"

"Shitty." The girl tried to suppress her fear with vulgarity. But Kiret was satisfied with the answer. A complaining, spewing or joking soldier in unfavorable conditions is a healthy soldier. If he doesn't do any of these things, then either something's wrong with them or are dead. This also applies to civilians.

"Relax, child, I will land in a moment."

Jenny didn't react to being called a child. She turned her head to the right and, resigned, watched the sea of deciduous forest, typical of temperate climate zones. "Maybe it's right that we are above Atla," she thought, "but probably somewhere to the north, because at Biffter's residence there are other plants and a warmer climate."

Keeping his hands on the control boards, Kiret pressed harder and harder to stabilize the flight. He probably wouldn't be able to lead the constantly descending machine to a flight parallel to the ground, but at least he would prevent them from dying in the crash, sticking the nose into the ground. If he lowered the angle of inclination a few more degrees, they would land in about ten kilometers. He hoped not in a broad river to the right.

He wondered which area of Atla they might have been in, since he couldn't see people. Nobody came to their rescue, contacted 'Perfarius', and it wasn't surrounded by territorial protection. Not to mention, autonomous vehicles should have flown into the vicinity of the hole in the atmosphere like wasps to sugar.

And yet someone did come - three Kandrok machines fell out of the tunnel.

The V-formation caught up easily with Perfarius and overtook it, flying higher like ravenous birds over their wounded prey. It turned back in a bend at cosmic speed, showing off its skills. From the very beginning, the pilots had triumphed over the defeated enemy, so they didn't kill it right away.

"It's them again!" Jenny squealed. "They've managed to find us!"

"I'm not blind," growled Kiret, angry in turn: at the enemy, himself, the girl. Drenched in sweat, he tried to remember everything he knew about the cybernetic people. Anything useful at the moment.

The machines as ugly as broken bricks vanished from sight, but reappeared. One fired into the ground, throwing a geyser of earth into the air that reached the underbelly of the ship.

"They are playing, shitty bastards ..."

"They will kill us, won't they?" Jenny whined.

"We have to crash the ship."

"So, it's over?"

"No, salvation."

The ground was fired again, this time it was treated with a long-radius energy cannon that cut it like a laser metal, which was like a fracture in the eight-degree Richter quake. An analogous geophysical device - so ingeniously named the Earthworm - had been once constructed by Earthlings as part of the HAARP program, around which a number of conspiracy theories had arisen. Originally, it had been intended to be used to dig depressions for collectors, open-cast mines or riverbeds, as well as to study the deep layers of the planet, but it ended up, as always, with turning the civilly useful thing into the weapon.

Kiret tried to open the lower emergency hatch from the cockpit, but it was stuck for good. He decreased the thrust of the anti-gravity drive. The machine slowed down, but began to descend faster and at a dangerously sharp angle, also deviating from what couldn't be called a course. Fortunately, they still had time.

The ships disappeared from view again, as if the unhurried pilots had flown to take a preliminary look at the planet.

They turned back soon.

The closest one fired at Perfarius so as to add a notch to the damage list, not intending to destroy the ship, but to humiliate the crew of two. And the enemy succeeded in it - Kiret couldn't remember the last time he had felt so powerless and humiliated. Probably hundreds of years earlier, when he had been forcibly drafted into the New Order Army in France and had had to pretend to Masonic officers that he had believed in the ideas and views he had hated. He had done it then in defense of the family. Now he had nothing: family, nation, power, achijes' trust and friends. He was fighting only for Jenny's life.

The interior shook as something exploded in the engine room and on the tail. The girl sobbed; Kiret shouted a stream of swear words. Smoke, like the whiskers of a large catfish, now trailed in tarry ribbons from the bow as well, obscuring visibility.

"Here you are, steer." Jenny was appalled as Necron pointed to the instrument console.

"But I can't!"

He gripped the girl's hand aggressively and placed her open palm on the control panel.

"Long ago, vehicles were built whose operation was learned for months. But for some time now, equipment has been made just like for idiots, that the monkey's intelligence is enough to control it. Just press down and keep your fingers like that, the back of your hand more to the right. Harder. More. Oh, that's right! It's easy, isn't it? Bear it so for a while. Don't change the pressure force."

"Kiret, why are you unfastening? What are you doing? What's this naval craft crashing about?!"

"I'll try to open the emergency hatch from the inside, the one in the engine room. We are going to jump into the water. If Perfarius shatters a moment later, we might cheat the enemy."

"They will immediately discover that we survived!"

The general didn't reply, just left the cockpit, holding onto objects along the way. Jenny's thinking was good. Even an idiot with primitive technology like lycans from Chulimal would have detected there were two people in the water. But he couldn't think of anything better. Maybe they'd have a chance if there were the moment when the enemy having a great fun decided to fly away again, and the swift current of the murky river below swiftly swept them away from the jump place. Outdoor water and air shouldn't have been toxic, since the area was overgrown with lush vegetation, including bio-indicator tree species, very sensitive to pollution and deficiencies of biogenic elements.

Kiret slid his hermetically sealed helmet over the rest of the armor. Bumping against the walls, even falling over once, he reached the engine room. Having closed the hatch behind him, he squeezed into a niche bordered by engine chambers.

Though he was sturdy and reinforced with the biometal armor, he was unable to open the little door by hand. The frame and leaf fused together, rendering the lever actuator useless. Even with a tenfold increase in force, it would have been impossible to smash the jammed hatch.

Kiret had anticipated this, that's why he had taken a combat plasma thrower along the way.

"What about Kandrok?!" He shouted, hoping Jenny would hear him. In haste, he hadn't thought to give her the communicator; the failure prevented communication with the cockpit through the helmet.

Silence.

Since the naval craft wasn't being jerked and there were no further explosions, it meant that Jenny, dumbfounded with nerves, was probably coping.

The temperature was rising rapidly. The Kiritian fell to his knees, leaned back, and, holding the weapon in both hands, opened fire.

With hot combat plasma, he attacked the hatch and frame. In the cramped room, the temperature had already jumped to over eighty degrees Celsius, but inside the armor it was optimal for the body.

Necron wasted gas from all six side magazines and managed to burn only a crack.

"Screw it."

He slung the strap of the weapon over his chest. The plasma would regenerate itself over time as a result of the autonomous chemical reactions inside the thrower's chamber, before he filled the magazines again.

Necron hurried back to the cockpit. Jenny sat stiffly in the same position he had left her in. Fear had eradicated all her previous hysteria.

"Where's Kandrok?" Necron asked.

"I don't know."

"We'll have to go ou..."

A shot.

Flash.

Fire.

Powerful shock.

Jenny was insured by the armchair's breast plates, but Kiret flew back against the console. The armor prevented him from breaking his spine and crushing his skull.

The enemy appeared over Perfarius out of nowhere. The badly damaged ship couldn't follow its movements, and the Kandrok members made even no effort to mask themselves, having a great time.

They unintentionally solved the problem of Kiret and Jenny's escape - the explosion destroyed the chassis under the propulsion chambers which were torn out along with a piece of the stern. The rear gate came off. Thanks to the hole that was created, part of the fire was extinguished, and a per mil of the toxins escaped outside. Unfortunately, the equipment needed for the survival of the crew also fell out.

Kandrok began making far turns again.

Perfarius was completely beyond the control of the pilot. It turned slightly to the right and began heading with its bow towards a treeless hill.

"We're escaping! This is our chance!"

Necron released coughing Jenny from the safeguards of the armchair. He pressed a found rag into her hand.

"Here you are, press it to your face. The air is still poisonous."

Struggling with the acceleration gravity, holding the girl with one hand and gripping the unevenness of the deck with the other, the Kiritian made his way to the gap.

Semiconscious, Sandstorm meekly obeyed all commands, but panicked as she saw the frothy river fleeing far below.

"I won't jump ..."

"Yes, you will."

Kiret pushed her off the board. She flew with a shriek, losing the cloth. He himself jumped right after a splash between the current and the shore sounded. If he had waited a few more seconds, they would have had to jump onto the boulder-strewn ground.

As he fell into the cool water, he thought that there were too many things he hadn't considered. That, despite his strength and the emergency air tank under the neck, something could go wrong and he would drown if the river turned out to be too deep and the current too fast. He hadn't asked the girl if she could swim. But the water might have turned out to be shallow, full of boulders and rocks. Or biologically contaminated. There were more negative factors that could be named, so Kiret turned off his mind to these matters. He had to rely on luck again, which he hated to do. Too many variables, too little role of man.

He estimated the depth of the river at four meters when he gently touched the bottom.

A bright flash nearby marked the spectacular end of Perfarius. Kiret felt sad, he liked this pioneer of the flight to Tamasul. A swarm of junk fell into the water. It bumped harmlessly against the armor of the Kiritian wandering on the bottom, but most of the debris floated away diagonally with the current. The world above the surface was pulsing with rippling black, yellow and red. Only now, as Necron stood and looked up, could he see the effects of using the elevator drive near the planet. He was grateful to the water that it limited this gloomy sight, for which he would have been lynched at once by the natives if they had found the perpetrator of the disaster. If any people had lived here.

Thanks to his helmet cover he had a good view of the underwater landscape, clouded by the silt and sand dragged by the current. He got entangled in plants with numerous crowns strung on the stems. He tore one from the bottom and brought it to his face. He recognized the subspecies of milfoil. Nearby, there was a swinging colony of underwater grasses, intensely green, with a translucent skin. "There are still not enough components to finally identify the planet," Necron thought. It could be any terraformed, where rivers were created, for the same species of flora and fauna were distributed everywhere, often as biological synthetic organisms called modificants. A private colonial exploration company even created animals that looked like taken from Karicon, the planets of the assassin Divinus: dragons, unicorns, and forms of centaurs, created by mixing a horse with a monkey. Genetics made it possible to create an infinite number of combinations, the only limitation was the imagination and human ethics.

The funnel bottom turned out to be relatively steep, but not very wide, so Necron quickly came out above the surface. The sight of several species of birds flying in droves in the direction opposite to the crash convinced him that he could take the risk and slide off his helmet. The air felt familiar, made him think of something so old and forgotten that the man was unable to come to the right conclusions, as if he had been trying to recall events from his childhood. He could spot no moons in the sky; the yellow dwarf illuminating the globe was setting slowly, lengthening the shadows.

"Jenny!"

He looked around as he walked into the shallows and flailed at the water with his arms. There was no shore on this side, the current had long washed it to the level of a clay hill from which the roots of coastal trees protruded. Further on, there was a young forest composed mainly of beeches, pines and birches. Over the crowns hovered puffs of gray smoke; Kiret estimated that the catastrophe must have occurred a kilometer and a half away. The other side of the river was overgrown with calamus ridden with water clubs, also duckweed lingered in layers. There must have been a ford, for the water reflecting the green of the overhanging branches was almost still. Necron noticed a crooked, crude pier made of stilts and wooden planks used by poor fishermen. So, there could be people in the area.

"Jenny!"

Having grabbed a protruding root, he climbed the quay over the wall of hardened sand. It looked over a small part of the area. There was no trace of the girl. The man scanned the ground with a nucleo-visor built into the helmet in search of biological traces, such as saliva, epidermis or blood. Having found nothing, he began to run down the river as fast as the weight of the armor and repeated protruding obstacles allowed him, with the majority of roots and the moss-grown remains of the wall. The latter was battered to such an extent as if it had been compressed by an enormous weight or smashed by an extremely powerful explosive.

He spotted the girl over two hundred paces away in a recess of a steep bank, in front of a short sand and gravel beach. Facial details blended together due to the distance, but it seemed to him that Sandstorm was sobbing. Maybe she was even hurt. He felt sorry for her.

He felt relieved as he stepped closer. The soaked girl was shivering a little, but the way she sat with her knees pulled up to her chin and the resigned expression on her face denied that something serious had happened to her physically. Nor did he notice any traces of blood.

"Jenny."

She turned her head towards him. She had an expression and florid face, as if she had actually been crying. She was tougher than Kiret had ever thought, but she was still much more sensitive than her mother. Not having much time to look after her, he had spoiled little Sandstorm, to which even more had contributed the Bidwell foster family, treating her like a sugar princess. Anna, being rebel, had had to hide all her childhood, follow military procedures and live with the fact that Kiritians could attack them at any moment. In that respect, Jenny lived like in paradise.

"Is everything all right?" He rather slid than descended to her over a low slope. He crouched down and hugged the girl.

He had expected her to scold him as usual and to explode, but she eagerly wrapped her arms around his neck, remaining resigned and upset.

"Are you fine?" He moved away.

"Yes. I walked a bit and didn't notice anything disturbing about the body."

"That's good."

"Kiret, what do we do now?"

"We will remain hidden for now. Then we'll look for some place where they have interstellar communication. I saw a pier, so there must be people here."

"Do you know where we are?"

Good question. At least now he could allow himself a moment to catch his breath and put the facts together. He got up. The pressure and density of the air didn't tell him much, because as a rule, they were terraforming constants, providing humans with optimal conditions on a colonized planet. The weight of the armor prevented him from accurately estimating gravity, but it didn't hinder him from picking up the nuances of his surroundings. Earlier it had been easier for him to run than on Atla. The sky was free of moons, and he remembered seeing two at once when he had landed for Jenny during the day. It hadn't passed enough time for the satellites to reach the other hemisphere at the same time. A thought occurred to him that made his heart beat faster. He had been considering it for some time, but had stubbornly dismissed it as impossible. Though ...

He saw boomerang-shaped planes on the horizon. The squadron, consisting of six units, was flying upstream at high altitude. It passed the two on the shore, ignoring it, although more likely not seeing, because they were both hidden in the niche, and the planes' geo-scanners might have been inactive. Necron recognized their models.

"F-314 hybrid fighters, with autonomous or manned modes. Damn, what dinosaurs. Looking at the way they are flying, I suppose these are with pilots. Not good." He looked nervously in the opposite direction, feeling that he was missing something important. Jenny rose and stood next to him.

"What's going on?"

"Seems to be a territorial defense. Stay here."

With a few long strides he climbed the escarpment and ran into the hilly forest.

"Go back, you morons!" He thought aloud. He waved his hands desperately. Aside from hoping to be spotted on a thermo-vision or a nucleo-indicator scanner, there was nothing else he could do. Giving light signals with shots of plasma upwards would have been too spectacular, and it would have certainly attracted the wrong eyes.

He heard shots at the same time as he saw flashes obscured by the crowns of beech trees.

Several minutes later, Kiret was at the top of a glacial mountain, with a sufficient view of the Perfarius crash site. Panting, he rested his hands on his open knees and tilted his figure, gasping for breath. After a while he hit the tree with his back and fell to the ground.

No longer one source of smoke stained the clean air, rising for kilometers, but seven. The orange-blue sky was cut by the gray nuggets of Kandrok's machines. They landed in no time, technically literally like flies on dung. Still trying to calm his breathing, Kiret watched as the microscopic pilots emerged from the machines and went to admire closely the work just accomplished.

He heard rapid breathing and the rustle of dry conifer needles and fallen beech leaves.

"You were supposed to stay in the hideout," he said to Jenny.

The girl, not too tired, stopped and looked fearfully at the plain below.

"I've never seen the aftermath of a battle," she commented in a whisper. She fell on the litter beside Biffter, and sank her fingers in it.

Necron was reminded of Batab Gareth's account of his escape from Kiritians' capital. The enemy hadn't been chasing a group of refugees then, and wanting to get rid of them and the plague in one fell swoop, he had dropped a kind of kinetic charge on K'otz'ib'aja, which had destroyed huge tracts of land, and had also sent a powerful shock wave into space. What if the standard procedure of Kandrok, who couldn't get its enemy or didn't want to look for it, acted on the principle of *Destroy everything if you don't find a target*? How would they react if they didn't see the remains of Kiret and Jenny among the wreckage, priority targets to be eliminated? Given the high degree of development of Kandrok, their procedures probably required proof and certainty that pursuit objects were destroyed. So, would they look for them all the way? If they didn't find them, would they destroy a big part of the planet with a kinetic charge, or they would take a cursory look at the crash site, declare the couple dead and fly away?

"We have to run away," Kiret turned to the girl. Even though he hadn't caught his breath yet, he got up and began running down the hill along a different route than the one he had taken to the top.

Jenny didn't ask questions, trusting the general's judgment. She hurried after him, grateful that she no longer had to see the seven death bonfires glowing at the disaster sites.

Kiret led her through the forest, at first near the river, later they went deeper and deeper into the forest. The trees grew away from each other. Low, moraine hills didn't cause breathlessness while crossing them, like the earlier hills. Overall, the terrain was not difficult to travel, but the armor bore hard on Necron, slowing him slightly. So, he turned on an exoskeleton muscle assist, about which he hadn't thought earlier. He felt a cover of lining plates and stabilizing tubes on parts of his body. From now on, the armor would take most of the load, and the operator would have to make only gentle movements to steer it. However, even with the assistance,

Jenny, who loved to run, was ahead of him. She had spent her entire childhood roaming the fields, meadows and forests of Atla, sometimes all day long. She had escaped Martin's gang. Few in the valley, where the colonial estate was located, had been able to catch up with her. After the incident with Martin and rumors spread that she was Forkis' daughter, she had left the Bidwells and moved to the other hemisphere of the planet to the Biffter residence, where she had grown up. Since then, she had run rarely. Now the cell memory of the muscles reminded the girl that she was still capable of high physical exertion and the development of great speed. More than once she overtook the Kiritian, anyway encouraged by him to flee as quickly as possible.

They ran a few kilometers from the observation hill.

"Do you think ... they will drop ... a kinetic charge on us?" Gasping, Jenny caught up with her companion.

Necron stopped, moved the plasma thrower, and leaned his back against a small beech. If it hadn't been for the armor, he would have been even more tired than Jenny.

"How do you know that? Anna told you?"

The girl crouched down next to him.

"I read it ... in your mind. Really. Somehow it worked out by itself."

"Telepathy after Forkis. Nice. It's a pity that you can't read the minds of our enemies, and at a great distance."

"It would certainly come in handy."

"End of the break. We have to go further."

They moved through the forest again.

Necron had never supposed that in power he would be in a situation that would require a long flight on foot. His subconscious mind told him that their efforts made no sense in the long run. Kandrok with its spy technology would surely find them. Maybe they knew about the fugitives, but first they wanted to investigate the downed F-314 fighters, which operated only on the planets of the Old Zone, from where humanity had begun further colonization of space.

And now Kiret brought the enemy to this region.

He came to his senses. He preferred to take nonsensical steps, so that there were any, then to give up and wait for death. Something could always happen, seemingly insignificant, which, however, changed a sealed fate.

Jenny often surveyed the sky anxiously.

The sparse forest was littered with stones and boulders of all kinds, from the size of gravel to colossi larger than a building. Remnants of a city knocked around the area, so old that nothing could be said about its past appearance. The destructive forces of time and nature had done their job, almost merging the products of civilization with the underbrush of the backwoods resurgent after some cataclysm.

After an hour's walk, the terrain became moister and spongy. The wet leaves stopped rustling beneath their feet, water emerged from the soil with every step they took. The trees thinned even more; the pines were completely gone; streaks of mist appeared. It darkened, but the contours of the surroundings were still visible. When it was completely dark, Necron would activate night vision in the helmet and would guide the girl, although she claimed that she didn't need it.

They already thought that the danger was over when a powerful explosion took place kilometers behind them. The shock of the ground knocked them both off their feet. A crimson glow bloomed under the sky as if during a gigantic fire at night. The forest they had traveled through previously disappeared under a dome of unidentified alien energy.

The shock wave turned out to be worse than the earthquake.

Pieces of the destroyed world were flying over the swamp.

After the ground fled from under the girl's feet, she rolled down a steep slope. She fell chest-deep into the marsh.

"Kiret ... Kiret! It's pulling me in!"

"Don't move. I'll help you right away."

"Do something!"

He had no rope with him and no movable equipment except the plasma gun and the X17A4 pistol. He looked for a long branch, but found none at hand. There were no trees nearby, and he didn't have time to look any further, because he didn't know the squishiness of the mud. He noticed boulders overgrown with moss sticking out of the slope, he used them as a support for his legs as he descended. He slipped on the first one and fell into the mud, managed to brake on the next one, covering a few meters on his back.

"Don't move," he instructed the panicked girl again, who, desperately trying to get to the silty shore, was sinking more and more.

The penultimate boulder couldn't support the Kiritian's weight and fell with him into the mud to the left of Jenny. Biffter felt a polished stone with a large, flat surface beneath him. He explored with his fingers the bumps of the engraved letters. He glanced at the boulders on the slope - which weren't boulders.

"Great, old graveyard," he thought, but refrained from commenting out loud. He didn't want the girl to become even more hysterical. A tombstone or not, it made it possible to lie on its surface and outstretch his right hand; Kiret winced as with his left one he pushed a human skull deep into the mud.

He didn't reach Jenny the first time. Alive a moment ago, she froze with her eyes bulging, as if she had become a corpse herself. Only after yelling at her, she begun to cooperate. Kiret leaned even further. He was all covered in mud, as was his companion, who managed to grab the extended hand after another attempt.

Necron pulled her onto the tombstone, invisible because the stone surface was several centimeters under the dirty water. Exhausted, Jenny however only thought about being finally safe; her clothes were completely damaged. The sky above them turned brown, like blood mixed with mud, trickling from her elbow and scratched cheek. The aberration tunnel in the clouds created by Perfarius was still clearly visible. The phenomenon, presumably letting the mixed radiation from cosmos into the planet, presented itself frighteningly, but also amazingly when combined with the color formed after the aliens' bomb explosion. The grayish mist that hung over the swamp had turned orange due to it.

The enemy could be lurking somewhere nearby.

Jenny couldn't stand it and sobbed as she snuggled against Biffter's chest who consolingly put his arm around her. The mud was everywhere, so she gave up on trying to clean her face and arrange her hair.

She was first to spot three black blobs moving soundlessly and high above the fog. They were flying slowly like Jumbo Jets in the twenty-first century.

"I can see it, too," Necron said, feeling her tense muscles.

"Kandrok members."

"I think they are looking for us because they didn't find the remains at the crash site. They are doing it meticulously, which is probably why they are drumbling so much."

"But they have already passed us. They must be flying south, if the star that set is their direction indicator. Why can't they see us?"

"I don't know. Maybe it's the mud's fault. Maybe they can't penetrate the fog with scanners or whatever they're using."

"Mud? Seriously? Are you telling me that the guys who fly between universes have trouble tracking down the fugitives who fell into the swamp?"

"And we as humanity are better? We wanted to colonize space, and we couldn't even cope with a cold, unemployment and tons of garbage. It is said that each omnipotent has some weaknesses, often very inconspicuous. It is not known what natural environment Kandrok live in, it is possible that there is neither mud nor fog. This is likely since they are a cybernetic people and some atmospheric factors may damage their metallized bodies and the electronics they use. But remember that I am theorizing, so don't take this information seriously." Kiret changed position, pushed away Jenny which knelt. They were both staring at the southern sky, where nothing else was visible except for the wisps of fog and the glow after the explosion.

"They flew away. Do you think they'll come back?"

"Hard to say. Let's get out of here." He got up, leapt from the submerged ledger to the hard quay. He grabbed Jenny's hands and helped her get to him safely.

"What if they turn back? Maybe there is really something to this mud and fog."

"You prefer to be stuck like this until morning?"

The girl looked at herself in disgust and shook her head. Kiret managed to clean the helmet cover so that he could use the vision.

A bit further, the slope was lower, though it smelled of stagnant water more. Necron indicated Jenny the direction and moved first. Slipping on a slope and slicked grass, they made their way to a stable ground, and after walking a certain distance, they found themselves on moss carpets. The fog had decreased almost to zero. Only after reaching the rise, they noticed how enormous damage Kandrok had done. The light on the moonless night was still being given by the bloody, electrified glow. The trees of the distant forest had vanished turned to ash; no stump remained.

"They wanted to kill us with some kind of thermal weapon, maybe kinetic-thermal." Necron rested his leg on a boulder, and his forearms on his knee. "Damn bastards. They didn't hesitate to destroy so many hectares of land to get two people."

"I take it you have a plan?"

"First we have to wash because we look like two swamp monsters." He tried to joke, but quickly removed the smile from his face, seeing that the depressed girl looked sadly towards the nonexistent forest. "Then we have to find shelter and rest. Afterward we'll go looking for some kind of comm center where they have interplanetary communication. Since there is a territorial defense here, there must also be key objects somewhere. We'll go that way." He pointed to wooded hills out of the shockwave range, behind which the yellow dwarf had set.

Jenny pressed her chilled hands to her chest, rubbed her muddy arms.

"It's getting cold."

"The whole area looks as if a glacier retreated from it recently. And where a glacier was, you'll find plenty of rivers, lakes and moisture. Be glad there are at least no mosquitoes. Come on." Kiret hugged the shoulders of the girl, who not for the first time looked anxiously at the sky. "I promise I'll do whatever I can to get us unharmed out of this mess."

2. Without logic, without physics

The crew stood speechless, unable to take their minds and eyes off a landscape that probably even Lieutenant Tsar Seymour had never seen during his biggest kick. The environment didn't make a big impression only on the assassin Raver Divinus Relagard, who hailed from Karikon, the reserve planet that had once been the experimental field of Nimja, where phenomena occurred equally strange as those on Amyrade Anfraktoris. Corporal Zira Aytar also tried to appear composed and indifferent, though in spirit she was as bewildered as delighted, but it was not in her nature to externalize her emotions, except perhaps anger. In turn, the youngest corporal, Darius Schindler, indulged himself completely - he fell down on a turkmenite-colored rock from the impression, with his mouth open. Geneticist, technologist, and physicist Sariel Jelinek had symptoms of photogenic epilepsy and wanted to vomit, but like a masochist, he stared wide-eyed at Amyrade's peculiarity, lest he missed the smallest detail.

The team of nine was on a poisonously blue rock. Nearby, there were two drop-spacers - armored rovers that could change geometry, named drops, and designed specifically for this mission. Several dozen meters in front of the crew, the ground gently turned yellow and there was a swamp, then there was a pink prairie and another strip of land smeared with bright colors, as if there had been an argument between the creators of Amyrade first, and then a battle with paint poured from buckets in streams. In the distance, a kilometer-high cap mushrooms bulged, under them grew trees spiral like a narwhal's fang, with colored pebbles instead of leaves, as well as spongy structures like truffles. Transparent rays with vessels and organs showing through the skin, luminous orbs and quasi-whales, whose bizarre morphology could best be called cosmic, floated under the caps like in the depths. If that was not enough, in the place of the clouds there was a ribbon of water iridescent like the Cairo Night stone exposed to light, above it a circum-horizontal arc twitched. Little, bouncing creatures unlike anything alive that teammates had ever encountered, moved across the ground marked by beautiful geodes. They weren't sure if they were moving plants of biology unknown to a human.

"Tell me you don't have anything to do with it," sighed Captain Michael Avadar, who was in charge of the expedition, and looked at Tsar.

"I don't." The corporal raised his hands in surrender, making an innocent face.

"Me neither!" Darius completed as the commander shifted his resigned look to him. It didn't fit Avadar, who was a gentle and indulgent man by nature, of the 'good uncle' category, but he could scream too, and he certainly never lost his self-assurance. From the moment he appeared on Amyrade, it had been as if his hidden self, had been revealed, of a person not very self-confident and melancholic. Darius suspected that to the state of the captain might have contributed this crazy journey understood by no one, except for Nimja, of course, which had arranged it and given almost no directions.

The members of the expedition presented themselves the same, dressed in full, heavy war armor. After the drops appeared on Amyrade, the gear worked for a few minutes. Jelinek barely managed to determine the parameters of the environment before everything conked out. However, by the term 'everything' one had to understand devices of digital technology. The drops stopped running on batteries powered by complex radiation, and they could run only on fuel, which was heavy water. Energy for work was provided by a chemical process in the engine sub-chambers, where deuterium was separated from oxygen. Out of the weapons, just mechanical, or ball one worked; as for optics, only binoculars could be used.

The crew was surprised at the moment of 'landing'. They just appeared on the blue rock. It seemed to them that the extragalactic journey, perhaps to another dimension or beyond the boundaries of the universe, took a second. The drops were not warm. The wheels didn't leave even a centimeter of trace on the sand-covered ground. When Jelinek examined the soil and air, to his amazement it turned out that the environment was optimal for the functioning of the human body. There were no further arrangements, because then the equipment failed. The confused crew members realized that unless condition changed, they would have to cope like people of the twentieth century. Nevertheless, General Kiret Biffter had prepared them for this eventuality and they had been trained. Therefore, he had ordered bullet guns and rifles to be brought along with deuterium water as fuel.

Heavy armor without markings turned out to be a drawback in the absence of digital identification. With their universal sizes and one-way mirror-type anti-radiation face shields, it was difficult to determine who was who, to make matters worse, with the assistance systems turned off, the crew began to overheat.

To the surprise of the rest, Tsar folded the helmet strobilus on the nape of his neck without further ado.

"I feel better at once," he said, smiling brightly. He ran his gloved fingers through his reddish hair and took a deep breath. He glanced at his companions staring at him in amazement. "What? After all, our doc examined the surroundings and everything is alright. Same air as on Morascrik, for real. Anyway, Div is walking without armor and is fine."

He waved his hand at the assassin with a neutral expression on his face, who nodded slightly to him. Div didn't succumb to pressure from Avadar and refused to be trapped with armor, preferring to remain in his dark blue hooded cape, leather garment and Karikon moccasins. Brought up in the world where a simple firearm had just been invented, he was not afraid of the possibility of irradiation, lack of air or the presence of pathogens, which, according to Jelinek, didn't attack organisms from other planets, because they were evolutionarily incompatible with them.

Darius slipped his helmet off right after Tsar.

"Indeed! Wow! The air is just perfect!"

"You'd better be careful, gentlemen," Sariel said mockingly. Though he had been kiritianized at twenty-six, his character and expression were more than once like those of a nervous aged scientist prancing due to his skills. "Maybe you feel well, but it is possible that negative changes have just started taking place in your body. There is no way to examine you. At most, I can shine into your eyes, tap or listen with a stethoscope." He winced at the thought of such an archaic form of examination. In laboratory conditions, a minute of scanning in a medical 'sarcophagus' was enough to have a list of all ailments of the patient. Its portable and analogous form in the field was a neuro-mogram, now inactive for some unknown reason. "Stay in the covers then."

He looked at the achijes with contempt when, right after his words, the strobili were slipped off by the technician Corporal Rasmus Darkoris and his subordinates - Lt. Private Tau Bradshaw and Private Kazuo Shimizu. Avadar and Aytar followed them immediately. Not wanting to pass for the black sheep on the team, Sariel sighed, shook his head, and revealed his face last. The cover electrified his blond hair, which stood on end. The intense colors of the surroundings made him feel even more sick. The spasm shook his body. The man went to the drop for an antiemetic. Puking in front of everyone was the last thing he needed. He wasn't in charge of the expedition, but he was furious anyway that his warning as the most educated person here had been disregarded.

"How do you explain that the conditions of Amyrade are almost perfect for a human?" Shimizu asked.

"Let's wait for Jelinek to come back." Avadar struggled with the scanner on the bracer. "He'll probably have an explanation." He added embarrassed, "Does anyone remember the detailed report based on Aggroteh's story? We don't even have a way to read it."

Everyone ignored reports or read them casually, and that was not the knowledge necessary for the brain transfer by an entraser. A fragment of interest in a given situation was always opened or when preparing for a task. Only where to find it was remembered.

"I remember something, sir," Darius said. "This, well ... I was a little nervous due to the expedition. So, in order to keep my mind occupied and not take ... sedatives again," he looked at Tsar, "I read Aggro's report on the Tamasul expedition over and over again. And there was something like this, "As I looked into the celadon heart of the kariban, I asked the Nimja member what Amyrade Anfraktoris was. Nanawak replied, 'Even I don't know that. I do know, however, that Amyrade is a location that cannot be reached in any way. Where there is no concept of the constant laws of physics. Where everything is changing continuously. Where time and space do not exist. Where the living are not allowed. Amyrade Anfraktoris means the Creators' Trashcan or the Processing Plant, because this place resembles a trial version of a created world, completely unsuccessful. A collection of everything that will someday be logical and arranged. Part of the atole also goes to the Processing Plant, before it changes its form."

"Nice. The character crammed the entire apocrypha dictated by the cat." Seymour nudged the boy's head, who raised his arm to block it too late.

"If there are facts in this Nanawak's words, it is possible that Amyrade's incredibly old dimension is made of non-baryonic material." Jelinek joined the team, folded his arms over his chest. He looked better now.

"Can you be clearer?" The captain asked.

Sariel glanced at Darius.

"The point is that we don't have to be surrounded by matter known to us, made up of particles like protons and neutrons. The world of Amyrade may have arisen in the early days of the universe we know, when baryonic matter didn't exist yet. So, we are dealing with an alien, unexplored, primary structure. Existing so far in theory. Speaking unscientifically: a form of chaos, another dimension."

"And what does this have to do with our mission?" The commander asked.

"That nothing should surprise us and we must be ready for anything, constantly vigilant. Keep our minds open."

"What are the orders, sir?" Aytar asked silent Avadar who thoughtfully looked at the creatures flying over the giant mushrooms.

The man finally encompassed the achijes awaiting his decisions.

"First, let's check the other two artifacts." He motioned to Darius.

The boy crouched down and carefully removed his backpack. They had lost karitan when they had arrived on Amyrade, as announced by Nimja. The artifact, active and pulsating with light, had dissolved at launch, then had simply vanished as if it had never existed. Kariban had become a transparent, faceted and cold ball with an extinguished core that could pass for a nicely made ornament. To the egg-like xik'iri called the Collector was happening something.

After examining the items, Darius hid now unnecessary kariban and focused on the Collector, whom he grasped with his hands. He got up.

"And?" The expedition commander urged him.

"It's slightly warm, I can even feel it through my gloves. As you can see, the inside is glowing red. And I think ..." He put the artifact to his ear. "Yes. It is buzzing. But you only hear it held close to your head."

"And do you ..." Avadar found it hard to pronounce the words, "have mental contact with it like in the base?"

"Nothing. Zero."

"And how does it work?" Bradshaw ran his hand over the dreadlocks.

Avadar looked at the technician corporal.

"Any idea, Darkoris?"

The man, with his face focused, shook his head, staring at the artifact.

"I'm sorry, sir. I'm trying to think of something."

"And you, Tsar?"

The lieutenant raised his hands and shrugged.

"I'm not Alphonso and Omega."

"It's beginning beautifully," disgusted, Jelinek whispered under his breath.

"Something else puzzles me." Div moved aside the tail of the cloak, revealing the case with the dagger. "See? The sapphire in the hilt is glowing blue like it did in the Cargoo base, although I haven't activated it."

"So why are you talking about it only now?" The captain asked. Taking Divinus on the mission had its pros and cons. The pluses were that of all those present here; he had the most resistant psyche when it comes to contact with scientifically unexplained phenomena. The downside was his introverted lawlessness and lack of Kiritian subordination. Avadar turned to everyone, "You are to report to me anything that catches your attention."

"But everything is messed up here and catching attention, sir," muttered Tsar.

"You know well what I mean."

Darius took a few steps to get a closer look at the assassin's dagger. Then his Collector lost its splendor. The surprised boy, inspired by a certain thought, stopped and began to move his hand with the artifact. As he moved it to the right, the light returned to its previous intensity.

Div frowned. He also began to wiggle his dagger taken from his case. The effect was similar to that of the Collector, except that the sapphire glowed bright blue rather than red, most intensely when the assassin extended his arm in the direction opposite to Darius'.

"It looks as if the Collector and the sapphire were showing directions," Aytar voiced loudly the thought of each teammate.

"So, it's something like hunt the thimble?" Tsar threw.

"May I?" She extended her hand to the assassin.

"Sure, Zira."

Aytar took the dagger and began to move with it. Also in her hand, the sapphire worked in such a way that the most intense glow was emitted from it at a specific position in relation to the terrain. She walked forward with her arm extended. The intensity of the light didn't change, it only dimmed when she moved her hand to the left or right. She gave the item back to Divinus and took the artifact from Darius, which immediately became dead in her hands.

"Then I'll try too," suggested Shimizu.

The collector acted the same in his case. Jelinek, Darkoris and Bradshaw tested it successively; the artifact also showed no activity.

"Looks like it is I who will have to wear it." Darius took the item from the hands of the black achij.

"The question is, what do these items indicate?" The assassin said softly. "How are we supposed to interpret this?"

"I guess you should know it best," Jelinek said with a slight reluctance, angry that he couldn't rely on his knowledge, and it was not him that the group's attention was focused on. Amused, Div summed up the words with a cool smile.

"In human civilization it has been assumed that red means a threat," said Darius. "But the heavy star knows what that could mean on Amyrade. Could this little crap really track down Forkis' atole?!"

"Alright," the captain said, clapping his hands. "Since we know more or less the surroundings, let's change into light armor, because heavy will be useless in this environment. It will only disturb and slow down our movements. We will explore the area with all available means and set off in search of atole, if we don't detect known threats. We will have to watch out for everything, take every step carefully, and have our eyes around our heads. Darius, you are setting the direction of the march, because for some reason only you are tolerated by the Collector. I hope at least it doesn't go haywire. But I emphasize a second time: we do everything carefully and pay attention to every pebble. After all, we don't know what xik'iri may indicate. Nanawak may have fooled Aggroteh."

"Can anything be done about it, Captain?" Bradshaw waved at the bland, colorful sights.

"I know that pain. You'd like to get a Daltonics attack," commented Tsar under his breath so that no one heard him. He smiled cavalierly. "Though the views aren't that bad at all! What if ..."

The achijes headed to the drops to change clothes and take kinetic weapons. Div went with them to have also something to shoot besides the dagger, throwing knives stuck in the notches of a leather belt, and a sword. His energetic plasma weapon, which Kiret had given him before the expedition, also didn't work.

"Where are you going?" Avadar asked Seymour, who was about to sneak behind the rock.

"To answer the call of nature."

"I already said: no lawlessness! We are not on Cargoo."

"I didn't want to attend to urgent needs in the presence of the lady." Seymour bowed theatrically to Zira.

"Go ahead," Aytar replied, not looking in his direction. With a disaffected expression, she viewed a multi-mode flamethrower assigned to her. "I've already seen worse things. For example, this Stone Age crap."

"I can assure you that the view would be rather pleasant to see," Tsar grinned. "If you want, you can find out for yourself."

The blue-haired Kiritian woman ignored the frivolous offer, shook her head in disgust and took care of the thrower. Despite the friendly relations between achijes of varying ranks, it would have still sounded strange if a corporal snarled at a lieutenant. Even if the lieutenant in question was an idiot.

"Tsar!" The captain exclaimed as Seymour turned his back on him again and began walking. "What are you up to?"

The lieutenant pivoted on his heel.

"I was thinking ... I mean, I have an idea. But in theory."

"Almost every idea you have concerns getting overdrunk."

"Oh, Mr. commander, why getting overdrunk! I want to test something."

"Then will you enlighten me, or I should give you an order to report?"

Tsar pointed to the monumental mushrooms.

"Not that I have something against such views, but some may suffer from neurological disorders." He looked at the back of Jelinek, putting on elements of light armor on his uniform. "Since we are in dreamlike, distorted Amyrade and everything works upside down, maybe if we take a little bit, looking at the totality will be easier?"

The captain sighed, shook his head.

"And what am I supposed to do with you, Tsar?" He said seriously.

"Let me test the theory in practice. You know me and that I will not hurt myself."

"You put me in a terrible position. If we were at home, you would be disciplined for getting overdrunk before the mission."

"But we're not at home. There is no one else here, and you, Captain, are supreme here."

"I wonder how you even managed to smuggle in drugs. Every gram of load was carefully checked."

Tsar stepped closer, made sure the rest was occupied, and lowered his voice,

"In the same way as you managed to smuggle a dozen liters of vodka in the drop's engine compartment. In the left cylinders."

The captain straightened up.

"Perhaps neither of us," continued Tsar, "apart from Technician Darkoris who didn't deal with the preparation of the drops for the journey, knows how to build them. So, everyone in turn came up with the idea that after the final inspection, would smuggle something in the element that was empty inside and looked like it was needed for the operation of the machine. Apart from the risk of explosion or frying equipment worth billions of uinals, in this way we have a lot of stimulants on both boards. Taking them was like throwing a guy over the edge of a building being renovated, who insults the builders on the roof. Because who normal goes on a dangerous mission without good stuff? Well, maybe except for

Div and Aytar fascinated by him. Nothing but fribble, my soul, there is no hell. Although about the fact that hell doesn't exist, I wouldn't be so sure." He looked around. "So, I understand you agree, sir?"

Amazed, Avadar said nothing. Whistling, Tsar took a small tube out of his pocket, poured rusty powder onto his hand, and sniffed it in front of the commander. He exhaled loudly with satisfaction. The captain waved his hands, went to change and get his backpack and weapons ready.

Seymour was the last to join the group. He put his hands on his hips and proudly looked around with his dilated pupils.

"Ha! I was right! All I can see is a red sky and orange soil of a plain stretching out fu... far away. There are a lot of boulders, some hills in the distance."

The captain thought for a long time, looking at Tsar with an ambivalent expression on his face.

"This will probably be the strangest order in my whole hundred-year-old life, but you are all to get stoned with the same thing."

"Can we talk for a second, sir?" Tsar asked him with an indulgent smirk. They went out of earshot.

"What's up, Lieutenant?"

"It was just a test on my part. Total spontaneity. Nevertheless, I was right, the world of Anfraktoris looks almost normal on a properly selected stimulant, but taking drugs in such a case can only be beneficial for Jelinek. See, Doc is almost green, as if he was about to puke again. He just pretends to be fine. He probably went to vomit behind the drop, so no one see it. We have no solution to his problem, since the electronic vision aid in the helmet covers has failed. Nobody foresaw that we would get high without getting high. So, Sariel can be given the drug, but the rest of the achijes and Div are coping with the environment. The view of the real is desirable during the trip, don't you think so?"

"Tsar is an amazing man," the captain thought. He always played the fool, but he always judged the situation perfectly and hit the nail on the head, even if he happened to do it by accident. He heard that every mission involving Seymour had apparently succeeded. The only time he failed was while searching for Emperor Forkis on Aj.

However, he had a different opinion about the participants of the expedition:

"Such views are normal for you, Tsar. You are somewhat immune to anomalies, which is why you were selected for the mission 'Revival'. But the rest feels uncomfortable, though no one will admit it. Maybe even Div is playing. If we see the alien dimension in the same form as the worlds known to us, it will be easier for us to work, we will become more efficient and effective. Mentally safer. Anyway, that drug of yours probably doesn't act too long."

"No, but it will affect me for a shorter time than the rest anyway, because we have been good friends for a long time. Others may have unpleasant side effects."

"Then you'll single out a smaller dose for everyone."

"I see you won't change your mind, Captain, and relieve only the suffering of the scientist who looks like a vegetable?"

Avadar stared at him hard.

"Well, your will." Tsar shrugged and smiled soothingly. And then he volunteered with his uncomfortable, undisguised honesty, "You're afraid, aren't you? You will feel better if everyone pops something, because it would be embarrassing if only the commander swigged?"

"Tsar, to the line," Michael replied sharply.

After half a terran hour, indicated by spring watches, everyone except Divinus, who despised psychoactive substances, and Aytar, who hadn't taken the stimulant 'in case', took the singled-out dose. The captain also drank a few sips of vodka for confidence, assured by Tsar that it wouldn't react with the drug. He was angry with Seymour that he had known his intention from the beginning.

"The drug is commonly called boatik, it's soft," Seymour explained to the group. "The plant it comes from was first bred on a Proxima Centauri e. It only causes hallucinations. And on Amyrade, as you can see, it works conversely than in our reality."

"After all, this place is a troll house of the gods," commented Shimizu.

"Do you think Anfraktoris really looks like this?" Asked Darius, who had taken boatik right after Tsar. "Why did we see exactly the pseudo-whales, mushrooms and some jumping beings?"

Jelinek put forward the theory:

"It looks as if the flexible surroundings wanted to adapt to the people in it. It is possible that we saw such unreal images because of Divinus, who sees elves, werewolves and dragons on Karikon every day. Our memories were synthesized and the local vision with the common denominator was created."

"Not in everyday life, but sometimes it happens," muttered the assassin from under the hood. His blue eyes seemed to sparkle like the sapphire obscured by the case he wore at his belt.

"Will you make it?" The captain wanted to make sure.

"These views do not impress me," Div replied indifferently.

"And you, Aytar?"

"It's good. Matter of habit."

"Such a visual dissonance can be useful for us when assessing the situation. So, it's time to take a look around. Seymour, you will take Darius and Zira. Darkoris, you'll go with the achijes of your company, Shimizu and Bradshaw. Jelinek and Divinus, to me. You will report to me, assassin, what you see. Communicators are not working, so we will call each other, use flares or smoke grenades. We don't have a way to check distances, so you will have to count the steps or estimate the measurements by the seat of your pants. Don't walk away from the drops more than ten kilometers. Shoot anything that wants to kill you. A lot can happen, so it is not possible to list all of the eventualities. That's why I'm counting on your survival instinct and intelligence. Everyone in the group has someone with a mechanical watch. I'll see you at the drops in four hours at the latest."

"Maybe someone should keep an eye on these drops?" suggested Div.

"The two artifacts are the most important. Without kariban we won't get out of here, and without xik'iri we won't find Forkis' atole. I will have the machines in sight. I took an antique sniper rifle, the vision of which needs to be corrected manually," the captain, used to electronic assistance, didn't refrain from uttering the remark in a biting tone.

They moved in three directions. Schindler's group followed the Collector's signal which led them in the direction opposite to the sapphire's guiding section of Divinus.

"Do you think xik'iri is showing the direction in which we should go to find the emperor's atole?" Darius walked with the artifact glistening red attached to his belt so he could use his hands to manipulate the rifle. He stopped and sighed. "This is all idiotic. What are we doing?"

"Well," said Tsar, walking in front of Aytar, "Amyrade made such a tart of the logic that we know, that it is a wonder that there is no brothel nearby. Although maybe one would be found. Right, Miss Corporal?"

Zira gave him a grudging glance, even before he turned to her, grinning. She didn't like men very much, but because of her work she had learned to tolerate their presence. She had managed to like only Divinus. Although he had grown up in the culturally different world, his past was similar to hers - he had had to fight in the streets for survival. The character and pyramid of values didn't differ much in the two of them either.

"I must admit that the area is interesting," she reported. "A purple tunnel hundreds of meters in diameter, with a turquoise-white light at the end. The walls are cloudy, blurry, as if you were looking into the depths. On the left and right, levitating spheres resembling puffballs of various sizes. Patterns associated with galaxy spirals on their surfaces. Luminous dust floating everywhere, possibly some seeds. Overall, the view is captivating."

"It must be so," Darius thought, for Aytar was rarely enthralled with anything, and she was certainly not in the habit of sharing her feelings with others, like Div, preferring to hide behind a mask of indifference.

"I haven't known you have the soul of a poet, Aytar. Damn. I'm beginning to regret the idea of taking drugs," Seymour groaned.

"These words don't suit you at all, boss." Darius smiled.

"Well, on a normal planet they wouldn't fit. But everything is pointless here, so I don't want to stand out either."

In Schindler's vision, they did indeed enter the huge tunnel, smooth, as if it had been hollowed out by an earthworm of a size none of the team would have wanted to meet. But empty, steel gray and monotonous. The light at both poles came from the scarlet of the sky.

Nothing disturbing happened during the reconnaissance, except for the visual anomalies. Ice bordered with lava like a river with a beach, the sky seemed to look like water, frogs 'swam' in the air, and when Jelinek stumbled over a boulder, instead of falling, he rose for a few seconds as in negative gravity. The visions of the assassin and the Kiritian woman took physical forms for both of them, for example, when Zira had a tree with moving pink branches in front of her, she could lean against its trunk. When surprised, Darius wanted to examine it organoleptically, he passed through it like through a holograph. The drugged group saw similar things to those seen by the sober couple, but more real and unadorned, as was the case with the tunnel in Aytar's vision.

After four hours, they all met at the drops.

"Do you have any idea what Divinus' sapphire might indicate?" The captain wanted to consult another unknown with the team.

"I have no idea," admitted Jelinek, "but we should follow the signal of the Collector, as intended by the mission.

"Because we will do so. There may be time to discuss the dagger if we find this atole first. Now let's take an hour's break, Jelinek will collect the samples and put them in containers, and then we will leave. Tsar, how long does this "blowjob" act?"

Darius, Shimizu, and Bradshaw bowed their heads and laughed softly.

"Boatik, sir," corrected Seymour with a smile. He was sitting on a boulder and tossing a Kalashnikov AKX-912's magazine, which was rising unnaturally high. He noticed that gravity changed character, was more like that of the small size and mass moons when a sharply greater force was applied to an object, regardless of the direction of the vector. "It depends. The bigger lightweight, the longer it lasts. But it shouldn't be less than five Terran hours. My condition is slowly coming to an end. We can be drugged non-stop for a week without harming our health. At least on normal planets made of baryonic matter." He glanced at Jelinek. "But if something goes wrong, there are detoxes in the drop. However, there is no guarantee that they won't work conversely. Someone would have to sacrifice and check."

"So, the old way," Bradshaw grumbled.

After an hour, they were sitting in their vehicles which moved one after the other, using two rows of wheels to move over hard terrain, perfectly coping with the indentations of geodes. The ceilings were pulled apart. Darius sat on the hood of the first vehicle, keeping the Collector on his crossed legs. Tsar with a Kalashnikov crouched in the rear and watched the terrain, as did Bradshaw and Shimizu with the other rifles on the second vehicle. Div and Zira acted as drivers, as the autopilot didn't work, while the captain, scientist and technician discussed obstacles along the route and observations of Jelinek in the second car.

The comfortable journey ended when they reached a field of narrow, pointed hills reminiscent of intestinal villi. They were so densely packed, and the terrain near them so treacherous and uneven that it was impossible to travel by drops any further. They couldn't fly either, because to change the geometry of the vehicles were required electronics and batteries with more power than the energy obtained from deuterium decay. Darius with Aytar climbed the highest surrounding peak, from where they saw its twins stretching endlessly. Zira could clearly see several full moons of different colors, a phenomenon that wouldn't have had the right to occur in known worlds, and in addition they hadn't noticed any stars around Amyrade so far. Schindler, in turn, saw only a uniform, infernal sky, horribly blending with the hills, which made it seem to him that they were standing in front of the entrance to the body of a titanic size.

As they both descended the steep slope, the Collector suddenly went out. The worried boy exchanged a look with Aytar, whose eyes, as usual, expressed nothing.

"Oh, that's not good," he muttered.

The artifact status hadn't changed at the drops.

"And back," said Tsar.

"Maybe it's just for a moment," Shimizu wanted to build up morale.

"If that flea-ridden Nanawak had said something more, we'd know what to do," Zira snapped.

"Maybe the artifact responds to a magnetic field or something like that," Darkoris suggested. "Maybe it is changing rapidly here. I mean reversals that last a few minutes."

"As long as there is any," Jelinek said. "If only our measuring devices worked ..."

He fell silent as the Collector regained its former color. It shone brightest now as Darius shifted it eastward, assuming that the hills were ahead of them to the north.

The eyes of the team turned to the commander.

"Let's wait a moment and see if anything changes. If xik'iri is indeed pointing to Forkis' atole, it might be moving."

"Which may mean we're going to go round and round," said Bradshaw dissatisfiedly. "Run after the target like a donkey after a carrot tied on a stick."

"But interestingly, the Collector and the sapphire now point in the same direction, although in my case nothing has changed from the very beginning." Div raised the dagger holding it by the blade above his head so that everyone could see the hilt.

The change in the direction indicated by the artifact gave everyone more and more strange assumptions, but at least the problem of the stagnation was solved.

They moved further in the drops, having a highland to the left.

Although it seemed to Darius and Zira at the vantage point that the hills stretched for hundreds of kilometers, after several minutes of slow and calm driving, the team left the highland behind. The sky turned cyclamen. They entered rocky areas with active volcanoes. Scorching rivers of liquid gold edged a flat road on which they drove. The air shook like a desert mirage, but neither the heat nor the materials rising from the craters and intrusion plagued the drops and the crew hidden inside. The less active mountains were being circled by archeopteryxes and griffins, astonishing some of the group as the rest saw the cones of extinct volcanoes and the black crust of the ground, with no sign of life.

Soon they found themselves on an open plain. The cones stayed far behind until they were finally out of sight. The drops' wheels crushed the dry, cracked, clay soil until they ran onto huge slabs of rock, adjacent to each other, as if someone had built a road here. The sky turned red again, visible to all.

A tall building appeared in the middle of the void.

"Skyscraper," Darius said, stepping onto the hood of the first drop after they had been stopped.

"I see a dark cathedral," Divinus whispered from the depths of the hood.

Then Zira spoke:

"Me, too, a cathedral, but an ordinary one. Very old, stone. As if from Earth from centuries ago."

"Also, I see what you see, sweetheart," Tsar added.

"An interesting matter," commented Jelinek, rubbing his chin. "Apparently, in this case Amyrade couldn't create the object we all came into contact with. Div has probably never seen an office building or a cathedral as we know it from our worlds."

"Logic is, rather, the last thing we should be using on Amyrade." The captain came off the drop. After a while, everyone was on the ground.

Darius was the first to approach the square-sectioned skyscraper, tilted his head up high. The side at the base was over a hundred meters wide. It consisted of a swarm of black plates reminiscent of solar panels separated by grooves a few centimeters wide. The tower at the top was invisible, and to eye it up, you had to walk away a long distance.

Avadar ordered his subordinates to inspect the building. Nobody found the entrance. Both the sapphire and the Collector glowed with equal intensity as Div and Schindler walked around the colossus once again.

"How can a cathedral not have a gate," muttered the assassin.

Mechanical watches showed the next hours, and the expedition stalled. Like the time of day, if you could put it that way - according to Nanawak, time didn't exist on Amyrade. The amount of light coming from the sky didn't change.

When Darius accidentally scratched one of the sand-stained slabs with the artifact, a mechanism clicked and burr started to come from inside the building. The boy froze, clutching the Collector with both hands like a last resort. With the face of an offender, he looked at the rest of the confused crew. Zira and Jelinek glared at him furiously.

Behind them they heard a hiss as if gas had been being released from dozens of siphons. Everyone focused on the building, and no one was watching the plain through which a dense fog was moving over the ground at racing pace. Avadar cursed his thoughtlessness in spirit. Accustomed to the technology doing nearly all the tasks for a human, he had forgotten that his wrist weather scanner was unable to detect a threat.

"Drops!" Darius tucked the Collector into the bag on the left side of his belt and raced towards the vehicles, followed by Shimizu and Bradshaw. They didn't make it. The furious fog, casting a sharp shadow engulfed them like foaming waves seashells on a shore. The three, cursing, turned and started running in the opposite direction, chased by the white death.

"All behind the building, quickly!" Cried the commander.

"Holy shit!" Tsar rushed towards Schindler, but by the time he reached him, the fog engulfed them both.

"Darius! Zira! Div! Shimizu!" He called. He could barely see the fingers of his outstretched hand. The phenomenon had no odor or mass, it was not known whether it was warm or cold, as well as whether it was sound conductive at all.

After a few minutes of wandering, the man randomly pulled a flare from his backpack, hoping that activating it wouldn't trigger an explosion. He had a bright pink beacon that, in addition to light, emitted foggy smoke, as if it had been competing with it for the title of king of chaos. The fog seemed to be winning this duel, because no one came to Tsar.

Despite the aid of light, he lost his companions, and he was also unable to get to the facility's wall or find drops. He took a Kalashnikov in his free hand, and with the other he dangled the flare like a bogey at a swarm of annoying insects.

Not long after the flare dimmed, something hard hit him in the back. The lieutenant grabbed the object, turned it towards him, and put the barrel against it.

"It's me!" Frightened, Darius held the active Collector. Tsar sighed nervously and released his arm.

"Have you seen anyone else?"

"No. Then I would rather not be walking alone."

"And my flare?"

"Not either. Nice Fuster Cluck, right, boss?"

"Your artifact is still glowing. Maybe we can find something with it. You will navigate."

After another minutes of walking blindly, they didn't come across any obstacle.

"Not good," hissed Tsar. "After all, I was twenty meters from the cathedral wall when this milk flooded me. I haven't been looking for you for a hundred years either."

"So, what's the plan, boss?"

"You know what? I don't know and I'm not ashamed to admit it. Extrapolation climbed onto the roof of this cathedral, jumped and committed suicide, overwhelming logic. All we have to do is go anywhere and keep looking."

"I think something is moving there ... Some gorilla is coming here!"

Tsar glanced at the new threat and saw a tall, beefy and short-haired Kiritian.

"Damn, Darius. Don't raise your weapon towards me, you weenie!" The newcomer aimed the barrel of his rifle at the ground with the pressure of the flare. "You've finally come." Relief appeared on Private Shimizu's face that was white like the fog around.

"Schindler thought you were a gorilla."

Darius smiled embarrassed.

"Just don't know if I should take it as an insult or a compliment," Kazuo said, in a tone indicating that he wasn't angry.

"I told the captain this boatik was a bad idea," Seymour purred. "Otherwise, everyone, maybe except me, would see the same. Okay, folks. We have to find the rest somehow. Div has the dagger so he should follow the sapphire light and go in the same direction as us. As long as it has not gone out."

"I screamed. Did you hear me?" Shimizu asked.

"No." Darius sighed. "That deluge of fog is probably my fault."

"Sure, kid." Tsar jokingly prodded his temple. "Because you knew from the beginning that if you touch the right panel, you will change the arrangement from boring to one conducive to playing hide and seek."

They moved on, keeping the glow of the artifact always at its most intense. They stopped calling companions when, after observing, they concluded that the fog didn't transmit sounds beyond two meters. Moreover, they couldn't know if the screams inaudible to them were being picked up by some Amyrade natives who didn't like intruders.

Soon they found Divinus, who, as Seymour had predicted, was guided by the blue light of the sapphire.

The ground changed. They were now walking on smooth, close-fitting tiles of rock, similar to white-gray marble, as if in a museum full of splendor. The fog had thinned, letting them see the nuances of the immediate surroundings, but far away it was still impenetrable like the walls of a glacier. The road, built with refinement, was bordered by branchy old trees without leaves, growing out of brown soil covered with moss and glowing spheres. At least Div and Seymour perceived such a view.

"Can I ask you something?" The assassin asked Tsar in a whisper at one point, taking advantage of the fact that Darius and Shimizu were walking a few steps ahead and talking.

The lieutenant noticed that his companion was a bit self-conscious, and it was quite rare to see the emotions on Div's face.

"Go ahead," he replied also quietly.

"It's about Aytar."

Tsar smiled from ear to ear involuntarily, for which Div glared at him.

"Is she always so ... wooden?" Relagard continued. "Something happened to her? Any trauma?"

"In a sense, do you have a chance with her?" Tsar said bluntly. "They say, she's asexual. Many people say that this is her nature, of a reticent orphan, acquired while still on her native Calvary. But I think Aytar's condition may have something to do with Forkis. She was kiritianized over one hundred and twenty years ago as a result of their short romance. A doozy. The wench was dying and they rescued her in Dr. Figam's infirmary."

"Forkis hurt her?" The assassin felt angry.

"On the contrary, he wanted to help her. When he brought her from Calvary, she was nervous, terribly composed. But something got messed up, very strange, in the emperor's apartments in K'otz'ib'aja. Whoever witnessed this had a selectively erased memory, including Kiret Biffter himself and the batab Gareth, commander of the city guard. So, you won't learn anything from them, Aytar will be furious if you ask her about it, and Forkis is as silent as a grave. But keep trying, brother." He patted him on the shoulder reassuringly. He leaned towards his ear and whispered, "I think she likes you."

Tsar winked at surprised Div and overtook him.

The road ended unexpectedly over a bluff that ran from left to right like a canyon or a planet fracture; tiles protruded shattered near the edge. In front of a high-tech bridge stood Private first-class Bradshaw with his rifle in hand, staring to the side. He was terrified. Hearing footsteps, he glanced at the group, then returned to the observation.

The four saw a semicircular tent made of skins near the bridge, where a large family could have lived. In the light breeze, pebbles were rattling, pieces of bark and bone ornaments on strings. There was a wooden table closest to the road, on which were lots of parchment rolls folded or held by boulders. A thin, silver-robed old man with a long beard and mustache leaned over them. The lieutenant's first association was with an Asian monk from Earth. The old man was writing something quickly on parchment, occasionally dipping his pen in ink.

Div raised an eyebrow, glanced at Tsar, who looked back at him and shrugged. Only they looked at the old man in surprise, as if it had been some sick joke, the rest stared at him with fascination and even religious fear, like fanatics at a dictatorial leader.

"Hey, Grandpa." Seymour walked over to the table. He held the rifle low, didn't sling it over his shoulder, to let the stranger know that in the event of an inconvenience he was ready to act. He glanced at the calligraphed characters; he had never seen such a language. "You probably don't understand me, but it's worth a tr..."

"Yes, I can communicate with you," replied the old man in a powerful but also jovial voice, as if amused. Amazed, Tsar opened his mouth. He turned to Div, who was looking at the stranger with a cool, distrustful look. Indeed, few things made an impression on the assassin who had lived on Karikon.

The old man put his pen aside, placed his hands on the edge of the table, and smiled brightly. When he looked up, it turned out that he had multicolored pupils.

"You're finally here. Now I can take my brother down."

"What?" Tsar blinked. "And how is it possible that you speak Kiritian, Grandpa?"

"I'm the material projection of your minds, the common denominator, as you stated in your previous brainstorming session. Avatar. I took a form that each of you has seen before. I don't understand your language and I don't know it, because when we saw each other a long time ago, people said differently. I could know your speech if in the real form, I touched the head of one of you. And we're communicating because we're using the resources of our own minds. This is one of Amyrade's many wonderful properties. My native speech is like this."

He uttered weird, screeching words that the lieutenant didn't understand. Also, the sense of the expression.

"What is this gibberish?"

"Lieutenant, please ... calm down. You are talking to God," Darius said frightened.

"What does the rest see?" Seymour ran his look over the faces of his companions. Darius, Shimizu, and Bradshaw were more or less Christian, so they saw either Jesus at the table or an old, powerful man with a lush white beard, mustache and hair. Div was skeptical about matters of faith; he described laconically that a monk was sitting there. "Another visual dissonance," Seymour thought, now completely drug-free.

"You want to go on, but you're lost," said the monk. He pointed to the bridge obscured by the fog. "You have to go this way; this is the only route that will change your position. Otherwise, you will wander in the fog forever."

"So, let's go, what are we waiting for." Shimizu walked away like a mindless sheep chased by its shepherd, astonishing Tsar.

"Are you crazy?" He grabbed his arm and pulled him towards himself. "You are to stand here and not move without my orders!"

"Something's wrong here." Seymour flinched as he heard the hissing voice of the assassin in his right ear, soft but full of threat.

"What's with the bridge and your brother?" The lieutenant asked.

Multicolored as a reflection nebula, the old man's eyes flashed playfully but also disturbingly.

"You'll be able to continue your mission across this bridge. But it is warded by my brother's guards who will want to kill you. You have to kill them first."

"Okay, old man, where's the catch? I meet so suddenly 'material projection of my mind'", Tsar raised his hand and bent the index and middle fingers a few times, "in the complete woods, who wants to help us selflessly? Since you come from our heads, you can't help us because we ourselves don't know what to do."

"What if my voice is your subconscious? You know you have to cross this bridge."

"Don't move," Tsar said to his people, who had shifted.

He glanced at Darius' artifact; it shone intensely when directed towards the bridge. The sapphire also seemed to indicate that direction. He frowned, gave the monk a grudging look, and turned away. With the crunch of stones being trampled with military boots, he approached the bridge and stopped a step ahead of the first span. The structure with thick pillars and stone arches, interwoven with metal stabilizers, looked solid enough for a battalion of heavy plasma tanks to pass through here, not only one at a time, but even one after the other. On the sides of the bridge, nothing could be seen except the dense white which, at the top, turned into a ghostly red like that of a sunset.

Div caught up with Tsar. The lieutenant wasn't surprised that the assassin, who had lived arbitrarily for centuries, didn't obey his command, but he was a person about whose safety and sanity he didn't have to worry at all.

"Do you want to go there?"

"Do we have a choice?" Seymour returned to the monk. "Maybe some guidelines?"

"These guards are monsters, demons, you must kill them all. You can also beat my brother, he's a moron." The infantile utterance didn't suit the old man with a prudent face. Tsar thought that if his appearance and behavior were components drawn from the minds of the five arrived, the words might have come from an impetuous Darius.

"There are a lot of them there? How are they armed?" He noticed that the monk had been most interested in Schindler from the beginning, having the attention focused most often on him. And it was not a friendly look, rather an appraising one, as if during the selection of the best merchandise in the market.

"About as many as you." He laughed, at which Div grimaced. The old man gave him a defiant look. "Anyway, you'll see for yourself."

Tsar nodded to the achijes, who followed him as if hypnotized, though he sensed that he wasn't the leader in this extraordinary game. While he was considering the real strength of the bridge that was not suppressed by successive 'brain projections', the assassin, apparently following his train of thought, climbed the span. He walked dynamically and started jumping up and down. For a moment he watched the area high above, then he peered over the railing towards the chasm.

"Looks fine."

"Come on, folks," Tsar ordered. "Helmet covers onto the mugs. No rushing, acting tough or doing stupid things. Maximum caution and thinking. Keep your weapons ready." He chattered the precept, though he was concerned about fulfilling half the things, especially thinking. And rightly so, because Darius, Shimizu, and Bradshaw were delighted to see each piece of the bridge as if it had been made of diamonds and gold. They seemed absent and deaf to the orders of the commander; they walked as if guided by entrasers hacked by Kandrok.

"I'm confused," Div grumbled, slipping the dagger into the case and pulling the sword out of the scabbard. With his free hand he grabbed the pistol Captain Avadar had given him.

"I got confused already many years ago, when Mr. Biffter came up with an idea of reviving the dead," echoed the lieutenant.

The assassin, watching closely the achijes in front of him, stopped, frowned.

"You sense something," noted Tsar, who also stopped. "Stop!" The achijes obeyed.

"One thing puzzles me," said Div. "Shouldn't it be you and me who should have the strongest visions, not stifled by drugs?"

"Schindler, describe what you see," Seymour ordered.

"The bridge made entirely of demon bones. Entwined with vegetation and flowers. They are beautiful." Darius brushed the petals of the blue bell dreamily; Tsar and Div saw him touch a marble brick. "Lots of birds and butterflies are flying around. Turquoise cascades are falling on the sides. We find ourselves in paradise. And paradise must be demon free," he added loudly and sharply.

Tsar abstained from raising his hands to the eyes behind the shield.

The rest of the lost team emerged from the fog on the other side, stretched in an extended line on the entire width of the end of the bridge. Everyone except Aytar wore folded helmets on their necks. Zira soberly and anxiously looked at Tsar and his subordinates. The latter kept their fierce, full of determination expressions visible behind translucent covers. Their dry, expectant gazes looked like those of a primitive mob ready to lynch.

"We have to kill the demons! May God guide us!" Shimizu shouted, echoed by Darius and Bradshaw. Those on the other side were screaming more or less the same, except for confused Zira who retreated behind the thick stone pillar of the bridge.

Seymour stared at the captain, hoping for his reaction, but when he noticed that the commander seemed as dumbfounded as the rest, he exclaimed:

"Stand and wait!"

"Kill the demons! Death to monsters!" Schindler shouted over him. He lifted the rifle and started walking, followed by his companions.

"Move one step more, and I will tear your legs off your ass!"

"They must be deaf to your commands," Div said, calmly, as always.

"What do you see, Darius?"

"Horned, four-legged, hairy beasts! Don't stand like that, boss, help us kill them!" He shouted passionately.

"Goddamn it," Seymour grumbled.

The three achijes started firing, the other side pulled on their face shields and did the same. The bullets missed, hit the targets, ricocheted in all directions.

Following the example of Zira, Tsar and the Div retreated behind the stone pillar on their side.

"That's why we insisted you don the armor." A bullet whistled past the lieutenant's head as he briefly looked around the corner.

"I can handle."

"They won't hurt themselves. It is lightweight biometal armor and the helmet visors are puronax. The bullets, on the other hand, are shitty. Unless ... Cease fire! Stop! Goddamn it!"

The two groups approached each other and started fist or bayonet fights if someone had it. In an aggressive, fierce skirmish full of screams, one tried to remove other's pieces of armor.

Tsar ran to the center of the bridge, released a few flares from his pack and began to activate them by hitting his knee with their poles. Divinus quickly understood what he was up to, stopped beside him and helped him throw them into the furious crowd.

"Without electronic assistance, they will barely see through that colorful smoke and lights. It's something." Seymour saw Aytar coming toward them. "Zira, finally! Do you have any idea why they see demons and we see normally? Everything is turned upside down now."

"I don't know." Gasping, the woman turned sharply as she heard more shots.

"They have to be quickly separated and neutralized," said the assassin.

Breaking through the smoke, they got to the dazed achijes in which even demonic forces entered. Avadar and Darkoris fought like berserkers with exposed, bloody chests. Fragile Jelinek was thrown by Shimizu's mighty arms and flew several meters. When Aytar tried to save the scientist from a bayonet stab, she was thrown away like a rag doll, and she wasn't a physically weak woman.

Tsar, trying to hold down struggling Darius who was dragging him behind himself, unexpectedly remembered the situation on H14 when they had first met Chimalmat. The Onkalot woman had used her telekinesis ability to create an army of skeletons brought from tombs and used them to attack a Kiritian squad. Aggroteh interrupted her incantation as he knocked her onto a block of the pyramid.

"Something's controlling them!" He called to Div, who, though of medium height and average stature, had swiftly toppled heavier Avadar and was now crouched on his back, driving a knee into it.

"The switch," the assassin blurted out suddenly.

"Be clearer, man, what you mean!"

Darius attacked Tsar. He hit his helmet with the butt of his rifle, as if he had forgotten that he wouldn't damage the puronax that was used to protect the cockpits of subspace velocity spacecraft. Pure, mindless fury burned in the corporal's green eyes; he screamed like a caveman trying to finish off his game. Or kill the demon.

"I think it's that monk," Div began to explain. "He changed our perceptions: now those who are not affected by the drug see the truth. The rest went crazy, he indoctrinated them somehow on a subconscious level. He controls their minds. But that's just my theory."

"Bravo, Div. Kiret made the great decision to include you in our team."

"I could be wrong," said dryly Relagard, who disliked praise.

"You're not! This old man called himself an avatar. Someone controls him, it is not our imagination. He lied to us!"

"What old man?" Aytar got up from the ground.

"The white-bearded decayed man at the desk on the other side of the bridge. Darius and the two took him for God," Tsar said. Schindler knocked him to the ground and they both started to struggle. Darius was taller and more massive than Seymour, and, driven by undefined insanity, had increased strength. "He was complaining about his brother and some army of demons."

"On our side there is the clerk with the tie who demanded the fee from the wrong twin." Jelinek wanted to jump on the woman, but Div quickly extended his arm and tripped him with his sword. "Thanks. He ordered us to kill the monsters guarding him."

"Sounds familiar," snapped Relagard. As soon as he got off the captain, he rose and attacked Darkoris fighting with Shimizu. Moving swiftly like a panther and not injuring anyone, the assassin sent the three achijes to the ground, using his limbs, pistol butt and sword hilt.

"It will not end by itself," pointed out Tsar, to whose throat Darius tried to get with his teeth. The lieutenant didn't have enough strength to resist him. "We have to deal with the source, not struggle with the consequences." He shrunk his legs and kicked the enraged corporal off with a powerful push. Out of breath, he got up and ran a bit so that Darius didn't find him amid the thick smoke of the still working flares. "Aytar, take care of the jack-in-office. Terrorize him or something like that."

He couldn't see the corporal, but he heard her answer amid the fiery rattle of the rifles:

"What about ours? When we leave, they'll kill each other!"

"I'll take care of it." Tsar flinched as the assassin emerged from the smoke next to his right side. He had a deathly expression on his face dirty with blood and an eloquent look. Seymour felt a shiver down his spine, but he didn't want to ask for details. "Go, Lieutenant, or it will get worse."

"We may be wrong."

"It's worth a try if there is even a shadow of a chance for ... normality."

Tsar ran out of the smoke. He looked back for a moment as he heard more shots, but saw no human figure.

He reached the monk sitting with his hands clasped defiantly over his chest; he had an amused expression on his face.

"I don't care about the rest, but you have to bring the boy to me," he said enigmatically.

Seymour raised his rifle and pointed it at his forehead. The old man looked indifferently at the blackness of the barrel.

"I don't know what's going on or what you're up to, but free my people from this madness," Tsar droned.

"I was wrong, I took you for someone else, but it doesn't matter anymore."

"Stop talking shit and restrain that fucking crap!" The lieutenant seems pissed off like never before during his service among the Kiritians, but hadn't been burdened with such a messed-up assignment so far. In addition, he couldn't trust his own mind, because Amyrade didn't belong to the universe he knew, where the laws of physics were constant and familiar to him. Maybe the gods did exist - whom Tsar considered to be the exteriorization of the human ego - and they had experimented here once, creating planets? He took his finger off the trigger guard and pulled the trigger lightly. "Stop these games and set my men free or I'll destroy you."

"You're not gonna hurt me anyway. You're talking to the projection." The old man laughed; Tsar replied with a sneer.

"Kiss my ass, you prick."

He sent a whole series at the other, so that he was thrown away, along with a ghastly chair made of bones of species Seymour didn't know, but also human. Instead of blood and guts, dust began to come out of the chopped old man's body, causing the entire false structure to shrink, which looked like someone was sucking his insides through a pipe.

Seymour pursed his lips in disgust. Only the skeleton remained on the damaged block of rock, it rose for several meters like it was held on an invisible rope - and fell apart. The dust instantly flew away like a swarm of black flies, perhaps accidentally in the direction indicated by the light signals of both artifacts.

The flares that should have acted for hours had exhausted their fuel extremely quickly. Tsar had grown accustomed to the idea that he shouldn't have worried about a lack of logic on Amyrade. Visibility began to improve. On the other side of the bridge, he saw a plain marked by various rocks, their facets and geode crystals reflected the red of the sky, which began to turn orange. He indeed associated the landscape with hell. As his chest began to burn, he realized that he had been holding his breath since the avatar was destroyed. His heart pounded with emotion and fear for the fate of the team, especially Darius'.

Tsar hoped he hadn't made a fatal mistake. After all, he couldn't know what chain reaction the elimination of the old man would cause. And he supposed that was just the beginning of the problems.

As he jogged across the bridge, he almost dropped his rifle, having seen the details of the bloody spectacle.

3. Jamal Ibn Yusuf al-Aswani

After two hours of walking, Kiret and Jenny saw a large glacial lake. The world turned intense gray in the evening; Necron put on his helmet and turned on statistically assisted night vision, allowing him to see the area better than a cat and feel like in front of the desktop of a flying machine. He was the first to go, choosing a path through a meadow dotted with dilapidated boulders. He ignored Sandstorm's statement uttered in a pretentious tone that she could see no worse than him after dark without equipment, and he tried to finally determine what planet they had crashed on.

They were too close to the surface to see the continents when they emerged from the node's tunnel, and the small stretch of water and land that was visible meant nothing to Necron. The failures of Perfarius made no identification possible. He had already received evidence that the planet was terraformed and inhabited. They certainly hadn't crashed on the experimental globe, as such were colonized to a limited extent. If the physical parameters allowed for it, the usually unfriendly to humans, original atmosphere was changed on them (or they created it from scratch in the absence of it), erecting multi-kilometer poles of paired synthesizers, or scattering modified thallophytes producing air with a specific composition, and preparing the ground for the construction of military-scientific facilities. So, plants and animals were not there at all.

They reached a sandy shore covered with a rush, swaying lazily in the light breeze. In the subtly wrinkled surface were reflected stars. Necron knew these constellations, he knew which planets looked exactly like this. He looked around the area and when he saw nothing suspicious, he turned to the girl:

"Go wash yourself. Scream if something happens, I'll be nearby. Or you know what, we better do it my way." He pulled the X17A4 out of the compartment and directed its butt towards Jenny. "Take it. You can go into the water with it."

"I've never had a gun in my hand."

Kiret smiled indulgently.

"Then great. Daughter of the nation's military emperor and oppositionist, brought up in the heat of battle, and can't shoot."

Sandstorm frowned on him.

"Then teach me."

"You hold it, aim, pull the trigger. And you already know how." Biffter did a water lily demonstration. "Don't worry about recoil, because the photon flux doesn't give it. Energy replenishes itself, like in my plasma thrower."

"Don't destroy the flowers." Jenny hesitantly took the gun, but when she held it for a moment, she aimed it at various objects, tossed it from hand to hand, and smiled approvingly. "It is light, you hardly feel the weight."

She moved away and quickly disappeared into the thickets of the wharf.

"You can turn on the flashlight, by the way," said Kiret to the nonexistent listener. He remembered Jenny saying something about moving in the dark. Maybe she hadn't made it up, wanting to get attention and show that she hadn't been so helpless. Forkis had used infra-vision in the dark and may have passed it on to his daughter. However, it had happened.

He started rinsing the muddy armor; his body inside was clean. He moved a dozen paces from the shore and stopped where the water reached his neck. He examined the ground. He soon returned to land, removed his armor and left it on the grass, then stripped off his thin uniform and went to take a refreshing bath. The water turned out to be perfect: cool, clean, odorless, as if untouched by human civilization. Necron dropped onto his back and, shifting his shoulders, allowed himself a moment to relax. Very short, because on the shore a calamus danced wildly, from which Jenny ran out with impetus.

"Something's moving there!" Out of breath, she noticed his things scattered on the beach. She flushed red, thankful it was dark.

Necron rolled over and plunged into the water, leaving his head and shoulders floating.

"Do you always so unceremoniously deprive people of privacy?" This time it wasn't a joke. He wanted to be alone a bit and think things over. Jenny's constant presence was starting to irritate him.

"Sorry, I didn't see through the brush that you were swimming. Something terrible is out there."

"I'll go check it out. Walk away, I need to get dressed."

"No way, I will definitely not go back there."

"You don't have to go to the same place, just step away."

"I'm afraid."

"Girl, you have the gun. Anyway, as you wish, you will see something terrible also here right away."

As he started to go out of the lake, accustomed to swimming together on missions in the field, Jenny, like a startled rusalka, ran into the trees instead of simply turning around. He heard a loud splash, then a curse. At first her behavior had seemed comical to him, but he realized that she might not have seen a naked man live before. He had never brought up such topics with her.

He put on his uniform and armor, took the plasma thrower from the sand. Then moved away from the shore.

"Jenny? Sorry, I didn't mean to scare you."

She jumped off the branch beside him.

"It's okay. You are all wet, you need to dry your clothes or you will get sick."

"What about the pig?"

"Pig?"

"You know ... I was scared of the pig. But it was weird. Hairy, huge and with big fangs. When I wanted to wash myself in the water, it went out of the bushes and started making sounds as if it had been the sign of an attack. I was so scared that I forgot about my gun."

Necron shook his head with a sigh.

"And?"

"Nothing. I ran to you."

"You must have been scared of an ordinary boar, girl. They are not found on Atla. However, I will go check, but you stay." He pointed his finger at her as she took a brisk step toward him. "Next to the beach you will find a landslide, uprooted trees form a canopy between the hill and the embankment below. Go there and light a fire in the niche."

"I don't want to stay here alone."

"Go and no discussion!" He said in a sharp voice of a commander.

Surprised, Jenny fell silent; Biffter had never spoken to her in such a tone. She knew him as a gentle, sometimes gloomy person. She took a few steps backwards, turned and walked towards the shore.

Kiret just realized why the girl irritated him so much - he was subconsciously angry with her for Skelver, Kandrok's informant. If she hadn't secretly employed him in the mansion, they wouldn't have been stuck in the wilderness of another planet, which, to make matters worse, had been also discovered by the enemy.

Using his vision assist, he easily found the watery path Sandstorm had followed through the coastal scrub. Numerous shoe prints in the mud testified that she was not the only one who had passed this way in the recent past, but they belonged only to animals.

He stepped out into an open space where small waves washed another beach; there was an intense musky scent in the air. In addition to the shoe prints in the sand, he also saw cloven hoof prints. He looked towards the forest and saw three adult pigs and a few piglets. They stood motionless against the background of vegetation and trunks similar in color to their hairs, presumably believing that the stranger would see them only when they moved. Necron had never seen such a type of hogs before, with a mottled ashen skin, quite long, floppy ears, and a thick mane like that of a warthog. The animals had little to do with slaughter pigs - the ones here were characterized by longer limbs and muscles so thin and poor that bones showed through them, which couldn't be the result of malnutrition, since the area was teeming with vegetation. He supposed he had encountered modificants. When he took a few quiet steps to see if the herd was tame, it scattered and run away with a squeak into the forest. Unlike Jenny, whom the boar wanted to drive away, it considered him a threat.

The sight of the animals reminded him that they had no food. On the way, he and Jenny had swallowed tablets made of high-energy cockroach milk that Necron had with him - fulfilling their role during static functioning in a spacecraft (they were then sufficient for a board day), but not in rough terrain.

He returned to Sandstorm and found her crouching by a briskly burning fire, visible only from the side of the dense forest. High above, three massive fallen trunks formed a roof, resting, on one side, on the wall of the slope, and on the other -

a hill. The girl on the sides made a construction of branches and leaves to further restrict visibility; the fire from spreading was protected by a circle of boulders.

"Not bad." The Kiritian sat down next to her. "How did you light the fire?"

Sandstorm smiled, picked up two stones.

"I read about it once in the holo-book." She threw them next to the fire. "Did you see the boar?"

"Yes. But I thought too late to catch it for dinner."

"Right, I want to eat." Jenny felt her clothes, they were getting drier.

"Me too." Necron stood up. "I'll have a look at the lake to see if I can shoot any fish. They should be in such clear water."

"Just don't let half the tank evaporate from your shot," Sandstorm joked. Kiret smiled.

"Sit back and dry yourself completely."

He went with the plasma thrower to the shore where he had been swimming before. He turned on thermographic vision. He crouched down and went still. He soon spotted a large shoal of several species in the deeper part of the lake, but there was no good way to catch them. However, while he was stuck so motionless, a few pieces looking like zanders flowed into a basin between coastal boulders.

Necron didn't remember the last time he had just made a human trip to the water and had been fishing in peace. The ancient way: with a lure, fishing rod, line, a hook and a bucket standing next to a folding chair. In a quiet, friendly area, with the ability to completely push away your worries while fishing. I guess it had happened in another life - when he had been still an ordinary person and had a family. Before he was forcibly recruited into the NOA, which was the duty of every healthy male under the global government.

As he wondered so, the fish came even closer. It was enough to quickly extend your hand and grab one of the quite big specimens.

Necron did so.

He was fast, but the fish turned out to be faster and escaped from the basin.

"Damn it."

On the second approach, he no longer waited like a cat on a shore, but stepped into the water up to his knees. He stood a little, aimed at the nearest fish that swam over, and fired. He looked up at the sky irritably as its battered remains spread beneath the surface, quickly bombarded by the school with its mouths. Despite the minimized stream of combat plasma, the next shots also did too much damage for a substitute for a meal to emerge from the smashed fish.

Necron heard a chuckle behind him.

"Really a barrel of fun," he said with mock sneer, having turned to Jenny. She sat cross-legged on a boulder and bit her lip to keep from croaking. "Why don't you try it yourself?"

"No problem."

"Then start the show."

Much to Kiret's curiosity, she handed him the gun he had given her as they passed each other. She took off her shoes, pulled up the sleeves and legs.

"Watch, general, and learn," she said kindly. With a smile, he waited for her to compromise herself to be able to bite back.

He ceased to feel like joking when, after a few minutes, three large fish, bouncing and caught with bare hands, lay on the shore.

"You surprise me, girl," he muttered, neither with appreciation nor a sneer.

When Jenny caught two more, she stepped in front of him and curtsied playfully.

"I used to run around forests and lakes as a kid."

Necron slung the thrower over his chest, handed the girl the gun. Remembering how his combat plasma fishing attempts had ended, he killed the fish by hitting their heads against a boulder.

The evening turned out to be calm - no uninvited guest wandered into the range of the shine of the deliciously crackling fire. The sky cleared, only to the east remained the infernal glow. Kandrok didn't appear anymore, just as any other flying machine. Necron wanted to believe that the enemy found them dead, but he was much more worried about how it would treat the newly discovered planet. He didn't know its priorities and procedures, but he feared the worst.

I don't think he could bear that.

From the stars shining through the ceiling of the hideout, he shifted his gaze to Jenny curled up, sleeping next to him under a rug of surrounding plants. He rested his head on his arms entwined in the back. He was glad that Sandstorm tried to be of help, she seemed to understand the seriousness of the situation, and stopped sulking. If their cooperation continued this way, they had a good chance of leaving the planet.

In the morning, Kiret felt rested, though sore because of the armor he had preferred not to take off in the strange area. Jenny woke up. They lit the fire again and ate the remaining fish's meat, roasted and trimmed with sharp stones. They had nothing to boil water in, so they drank straight from the lake. They would worry about possible parasites or toxins later, when they found a medical center.

They moved on shortly after sunrise. Necron would have loved to explore the area at the fishing pier seen the day earlier, but Kandrok had destroyed the entire region. If there had been people there, they were probably already dead. About going back to the wreckage of Perfarius, he could forget. So, they could only go as far as possible from the crash site and hope that they would find help.

They went outside the forest area. The bald, open space at the edge of the field of view was framed by hills or low mountains, which seemed no less real than a mirage. The ground on which they walked looked very degraded. They crossed the fords of shallow, narrow and numerous watercourses, passed boulders resting on soils of various kinds, from sand and clay to black and brown. Fragments of the passing city, mainly the pressed foundations of buildings, couldn't be attributed to any civilization.

"You think a huge space shuttle has landed here?" Jenny asked as she caught up with Kiret on a hill overlooking the total, anonymous destruction.

"Good thinking, but not enough. See, if something had landed here, it would have crushed everything completely, and not mixed up the soil from different regions and in addition brought a lot of foreign matter. It looks more like a gigantic flood that took place several decades ago, estimating by the age of the passing trees. It is possible that we are in a depression the size of a country that it once flooded."

"Where is the water now?"

"Maybe it soaked up, maybe it evaporated, maybe it flowed down in newly formed rivers. Are you tired, do you want to rest?"

"No."

"Then we're going on."

"Do you already know where?"

"We certainly won't find out if we stand still."

***

In the late afternoon feral Beaucerons got them. At first, they mistook them for wolves, because they looked so from a distance. They were surrounded by a pack while searching the ruins of a mosque nearly razed to the ground. Necron recognized it only because the mosaic of the floor and the crescent fallen from the dome were well preserved, while the rest of the building had been spread over many hectares by some great force.

In the colors of the sky turning red, the dogs were associated with ghosts, a black and red, hateful death with bared fangs. Stiffened, Jenny said nothing; Necron was also silent. They stood back-to-back.

One of the Beaucerons lunged at the intruder he thought was easy. Kiret killed it by melting its skull, spine and insides with plasma. Shaky, Jenny turned her head grimacing as the carcass slapped the ground with a wet splat.

The rest of the animals moved away, looking at the scrap. They still snarled and barked at Necron, wagging their tails in warning, but already with less enthusiasm. They bared their teeth, but none of them broke a formed circle.

Jenny's heart was pounding like after a half-kilometer sprint. She was afraid that her unpleasantly soft, trembling legs would fail her. Even though she had the pistol, she was unable to fire it. "Giving a civilian a gun is not the same as training them mentally to use it," Kiret thought. As a veteran and participant in many battles, he was slightly nervous, which was related only to the safety of the teenager. Even if the dogs had attacked him in swarms, his armor would have saved him, but Jenny had no cover.

The dogs didn't know how to behave. Previously, no one had fired such a gun at them, and the man holding it was protected by a shell like a turtle. Another of the more impulsive, overgrown puppies decided to test the durability of this protection. Announcing an attack with barking, it lunged at the Kiritian from the side, as if it had forgotten about the fate of its companion.

The girl cursed.

Kiret pushed her away. He didn't fire. Instead, he pushed the blades out of the back of the glove and hit with it the throat of the dog leaping at him. Metal pierced the tissue and bones with a hideous crunch, exiting under the last cervical vertebra. Blood splattered over Kiret, Jenny, the animal hanging from the blades and the mosaic of the old temple.

Supporting himself with the barrel of the weapon held in his other hand, Biffter slid the carcass to the ground.

"Go away, maggots!" He shook the four bloody blades sticking out above his fist. The rest of the Beaucerons were effectively stripped of self-assurance. They already knew that this individual had more than one deadly tool.

The Beaucerons flocked and retreated beyond the ruins, abandoning ill-considered hunting. In the open, they ran towards the woods at which Necron and Jenny had camped the night before.

Jenny was frightened to see that her companion felt worse. He grimaced as if he had been fighting the pain, though he wasn't hurt. He staggered for a moment.

"Is everything alright? Are you fine?" He asked.

"Aha," she said, and nodded. She didn't return the question, sure that Kiret wouldn't deign to answer her about his health anyway.

"These animals were almost mad with hunger. It doesn't look good." He wiped the blades on the skin of the skinny dog and with a soft click slipped the metal into the compartments. "The evening is coming. We must find a good shelter."

They found the path least cluttered with rubble and moved along it towards the hills.

They decided to spend the night in an abandoned village, so primitive that Necron thought they had traveled back a thousand years in time. The Earth had undergone a technological revolution mainly in the first centuries of this millennium, many new inventions had been created, but over time scientists had focused on everything that had served space exploration, mainly on spacecraft propulsion, creating materials harder than diamond, as well as on medicine. Many solutions from centuries earlier hadn't changed according to the principle that if something worked well, why change it? The same was true of certain social classes. The countryside was a good example of this, where a healthy, peaceful and ecological life was preferred. Only modern agricultural and transport machinery was purchased, and androids were used in richer ranches.

As for the ghost village, where the two of them found a refuge, it consisted of a few shabby, dilapidated cottages made of wooden logs and boards. Their curves and imperfections indicated manual, not machine work. Estimating by numerous traces, such as the thickness of the dust in the hallways, the inhabitants had left some time earlier and taken all their useful possessions with them. However, someone else had visited the village afterwards. In the room of the house Necron had chosen, there were household waste and blankets. He judged by their condition that someone had been there in the past few weeks. He would have loved to know who the nomads were and if they might have come back. While Jenny was resting in a chair and eating blueberries and wild nuts, he went out to survey the hilly area. To the east he saw the beginning of a mountain range; to the south of the village there were miles of open space all the way to the wall of trees; in the west there was a young forest, the north was also marked by open space, but of degraded fields. Necron was concerned by bullet marks visible on the walls of the houses.

On the way back, he hunched and almost fell over when he suddenly felt weak. He leaned his arm heavily on a low lintel, activated the bio-scanning with the neuro-mogram mounted in the bracer. He tapped his forehead on the wood, seeing the unsatisfactory result.

"Just not now and not here," he muttered in frustration.

He entered the hut when he felt better.

For dinner, they ate wild apples; although they had plenty of them, they didn't eliminate hunger. They couldn't count on anything else, especially since weakened Necron was unable to come out and hunt something, and he didn't want to let Jenny herself outside.

The night turned out to be cool and damp. Kiret forbade making fire in the chimney or next to the hut, frustrating his companion, and made her almost his enemy when he told her to lie down on the boards and wrap herself with dirty rags. The cold finally won over the disgust: offended, Sandstorm muffled herself up in blankets and tried to sleep. Kiret lay down directly on the threshing floor; the aided armor provided him with the temperature optimal for the body.

He congratulated himself on not agreeing to light the fire, because there had been a shooting during the night. The cannonade came from the mountains, then moved south. There were muffled human screams, too distant for language to be recognized. The Kiritian, leaning his head on his clasped hands, had been unable to recognize the models of the weapons being used. He knew for sure that they were shooting each other with bullets, not with self-renewing energy.

"Will they come here?" The girl asked with mock indifference. She couldn't sleep either.

Kiret turned sideways towards her.

"I don't know. Hopefully not."

"Who are they?"

"It's hard to say. But they are definitely two or more sides of the conflict."

"When do you think we'll find some help?"

"Given that there are the villages, people, and feral dogs, it should be soon. However, we must be very careful." Kiret glanced at the window opening where the dim glow of the tiny sickle of the moon and stars fell into the room.

A small smile bloomed on the girl's face.

"But you will destroy everyone. Well, maybe except for Kandrok, but it is rather not here."

Kiret chuckled.

"You glorify me too much, baby."

"At your service, baldie," she bit back for "baby". She lied because Kiret, who had had no way to shave, had gotten stubble, and on his head had appeared short hair in the deepest shade of brown, both interwoven with gray.

She got up in the morning, feeling cold and sore, and there was also anxiety and concern. Walking to a nearby pond, Kiret was moving slowly, as if he had been sick, his skin pale from kiritianization turned white as lime. His eyes were black, and heavy breathing was spluttering in his chest.

"It's high time to tell you everything," he said as he returned in front of the cottage. He smiled reassuringly, seeing the girl's worried expression as if he had been inviting her to his own execution. "As you probably noticed, I don't look the most beautiful. But don't worry, I swear on the Kiritian truthfulness that I'm fine. I've been through the dozens, if not hundreds, of times. You will have the opportunity to see live both the dark and the light side of being Infected. The super virus works so that, on average, every few Terran years - time correlates with the annual cycles of the planet where a Kiritian lives, frequent travels can obviously disrupt the biological clock - rapidly rejuvenates the aging body. In the newly kiritianized, this process is unnoticeable, but in someone who lives for several centuries, the physical aspects of the rapid changes are clearly visible. My body should have died already a long time ago, but the pathogen is violently, ruthlessly and effectively eliminating the process of decay of organs and the rest of the body. It will always win. Colloquially speaking, the process is that at some point the programmed super virus starts working weaker, then the natural biological processes of the body turn on that want to kill it as soon as possible. This causes increased activation of the pathogen, 'turning back time' and starting repair processes. Anabolism starts to prevail over catabolism again. You're probably asking why the super virus can't just work the same all the time. Well, the body would not be able to withstand it, because there must be changes in it, cell replacement, copying, regeneration. According to the ubiquitous principle that everything is moving. The described process is a ridiculous price to pay for immortality, and I have to struggle with this weakness every few years, for several days. I will be weak and moody, looking sick, but I assure you that you don't have to worry about being left alone. Have you gotten any of what I've been saying?"

"I guess so."

"As long as I still have the strength, let's practice using the pistol. You'll have to look after me." Necron grinned.

Making sure that the area was empty and safe again with his scanner, he took Jenny under cover of young, dense trees. He sat down on a fallen tree and began with an erudition on the use of weapons, giving examples of various situations. He sensitized Sandstorm to the need to overcome her fears and become resistant to stress. Then came the easier, practical part with the use of the almost fully automatic pistol, because from the manual part the user only had to pull the trigger, aiming at a specific target. Soon the girl managed to shoot a rabbit for dinner.

In the afternoon, sitting close to each other on the same fallen log, Kiret practiced telepathy with Jenny.

"Pear," she said after a minute of slight mental effort. She yawned long and wide; the brain had worked a bit in the last hour.

"Be careful, a fly will get into your mouth."

Sandstorm smiled briefly.

"You're thinking about a pear."

"Correct again. It's time to start something more difficult, this time without individual items."

They looked in each other's eyes again, like monuments facing each other.

"XRS-14," she replied. She wiped her wet forehead with her hand. "The White, my mother's lost fighter in outer space, in the background of some planet."

"Specifically, it's Eos Endymion and its moon U1. Damn, you're good. Seriously. You are making progress. But now you're gonna fall over."

"Come on, we'll see."

After a dozen or so minutes, Kiret laughed, seeing her face twisted with futile effort.

"You're giving up?" He asked with a smile.

"Uhhh ... I'm fed up."

"I could block my thoughts from Forkis, so I can also from you."

"But I guess you have to want it, you focus, it doesn't come to you spontaneously. So, if you don't know I'm probing you, I'll read everything in your head?"

"It's a little more complicated ..."

The expression on his serene, relaxed face changed dramatically. He leaned forward sharply, grunted, and grabbed his chest. Jenny got to him immediately.

"What's wrong?!"

"It's not dangerous. I know this state perfectly well. I'm feeling bad. Can you help me get back to the cottage?"

The girl wrapped his arm around her shoulders, grabbed his waist. They made their way at a slow pace to the wooden house. Kiret lay down heavily on a makeshift bed padded with blankets they had built from branches and furniture scraps in the morning.

Until the evening and for the following day he lay as if in a high fever. Jenny wiped his face and torso with a wet cloth, changed compresses. She fed rabbit slop she had managed to cook in an old saucepan, against Kiret's prohibition not to light a fire.

At night, shots were heard again, but also this time the warring bands didn't become interested in the village.

Early in the morning, Kiret got up very changed. The hair and stubble turned fully dark brown and glistening with health in the early rays of the sun. Hazel eyes brightened with determination, as well as the melancholy that had been present in Necron for some time. The skin no longer frightened with corpse white like in a cave amphibian. "The ex-emperor does indeed look like his thirty-four years in which kiritianization preserved him," the girl thought with delight.

"And, are you ready to go?" He smiled with satisfaction as he slung the plasma gun strip over his torso.

"Absolutely," Jenny replied enthusiastically.

They went on to look for signs of civilization where they could finally get help. The mysterious night shooters faded away like heavy morning mist, no longer disturbing them. When they left the grove and found themselves at the foot of a vast hill, Kiret, who had been optimistic in the morning, was shocked. He took a few stiff steps as if he had been sitting in his armchair for half a day, then stopped again. To Sandstorm's amazement, he fell to his knees as he saw the golden reflections of the sun on enormous towers that dominated with the bulk over the area. Jenny didn't understand her companion's behavior, she herself saw the extravagant construction that didn't fit to the dilapidated, barren surroundings. Amazingly complete. For Kiret, this miracle must have meant a lot, because he was no longer on his knees, but was stuck on all fours with his head bowed as if exhausted. The girl came up to him, crouched down, put her hand gently on his shoulder and asked with concern:

"Necron, what's going on?"

"Earth. Chaponost."

She looked at the ground around the boots.

"What about the earth?"

Necron turned his head toward her.

"We are on Earth, near Chaponost in New Arabia, former France. It must be Chaponost ... But the area doesn't look like Chaponost at all!"

If it hadn't been for the wind whistling between the three monuments, there would have been perfect silence.

"Please elaborate," Jenny broke it. "I only know this planet from education and stories."

"This is the Freedom Monument, erected after the Fourth World War. We are in my former homeland." Necron sat on his boots, looked at the tops of lithium steel poles protruding a hundred meters above the ground, containing stone and metal in a ratio of half and half. The ends had been bent like the tips of crowbars, they had been merged with a large hoop, giving the whole the shape as if of an umbrella stand. It had once been considered modern art. The structure of the monument was simple, the creator had put on austerity and monumentalism. Long ago, flags had fluttered at the top: with a dove meaning peace, French, Arab and of the United States of Europe. The entire structure had been covered with a transparent film of something that had looked like ice, which had made the metal appear iridescent in the sun with fresh, factory-made silver. "Now everything is completely distinct. Different than I remembered. The people, cities, life ..." He unconsciously grabbed Jenny's hand and squeezed it so tightly that it hurt the girl. "Everything is gone. All the past. Only the monument has remained."

Sandstorm could only guess what felt Kiret, of whose former reality only memories was left. She pulled her hand out of his grip, after hesitating briefly, wrapped her arms around his shoulders and pressed her cheek against his armor. She was grateful that Kiret, lost in thought, had ignored her boldness ... or simply agreed silently to closeness and sympathy. He probably needed it, though his pride kept him from saying it aloud. Jenny had often thought about the psychological aspect of kiritianization and immortality - whether after centuries of life a person emotionally turned into a low-generation, insensitive android. Now she had her answer, and was relieved to find that her assumptions were wrong.

She wanted to gently touch his mind to find out nuances about the Kiritian's past, but encountered standard nothingness, as if she had been staring into the unlit depths of an ocean. Apart from practicing together, Kiret didn't let her into his thoughts. She came to her senses and felt ashamed. She couldn't help it that wanting to know as much as possible about him overwhelmed her more than once.

The man slipped out of Jenny's embrace, walked to the base of the structure, and touched one of the pillars with his hand. He stroked it tenderly like a beloved pet, tapped his finger against a transparent layer that he didn't recognize.

As they descended the escarpment sometime later, before their eyes widened in disbelief, appeared a sad, gray, pressed city. Most of the buildings were razed to the ground, a small district in the east had been preserved: a historic castle, a lonely spire, a fragment of a wall, a monument, some official buildings. As in the case of the Freedom Monument, each piece of metal, wood, stone or alloy was covered with the transparent coating. There was no sign of any life except the newcomers.

"Better not touch it," Kiret sensitized the girl, when she wanted to examine a fragment of the wall with her fingertips. "Could be toxic or contaminated or hell knows what."

"You touched it yourself."

"I have gloves."

"Is that Chaponost?"

"Yes. There should be nearby Lyon, the bigger city."

Jenny was appraising the area excitedly, unconsciously shaking her head.

"What happened here? Kandrok? Earthquake? Asteroid?"

"There would be fresh traces of Kandrok, assuming ... that it was I who brought them to Earth. An asteroid shockwave would have wreaked total havoc, and many objects would have been flooded and burnt to ash. After a strong earthquake, there would be a lot of ground fractures and sinkholes. The city looks as if conserved with something, but it has been destroyed anyway. All I can think of is ice."

"What?"

"You saw how many swamps, rivers and lakes we passed. There was water everywhere. Either there was a great flood, or a mighty glacier descended from the Alps and changed the topography of the area. Such an approximation on my part. Another evidence for this theory is the young trees themselves. Probably none of the passed along the way was more than several dozen years."

"Chaponost itself looks as if ice-covered. It is like a tomb."

"More like an icy desert."

They walked on a cracked street littered with boulders and fragments of buildings, silently searching for animals, plants, people, bodies - anything made of proteins. There were even no vehicles here.

The blue sky was clouded over, and the two were again accompanied by a neurotic wind blowing through the dead, poorly conserved neighborhoods.

After a dozen or so kilometers they reached Lyon. Here too, little had remained of the splendor of the agglomeration with a population of two million in the twenty-sixth century. The Rhone and Saona rivers were connected by a huge lake that swallowed up most of the buildings. Colorful buildings with narrow streets on the hill were best conserved, while in the lower parts of the city it was rarely possible to find anything higher than two meters. Here, too, the transparent layer covered all objects created by human or robot hand.

Kiret managed to find a landing field using his memory; while still living on Earth, he had visited this city several times, the center of which hadn't changed much over the centuries, because the builders had put on the expansion of the periphery. He quietly hoped that the territorial defense had taken off from Lyon. However, the airport turned out to be closed and unused for a long time, and they didn't find a living man or machine here either. Instead, they found several conserved bodies that were preserved as if they had died an hour earlier. No trace of a fight or flight, on their faces had frozen expressions of resignation and reconciliation with fate. They appeared to be the homeless, drug addicts and drunkards - no rich or middle class.

"So as always," Necron droned grimly.

Jenny leaned against a birch tree with a sigh.

"What we gonna do now? The evening is approaching."

"We can go north to Mâcon, or more east to Geneva," said Kiret indifferently, looking at the sky turning a dark shade. He felt nostalgic to recognize the first constellations he remembered well from his youth. "Both had spaceports. But on foot it will take us even three or four days, depending on the chosen city. Moreover, I have no idea what the region looks like now, and we will certainly encounter difficulties in the field. However, I feel that going to old metropolises doesn't make sense. Probably in others it is the same as here. But we have to look further, we will definitely find something," he added firmly, realizing that as a guide and a hope for Jenny, he shouldn't have been picky and complain.

On the outskirts of the city, they found recently built, abandoned wooden houses, similar to the one in which they had spent the nights before. There was a lot of waste as well as more and less useful items on the planks: nonfunctional bullet guns, ammunition wrappers, knives, animal bones, fragments of robots, rags stinking of urine, broken tools, pieces of furniture that had probably been looted from Lyon. They chose the cleanest facility with a table and bed padded with dry pine branches. A hole had been cut in the ceiling, and a hearth surrounded by boulders and sand had been built underneath it. Kiret replaced the pines with young birch leaves, which were not lacking on the shores of numerous ponds abundant in waterfowl.

For dinner, they managed to catch two little ducks. They took a risk and lit the fire in the hut for the time necessary to roast the meat. The windows had been boarded up tightly by previous tenants, and the only trace of human existence was smoke rising through the chimney, barely visible at night. Kiret doubted if anyone in the area used thermal imaging or equipment that allowed vision through walls. He considered whether it would have been better to give up the chosen strategy and instead of hiding, just flaunt their presence by lighting a fire outside. Someone might have come and helped them. On the other hand, he didn't know the situation on Earth and had no idea how the natives would have reacted to the presence of a Kiritian.

Before going to sleep, they washed themselves in a stream.

Having practiced telepathy with Kiret, intimidated, Jenny fell asleep on the bed. Necron padded his pallet with leaves and branches at its foot, although the girl with evident shyness, but also virtuous hope, insisted that he sleep with her, explaining her request with trauma and cold. It wasn't the first time that Biffter pretended to be blind and not seeing her signs.

***

In the morning, feeding on the leftovers from their supper, they agreed that they would go to nearer Mâcon. They looked down the hill at the city skyline for the last time and, after a moment of contemplation, set off. Being warmed by the sun from the cloudless sky, they headed north. They left the last pressed buildings of the suburbs behind, entering a forestless plain, full of puddles, lakes and watercourses. Far to the east, the blue outlines of greater hills were visible, but to the front there was nothing but a barren, increasingly drier countryside.

The ground seemed to lower as if it had had the shape of a gentle funnel.

Three hours later, they reached a crack in the ground. It was not a rift from the quake, but a canyon, as if the area had been struck by a cataclysm of thirty on the Richter scale. Such an amplitude was rarely observed on terrestrial planets - the destabilization of the crust on this scale came rather from outer space, after an object impact, for example. However, Kiret saw nothing that indicated an extraterrestrial cataclysm. Visually, the bottomless chasm with rock and clay walls was more than half a kilometer wide, stretching from west to east, as if from the Atlantic Ocean to the Alps. Miniatures of Pteranodons, with the wingspan the length of a man's arm, circled over the bluff. The reproduction of extinct species had been mastered centuries earlier, with a Siberian mammoth being the first to be restored. Creatures from the past had been kept in laboratories, zoos, and amusement parks, but some had been introduced into the ecosystem through oversight or deliberate action. Fortunately, these were small animals that blended into the environment and didn't upset the ecological balance.

Necron and Jenny had no interest in the Pteranodons, however. They stared in amazement at the unexpected obstacle.

"What a big hole," the girl broke the silence. She took a few steps back, having realized that the ground near the edge could be unstable. "There are such things on Earth? Hey watch out, or you will fall in!"

"There shouldn't be." Necron stood right at the chasm and leaned his hands on his knees. He tried to pierce the absolute blackness with his eyes. "Looks like an old sinkhole. Pass something heavy to throw."

Jenny found a boulder the size of a pineapple and handed it to Biffter. The latter threw it into the abyss. A minute passed, then two, and you couldn't hear anything except a whistle of wind in the open space and the occasional screeching of the flying reptiles. Some of them dived into the abyss and caught their claws on the canyon wall to rest.

The Kiritian and the girl looked at each other.

"So, we're screwed."

Necron looked resigned from left to right.

"What could have made such a chasm?"

"I have no idea, Jenny. I have seen cracked mountains on Earth, for example the Ural Mountains, or bottomless pits the size of villages, created by mine work, weapons tests or tectonic plate displacement, sometimes for no reason, but never anything like that. Relatively even walls may indicate that a human had their fingers in it. You can even see glass here and there, which is the result of the use of high temperature."

"So how do we get to the other side now?"

"We have to go along, all the way."

"If so, let's go right." Jenny chose this side because of the mountains, as depressive emptiness yawned on the other side.

"I think so too."

"You think we'll find a viaduct? Because air transport would rather be unrealistic comfort."

Necron pulled on his helmet and zoomed in.

"I can't see anything, but maybe farther there will be something."

They wandered with breaks for hours. The canyon began to arc as if it had coincided with the south-eastern border of old France. The ground was becoming more even, it resembled a land for development. Erratic blocks, swamps and petrified heaps of wood in old forests had vanished.

Instead of the viaduct, they found mysterious plaques stating that the area was guarded and that entering it could be fatal. On the titanite there were crossed-out images of a wolf, a bear, and a beaver. They circled the area in a wide arc and began to move away from the canyon. After using the thermo-vision in the helmet, Kiret noticed defenders with the appearance of lighthouses several meters long. The bright colors indicated that the defensive turrets, often placed on the outskirts of a facility instead of a fence, had power and were ready to turn intruders into dust.

"Since the turret AI hasn't noticed a threat in us so far, they should let us pass," Necron said to concerned Sandstorm. "They're old models, I know how they work."

He wondered what decision he should have made. He had no way of determining whether they had found a military or a civilian facility - there was nothing else in the sight and vision range. He must have missed something, because who normal would have set up defenders in the middle of nowhere? If they actually operated autonomously using AI, did the operators monitoring them already know about the presence of the newcomers? Maybe it was an abandoned installation, and there was no living soul in the area?

Jenny looked around and shifted her gaze back to the towers.

"Why hadn't we seen them before? They are quite tall."

"It makes me wonder too."

As Biffter appraised the defenders on close-up again, the heads turned with the cannons towards them. A shot was enough to destroy a target. There was another nuance he had previously taken for a foreland - buildings.

"Are we taking a risk?" The girl asked as he indicated her the objects.

"It would be worth checking, since we are sure that we will not be shot dead."

"And how do you know that? Because you saw the defenders through binoculars?" She said without malice.

"I've seen something like this a thousand times, and I know how these towers work."

True, Kiret was an ancient Kiritian after all. The girl felt stupid, but she didn't show it.

"They might be broken. Or someone has configured them custom."

"They're operational. Aside from those unfortunate territorial defense planes, this is the first oasis of human existence where someone might have survived. I can't catch the silhouettes with the helmet thermo-inductor. But since someone has made an effort to set up the towers, they might also have secured the buildings from spying. Although it's weird. As far as I know, on Earth the Kiritian technology isn't used, but archaic one, so my hardware should be able to handle security."

"What's the problem to buy something extraterrestrial and bring it to the planet? Probably also on Earth some discoveries are constantly made, and defense and espionage technology is being developed."

"Good thinking, Jenny. However, the first issue is the economic and logistical problem. People in the Old Zone are not as rich as in the rest of the Zodiac Universum. As for research on Earth, I don't know anything about the news, Kiritians would be the first to know about controversial inventions."

"You've kind of lost control of everything lately." Jenny smiled apologetically.

Necron ignored this nasty fact.

"Wait here while I ..."

"I'll go too. There is nowhere to hide anyway."

He thought that, in fact, it didn't matter whether he would leave the girl on the outskirts and walk towards the buildings himself, or they would go there together. Probably their presence was known and their every step was followed.

Kiret slipped off his helmet, didn't reach for his weapon, wanting to show a possible observer that he had no evil intentions. He moved calmly, looking around as if a masked army could emerge from the ground at any moment. Sandstorm followed him closely.

It quickly became clear why the defenders were out of sight. They were surrounded by a dome of gigantic diameter bending light waves, and Kiret and Jenny had accidentally gotten in through one of the entrances and found themselves in the line of fire of the four visible towers. Soon Necron ran into a second, smaller dome, which looked to Jenny as if he had hit the air. Running his hand over the transparent material, he found an entrance. It was through them, with the right arrangement, that they had seen fragments of buildings before, but now they could see them in all their glory. There were gravel or stone slab paths, a few buildings, and a small landing pad with bigger and smaller flying machines. The whole was indeed reminiscent of oasis, as Necron had previously described it. The towers could be arranged on a circular plan around the residence, which couldn't be seen due to the cover. Probably during the day, the entrances were opened, but after dark everything was sealed. The area might have belonged to a rich man who could actually afford the extra planet protective screen that banally removed visual, infrared, and thermal signatures. Palm trees of rare varieties, the ubiquitous marble, whitewashed sandstones, limestones, a swimming pool and a mass of tropical flowers, which must have been extremely expensive to keep in barren areas, also testified to the splendor. Only on the north side was chaos - the ground resembled a training ground or an air raid site, but the latter was unreal due to the protective screen. Kiret associated that it might have been the result of the ground fracture a few kilometers away.

Buildings with flat roofs and small, tall windows had cream shades. The largest one in the center boasted the rich ornamentation of the gate. Three young women wearing blue and green al-amiras tended plants. At the sight of the newcomers, they took a break from work and straightened up like astonished meerkats.

From below, both protective domes were clearly visible to the naked eye. The structure resembled plastic, stylized as honeycombs; this seemingly filigree structure could withstand rocket bombardment.

Several armed men and an elderly woman emerged from the buildings. The faces of girls not much older than Jenny appeared in the hallways, they had long black hair, simple clothes, but a lot of beads and bracelets. The last one to appear was a curious man in his fifties in a traditional Arabic outfit, unchanged for centuries: a white jellabiya behind his knees and a light brown keffiyeh held by an agal on his head. He wore a belt and chains adorned with precious stones, but gold was the most abundant.

"Jenny, please don't speak," Kiret whispered to his companion. "From now on, do only what I tell you, okay?"

Sandstorm nodded, which Biffter couldn't see, looking at the master of the house. The latter waved his hand to the men to stay where they were and lower their weapons, then smiled heartily at Necron.

"Hello, brother, in my house," he said in Arabic, spreading his hands as he stepped closer. He was accompanied by a heavy, suffocating, woody scent of perfume. He nodded slightly to Jenny. She returned the gesture, not understanding a word or knowing how to act, but she sensed that it was a cultural norm that Kiret knew as well as Arabic.

"My name is Jamal Ibn Yusuf al-Aswani. I have settled here in the former lands of New Arabia, coming from Egypt."

"I'm Matthew Rain," Kiret introduced himself by his old pseudonym. "And this is my wife, Jenny." He pointed to Sandstorm without looking back. "Forgive me for entering your homestead uninvited, but I didn't see it because of the protective screen."

"Indeed." Jamal glanced at the top of the dome high above his head. "It's nice to hear that my choice turned out to be good and the money wasn't wasted. I had the materials imported from outside the Solar System, I didn't want to look for them in Wakanda, because ones of equally good quality are produced at most there, in the heart of Africa. Generally, anyone who can afford it prefers to buy goods from exoplanets. If Allah brought you to me, it means you are a good man. You belong to Kiritians, right? Judging by your armor." The man smiled enigmatically. "We rarely see Immortals on this planet, and in the Old Zone in general. You have a very strange accent and your speech is a bit archaic."

"Yes, I'm a Kiritian, but no one important. I learned Arabic a long time ago. I have found myself on Earth by accident." Necron grinned. "I'll pocket my pride and say straight out that I'm lost."

"You don't have to excuse." Jamal waved a hand at the men behind their backs as if chasing hens away. They turned and soon disappeared into the hallways of the bright buildings. The women also returned to their garden tending activities. Kiret noticed that they were all well-groomed, calm and richly dressed. He was pretty sure he had come across the religious family of Muslim traditionalists, but not radicals. "You and your wife are probably tired, since you got here on foot."

"I lost a flying machine, it crashed. But I didn't realize that the planet looked like this now, and many cities had disappeared. I was hoping to get help in about an hour."

Jamal touched Kiret's back with his hand.

"These are not matters that are discussed in a hurry and standing up. I cordially invite you to come inside."

"How can you be sure that I will not mess up?" Necron managed a slight smile. Rather, he was not afraid of an ambush, but if something had gotten complicated, he believed in his centuries of military experience, the thickness of the armor and the firepower of the weapon. He would have defended himself for sure, but the weak link was Jenny. However, it was not right to reject hospitality, especially since he couldn't know when he would have the opportunity to meet people again on this planet completely different than he had remembered.

"Allah has never let an evil one into my household, he favors those who obey his laws. If you were a threat, brother, my guns would have eliminated you. They won't let in anyone, in whose head are undergoing chemical changes not approved by algorithms."

"Come on." Necron spoke to Jenny in Kiritian, grateful that she behaved passively.

Jamal took them first to a bathhouse called hammam located in a high building, separate for men and women, to refresh themselves. It was a room mostly filled with turquoise water due to the lighting. Marble stairs led to the reservoir, from which protruded columns topped with arched vaults. The walls were decorated with colorful mosaics with patterns taken from nature. Incense filled the air with the aroma of agarwood. The women's hammam was similar, although smaller.

After a half-hour of ablution, Jenny went with the women to another room, while Jamal invited Kiret to a guest room - the part for the householders was inaccessible to strangers - which, unlike the building's bland exterior appearance, overwhelmed with colors and splendor. A scent of a few incenses' fragrance was coming to the nostrils, intense but relaxing. In the center, there was splashing water in a marble casing. Heavy, patterned and gilded furniture obscured two walls of the octagonal room, while the rest was occupied by coats of arms, mats and oriental carpets. The shelves were full of ornaments of all kinds, especially gold and crystal animal figurines.

Kiret sat down on a couch in front of a table for many people, where cups and saucers had previously been placed. The man, introduced as Jamal's son, with a name that Biffter instantly forgot, brought cigars, tea and fare consisting of herb pies, vegetarian tajine, vegetables, cheeses, and yoghurts, then left. Necron felt uncomfortable, was constantly vigilant, but skillfully hid it under a mask expressing appreciation for the owner's tastes. Though he remembered that French Arabs had been very welcoming and affectionate, at least during his time on Earth, he was surprised that, as a stranger, he had been allowed into the house in the middle of the wilderness with the gun. Some Arabs were very religious, which hadn't changed over the centuries, but somehow, he didn't buy the excuse that Allah sent Jamal the vision about the guests. It was possible that he would offer him something that would involve radical measures, because he had glanced at his plasma gun more than once.

While the host puffed on his cigar with delight, Kiret looked around the oriental room. He quickly caught details of modern technology that a civilian would have not noticed. Decoration hangers were masked mini-cannons, ready on a verbal command - maybe their AI was using autonomous software - to shoot a dangerous visitor. Niches in the walls, covered with wooden flaps, could conceal maintenance robots capable of producing from atoplaxal molecules - called stem cells in the world of technology - any repair substance. And there would have probably been found many more nuances if Jamal hadn't started a conversation, drawing his attention. That's why he had let him in here; the house only appeared to be traditional. Living in the midst of the inhospitable wasteland, the Arab was confident in his safeguards, even with regard to the armed Immortal.

"Tell me how you got here, Mr. ex-emperor." Seeing Necron's astonished expression, Jamal smiled indulgently. He released a thick ribbon of smoke and lay comfortably on the couch set perpendicularly to the one occupied by the visitor. "First of all, you turn to me casually, so you either downplay the norms of politeness or you have to be a key figure used to talking to subordinates. Generally, many Kiritians speak to each other directly, that's your trait. The second thing. Although Morascrik is about five hundred and forty-five light-years from Earth, I know what the dignitaries there look like. I'm interested in the politics of exoplanetary colonies, and K'otz'ib'aja influences all of them, at least it did, so how could I not know famous Kiret 'Necron' Biffter? But I understand your situation, brother, and that you had to create a second identity for yourself. Sensibly. Due to Kandrok and electronic silence, less and less messages are reaching us from outside the solar system. So, I'd love to know your story."

After Necron too, helped himself to a high-quality cigar, he began to talk about his adventures from the moment the enemy had tracked them in space. Jamal interrupted him as he reached the canyon.

"Ahhh, this. We called the crack the Border. It stretches through the southern parts of almost all of Europe. It is the brilliant idea of the Haunted Zone eggheads to physically halt the growth of an ice sheet that they themselves may have created through their irresponsible tests on the Earth's atmosphere and the planet's core. For about three hundred years, from 2615, when glaciers came from the north and flowed down from the higher mountains, there was a small ice age that covered most of the northern hemisphere. This resulted in one of the greatest migrations of peoples in the history of the planet. It's funny. Once, the poor fled the southern hemisphere, mainly to the developed US and Europe, because life was most comfortable there, lived off handouts with idiotic social standards, and then it turned upside down. Now, as you may have noticed while traveling, the climate has warmed up again. The seasons of the year have shifted. It is January, and trees have had green leaves at this time for many decades."

Kiret couldn't hide the shame visible on his face.

"I haven't known ..."

"When you are lumbered with so many colonies and rebels, and recently also Kandrok, it is no wonder that you don't think about the Old Zone, which has long since separated from the affairs and politics of K'otz'ib'aja. Space is no longer interested in Earth. People flew away from it and forgot about it. Everyone did so, deluded by the conviction of the space dream, which, however, came true for many. Only a handful of patriots and the poorest, those with no prospects, have remained on the blue planet. The population is now perhaps a billion citizens."

"What is the Haunted Zone?"

"That's the local name for CERN. Once the cradle of the most powerful minds in the world, the craziest experiments and religious rituals, today it is a land of ghosts, the living dead, savages, mutation and deadly vegetation. Apparently the most dangerous place on Earth."

Kiret preferred to think of the sentence uttered with a slight smile as a metaphor understandable to the indigenous people. He remembered that Dr. Maximus Figam, the wisest mind cooperating with the Immortals, had been working at CERN for a while, even before the Ice Age. The center, festooned with certificates, had been one of the unrivaled at that time. Just as being president had been the culmination of a political career, working there had been the top dream of every outstanding scientist. Bolder and bolder experiments, which had bordered on scientific fiction, had been carried out in it. Necron, however, wanted to make sure they were thinking of the same place.

"Is it about CERN near Geneva, founded in the twentieth century and operating for hundreds of years?"

"Correct."

"And it helped?"

"What helped?"

"The creation of the Border."

Jamal shrugged.

"Some say - yes, others say no. Although it is a very strange method of stopping drastic changes. So is the covering of derelict cities with a layer of hyper-resilient cladding of atoplaxal particles visually resembling ice to prevent the annihilation of streets and buildings. Nevertheless, the ice sheet crossed the Border a little and began to retreat. The climate has warmed. The moist, fertile area was quickly taken over by vegetation, animals returned, and many new lakes and seas were created."

"No wonder I had trouble recognizing the Earth from close orbit. Moreover, my ship was damaged and I couldn't scan. What about the original population of these areas?"

"As I mentioned, everyone escaped either into space or to the southern hemisphere, mainly to Africa. As the ice sheet and glaciers retreated to the mountains and the North Pole, the refugees began to return to their ancestral lands, like me. I'm the first in the region ..." Jamal sighed nervously, "or at least I thought so. I moved in only a week ago."

Necron looked around the room.

"Week?"

"The entire residence was printed by 7D machines in a few hours, even real plants. The flora is easy to create, because it is a cluster of totipotent cells that multiply rapidly. However, this technique cannot be used to build living animals, especially humans, unlike flora, they have souls, something that is still beyond the reach of modern science. Soon, the area will swarm with more settlers, because the soil is fertile and so hard after the thaw that heavy buildings and installations could be erected without the costs of stabilizing it. We will recreate the cities, the New Arabia, often referred to as European Arabia, will be reborn. We will rebuild the mosques. We must make it before the Visegrad Group and the Asian Federation, because they also look at Western Europe with a greedy eye."

"Whose land is it?"

Snorting, the Arab raised his hands and lowered them, flicking onto the table the ash of the cigar which made him feel more and more relaxed.

"Nobody really knows it. The great powers are arguing about it, showing the world ever new, alleged documents of ownership." He scooped up the ash with a napkin into an ashtray. "It will turn out that the first and the stronger is the better. However, I hope that it will not end with another world war, I don't even know which one."

Necron helped himself to the herbal pie. He was a little relieved at the thought that even the indigenous people were lost in the politics of their own planet.

"Can you summarize the current political distribution? How are Kiritians perceived?"

"So, it's like that." Jamal assisted himself by gesturing. "Apart from Muslims who see you as exceptionally good warriors who seized power in the cosmos, half of the rest of humanity doesn't care about you, and the other half doesn't like you. The latter are mainly descendants of the New Order Army and sympathizers of global government. They liked socialism and a totalitarian regime, when no citizen had to worry or think about anything, since the only right government did it for them, and you spoiled everything," he said ironically. "The Visegrad Group, with Ukrapol, i.e., the United States of Poland and Ukraine as the leader, doesn't give a damn about you. The old-world hegemons don't like you. The nationless persons don't like everyone but themselves. USA doesn't like you. Wakanda and rich African neighboring countries don't care about you. Arabs like you, and maybe also the Indians of the Southern Continent, remembering that many patterns in your nation come from their culture. At least that's what they think."

"It's more about Onkalot culture, as Forkis was an Onkalot, but humanoid jaguars from H14 and terrestrial Indians have a lot in common." Necron put the ash accumulated on the cigar in the ashtray. "Who are the nationless persons, the Indians of the SC and Wakanda?"

"The former, as the name suggests, are people without a nation. Criminals, sectarians, migrants, nomads, traders - they are divided into different factions sticking to their own members. They are constantly on the move; some are wild and unpredictable. They cannot be trusted unless you have platinum or gold to offer. Wakanda is the most socially and technologically developed country in the world, but it is not a hegemon, rather a friendly country of progress and scientists, but dangerous for anyone who would like to cause problems for it. Pissed off or threatened, it can send an intercontinental missile and destroy a hostile country with one shot. The rise of Wakanda has a funny story, namely a group of politicians-jokers created the state by taking its name from pop culture. Amazingly, the country that seemed to collapse within a few years began to expand and develop. Africa is generally an interesting continent where you can see the entire evolution of human culture. Next to clay and straw villages where almost naked inhabitants pray to lions, there is a spaceport guarded by androids. In turn, the SC Indians are the peoples of South America who have combined their ancient culture and beliefs with modern technology. If nothing prevents them, they will soon become a force catching up with Wakanda. But for the time being they are fighting the United States, whose citizens emigrated to Mesoamerica because of the glaciers, driving out multigenerational families from there."

"Who is fighting with whom?"

Jamal chuckled, put aside his cigar.

"Someone always scraps with someone, makes up, then scraps again. Arabs with Wakanda. USA with Indians. The Visegrad Group with the Asian Federation led by Russia and China. East Islands with the Federation. Oceania with Australia. The Federation with the USA. East Islands with Oceania. A Federation falls apart, its former countries skirmish. Then another Federation is formed, with a different composition. When the glacier covered half the globe ... huh, what was going on here, bro." The Arab waved his hand in a gesture of "come on!". He drank some aromatic tea from a cup.

"And the territorial defense that attacked Kandrok?"

"The closest is in the Faroe Islands. There are bases responsible for defending the globe against unauthorized aliens, multinational and neutral. Could I see your gun, brother?"

Necron handed him the several-kilogram plasma gun. Jamal placed it on his lap, began to turn, examined the narrow barrel, the dhursteel casing, the melting light energy particle generators, and the two rows of hot war gas tanks. He lifted it and checked the balance. He got up, grabbed the gun in a combat position.

"By Mohammed... This is like a cannon! Even Wakanda doesn't have such a weapon. Now I understand why you are not afraid to walk alone in New Arabia, only in the company of the woman."

"I heard some people at night, I think they were shooting at each other."

"Probably hostile groups of the nationless persons met. What is the puncture strength of the plasma gun?"

"You won't be able to melt the armor of Kandrok's ship with it - diarduk, or their metal, in general, is resistant to our weapons - but it can handle almost any man-made material in the Zodiac Universum. Unless Wakanda came up with something we don't know. Which I doubt. Our intelligence still works."

"I don't think they have. Kiritian weapons are still the best." The Arab gave the plasma gun back to Necron.

"Where do I find the closest ship to leave the planet? Rather, I mean something of a better quality."

"Well. You will find nothing on Earth to stop Kandrok's attack, hide yourself from them, or escape them. Nevertheless, the machines from CERN are closest to your requirements, or at least they were. In the early days of the Ice Age, when the corridors were in danger of collapsing, all personnel fled, though there is a conspiracy theory that something or someone smoked them out. Maybe even killed. Many didn't return, and the accounts of the survivors were contradictory. Those who tried to investigate the abandoned research facility also disappeared. I don't know anything else. If the spaceport has survived, maybe you will find what you need there." Jamal gave his interlocutor a warning look. "But I wouldn't go to CERN if I were you. It would be better to visit the Faroe Islands, it is more likely to get a ship there."

"It's a long way for today's standards. I don't have that much time. My subordinates don't know what is happening to me. I have to inform them as soon as possible, because they are probably already looking for me in space. CERN is only a hundred kilometers away, if I'm not mistaken?"

"You're not, brother."

"How is your interplanetary communication?"

"Lack. I just moved in and didn't have time to mount many installations. It will take me months. A personal communication center cannot be printed with a 7D printer for private use. In addition, such communication now requires an international license, access to it is limited and controlled. It's all over Kandrok."

Kiret scratched his chin. He didn't catch a note of resentment or accusation in Jamal's words, so he took it as a statement.

"So, CERN remains."

"As long as anything works there and it exists at all. No one prudent who respects their life ventures there."

"But I'll take a chance. Could you take me there? I saw you have the flying machines."

Necron already knew what the answer would be, seeing the frown on the Arab's face before he looked away.

"Don't get me wrong ... It's not that I want to refuse help to anyone in need, but going to CERN is too dangerous. I don't want to involve you in something that I have no clue about. Until you know your enemy's name and identity, you don't know how to fight it. It's too much risk."

"So at least lend me a machine. I promise that I will return it, although I don't guarantee that it will be intact."

"You could lose the equipment, and I don't know when I will have the opportunity to buy something new in Africa. See, we're grounded, we've gotten ... a little problem. Only the low flying equipment is operational, the heavy ships have been smashed." Jamal clenched his fist. "We have a crisis caused by a fool and we have to keep an eye on our belongings. Machines, as well as communication stations, must be built, they are not printed."

"Okay, and is it possible to cross the border somehow differently?"

"Only by air from here. All the bridges across the canyon were removed long ago to keep the crap from CERN from spreading to the southwestern part of the continent."

Kiret sensed that further discussion would be futile. Something was not right to him. Jamal told him less than he knew, or lied for some reason to conceal the facts about the center. Perhaps he was afraid of something, and it was clearly human - Kiret didn't believe there were any monsters at CERN. Maybe it was about smuggling technologies and research records from the nether regions of the facility by looters?

"But would it be possible to cross the canyon with one of your machines? Do you have skulaks? With a strong momentum and anti-g jump it could cover the distance separating the edges of the Border."

"Yes, three."

"Once I reach my people, I will make a point of rewarding you for your help. I am a Kiritian, we keep our promises. If I destroyed the machine, I'd compensate you with ten better ones."

"Look, it's not about money ..."

Necron got a little nervous.

"Oh, you are afraid of something? Maybe a strong sovereign who dislikes Kiritians and whose right hand you are?" He said aloud the earlier considerations.

The Arab laughed softly, friendly. He followed with his eyes the meanders of mosaic patterns on the carpet for a moment before looking at his visitor.

"Sort of."

"All right. I see. I won't dwell on the subject so as not to cause you trouble.

"I'm sorry. However, I am happy to offer you transport to the Faroe Islands ..."

The men were surprised by the sound of an alarm. They looked at each other: Kiret was surprised, while Jamal's face was filled with frustration, as if he had known perfectly well what was happening and it had had nothing to do with the threat to his life.

The Kiritian stood up, holding his gun.

"Protect us, Allah, everything but not this ...," said the Arab.

He cursed as their ears were reached by the clattering, muffled sound of a volley of several rifles. Kiret recognized immediately that someone outside was using a cheap, archaic bullet gun. However, its universality on Earth was not associated with backwardness, but with foresight and its history - it was a relic from the times when, due to scientific tests, the planet's magnetic field went crazy and more CME clouds from space came, which resulted in disrupting the work of energy weapons.

Jamal's son, nervous, ran into the room.

"Sajid again?" Father asked.

"Again," he said dryly from the threshold, then walked away.

"And I was sure it was over. Let me get that goddamn Hebrew bastard!" Angry, Jamal got up and followed Sajid briskly.

Necron hurriedly moved after his host.

As they reached the open ground on the north side of the property, slightly pale and sweaty Jamal turned to Kiret and told him in the face:

"I take back what I said. I'll give you a skulak. Even one also for your wife, but in return, I'm asking ... no, I'm begging you to do something about this crap! Your gun should do well."

4. Led to death

The official's projection that the rest of the team met on the other side of the bridge - at least not drugged Aytar saw him - disappeared, as did the monk killed by Tsar. Zira crouched next to Div sitting on a rock block and dressed his wounds with accessories taken out of the backpack. She looked resigned; the assassin's indifferent face could mean anything.

Darius was sitting on the ground, leaning his back and head against a carved pillar, staring unconsciously at the sky. He looked like he was crying. He was the only one who left the skirmish completely unscathed. Avadar was stuck, leaning tightly on the flat boulder and pressed his clenched hands against his white crew cut. He had a lot of blood on him, it is not known how much of his own and how much someone else's. Bradshaw sobbed at Shimizu lying still. Darkoris and Jelinek also didn't show any signs of life.

Tsar left the bridge, walked briskly to Div and Aytar who were closest. The man looked at him, and when the lieutenant looked at the lying people, he shook his head.

Seymour sat down next to the captain. They were remote from the rest, out of earshot.

"You were right," began softly Michael who must have shed a few tears as well because he had wet marks on his face. He rested his elbows on his thighs and pressed his clasped hands below his mouth. "Why I didn't listen to you ..."

Depressed, Seymour was not surprised by the behavior of the achijes, who had never lost a battle in their power, at worst flying away tied with zero or almost zero loss of lives. They were not used to the defeats and deaths of comrades with whom some lived for centuries and treated them like family. Tsar couldn't help but reflect on the paradox of Kiritians' existence: they didn't die of any disease, they didn't age - but they could die from injury like any mortal. Now for the first time they fought the enemy whose essence they didn't understand.

"And who could have foreseen ..."

"No!" The captain looked at him sharply. "I was unfit for this mission. I felt that I couldn't handle it. Do you know why I'm here? For those who are better than me were either sent to the borderlands to protect the frontiers of the Universum in a poor way, or they were killed by Kandrok, who directly attacked the capital on Morascrik. General Biffter found the random captain available, and here I am. Amyrade showed me what I really am like. It showed my true face. Kandrok at this plane is like crossing a fragrant meadow. Because of my stupidity, the wrong decision, I killed half the team!"

Tsar didn't recognize him. Amyrade's unidentified influence must have shaken him emotionally.

"If it hadn't been for boatik, Darius wouldn't have activated the gate at the building and we would have been stuck in some wasteland. Captain ..."

"I can't do that anymore, Tsar," Avadar interrupted him again. "I'm resigning. From now on, you lead the party as the next in the chain of command. You're ten times better achij than I am."

Shaken, Seymour stood up.

"But it's not the right thing to do! Who returns their medal ribbons after one defeat? You know Aveo Lacetti well. He had once been a rebel commander, lost many battles, but became president of Nephrida anyway."

"Don't compare Kiritians with the rebels. You are doing much better here than I am. You figured out how to end this bridge madness in no time. The flare idea was perfect too, without the limited visibility there might have been more casualties."

"In fact, with the idea with this mind-controlling monk I came up with Div. So, he too deserves a compliment."

"No wonder, your reasoning is a bit different than the rest's, which is the most useful feature on this trip." The captain looked sadly in the lieutenant's eye. "Continue to lead the journey, Tsar. I don't know how you do it, but you always cope."

"Captain," Seymour said softly as he sat down again. He couldn't remember the last time he'd said something in the sincere, serious tone of a teacher explaining a lesson to a child.

"You're in shock. Full of anger, sadness and regret. It's possible that this goddamn place is impacting your mind. Please give yourself some time and calm down. One shouldn't make decisions under the influence of emotions." Tsar poured out all the doses of the drug from the leather pouch. "Nobody's gonna take that crap from now on. We need to see the same thing and act coherently."

They waited for boatik to stop working on each of them. The flare smoke and fog had vanished completely, revealing the barren countryside in all its glory. They placed the torn, bloody bodies next to each other.

"We're on Amyrade, we're looking for Forkis' soul, we want to revive him, and we can't do anything for our own comrades," whispered Bradshaw, sniffing. He crouched down and closed the lids of Shimizu, Darkoris and Jelinek with his fingers.

"It's probably can be done, but we don't know how," the assassin said helplessly. He looked at the sapphire of the dagger hilt that still set the direction of the march. Following his gaze, Darius also glanced at the red of his artifact.

"We should go on," Seymour said. "We don't know where the drops are. That's all we can do now."

"We can't leave them like that." Tau pointed to the bodies. He looked around for small stones. There were a lot of boulders and blocks of rock around, as if torn from a structure, but without heavy equipment they wouldn't move any even a centimeter, even if they were pressing against one collectively.

"I have a flamethrower," Zira said.

Bradshaw looked at her incredulously.

"No." He shook his head emphatically. "We're not sure if they are dead or what death on Amyrade is. How can we know if a soul is not staying in the body, and if by burning it, we are not condemning the owner to annihilation? Moreover, burning the body is a sin and one of the greatest crimes against God's creation! Cremation is an invention of Satan. The body must be respected. The remains of the dead await the day of resurrection, as it happened with Jesus. A man cannot destroy them."

Darius concluded the words with a nod of his head.

"But we can't leave them like this," he said sadly. "If there are any animals?"

"All right. So, what do you propose?" Aytar asked calmly.

"We have to move on. Maybe we can get back the same way," the captain announced.

"As long as we survive," said Div grimly. He patted Bradshaw comfortingly on his shoulder.

"Thomas." Seymour nodded at Schindler. "When I was killing ... annihilating that old man, he said that he needed only you. As if you had been someone important. He wanted me to bring you to him. I think someone might have directed the avatar. But who?" He looked at the artifact, took it from Schindler's hand. The glow went out immediately. "Maybe this is the answer; the stone is leading you somewhere. But why?" He gave him the Collector back. "Maybe you shouldn't come with us."

"What am I supposed to do? Where to go?" Darius' tone showed that he didn't intend to abandon the mission.

"We'd better not split up," the assassin announced.

"We will protect you." The captain tried to make his words sound convincing. They gathered in front of the bodies, Bradshaw gave a short prayer, then they set off, gloomy. As the signals from the Collector and the sapphire indicated the same direction, the depleted team had no problem continuing its journey. The terrain was favorable to them. They could all see an equally dry, cracked plain the reddish color of the sky. Here and there were protruding skeletons of thick, twisted trees and lonely cones of rock. The dry air thickened as if clouds of sand had risen to the skies.

Soon the pavement became similar to the annihilated avatar next to the bridge, with precisely arranged and level sidewalk blocks. There were also columns even tens of meters high, their rolled walls were marked by symbols unknown to the team members. Even more attention was drawn to a distant rock mass, taking the form of levitating islands that could be driven into the air by force like a powerful explosive weapon or an asteroid. What went up didn't fall from there, as if a vacuum or zero-level gravity had begun above a certain height. "Another bizarre phenomenon," Seymour thought, which they could only acknowledge, not explore its meaning and origins. Nevertheless, he found an explanation. He remembered Jelinek, which shortly after arriving at Amyrade had fallen over and flown up. So, he concluded that the dimension could divide into zones where gravity acted differently in each of them, and force had to be used to jump to another zone. But what the red power poles that joined the highest levitating islands and the sky were, he had no idea.

They went out to an open space fenced with a natural, vertical rock massif. In the center was a hexagonal high building made of green bricks that could be used for anything. But it was most like a temple of evil - up close, you could see many sculptures and bas-reliefs stylized as bones, skulls and demons. Visibility had deteriorated due to the dust suspended everywhere, as if you had been walking on the bottom of a silted lake. Within their field of vision irregularly spaced pillars protruded from the ground. It looked a bit like brackets for an indoor parking lot for thousands of vehicles, where a roof had never been built.

Either Darius' imagination worked or he heard deep, evocative growling coming from nearby.

"I can hear it too," Div informed him, seeing his uncertainty.

The team members stood back-to-back; each one raised their weapons. Bradshaw had two because he had taken the one from Shimizu. They were silent. They listened. Everyone tried to spot a move in the yellow-gray, odorless suspension.

The nightmarish growling came again from a place little closer.

The ground began to tremble. Nodding, Avadar signaled them to go to the wall of the building, which they immediately did. They clung to it with their backs.

Two monsters emerged from behind the corners at the same moment. Sloping, two-legged, reptilian, and at least ten meters tall. Their dry, thick skin, gray in one of them and brown in the other, resembled a mosaic of cracked stone, arranged in colorful patches on the back. The hind limbs were as thick as columns, and the slightly longer forelegs ended with spiked tubers. Bone spicules protruding at different angles grew also over the spines, shoulder blades and heads. The creatures had no eyes, or were so small that they blended in with the furrows on their mouths, but they noticed the intruders and began moving toward them at a speed contrary to the law of the scale. And with anger.

"Seriously?!" Seymour called.

"Disperse!" Avadar shouted.

The achijes and Div splashed in all directions like a startled school of fish just as the brown creature hit with its limb the wall of the building like a demolition ball. And with the same effect - remnants of bricks fell from the dented wall.

On the captain's order, they started firing. Bradshaw, screaming, was drilling from two barrels at once. But they might have as well tried to destroy two great movable rocks. The rifle bullets either bounced off or crushed the creatures' hard skin without doing the slightest harm to them.

Enraged, the giants attacked even more aggressively. Trying to catch the intruders hiding behind the obstacles and shooting, they smashed everything in their path. Avadar tried to get into the building but found the gate slammed; the giant's earlier blow hadn't pierced the wall right through.

The creatures moved at the same speed as the escaping, but they stepped sluggishly and had trouble changing direction and maneuvering.

"It's pointless!" Out of breath, Darius was pressing already the fourth magazine under the Kalashnikov's chamber. From the backpack damaged during the fight slipped kariban and fell to the ground, which the corporal didn't notice. The artifact was extinguished, so difficult to distinguish from rocks and stones. "We didn't even harm them with that crap weapon!"

Throwing flares and grenades was also useless, only the visibility worsened more. People figured they were trapped - the ravine through which they had gotten there either had disappeared or been perfectly masked.

"How I hate this shitty dimension," Bradshaw growled.

The gray creature stumbled, lost its balance, and damaged a stone pillar larger than it. After picking itself up, it grabbed the largest piece and threw it at the intruders. The stone span shattered, hitting the ground.

With no chance of escape, Darius fell to the ground automatically. Tons of rock leapt over him like a murderous, huge ball, missing by centimeters. However, the captain, driven under the rock massif, had no chance - a dozen tons of rapid death crushed him into a cake. The boulder was stuck against the wall, not revealing the macabre contents.

"Jesus Christ!" Bradshaw blurted out.

Darius couldn't move from the shock for a moment.

Everyone was desperate, terrified and tired, even Div, who showed nothing.

The ammunition was almost exhausted.

"Dude, move your ass!"

Schindler realized it was Seymour calling him. Lieutenant shouting, "Hey, here!" and waving his hands, provoked the brown giant, who stopped only a few meters from Darius.

The creature swung its long, heavy paw. It seemed uninterested in Darius, for it moved its arm over him and sent Tsar, who didn't have time to escape, dozens of meters horizontally, as if he had fallen from a speeding skulak.

The spinning lieutenant hit his side on a rock protruding from the ground. Despite the armor, the left leg broke off at thigh height and flew away.

Marking a bloody path behind itself, Tsar's body stopped in the sand. The scream died in the man's throat, who couldn't grasp what had happened at all. He rose on his elbows, looked at the stump, then cursed and, resigned, fell to the ground.

Aytar quickly got to him. Despite the creatures walking towards her, Tsar's protests and groans, she cauterized his wound with a narrow stream of the flamethrower. The man almost fainted.

"Otherwise, you would bleed out," she said, kneeling down and resting Tsar's back against her torso. "There's nothing else I can do now. As soon as we get into the drops, we'll restore your leg. Lieutenant, don't space!" She patted his face. "Now you are in charge."

"It will go haywire anyway," he droned, struggling with the pain.

They didn't see what was happening to the rest of the team. They both looked at the approaching creatures, emerging from the dust like ghost ships out of the sea mist. Tsar raised the rifle with several dozen bullets left in his last clip.

On the way of the creatures grew Div.

He angrily threw away his empty weapon and, in a gesture of honor, not caution, reached for the dagger. The beasts also stopped; they seemed curious about the object in his hand. The sapphire of the hilt glowed a dazzling blue, astonishing the assassin himself. Brightness dominated the environment, breaking easily through the suspended particles in the polluted air, creating long streaks. Div saw Bradshaw's body lying among the stones. Darius screamed that he had lost kariban and threw himself into the search, taking advantage of the inattention of the giants.

The creatures raised their arms as if to shield their invisible eyes from the monstrous glare. The assassin's eyes, in turn, flashed when a thought occurred to him. He took a few steps forward, swinging his dagger like a flare. The giants began to worry and back away. Div unexpectedly and daringly ran towards the leg of the purple creature, located closer. Before it could pull it back, he drove the blade into the hard skin as easily as into cream.

The creature howled pitifully.

"It is a weapon," Aytar commented in surprise.

"That's what daggers are for, as a rule," Tsar replied. His words slightly improved Zira's mood. The mission would have been a final disaster if Seymour had stopped joking.

"You don't understand? The sapphire must also be an artifact, not navigational, but offensive. Apparently, Nimja can make such devices from any object, as well as living organisms. Div was in possession of the alien artifact all the time, and he didn't know it."

"We too."

"The sapphire was pointing to the greatest threat from the very beginning, having tracked it down. Or it was created to exterminate similar creatures."

"Good theory like any other." Seymour grunted. He moved his good leg as if he had wanted to get up, then, with a grimace of pain on his face, he froze in Zira's arms.

"I can't find it!" Their eyes turned to the running up Darius. There was horror and confusion on his face. He stood still and looked up.

The giants dropped on four limbs, causing the ground to vibrate, moved closer to each other - and began to merge. It was like the double vision of a drunk who starts seeing normal again after taking a detox. The difference, however, was that the chimera began to change at the atomic level. It grew to the size of a small mountain, so that it could no longer rise to two legs; its skin turned carmine. A metallic spike structure came into being on the spine, resembling an inverted cage securing ancient lamps hanging from a ceiling. But instead of a light bulb, a red ball of power started to form there, pulled from the energy pole trembling closest to the levitating islands.

Even of astonished Tsar's mouth didn't flow out any drollery, he shook his head.

"Do you have an idea of what's going on?" Aytar asked.

"I have no idea, Corporal."

The transformed giant temporarily lost interest in people, turned to the group of stones and focused on a specific one. A bolt of lightning rushed from the ball on its back, hit one of the objects that exploded turquoise, flooding the entire area with a blinding glow and a wave of heat for a second.

"Fuck, kariban! It was lying there all the time!" Darius grabbed his head, curled up and touched the ground with it. "Sorry ..."

The Kiritians were shocked, everyone was thinking about the same - if they survived, how they would get out of Amyrade now.

"The giant must have seen kariban with its senses, considered it a threat like the sapphire Div, and destroyed it," Tsar said. "The beam must have been excruciatingly hot ..." He grimaced, remembering Aytar's treatment from a moment earlier.

"I fucked up," Schindler whimpered, with his forehead still on the ground.

"Darius, don't break down, it was an accident, you can't see anything in the dirt in the air," Aytar said to him. "We'll find a way to go back."

"The ball of power ..." Div seemed to have come to another conclusion. Before the giant turned its attention to the intruders again, he jumped on its tail, got on its back over the protrusions - and drove the dagger up to the hilt near the throat.

It flashed again like during the earlier lightning, this time blue.

The creature howled in pain, began to throw its head sideways like stunned. The energy from outside ceased to flow to it. It was too stupid, too clumsy for its size, or too heavy to kill the assassin by turning over.

Div yanked the blade out. He slipped, lost his balance, but managed to grab a metal yoke and not fall from above.

He managed to climb to the top of the back, where between the bars of the guard, he threw his dagger at the ball of energy. He immediately began to descend from the bulk to the ground.

The giant started to be heating up from the inside. More and more it resembled a sculpture made of volcanic rock with numerous grooves and furrows through which lava could be seen.

"Oh ..." It was all that Tsar managed to cough up, certain that an explosion was about to take place and the shock wave would kill them on the spot, eventually putting an end to the unsuccessful mission 'Revival'.

Darius sat on his feet, began to stare, forgetting about kariban.

The creature tilted to its side and fell with a thud, raising clouds of sand, stones, and dust. The earth shook. It froze, a rocky tongue, three men long, slipped out of its enormous maw.

The carcass faded.

Nothing exploded.

The assassin fell from a height of several meters, but apart from the momentary loss of breath after hitting the ground, cuts and bruises, nothing happened to him. Reclining and panting heavily, he reached behind his bosom and outthrusted the chain with the green actinolite pendant. The stone was intact. Div breathed a sigh of relief.

The walls of the arena that had trapped them so far shrank in one place, revealing stone steps leading to the nearest levitating islands. Darius got up, immediately ran towards Tsar.

"Lieutenant, Christ ..." As the dust slowly dropped around his body just like adrenaline level in his body, he sank to the ground again. He was terribly tired, desperate and close to a nervous breakdown. He had just seen Avadar and Bradshaw alive and fighting, and Tsar fully recovered. "I'm so sorry. I screwed everything up."

"Dar, I don't want to hear this anymore," Seymour said. "It happened, let it go."

While Schindler was busy patching up the cavity in the backpack with repair glue, the assassin joined the three that had survived.

"Well done, Div," Tsar congratulated him.

"Are you alright?" Relagard turned to Aytar with concealed concern.

"I'm fine."

"I guess you have been right. My dagger has always been an artifact - not a portable lamp, and its operation has nothing to do with Karikonian magic. But I don't understand why it didn't work as it does now when I was under threat on Karikon?"

"Better give up on the inquiry, you probably won't find an answer," Zira muttered. She looked at Tsar. "It's just Amyrade. The dimension in which we are intruders." Seymour grimaced as she injected him with a painkiller taken out of the backpack. "How did you figure it out, Div, how to kill the creature?"

"I just noticed that it was afraid of the dagger, also kariban. I decided to take a risk and attack. The throat and abdomen are usually the softest areas of most creatures. And with this ball it was improvisation. In my time among you, I have learned that the weakest link in a machine is its heart, like a generator. Damaging it can destroy the entire device, so since I wouldn't have broken through to the beast's heart ..." He shrugged.

"We are lucky that the reptilian didn't explode after death like a bomb," Tsar pointed out. "Then all the rocks around would shit with our guts."

"It was terribly risky and arbitrary, Div." Aytar scolded him with her eyes. She relaxed as the assassin smiled briefly and gently with the left side of his mouth.

"Hit-and-miss, as you say." Darius looked at the place where the captain had fallen, then at Bradshaw's body covered in dust and stones. Biting his lip and struggling with emotion, he shook his head.

"What we gonna do now? Because of me, we only have one Nanawak's artifact left. We have almost no ammo. The drops can be anywhere, and so can another threats."

"Darius, get a grip. The collector still works, so keep on with your mission," Seymour said. "I'll stay here."

"And I with you," Aytar declared immediately. "Kiritians never abandon their wounded."

"How do you imagine it? Will you hold me up while I hop on the healthy leg? If something attacks us again, we'll both die."

"You can prop yourself up, Lieutenant, with the empty rifle," Darius suggested.

"Yeah, right, and what else, genius?" The man replied half-jokingly, half-mockingly.

"I just wanted to help."

"In this state, I won't limp even ten meters. I feel like puking, I'm weak and everything hurts."

"I won't leave you alone," Div turned to Zira. "Darius can continue the mission alone."

"You must be crazy," Schindler couldn't bear it. "Let me remind you that we're still a team, which keeps going out of your mind."

"Why, Div? Do you think I can't handle it?" Aytar answered firmly.

"Yes, you can't handle it," the assassin replied. "Unless, while on Amyrade, you acquired some super abilities that will replace the empty magazines."

"I will definitely not go further; we are not leaving our own. Remember the account of Forkis missing during the battle with Commander Aveo Lacetti while fighting the rebels? We were ready to scour the entire Zodiac Universum, planet after planet, to find him. For one man only. Not for the emperor - for an achij like all of us. Because everyone is important and everyone must be saved, this is the fifth point of the Kiritian decalogue." The woman looked at the ground and shook her head. She lowered her voice. "Only recently, among the survivors of our army, something went wrong ... The selection for the better and worse began. The more important ones that need to be protected and those that can be sacrificed ..."

"Can you kindly shut up?" Tsar interjected. "In case you didn't notice, I am in charge now and you are to obey me. This applies to you too, Raver Divinus Relagard."

Div and Zira ignored him, looking defiantly in each other's eye.

"Then I am staying with you," said the assassin more calmly.

"I think I know how to solve your dilemma." Tsar directed the Kalashnikov's barrel towards his temple struggling, as the weapon was several dozen centimeters long.

"No!" Darius and Zira shouted simultaneously. Div grabbed Seymour's gun.

"I'm kidding." The lieutenant smiled sardonically. "Suicide fits oderses whose lives are short, and who have self-destruction in their blood. The life of a Kiritian is sacred. I'm also going to survive, though maybe in my current state I don't look like a terribly dangerous guy. Did you really think that I would take my own gift of immortality? And who would continue to lead the section, because not the team, since Schindler and Aytar have the rank of corporal?"

"Poor way to soften an argument." Div encompassed him reluctantly.

"At least you shut your mouths. Relagard, keep going with Darius. Protect him as much as you can." Tsar looked at Zira. "This will probably be the best compromise."

Div sighed, looking at the giant's carcass.

"I don't think we can figure out anything else. What do you think boy?" He turned to Schindler.

"You could suggest something, because you are quiet all the time," added Seymour. "Maybe you have an idea worth taking into account?"

"We should leave as soon as possible," Darius replied hesitantly after a brief reflection. The behavior of his companions worried him. It was as if the world of Amyrade had been exploiting from the buried meanders of their selves the true nature they preferred to hide - or completely changing their personality. He heard Captain Avadar confess to Tsar that he felt inferior to the other commanders and weak. Usually silent, Aytar gave a monologue about brotherhood, support and closeness, which she had reportedly lacked in her childhood. He had never seen her open up like this to anyone, she was as if different person. Tsar was too serious. Jelinek's pride and a sense of superiority went to his head more than usual, and Bradshaw, considered a tough guy, cried like a baby. Darkoris and Shimizu were nervous and aggressive. Only Divinus seemed to be okay, but it might have had to do with the paranormal phenomena on Karikon to which he was accustomed. And finally, he himself - he didn't see any changes in his character. Could it be thanks to the artifact that somehow protected him, which could also be the case with the assassin and his dagger? Maybe it had something to do with the phantom old man killed by Tsar? "Otherwise, we will all go crazy here."

"I'm glad you're bearing up somehow, man," Seymour said to him.

Darius just nodded. He would have liked to say something encouraging and comforting to the injured lieutenant, but whatever he would have said, would have been a lie. They couldn't count on anyone's support, most of the team was dead, the drops may have been lost. And it was not known how long they would live themselves. If the Collector led them to another powerful enemy, they were unlikely to survive.

Div collected all the magazines from the fallen, with at least a few rounds left, and brought them to Aytar. The woman placed Tsar in the most comfortable position between the fragments of a crushed column and gave him something to drink.

They honored the memory of the next victims of the expedition with a moment of silence.

"Come on, kid. It's time to go," the assassin announced.

"But without a plan?" Darius protested, spreading his hands.

"What's your plan? Do you know the terrain? Do you know what to expect? Unfortunately, we have to go rogue." Div looked at the woman. "Take care." He shuddered almost imperceptibly, wanting to hug her comfortingly, perhaps to say goodbye for good, but in time he thought it would have been frustrating for her. Especially in front of witnesses. Aytar thought the same, because she also moved, and then pretended to be changing position. "We will try to do everything to get back here as soon as possible."

"Good luck," she said.

"Same to you. We go." The assassin motioned to Schindler and they set off.

They walked several dozen steps, when Div realized something important and abruptly turned back, Aytar also started up. They quickly approached each other and ran into each other's arms, then kissed.

"Wow." Tsar shook his head. "And yet they did it in the end. I thought Aytar would be without a man for eternity. At least so much good in this crazy journey ..."

As Darius looked at the couple, Jenny Sandstorm came to his mind. He realized that he must have sincerely loved her since he thought of her at the moment when his life might have hung in a balance. He regretted that he had never had the opportunity to be as close to her as the assassin and the former Calvary thief had managed to be.

"Hey, and me, nobody will kiss for consolation?" Pretending to be disappointed, Seymour raised his hand and lowered it.

"Darius, give me your mouth. You have to be content with what you have."

"I don't think I will use it." Schindler smiled kindly. Since the lieutenant was still in good mood, he wasn't that bad. Even if he was pretending, it was probably not to worsen their moods more and not to focus on the lost leg.

"If Alice were here ... Ah ..." Seymour dreamed.

"So, you still remember that girl, Lieutenant, out of the hundreds you've had?"

"Such as she, are never forgotten. The daughter of enemies' president will always be a tempting catch."

"Yeah ... careful, I might believe that it was all about status. Rather, about it that she was hard to get. You must have a real affection for her, boss," Darius suggested, thinking of Jenny.

"Alright, and now get lost," said Tsar, as Aytar and Div stepped away from each other, "or I will puke a rainbow, which on Amyrade might be found normal."

Zira returned to look after Seymour while Div prodded Darius' shoulder, and the two of them walked towards a dent in a valley wall.

***

Rocky islets, looking like huge breaches in the bowels of the planet, levitated at different heights. The shortest distance between one and the other was tens of meters. Darius looked frustrated for a bridge, an elevator, a rope, an aerial springboard - whatever. They had to get to the top if they were going to follow the direction of the Collector glowing mad-red. Schindler wasn't convinced that they should have not considered an alternative solution, remembering what Divinus' artifact had indicated them.

"The trip is over. We're stuck."

The assassin studied the islets. He remembered Jelinek's sudden stumbling, then jumped up vigorously to test a possibility. He hadn't expected anything concrete, but to his and Darius' surprise, he began to rise, as if after the jump a very low gravity had started acting on his body. He reached twenty meters vertically, then descended and fell gently to the ground next to the Kiritian. Schindler walked back and forth, focusing on the legs and the ground.

"You don't feel anything. You walk normally."

"You have to jump up sharply. This is how some kind of low gravity tunnel or something goes on. Perhaps it works easier in this zone with islands."

"So, another thing to do and not think about, because the brain will explode from overheating."

Darius walked away as if he had wanted to make a long leap, ran a bit and jumped up. He rushed like from a cannon. The despondency left him for a few moments, he wanted to laugh from the wild pleasure of flight.

When he reached another island and flipped in the air, he lost control of the body. He began to wave his limbs desperately. He smashed his seat hard against a rock. Div landed right after him, cushioning the not-so-strong fall with his hands and knee. He got up and looked around. The levitating rock with shades of brown creating mosaics was flat on this side and the size of a small landing field. There was nothing on it except for a few loose boulders.

Darius dusted himself off and looked at xik'iri. The artifact was still shining brightest when lifted above the head. He attached it to his belt. He looked at the islets forming giant steps that climbed through the red of the sky to the dark, starry firmament they had first seen on Amyrade. Although everything around them was a physical exteriorization from their memory, the newcomers didn't recognize a single constellation.

With better and worse controlled jumps, they got to the next islands, bigger and more distant from each other. Men already experienced with this plane were not too surprised that there was no wind at the height, and space was approaching surprisingly fast, as if the layers of the atmosphere - if there were any - had ended a few kilometers above the land.

When they reached the highest, asteroid-like, several-kilometer-long rock and looked down, they didn't notice the elements of the earlier route. A cosmic void stretched around, where you could breathe, move normally and hear sounds. They missed the moment as the stars began to move backwards, forming white blurry lines, as if the rock was flying at its fastest subspace speed.

Surprised, Div and Darius didn't speak to each other, watching their surroundings closely. The low-gravity tunnel was not working at the top, and there was nothing else in sight to get onto. Glowing red, xik'iri pointed to a cluster of lights on the far right, somewhere on the edge of an eggplant asteroid. So, they moved there, armed only with throwing knives and a half magazine.

After a quarter of an hour, it turned out that the lights were the external illumination of a grayish spaceship in the shape of horseshoe half integrated with the second, rectangular deck. The dark blue glow of the nozzles burned at both ends of the bail. Darius knew this unit - a small Kiritian scientific observation shuttle that could hover long above the surface of a planet. Div had seen it once, too. They walked over a rocky pier and watched the craft move at the pace of an asteroid, slightly away from it. Empty corridors and the captain's bridge in the middle loomed through the transparent covers. There seemed to be no living spirit around besides them. The artifact still indicated that they should have gone higher, perhaps to the roof of the ship, but gravity here too had a force like that of an Earth-type globe, making it impossible to jump far.

If there were still few obstacles and unknowns, it turned out that Div couldn't come to the edge of the pier, because he encountered an invisible wall. It was as if the abyss of space had been encased. Meanwhile, Darius could normally stick his arm or leg out behind the edge.

"Interesting," muttered Relagard after more fruitless attempts to break through the barrier. And they tried to smash it with the artifact, knives, boots, arrows, and also feel for any damage in the perfect, supposedly glass facet. "It is as if something was holding me back."

"Don't even say that. I don't want to stay here alone!"

"Don't panic. We don't know how to get to the ship anyway, and I think it is where we should go." The assassin nodded at the artifact, radiating like light torn from the outer hull of a ship. "At least you should."

"Div, look!"

Below the pier there was a metallic glow that quickly grew larger and took the shape of a Kiritian transporter for several people. It moved vertically upwards, between the 'horseshoe' arch. There were red and white reflections on the cobalt body.

The unmanned transporter hovered for a moment above the shuttle, then fired two drives and flashed forward. Soon disappeared into the depths of space.

Darius didn't have time to ask, "What was this supposed to be?" when another similar transporter appeared below the pier. Five minutes elapsed before it disappeared from view making the maneuver identical to its predecessor.

The cycle was repeating itself.

The assassin and the boy silently came to the same conclusions.

"You must be kidding," Darius grunted, reading everything from the assassin's gaze cold like the space around. "I'll kill myself."

"Do you have other idea? Xik'iri's light shows unfortunately this direction, where the next transporters are flying."

"If only we had an influence on the appearance of the environment, since every element of it comes from our heads ..."

"Then try to change something."

Schindler closed his eyes and imagined a quiet area, with rustling trees, hot sun, a burbling stream and a lake full of floating flowers. By the force of his will, he tried to exteriorize the vision. When he opened his eyes, he could still see the asteroid, the shuttle, and the transporter overtaking everything ever and again.

"You think I haven't tried it?" Relagard said. "However, Amyrade works, we have no control over what is happening here and what the terrain looks like. At least we cannot consciously influence our surroundings."

"I'm also concerned that we haven't seen any ghosts so far. Or atole, as Aggroteh used to say. Whatever you call it," the boy said irritably. "And that's only why we're here: to be phantom hunters."

Div surveyed the cosmos.

"They may be everywhere, but we don't see them." He raised a hand and rested it on the void as if it had been puronax. He walked away a bit, took a short momentum, turned and hit the obstacle with his shoulder. "I have no idea how to get rid of the problem. I have to stay here."

"So, what are we going to do? There is no way back, it is impossible to go on."

"I can't, but you can. Just take a run-up and jump on that transporter at the right moment. Rather, you will have only one chance. I'll try to think of something to get back to Zira and Tsar."

Darius made a sad face, looked around, thought and finally looked proudly at his companion.

"Alright. Good luck."

"Same to you."

"We have to bring the mission to a close, whatever it is like."

The assassin nodded. They squeezed each other's forearms.

"Okay, Div. Let me know when to start. When I begin running, the edge of the asteroid will block my view, and I won't jump that far from the spot."

Schindler walked away several meters, breathed on his gloves and rubbed his hands. Then made a couple of jumps.

The assassin raised his hand, looking down into the space between the bow of the second deck of the shuttle.

"Wait, you can't see anything yet. Not yet ... Attention. Now."

He waved his arm.

Darius started to run.

He stopped abruptly half a meter from the chasm, knocking down stones. He would have flown with them into the black abyss if Div hadn't held him down.

"Sorry, I've chickened out ..."

"It's okay. After all, you're risking your life. I'd be afraid too if I were you. But I don't think the artifact wants to kill you by leading you astray. You'll try again in a few minutes."

The Kiritian returned to his position, watching the transporter as it went up and away, perhaps the same in the constantly repeating cycle.

"Get ready." The assassin raised his arm.

Doubts appeared in the boy's head. What if it was a phantom and he fell into the void? Would he reach Amyrade and crash into the ground, or would he float forever in space? Or maybe the transporter would explode? Or someone would come out of the cockpit, pull him in, and he would never get out of there? He would someday reach normal reality as a frozen mummy ...

"Stop thinking about nonsense, because you are unnecessarily getting excited," hissed the assassin, barely glancing at his facial muscles tightened by anxiousness. "Attention ... Now."

He lowered his hand, cutting the Kiritian's nightmares.

Nervous, Schindler rushed straight ahead, as if his legs had been racing without his will. He thought of the captain and the rest of the fallen, wounded Seymour. Zira was his last chance from the bloodthirsty dimension. He had to get a grip, sacrifice himself for them. This time he overcame the panic. He jumped far from the edge of the rock.

With a scream and the pounding heart, he began to fall, waving his hands.

He fell hard on all fours, on the real cobalt armor of hyper-resistant Kiritian dhurnstal. He peered through the canopy into the cabin, in his imagination turned up by the events expecting to see a corpse there, but the interior was empty. It was also hermetically sealed and couldn't be opened from the outside.

The transporter was constantly hovering. Schindler regained his balance and, slightly hunched over, stood on the armor with his legs bent as if he had been surfing. He drew level with the rocky pier and Divinus lifting his thumb, then left him below to the right.

The machine stopped for a few seconds above the shuttle - then moved in a jiffy towards the blackness of the alien dimension.

5. Darius 2.0

Darius couldn't feel the momentum or its effects, as if he had been standing in a closed room on the surface of the planet. He was breathing freely. Not a single hair twitched; he hadn't put on the helmet, since the rest of his companions didn't wear them, which didn't end with serious consequences. He looked back and saw the asteroid moving away, along with the shining shuttle against the abyss of space. For some reason the fear began to leave him, though not the affect associated with the unreal voyage into the unknown. The artifact gleamed at his side like a miniature supernova. Schindler allowed himself to be carried away by the moment, straightened up, smiled haughtily, and raised his arms, arranging his body into the letter Y. The fleeing stars were smudging around into long lines like luminous projectiles. He didn't even try to interpret logically the overturned laws of physics here; he was over this dizzying stage. With his level of knowledge, he wouldn't find an answer.

He had never experienced anything like that in any dream, in any virtual projection, even on the craziest drug.

After a journey time that Darius couldn't estimate, as if time had also ceased to exist, he noticed a blood-orange blur of a nebula in the darkness of space. The transporter was heading straight for its pulsating epicenter; the artifact sparkled even brighter, it downright blinded the boy, who finally pulled on the helmet. However, he immediately found it pointless and folded it - the cover without electronics didn't improve visibility at all. He wrapped the stone in torn material taken out of his backpack, revealing only a fragment of it. He didn't want to hide it inside because he needed navigation all the time.

The nebula turned out to be a very small world surrounded by something like gas, a flat earth towered above by a bricky and titian sky. The naked rocks were also of similar color, as if they had been composed mainly of iron oxide. As the decelerating transporter approached, Darius saw more stunning details: stairs, a tiled road, torches, braziers with fire, idols, the faces of fiends carved into columns, and it was all made of rock and stone, including a building located a few hundred meters from the edge of the anomalous world.

The machine finally docked to the extended pier and flew away as soon as Darius jumped with the rifle in hand onto the ground dotted here and there with planetesimals. Apart from the warmth of his surroundings, he could feel nothing else, not even smells. All he could hear was a creeping fire. He didn't spot anyone alive. From the uniform sky, was falling densely like snowflakes, as if incandescent dust from a fire.

He moved cautiously down a rocky walkway towards the temple of evil as he mentally named the structure because of horrific stone carvings, in the direction set by xik'iri.

The façade of the building turned out to be a lonely wall as high as a large tree; after crossing the gate, Darius found piles of rubble. Navigating between the great blocks of rock, he stepped onto a path formed by pillars with flaming fire. The area resembled his last road section from Amyrade, which he had traveled with Div, except that everything here seemed to be created on a grand scale, especially the microworlds levitating at the edge of the field of view - clones of the main one. However, from the surroundings breathed a depressing emptiness like the breath of death; Darius had never felt so lonely, even while hunting lycans in the Chulimal jungles after the murder of his family.

He also stumbled upon death. On the ground he saw ragged skeletons of humanoid creatures, armed with sophisticated staffs, if one can say so of the dead. Looking at the degree of bone erosion, he concluded that the creatures must have died much earlier, and whatever had killed them, had probably gone. At least it should have. The number of skeletons and their arrangement indicated an engagement fought. But Darius took into account that Amyrade, if he was still there, was governed by laws that were incomprehensible to the poor human mind. He kept his weapon ready to fire. If an enemy showed up, maybe this time they would be vulnerable to bullets.

He started climbing a hill towards a cave with a foreground littered with tablets. Here, too, the fire lit up the twilight, as if of the late evening; the fragment of the artifact peeking out from under the cover turned out to be the brightest object. The boy noticed on the boards, walls and other surfaces, entire mosaics of picture and cuneiform writing, so small and detailed that he probably wouldn't have been able to trace even a single detail.

As he got closer, the grooves turned the red color of the artifact, peculiarly illuminating the path as far as the entrance to the cave.

Darius swallowed. With his heart beating hard, he walked in that direction, thinking of forms of brutal traps and bloodthirsty enemies that he might not have been able to see.

When he stopped in front of the den, the fear left him on the spot. He heard soothing words spoken in baritone in his head. He didn't understand any, but subconsciously knew that they promised security. The second voice, of his self-preservation instinct, screamed admonishingly, but the former had completely dominated him, making Darius a puppet.

The chamfered interior of the small cave lit with fire and activated signs was simply arranged. It was like a natural chamber full of colored crystals, mostly amethyst colonies; stairs and cornices were carved in the rock. There was a sarcophagus against the wall. At least, Schindler associated so the detailed, pale blue object three meters long, especially that beside there were bottle-shaped containers that looked like canopic jars.

Unsuccessfully resisting with the remnants of his will, he moved forward like a controlled robot. Something told him to put away his backpack and gun, which he did, having completely lost control of his body, and he moved closer to the malevolent object with the artifact now as warm and bright as if it had been about to explode. He put his hand on the cold metal. He had never seen one like this, it was very different from the alloys made by Kiritians. It was the first element foreign to Darius; since he was alone here, Divinus' mind couldn't influence the appearance of his surroundings. So far, the world of Amyrade had had an ancient character due to the presence of the assassin from the primitive civilization. So why didn't the landscape change if Darius had grown up as a child in the bustling jungle and been then taken in by the nation approaching three on Kardashev's scale? Where was this wasteland, rocks, sand and ruined buildings from? And who sustained the fire?

He was no longer allowed to consider it, for whether he wanted it or not, his hands unfolded the material that dampened the Glare of the Collector, and then placed it in the opening on the sarcophagus carapace.

Details of the great chest glowed laser red. Belts of red energy began to move across the room with the hum of a working device, which Darius associated with scanning.

The artifact suddenly went out - and disintegrated like old, charred clay.

"Oh no ..."

Frightened, Darius held his breath for a moment. He realized that he had regained complete control of his body and mind. He would have liked to bolt not to expose himself to unknown radiation or biological hazards, to hole up somewhere and think what to do next, but curiosity made him take just a few steps back.

Inside, a mechanism sprang into action, and although the shell of the sarcophagus remained intact, all the apparatus inside got activated, clicking, shuffling and whistling. The red glow dimmed.

The carapace split into several pieces which stuck to its sides.

There was a neurotic silence, interrupted by deep, steady breathing. It didn't belong to the Kiritian.

Darius peered cautiously inside, most anxious to see the corpse, contrary to what he had heard. Completely dead and harmless. Could it be that the artifact actually led him to material Forkis?!

In the sarcophagus - which turned out to be a survival capsule - lay a humanoid creature resembling a large cat, almost twice the size of Darius. Its uniform had been worn out with the passage of time, and the colors had faded. The body itself looked no better. The short red fur had faded, the drained skin reminded of a mummy, so that if Darius had overcome his disgust and grabbed one of her dried flaps, he would probably have taken it loosely off a bone.

He shuddered as the creature opened its silver eyes, obscured by cloudy tissue, with barely visible pupils. Then, with a grunt and crackling of her dry joints, she sat up straight, snapping her teeth and moving her blue tongue as if she had been struggling with the fur in its mouth. It rubbed its head and protruding ears with a clawed hand, looked around half-consciously. Then said something in a foreign language, having noticed stunned Darius with the gun pointed at it.

As she began to stiffly go out of the capsule, some flesh indeed fell off its chest and arm, exposing bones. Schindler felt like vomiting.

The being barely glared at him with its eye, and he immediately dropped his rifle and raised his hands as if in surrender to a stronger enemy. Now he was no longer stunned, but terrified, not understanding what was happening to him and how it was possible that the crumbling alien was in complete control of his body. The demonstration of the possibilities, however, must have cost it a lot, especially since it had just risen from the dead, because it closed its eyes when it felt a pain, grabbed its chest and, spluttering, dropped to its knee.

The anthropomorph with a crunch of frozen joints extended its arm and reached for the canopic jar, then tapped a sequence with its finger on its rough surface. The egg-shaped device opened at its upper pole like a flower bud, the alien took a tiny ball out of the mucilaginous interior. It placed it at its feet, then leaned on all fours and lowered its head.

The lump scanned with a beam of energy first it and then Darius, who still couldn't move.

What happened next, Schindler completely didn't understand. It contradicted the law of conservation of mass, as well as all laws of biology and physics, even by Amyrade's standards inside-out to the nth degree.

The blue-gray ball began to enlarge, change shape and texture to take the form of almost a copy of Darius in less than a minute, along with the light armor protecting the body. Except that instead of the original's dark brown hair, she had gold, and her eyes remained as silver as the stranger's.

The anthropomorph rose, hunched tightly, so that its eyes and those of the creature half as tall as it were on the same level.

Whatever happened, the short-lived phenomenon was impossible to register by the primitive human brain, for Darius could only see the dried alien flesh fall with a hideous clatter to the ground, where it quickly turned to ash.

The second Schindler, on the other hand, came to life. His face was resentful, focused and inhuman, emanating a sense of superiority. He extended an open hand towards paralyzed Darius and placed it on his head.

Schindler screamed in pain and fell to his knees. Fortunately, the torment was as short as earlier the transfer of the alien self into the new body. The corporal was stuck on all fours for a moment, staring at his gloves and panting as if he had taken first place in a five-kilometer run among thousands of runners.

"I am a Nimja member, the Seventh Minister, called the Bone Crusher by Onkalots," the doppelganger said in Darius' voice and fluent Kiritian.

Schindler tried to get up, but found himself on the ground again from the impression. He raised his head and looked at the stranger.

"Who are you? How on earth ... do you know my language?"

"I know the same as you do. I know both your biography and your story. You were involved as the Infected. I can use your speech, associations, references, colloquialisms - anything that enables us to communicate. I took everything out of your head." The clone studied his human fingers, flexing and straightening them. "Such a long time. Thousands of years in the chest. But at least I'm alive."

"Wait ..." Having noticed that he had fully regained control of his body, this time lost due to his own powerlessness, Darius rose cautiously. He was holding the rifle in his right hand, and with the left index finger, he was pointing at the interlocutor. "I know you! You were mentioned in the report we had to assimilate before going to Amyrade. You had left notes in Tz'aqol's temple on H14, thanks to which we tracked the planet Tamasul. There Aggro met Nanawak. He killed you! You died in some kind of fratricidal war!"

"What a beautiful war it was. We destroyed each other's worlds," said the double proudly. Darius had a feeling he wasn't going to like him. Not knowing what to do with his hands, he tightened his grip on the weapon.

"Why do you look like me?"

"Your atoplaxial particles, thanks to which you can create a small object of such a huge density, separated by a bubble with the properties of another dimension, so that you walk on ships like on planets, is a primitive form of b'itol. We invented it about a million years ago. If I combine it with the qualities of Amyrade and my mind, it gives me divine possibilities. I can create a new body, ship, planet. Everything! I'm not limited by any rules!" The stranger spoke with increasing aggression and emphasis. "Indeed, it must be a megalomaniac Nimja member," Darius stated embarrassedly. Aggroteh similarly described the behavior of Nanawak, who had talked an awful lot. "I would very much like to stay here if Amyrade wasn't a dead protoplanet. Because what's the point of governing a depopulated land? Nobody intelligent lives here, hardly anyone shows up here and almost always by accident. This is no place for the living, dangerous and deadly, where you lose your mind at best." He smiled slightly. "Unless you are a Nimja member."

"Why did Nanawak say you died? Supposedly you are immortal."

"We are just like you, Kiritians. Old age or disease will not kill us, but we can be annihilated cause our bodies can be destroyed. There was a war between us, the issues of which I will not explain to you anyway. All I can say is that it was about power. Nanawak was sure I had died because I had arranged my own death. I had hidden in the only place in which he probably wouldn't have been looking for - on Amyrade. It is an extra-material dimension, at least there is no matter that you had known from birth. A very flexible place that adapts regionally to the needs of the resident. Even Nimja avoided this plane because it understood little of the rules that governed here. It is as if you retreated from your enemies and hid in the core of a star. During my exile, I did research on Amyrade, experimented and learned a lot. I suspected that Tepew and Nanawak had found some clue indicating that I was alive. I was especially afraid of the Observer, who mastered best the ability to monitor in real time the entire cosmos we know thanks to quantum entanglements, as well as his ability to penetrate space with the mind. To minimize the chance of detecting my brain activity and bodily signature, I had my minions put me to sleep, moved me here, and guarded the false sarcophagus until I was forgotten by those who wanted me dead. The guards, however, died, killed by wild creatures from other dimensions. You saw their remains outside. I couldn't afford to set an automatic anabiosis termination as I might have woken up at the wrong time and been tracked by the Observer.

"Why did you look like a big cat and now you appropriated my appearance without asking?" Intrigued, Darius asked the direct questions, ignoring that they sounded infantile and somewhat insolent.

The Crusher began to walk around the cave and pick up the sparse items in it one by one.

"Conservative Nimja members like Nanawak always take the form of the final evolutionary phase of resiba, a canine creature we come from, even though we have mastered the ability to transfer self to another body to perfection. For traditionalists, such a thing is blasphemy. However, many of us like to use this skill, usually for entertainment. I once took a form similar to Onkalots, because it is my favorite species," the alien's silver eyes narrowed into ominous slits, "which you extinguished. But I don't harbor hatred towards you, after all, you followed a program that was written in your genes. What happened had to happen. I'm too low in the hierarchy for me to change anything," he added quietly and as if to himself.

Amazed, Darius blinked.

"What?"

"This can be translated into the old language of computer science. As a civilization and each of its representatives, you have no will of your own, although you think so. You function according to the program. At the same time, you are the program, you only fulfill a specific role. Your goal was to create and develop the civilization based on digital technology, and it happened. And I took your form, because the cat was falling apart with its old age, and only your pattern was at hand. What I didn't take into account was that I would spend so much time in anabiosis."

"They say time doesn't exist here."

"Because it doesn't, however, it doesn't prevent the use of this concept in relation to changes taking place in space to facilitate the conversation. I already mentioned Amyrade's flexibility to you. The place where I had settled had adapted to my body." The Crusher walked over to the canopic jar, picked it up, and began to rotate in his hands."

"And if it hadn't been for you, I'd still be trapped." He turned to Darius.

"I didn't do anything."

"But your artifact did. Nanawak didn't tell Aggro everything about it. It had other properties besides finding souls." Nimja smirked. "It's also a great locator. Anyway, I sensed its activity when you turned it on in Cargoo's nether regions."

"How did you sense it? You were almost dead! And why were you probing the area, leaving the mental signature when you supposedly wanted to never be detected?"

"It will be hard for you to understand. Nimja's might is based on the power of the mind. Psionics has become the foundations of our civilization. We have created artifacts as artificial, material analogs of our abilities, so we are sensitive to their action. Only q'umaraq didn't come out of our hands."

"What about distance? From here to Cargoo must be bazillion kilometers! Due to the revelations with which his mind was still bombarded, Darius got rid of all his fear. He got really into the swing of it and had to admit that he had enjoyed listening to this chatty Nimja.

"On Amyrade, there is no concept of distance, nothing is near or far away. So, it is similar to time. Therefore, I can operate my mind from here over a vast area of the cosmos. I knew that this chance might not repeat itself and took the risk of considerable mental activity. I made xik'iri work only in your hands. Once you were on the protoplanet, it was downhill. I reset its search program and gave a new one, told you to come to me."

"Is there something special which I stand out with?"

"You are the youngest, most impulsive participant of the expedition, you have an open mind in a youthful way and it is easiest to manipulate you. Why do you have such a dissatisfied expression? Cheer up! After all, you were chosen. I got to know your minds, created your psychological models and knew that only you, driven by curiosity and the desire to experience a great adventure, would open the sarcophagus. Others wouldn't have touched it; they would have been afraid to release something that might have been inside."

"After all, xik'iri signal would have indicated exactly your sarcophagus. Captain Michael Avadar would have had it open. He would have thought it had to do with Emperor Forkis."

"He wouldn't have opened it, especially since Jelinek would have had doubts about the safe contents of the chest. The captain would have ordered it to be taken to one of the drops and you would have easily returned with the help of kariban to Cargoo, because in the original course of events the artifact would have still existed and you wouldn't have lost the machines. If you had been able to wake me up in feline form at

Cargoo base, Nanawak would have surely found out about it. So, you had to come here alone. The rest had to be liquidated."

An icy chill shocked Darius, he shook his head in disbelief, unable to comprehend the being's indifference to the loss of life. His hands in gloves turned white as he clutched them tightly on the weapon. The alien's words sounded as ordinary as if he had been talking about throwing out garbage.

"What? So, it was all rigged?!"

"That's right. Everything you've experienced since the reprogramming of the artifact is my interference."

Schindler saw in his mind's eye the massacred body of his commander and the corpses of other team members.

"You larva!" He didn't stand it. "You killed my comrades! You smashed our mission! You could have killed me too!"

"Otherwise, I would be stuck in the prison of my own choosing," the Nimja member said calmly. "You wouldn't have died, I had everything under control. Remember that you left each incident unscathed, scared at best."

"You're a monster! Murderer!" Darius wanted to fire at the Crusher, but without blinking an eyelid, the Crusher took control of him again and made Schindler drop the weapon and freeze.

The stranger laughed, rippling for a moment.

"Dear funny boy. There's no reason to be nervous. I'm a god on Amyrade. I will bring them back to life without any problems. I had exhausted all the power from your artifact so that I could wake up and regenerate my previous body after a fashion, otherwise it would have fallen apart even before using b'itol. But I can fix it all and get back that Forkis of yours. Now get a grip, or I won't let you move."

"How do you do that?" Darius came to his senses. He was still furious with the stranger, but had already had a taste of how easily the stranger could pacify his anger and aggression.

"Nimja members have a lot of skills. I can boast that it was my idea for each Onkalot to inherit a molecule of what their creators can do."

Though it was not necessary, the Crusher snapped his fingers to enhance the effect. The Kiritian had his muscles so tense in his struggle with another round of helplessness that freed from telekinesis, he almost fell on his face. Having finally found out that he was only an ant that wanted to fight an elephant, sighing, he slung his Kalashnikov strap over his torso.

"I'm not saying this gratefully," continued the Crusher, "because I don't like people, but thank you for indirectly setting me free. I will repay you."

"Nanawak could sense you. Maybe he's already on his way to get you."

"After so long, I have certainly been forgotten. Nobody's looking for me. I think I can function freely on Amyrade. Anyway, the activity of my mind perfectly suppresses your body." The look-alike patted his chest. "You humans, just like Kandrok, have poor mental coherence with the forces of the cosmos, even if the avors are religious fanatics who have developed severe brain neurocytosis. You have both gone into digital technology, and the more metal and devices in a civilization, the lamer spiritual development. Nevertheless, this was Nimja's plan."

"And yet you sensed me at Cargoo base."

"Just because I'm on Amyrade. When I leave it, I will lose more than half of my unnatural abilities." The look-alike made a face of disgust. "I am the only Nimja member who has learned to use the possibilities of this amazing protoplanet, despised by its countrymen. They claimed that there was no potential that they expected to create here, which is why one of the synonyms of Amyrade is the Creators' Trashcan. But I am of the opinion that they were simply afraid to experiment in the divine, although it was always divinity that Nimja wanted. Therefore, they tried to recreate the conditions of Amyrade, related and in a weaker form, on other planets like Karikon, where it was safe."

"Divinus' home planet," Darius muttered. "Full of anomalies."

"Anyway, I'll show you something." The stranger picked up the canopic jar and waved it. "Let's go outside."

At the entrance to the cave, he put the device on a beveled boulder, rested his fists on his hips, and breathed freely, deeply and for a long time.

"Beautiful view. I've missed it," he said with sincere satisfaction.

"Is the appearance of the surroundings your doing?" Darius stood next to him.

"That's right. Nimja took a liking to technolitic culture combined with monumentalism. We adore stones. Usually, we style our matter transformants as them, which you call artifacts, and less often we change living organisms into them."

The boy responded to his words with a nod. It would be correct. Nanawak of Tamasul lived in an enormous fortress on top of a rocky mountain, and had his laboratories located in its gut. Apparently, the structure didn't look like the property of someone who, from a human point of view, had divine faculties. Since the double, even in deep sleep, had a total impact on the appearance of the environment that fully aware Darius couldn't transform, he could indeed be powerful enough to bring the killed team members back to life. He wished he hadn't acted impulsively and threatened him with the gun, judging him by his human standards. After all, what did he know about Nimja other than the rudimentary information in Aggroteh's report? Darius didn't trust the Crusher, especially after what he had done to the team and confessed about people, but he had no choice but to accept his help.

"You do well not to trust me," said Crusher amused, probing the interlocutor's mind without hesitation. "It is a characteristic of mankind. We don't take minor species seriously unless we like one of them, but we can keep our word. However, how we act depends usually on our humor."

"That matches the report as well," the Kiritian thought. Nanawak had helped Aggro only because he had entertained and amused him.

He constantly felt strange and uncomfortable arguing with the improved version of himself.

"You're also a telepath like Forkis used to be." Darius must have been careful with his thoughts somehow. Apparently, Kiritians during the reign of Forkis had been able to control them so as not get into his black books. Schindler had never developed this skill because he had joined the militarized nation after the death of the First Galactic Dignitary.

The Nimja member laughed shortly.

"Of course, you can't hide anything from me. But don't worry. There is nothing in your head that I have not come across a million times before. Everything will make a zero impression on me. Now admire the power of Nimja."

The Crusher took the second ball, previously referred to as b'itol, out of the canopic jar and threw it energetically into the open terrain. It bounced a few times, bowled on the ground and rolled into a small basin filled with sand.

Darius had been sure that on Amyrade, nothing would surprise him more than seeing himself in version 2.0.

He had been wrong.

"Oh shit ..."

"Everything you see was packed in b'itol," Nimja explained as the spaceship began to grow fragmentarily out of the ground, as if built by armies of ants from the undercarriage to the top. "The particles are expanding, recreating the object stored in its memory. Size and weight don't matter here."

It was beyond the boy's ken. With his eyes wide open, and his mouth probably not less ajar, he watched the process of the object's formation. Kiritians used automated cosmodromes and factories to build machines, in which they had to obey the laws of conservation of mass and energy, and above all, have the materials supplied. What the Nimja member was demonstrating, in their world was achieved through atoplaxal particles that imparted physicality to holographic projections in a diluted form. Darius liked to play games that seemed to be reality with Tsar from time to time, you could even get seriously injured in them, on a higher difficulty level. But he was still dealing with a mirage. Now, once again, he witnessed the violation of the laws of physics known to him, and with a banally small amount of own work. It was enough to save the pattern of an object in the memory of b'itol. He wouldn't have been surprised if the Nimja member had made the record by means of his thoughts, since he had such a powerful mind.

"Dr. Figam would be delighted," he commented in a whisper.

The final appearance of the ship, however, disappointed him - he saw the most ordinary Kiritian medium transporter in the shape of *Turritopsis nutricula*, a jellyfish whose phenomenal biology had once inspired Figam to create the super virus. This model was used by the Immortals for interplanetary travel. He looked questioningly at the double.

"We don't use machines when we travel," explained the Nimja member. "We move differently from place to place."

"Porters," the boy guessed. "You have overcome the limitations of space." He remembered the mention of the alien conveyors from the report about Tz'aqol's temple and the history of Forkis, who, being an Onkalot, had avoided death on Chulimal during a colonist raid by accidentally transferring himself with Aggroteh to the planet Aj, using a porter.

"In porters too. But not only. However, now I have created something that is well known to you and will provide Kiritians with the comfort of traveling. As you expected, I made the transfer of the pattern and the writing on the b'itol matrix with the help of my thoughts."

"Comfort of traveling? Does it mean you're taking us somewhere?"

"Without me, you will be stuck here forever. I am the only entity currently on Amyrade who can help you. Unless you prefer to stay."

Darius felt a little uneasy. He didn't know what to make of any of this. Yes, he had saved the Crusher not fully willingly from falling apart or being stuck endlessly in the trap, but Nimja's involvement in helping Kiritians seemed suspicious. He quickly broke off these thoughts, aware that he might have been probed, which in turn could have resulted in receiving deceptive responses. Not having much to say in his fate anyway, he decided to surrender to the course of events for the time being.

"No, thanks a lot," he replied. "I mean, yes, I want to get out of here as soon as possible. But what about Forkis' atole? We've lost all artifacts."

"It will also be child's play. Go onto the ship, I'll be right there."

The gangplank slipped out of the airlock as the corporal approached it. The appearance of the transporter inside was also well known to him, so he quickly reached the cockpit, having traveled the short deck. The bulkheads swung open in front of him and the lights came on automatically, adjusting the color and intensity to suit his body's needs.

Soon, the Crusher returned, and behind it the rest of the canopic jars, the wrappers of b'itol, were levitating in a row. He held xik'iri in his right hand, strong red coming from it was flooding the cockpit. At Nimja's mental command, the canopic jars slid into a compartment in the left-hand wall, only one landed at his feet.

"You haven't said that you have the second artifact!" Schindler said too sharply.

"I just created it in the cave, I used as a template the remains of your destroyed one. It's a copy of the original, but it works the same."

"It will continue to search for Forkis' atole?" Darius asked hesitantly as the Crusher placed xik'iri in a perfectly matching recess in the center of an instrument console. The veins of energy dispersed centrifugally from it in a brief flash, similarly to the way it had happened before in the cave with the original version of the artifact.

The Nimja member gave the boy, who sank in an armchair, a forgiving smile.

"It is not far away. Looks like your xik'iri had been drawing it before it was annihilated. Then it lost momentum and began to act erratically, ripped from its natural program sequence, but as I made a copy of the artifact, it moved towards it again. Xik'iri paired with atole works in such a way that one attracts the other. Your team guided by xik'iri was moving towards atole while it was approaching you."

"As usual, I have understood only a part. I'd rather not ask how you managed to retrieve the former emperor's DNA from the ashes, but explain at least," Darius pointed to the console, "will this transporter fly at all if the electronics don't work on Amyrade?"

"Yes, because it is not an electronic machine." The Crusher smiled, seeing a surprised expression on the interlocutor's face. "As I said, I created the airframe in the image of your vehicle to make you feel comfortable. Besides, Nimja has never used digital technology."

"Why can't it be used here?"

"The protoplanet behaves like a huge Faraday's can or a powerful EMP emitter, breaking through Kiritian safeguards. But it has nothing to do with any cosmic rays."

"Then what technology do you use?"

The Crusher chuckled softly.

"You ask a lot. I can only answer you colloquially, using the terminology you know. I don't want you to find out too much about us." He stared into the distance with slight interest. "You wouldn't understand much anyway, it is more likely that you'd lose your mind learning about things not intended for a being just above two on Kardashev's scale. Nevertheless, Tepew would be furious if he witnessed our conversation."

"Isn't that the guy on the Chulimal records?"

"Onkalots called him the Off-kilter Fang. He used to be our leader, but then everything went haywire. He tended to break the fundamental laws of Nimja. He perfidiously got some of them on his side and indoctrinated them. A terrible war ensued, the effects of which, only a fraction, Aggroteh saw on the surface of Tamasul: the planet died and became a frosty, rocky desert."

"What happened next?" Schindler asked, seeing the silent Crusher watching something beyond the canopy.

"After the war, wanting to prevent the autocracy from returning, we unanimously decided that no Nimja member would be elevated above the other. We will all be equal and divide power in space into areas. We will not get in each other's way. We are too rare and precious to be annihilated.

But Tepew - if he is still alive - doesn't belong to Nimja members who would easily relinquish the absolute power."

"And what would upset him so much about our conversation?"

"That by giving forbidden information, I might accidentally interfere in your development, determined long ago. In short: you would be ahead of the time. You would break out of the cosmic program."

Having realized that he was indeed asking questions like a few-year-old admitted to an astronomy center, Schindler waited for the continuation, but the Nimja member didn't speak. Having grunted as he changed position, he also stopped his look on the red sky behind the canopy, slightly obscured by tall, columnar rocks.

"Do you see anything inaccessible to my eyes?" The Kiritian didn't endure in silence for a long time.

"Yes. Souls."

Darius rose slowly with his heart pounding.

"And I ... Could I see too?" He asked the question with a powerful, primal fear, but not of the kind that involved disturbing physical pain or the awareness of impending death. It wasn't about the body. Darius suspected it was a fear of knowledge that was not meant for humans. Although, despite many tragedies, the Revival mission proved to be a fascinating adventure, he increasingly tended to think that he might have asked the command to leave him at the Cargoo base.

"But since he had gone so far, experienced so many strange things, it was a sin to surrender out of fear. Not to know answers to the questions that have been troubling mankind for millennia.

"Are you sure?" The Crusher replied as usual, knowing his thoughts. "It is one thing to hear about something in reports, read on reliefs of temples, which are analyzed in the realms of myths and legends, and quite another to see that it really exists."

"A moment ago, I saw the two-and-a-half-meter cat steal my image, and then the transporter with the aliens' propulsion grow out of the chestnut-sized ball. Do you think something else will surprise me after that?" He babbled to give himself spirit. "I'm a Christian, I believe in God. The certainty of a soul existence is part of my faith."

"Despite this you are still scared." The Nimja member smiled. "But as you wish."

Using telekinesis, he lifted the canopic jar from the floor and took out another b'itol from inside. He hung it in front of Darius' left eye, then in front of his right; the boy heard a soft buzzing noise and felt the air vibrate under the influence of the heat. When the process, incomprehensible to him, was over, the Nimja member posted the ball towards the cockpit cover. The device changed density and color, then splashed on the cover in a transparent puddle, as if it had been made of bonded, densely packed water molecules, so as to ultimately leave no trace.

Outside, the Kiritian began to see hundreds of thousands, if not millions, of dots of color circling uncertainly around each other like protozoa surrounded by repellants. Some bounced off each other. Others gathered in groups or were flowing in the air in swift streams. The blaze of colors made him so sick that he had to lower his head. He rubbed his eyes and looked again.

"They are ghosts? This is what they look like?" He asked with fascination.

"They look like that to you. I have optically modified the cover so that you can see what is familiar to you and fits the concept of atole preserved in your imagination. They are everywhere, also on board the transporter, because they are not limited by matter, but you can only see what is behind the cover. Your brain has too little computing power to see more, even for Amyrade's conditions."

"Do you always see these ghosts or only here?"

"Every Nimja member sees atole. Our brains allow it, as well as experiencing many other phenomena. We also see different types of radiation and we can ignore them so that our abilities don't interfere with the comfort of everyday life."

"So Nanawak saw them too, every moment he spoke to Aggroteh on Tamasul." Darius tried to imagine how a Nimja member could see, and he couldn't think of anything better than the superimposed visual filters in his helmet or spacecraft cockpit.

"Atoles are not everywhere. Amyrade acts as a reservoir for them, and at the same time a sorting facility before the continuation of their journey. Space doesn't apply to them, while time - partially. Therefore, after someone's death, they simply disappear, port themselves, which is a natural cosmic process, programmed before matter was even created. Simply put. It would take a long time to explain for you to understand it after a fashion."

"I think my brain is going to evaporate right away."

For the next minutes of blissful silence, Darius watched, with a sentimental smile, the multitude of moving lights behind the canopy, already coping with the dizziness. The mesmerizing sight was as calming as looking in an aquarium with tropical fish, but the effect was tens of times stronger. He felt lucky to have the opportunity to see things that his species would discover only thousands of years later - unless Kandrok or another enemy killed all mankind before.

A red atole appeared in sight, brighter than all the neighbors, and moved like along an invisible line towards the transporter. As it crossed the barrier of the canopy, it disappeared to Darius' eyes, but the Nimja member indifferently followed the slower and slower path of its flight until his eyes rested on the copy of the artifact.

Xik'iri went out. The Crusher pulled it from the cockpit console and placed it in a casing resembling a small steel-blue rugby ball before handing it to confused Darius.

"Done," the Nimja member announced.

"Just like that?" The corporal felt the cold of the metal as if he had been lying in the frost.

"Just like that," said the Crusher, amused, seeing his disappointed expression. He cocked his head. "That's probably not what you expected."

"Well ... I admit I thought it would look more spectacular. As we set out on our journey, the artifact nearly smashed Cargoo's nether regions."

"You were given the dangerous toy, but if I know Nanawak, he didn't deign to tell you exactly how to handle it. You don't know anything about merging."

"Please, no brachylogy." Darius twisted the wrapper, examining its surface. "You must have forgotten that I'm not a telepath."

"It is about unnaturally connecting a soul with a body."

The corporal frowned, looked up, pressed his lips together, and shook his head helplessly. Then shrugged.

"That's all Nanawak. He didn't tell you the most important thing - how to use xik'iri, and instead he delivered a whole bunch of nonsense about the conjunction of the planets or the activity of the pulsar, without which, karitan would allegedly not take you to Amyrade. He was making fun of you. By the way, I can see that as a Christian you accept what is happening around you moderately gently."

"I'm a believer, but not a radical. What I am dealing with now is amazingly filling in the gaps in my faith, not contradicting it." Darius smiled briefly. "Maybe General Kiret Biffter received guidance from Aggroteh on the use of xik'iri. I'm just a rank-and-file mission contractor, and I probably know as much as I should know. So almost nothing. My job is to deliver the artifact with the atole to the general. What will our next step be?"

"I'll take you to the rest of the team. I can revive the dead." The Crusher smirked. "On the way, I will explain to you how to use xik'iri. Don't be afraid, it is not difficult," he added, seeing a hint of anxiety on the boy's face. "Then I'll meet General Biffter because he's in charge of you now."

It was not surprising to Darius that the Nimja member, who had some six degrees on Kardashev's scale, had decided everything himself, without consulting anyone on the team. Even Seymour, in charge of it now, could only passively obey his orders. Because if he refused to cooperate, the Kiritians and Div could get stuck on Amyrade for good.

"Onkalots called you the Bone Crusher. What is your real name?"

"What a long fuse, boy. I'm Nacxit." Darius smiled apologetically. "Nice to meet you. Does your name mean something?"

"A ruler. One of the Mesoamerican nations on Earth identified me with a supreme deity, the Feather Serpent. As well as peoples from other continents associated me with creatures or animals that they worshiped, characteristic of their region."

"Oh shit ... I'm sorry. So, you visited Earth ..."

"Several times. In a human form. As you already know, we can easily impersonate various organisms that we treat as avatars for our minds. We can stay in them for a while or whole millennia."

This time Darius had to sit in the chair and digest the information. It was too much for the tolerance range of his faith, an intense rain of too many elements that didn't fit into the mosaic he was completing, so he preferred to change the subject. They didn't have to rush to travel, since time didn't exist here, and he had a great conversation with this megalomaniacal alien, either way. Separated for long from his life, Nacxit was also talkative and so desperate that he chatted with the low-level achij.

"Why don't you like people?"

Nacxit sat down and stretched out in the other chair.

"Long ago, we refined various dominant species of animals from different planets, turning them into thinking beings that will one day create different civilizations. Unfortunately, the stronger Nimja member, with higher prerogatives and greater splendor, the better and more perfect the species they could create. It was the law of hierarchy and possibility. I created the Onkalots that you humans destroyed."

Darius sighed, looked straight ahead for a moment. He tried hard not to interpret these words in terms of his faith.

"I'm not responsible for what the long-dead people did. My ancestors may have had nothing to do with the colonists. This is probably true of most Kiritians."

"Kiritians are a specific nation. For centuries, you were commanded by the Onkalot, Xajb'a Kej, whom you knew as the First Galactic Dignitary Forkis. He gave you many standards and values that are characteristic of humanoid jaguars."

"So, one can say that you like Kiritians more or less?" Darius asked playfully, turning to him. Nacxit played telekinetically with a rock that orbited around his hand like a moon around a planet.

"Unfortunately, as for the species, I feel an animosity also towards you, but it doesn't affect the sensibility of my decisions at all." By willpower he changed the stone in the sand, it scattered over his legs. "I read from your head that when Forkis had died, the empire had begun to crumble, and with it, the nation's Onkalot values had started to collapse."

"Then you probably understand that bringing Forkis back to life and power is our priority."

"This is your concern, but I will keep my word and help you a little."

"It doesn't make sense ..."

The Nimja member leaned his head against the headrest and closed his eyes.

"Say it out loud. What has been bothering you for some time."

Darius didn't even try to cheat with his thoughts with such a powerful being, although looking like him. Moreover, he had been trained by the nation famous for its truthfulness. He started to turn the artifact wrapper with his hands again, which eased his tension a little.

"You guided me like a puppet. You smashed our mission. One could say that you freed yourself when you sensed the suitable tool nearby." He looked at the interlocutor. "So why do you want to resurrect Forkis? I don't buy the reason that you like Onkalots. Why do you want to take us away from here? What do you need Mr. Biffter for? I'd rather know the truth before I lead you to my companions. I don't want to hurt them."

As the Nimja member started laughing out loud, Schindler realized what a blunder he had committed, as if he had been in control of the situation.

"You might not like the truth, boy." Nacxit opened his eyes and shifted his position. He began manipulating the matter of the stone again, lifting it at his face and changing its shape and density.

"Nevertheless, I do insist that you reveal it to me."

With the rock being tossed in his hand, the Nimja member began to wander in the cockpit.

"Kiritians are playing their game, and I also want to return to another game, for now anonymously and secretly like the assassin you have in the ranks. Let me just say that I would like to see the defeat of avors created by Tepew."

"You used that word once."

"Avors are Kandrok's super-collectivity of semi-autonomous beings. All together as one. As you are humans, they are avors."

"You should've said so from the beginning." Darius smiled, displaying his well-groomed teeth. "And that was to make me angry that you want to help us beat the enemy? Then we're on the same team."

"Rather, you will be angry that you have no free will. Everything that happens to you was planned. You are operating according to the program encoded in your genes. You were to kill Onkalots, you are to be killed by Kandrok. But even among Nimja members, the fundamental rules that we were to follow were broken, which means that all the rules of the macrocosmic game collapsed. At least I think so. That's why I want to meet Biffter to find out more. All I have to do is stand next to him and collect information telepathically. Satisfied with the answer?"

Darius felt as if the artifact had suddenly increased its weight to tens of kilograms. For some time, he stared at wandering souls, which appeared to him behind the canopy as colored spots moving along designated paths. Everything became so unreal, more unbelievable than the stupidest dream he had ever had. Schindler didn't know if he could still trust his senses; all boundaries between fantasy and reality had become blurred. It was giving him a headache. It was only because of Tsar's narcotic school that he endured. Could he trust this Nimja member, take his words seriously? He couldn't, but he felt something was up. Even if he might have not like it. In any mythology, cooperation with a god or any powerful being usually ended up catastrophically for a mortal. Maybe this is what the myths had always been about, so meticulously perpetuated on indestructible, timeless media, in the style of stones? A warning to future generations against the beings from the stars? Now he had no choice but to wade into the episode in which he was involuntarily involved.

"I've always thought," he began, staring blankly at the niche that was the entrance for the artifact, "that everything I saw from birth was made for us so that we could direct our fate as we saw fit. That our achievements were only a consequence of our actions, and that as people we had control over everything. Now here you have told me that life has no meaning ... that everything is the program and creation of the powerful intelligence. That our every thought is predetermined, that we are puppets who will die collectively anyway, whatever they do in the meantime." He shook his head. "After tens of thousands of years of *Homo sapiens* existence, I, Darius Schindler, a simple achij, would-be farmer from H14, is the first person to learn what the meaning of existence is. So, it's not there ... Wow ..." He looked at the Nimja member without enthusiasm. "It should be a lofty moment, shouldn't it? And somehow, I don't feel winged or enlightened. Honestly, I don't feel anything. I would at most have a drink."

Nacxit patted him on a shoulder with mock sympathy. Still unacquainted with his abilities, Darius was surprised when he handed him a glass of clear liquid, which is unknown when and how found itself in the Nimja member's hand. He drank and tasted weak vodka, which quickly sobered a mind, although it didn't give a too strong kick in an esophagus, stomach and blood. This was exactly what he needed.

"It's probably better now?" The Nimja member, knowing the boy's thoughts, asked the polite question to keep the conversation going.

Schindler nodded a few times, handed back the vessel, which hovered above Nacxit's hand and instantly dematerialized.

"Be careful, boy, because from this philosophizing, you will grow a knee-length beard right away, and your head will go bald."

Darius answered to the words with a spontaneous smile.

They took off.

The transporter rose soundlessly above the peaks of the tallest structures. Soon they were moving at a dizzying speed, but Darius, as during the previous journey, felt no gravity force. They might have as well still been stationed on the ground.

"You said," he spoke, "that Nimja's knowledge was not meant for humans, because we might have advanced too quickly. And you've just given me so much information full of contradictions."

"Only generalities that you couldn't use in any way."

Darius folded his hands into the basket and looked at the canopy. From the reddish enclave of techno lithic ruins and caves, they slipped into outer space, full of fleeing stars, tinged in the distance with a spectacular nebula. Atoles thinned like antibiotic-treated bacteria, the corporal only sometimes noticed occasionally wandering spots.

"If you came in on our cause," he replied with a sigh, "it would certainly give Kiritians a strong boost in the fight against the enemy. If Figam and HQ don't come up with something, we'll definitely be doomed."

He said it on purpose, in his naivety, thinking that maybe he would make the Nimja member reflect. Or cause any reaction that would favor the Immortals. The stranger, however, stared at the stars with the steadfastness and coolness of a superior being.

***

They didn't find Divinus on the asteroid. It turned out that he had managed to find an anti-gravity tunnel, through which he again got onto the protoplanet Amyrade, then returned to the place of the fight with the giant.

The moment Darius and Nacxit hovered in the transporter over the arena, there was a blizzard and a gust of wind, born of the gloomy moods of the Cargoo crewmen unaware of it. The giant's body was covered with snow, making it look like a small hill. Aytar with Seymour and Div managed to enter a green building in the center; all its gates were up now. However, it didn't do much, because in the completely empty building, it was impossible to hide from the gale. Partial protection against the snow chopping from everywhere was provided by pressing oneself against one of the internal corners of the building.

The transporter, flooding the surroundings with streams of blue, landed on a white skin. The confused remnant of the squad froze, seeing two Darius who were not very different from each other emerge from the machine that looked electronic and somehow worked.

"Come on ... I'm begging, no more anomalies!" Leaning on Zira's knees, Tsar raised the rifle, ready to squander the last bullets.

There was a neurotic interlude as the arrivals stopped at a distance in front of Div and the two Kiritians.

"Eeh ... Hi, I'm back," Darius broke the silence.

Tsar looked at the face of one Schindler and the other alternately. He winced as he moved the stump to make himself comfortable.

"Did you multiply by budding or dividing the thallus? How do I know you are you?"

Schindler grinned. He had heard once that a complaining soldier was a soldier in good shape, and if they were joking, they were rather fine.

"I present to you the truest, alive Nimja member." He pointed to the double with his hand. "He's Nacxit, the Bone Crusher himself. The one mentioned in the report."

"He doesn't look like a Nimja member to me, his appearance is a little too human," Divinus grumbled sarcastically. He gave Schindler an accusing look. "Why did you bring him here, straight to us? It could be another dangerous mirage."

He managed to narrow his eyes distrustfully, but he couldn't contract his muscles for a potential fight, as he was almost completely telekinetically paralyzed when the alien took a few steps towards him. He could only breathe and move his eyeballs. Aytar and Tsar also froze, by no means from amazement.

Nacxit stood astride before Div and folded his arms behind his back, psionically examining his mind.

"Nexval didn't look like an elf?" He said. "And he was the realest Nimja member, though terribly mischievous and fond of playing tricks on others. We can assume the form of any rational being."

The words of the stranger made an electrifying impression on the assassin, because here the Nimja member revealed the fact from his life, about which only four people knew, in addition related to Karikon. He was about to ask if he was Forkis, somehow recovered by Darius, when he remembered that the former Kiritian Emperor was only a telepath.

"Telekinesis and telepathy are few of my talents," Nacxit said with satisfaction, seeing the impressions he had made on the new interlocutors. To intensify the effect, he made an arc with his hand, causing the wind and snow to hit the invisible barriers of air particles created at each entrance. "It is nothing supernatural, although you probably think so, because you don't know scientific explanations for these phenomena. These are naturally developed features associated with higher control of matter and energy. I already know everything about you. It was enough for me to stand by you."

"And in my case, you had to touch my head," Darius said.

"Back then, it was about learning the language faster, that is, a significant interference. Touch, gestures in general, strengthen the action of our minds. It's like using your muscles to push a drop versus the arms of a three-ton walking robot."

"He really likes to talk." Schindler pointed his companion with his thumb.

"Maybe you will deign to explain to us what this is all about?" Aytar asked.

Darius summarized recent events. The companions were as agitated as he had been before on hearing about the alien deliberately killing the teammates. They took control of their nerves to some extent when they came to the same conclusion as the corporal earlier - that the thinking of man and being about divine possibilities was radically different from each other. Especially when it comes to understanding death.

"Thus, our mission was saved!" Schindler proudly lifted the wrapper with the charged xik'iri's atole after his coverage was over.

"Since you are a mind control master, why didn't you just mentally convey us this information, but Darius had to tell?" Asked the assassin doubtfully.

"I could have done that," said Nacxit, "but it would have been a shock to your brains. I would first have had to improve them evolutionarily, so that telepathy between a man and a Nimja member was possible at all and went freely. At this stage, you might have gone mad or gotten neurological damage. My skill is a more complex process than information transfer from an entraser."

Darius looked at Div and shrugged.

"Great!" Tsar, in turn, looked at his subordinate. "In short: this boaster looking almost like you has superpowers, and when you do something against his will, he hurts you and can even kill you?"

"More or less." The Nimja member smiled slyly.

"Then will you help us get out of Amyrade? Can you heal him?" Aytar nodded to Tsar, then added hesitantly, as if words couldn't pass through her throat, "And revive our dead?"

To their surprise, Nacxit nodded briefly.

He knelt beside Tsar, bent out the remnants of the biometal armor around the stump, and put the torn piece of b'itol to the wound of the grimacing man.

Everyone except the Nimja member, who kept his expression indifferent, even bored, watched in disbelief and fascination as the achij's leg grew back like a lizard's tail after autotomy on a very accelerated visual recording. By itself, without putting the patient into a bio chamber, scanning, injections, adjusting the portion of molecular glue in the form of slime from stem cell modificants.

After a minute, during which Tsar felt only pleasant warmth, he had a leg as before. Nacxit gouged out more b'itol of the ball and replenished the biometal sliver in his armor, which grew, covering the limb - showing that he had the same control over organic and dead matter. The military boot was also restored.

"Dude, thanks!" Tsar blurted out happily when he stopped goggling. He immediately got up and walked a little, then trotted from wall to wall. "It's like nothing happened to me!"

Nacxit turned to where Captain Michael Avadar had fallen. The rest of the team, like a group of sheep, followed him, crossing the barrier straight into the fury of the self-indulgent snowstorm. Only Div stayed behind, completely distrusting the stranger. He had seen similar phenomena on Karikon, so not everything was new to him as it was to the Kiritians.

"Such things happen when people lose hope." The Crusher looked up at the sky and waved his hand. The snowstorm and the wind stopped immediately, and the firmament turned red and ominous as in the enclave with the tomb. Darius thought the Nimja member must have liked that color.

He expected that also this time the stranger would again use his balls to work with biomaterial, but to his surprise, it is not known which time in a row, Nacxit knelt down and got to work with only his hands raised above the remains. The body and armor fragments began to rise, transform and merge.

Soon on the heated ground, rested the captain's body lying supine.

In turn, after another minute of Nacxit's focus, the man came back to life.

He opened his eyes, sat up abruptly, as if someone had jerked him forward, and began to run his unconscious eyes over the people and surroundings. Gradually, the gaze became sharper and panicked.

"Oh shit ..." Schindler's respect, who fell to the ground, grew even more for the stranger. "He can really do it... Jesus Christ..."

Tsar looked like he was preparing to get rid of all his drugs.

Aytar got moved at the sight of the recovered commander. She crouched down and hugged Avadar as if a father healed from a serious illness. The gaze of Div standing with his arms folded over his chest softened a little. Confused, Michael mechanically returned the hug, completely not understanding what was happening around him.

"Relax, you're safe." Zira rose and helped him up. "Welcome back, Captain."

"He'll be fine, he's just a little shocked," Nacxit said. "He remembers what happened until his death."

"How is that? My death?" The commander was surprised. "Darius ... Why are you double? What happened?"

"Transferring information to the brain would be very useful indeed." Tsar nudged Nacxit's side, the latter glared at him. "Let me do it for you," he interjected happily, seeing Darius open his mouth, again preparing to explain. "Forkis' atole has been found, sir. Other Darius is like a god, he raised you, healed me, and he will revive the rest of the team as well, and then as a happy family we will return home. Understood, Captain?"

Michael blinked twice in response. With a confused expression, he looked at Div, now presenting himself most seriously of the company, but the assassin merely lifted and lowered his hands helplessly.

"How did you get the captain's atole back without the artifact?" Darius asked Nacxit, looking at him again with the same fear as when they had first met.

"He died recently. His soul still hung over his body. Such is easy to turn back, as long as the body can take it. Death only occurs when the body, or its vital link, is too damaged to function properly. Anyway, as Kiritians, you should know it well."

"The death part, we do. And b'itol? In the case of Tsar, you used it, and of the captain, you didn't."

"Since the leg and armor of the lieutenant were lost somewhere, I didn't feel like telekinetically searching for their particles, so I created new ones. But you can't create something out of nothing, even on Amyrade, which is why I used transferer. All the matter necessary to recreate the captain's armor and body was gathered in one place, albeit in a distorted, fragmented form. I put it together telekinetically and revived your commander."

With Private Bradshaw it went even faster, because the achij kept his body, he had received only deep wounds. Nacxit brought the atole into the organism healed by telekinesis with the ease with which he seemed to do well everything.

The private was in the same condition as the captain: he moved normally, felt no pain, but he stared at everything in disbelief and fear, especially at two Dariuses.

"Now let's get back the rest of the team as well as your lost vehicles." The Nimja member indicated the transporter. "I invite you, miss and gentlemen aboard."

Also, this time everyone, except for Div looking at the Nimja member with a skeptical eye, moved after him like sheep after their shepherd, still unable to shake off their disbelief. The captain gave Nacxit command.

After taking off, they quickly found themselves in a zone conquered by thinned fog. Soon before their eyes appeared the ill-fated bridge, where the fratricidal shootout had taken place. Fortunately, the bodies of Shimizu, Darkoris and Jelinek were found in the same condition in which they had left them: whole, resting in a row, with the lowered eyelids.

The Nimja member landed nearby. Once the crew was outside, he crouched down beside Shimizu and set about reviving him.

"It's good that you didn't burn the bodies." He turned his face towards Aytar. "You would have broken the connection with the soul and it would have dispersed. It is forbidden to burn a corpse, it is primitive and barbaric, resulting from ignorance of the flow of matter and energy. Better to dissolve it into organic form than to destroy the divine coding that would naturally and properly return to circulation."

Zira froze.

"You remember that he reads minds?" Darius spoke to her with a reassuring smile, easily guessing what was the cause of her anxiety.

"I'm sorry, I didn't know."

"That's okay. Sincere ignorance is an excuse. This is one of Nimja's sayings." Nacxit turned to Schindler, "And you, boy, be prepared to have to explain to your friends again what happened."

"I think I'll start charging for it." Schindler sat down on the ground next to him. "How the hell do you do that?"

"The whole process of resurrection is nothing but telekinesis," the Nimja member explained, holding his hands over Shimizu. "It is enough if someone died recently. The atole still hangs over the body which hasn't had time to change its form. In order to turn the soul back, it is necessary to repair the shortcomings by restoring the correct atomic bonds."

"Would people be able to do something like this?" Aytar asked anxiously about what everyone was thinking now. "It would be a shocking acceleration of the development of necro-medicine."

"I have to clip your wings, dear people. I already mentioned that evolution had endowed Nimja with powerful minds, thanks to which we have learned to influence matter and energy with our power of will. You, like Kandrok, have gone into technology and machine building. Your bodies have almost zero potential when it comes to mind control. You would do a little better if you contributed to religion and the advancement of your spiritual life, but many of you go exactly the other way. Paradoxically, the closest to Nimja are Onkalots in terms of psionic skills, though very primitive civilization."

At that moment, Kazuo Shimizu opened his eyes. "Done."

The three revived men also needed time to recover, which wasn't favored by Darius' story about what had happened after their killing.

"I'm sick of Amyrade! I don't want to stay here any longer than necessary!" Jelinek announced with exaggerated anger. He tried to avoid glancing at Schindler-looking Nacxit, feeling uncomfortable in his company and even more envying him knowledge.

"Neither do I," echoed his commander. "Can we get out of here as soon as possible, or does something else stand in the way, Mr. Nacxit?"

The Nimja member smiled crookedly.

"You forgot about your vehicles. Unless you don't want them."

"Mr. Biffter would be fussing at us if it came to light that we had abandoned so damn expensive toys," Tsar replied.

Everyone went on board the transporter. Nacxit took a seat in front of the instrument console, surrounded by seated or standing observers. Since the machine's cover had been neurologically and optically modified by the DNA of Darius as a human, each crew member was able to observe souls coming to Amyrade from various corners of the cosmos as onto an immeasurable, and therefore limitless, plane. The short journey was accompanied by numerous comments and all kinds of expressions of delight and disbelief.

Side by side, the drops found themselves in an area where the team had experienced the collective but material hallucination associated with the office building or cathedral. The barren, broken ground where they landed was now completely empty. Nacxit brought the vehicles into an open hangar, once again using telekinesis. Though the show itself was as unusual as anything the Nimja member got to, Captain Avadar watched it with a gloomy expression. The two mobile fortresses bristling with weapons and the latest technology turned out to be useless in the face of Amyrade's power unknown to Kiritians. Paradoxically, the mission 'Revival' was pushed forward by heavy, mechanically processed water, a recipe from centuries earlier.

"The next stop will be Earth," the Nimja member suddenly said. "I've found your leader's ontogenic signature there."

Except for Div, sitting on the console in the corner of the cockpit and twirling the dagger with his fingers, the crew members looked at each other as if any of them could give the rest an explanation.

"Are you sure?" Avadar asked.

"What the hell is Biffter doing on Earth?" Tsar looked into the brown eyes of Bradshaw standing closest. "He doesn't even like it."

"How am I supposed to know it, Lieutenant?"

"I'm just thinking aloud, you fool!"

"I assure you there is no mistake," Nacxit calmed them. "I have tracked your general's signature flawlessly. All information about him, starting from the detailed appearance, I took from your minds."

"What?" Jelinek shook his head in disbelief, he couldn't not smile wryly. "How can you find anyone who is in another dimension? Perhaps a billion universes from here, if anything can be counted on Amyrade."

"He has almost six degrees on Kardashev's scale," reminded Darius. The scientist paid no attention to him. Schindler said to the Nimja member, "I thought you weren't an Observer like Nanawak."

"Because I'm not."

"Will the journey to Earth be safe?" Avadar wanted to know. "Kandrok can track us. You were also supposedly wanted."

"I am not afraid of avors." Nacxit turned his seat toward the console. "Outside of Amyrade, my skills will deteriorate significantly," he admitted reluctantly. "Now you understand what my keen sense of observation is all about. But I should cope anyway in the event of Kandrok's attack. The genome nearly identical to Darius and the counterfeit transporter make an excellent cover for the mind probes of other Nimja members, especially since no one is looking for me. In addition, we will not be flying through space," he added after a short pause. "We will port ourselves directly to the nether regions of the planet, where the conveyor is located. Someone just activated it."

"Wait ... what? There is a porter on Earth?!" Jelinek shouted near Shimizu's ear, so loudly that the private flinched. "You're wrong! This is some mistake. A man has never mastered the art of portation. We can only do it with messages thrown through space, i.e., with sound, which more falls under amplification anyway. The best we have come up with was a subspace drive, built on the basis of the improved Alcubierre's drive design!"

The Nimja member gave the young scientist a poisonous smile.

"Everything is correct, for the construction of the porter wasn't born in the human mind. Now sit down."

Darius thought of a portation method with the use of Kandrok's elevator drive. If there was a celestial body near the take-off or destination node, it could be torn at worst, and locally damaged at best.

Before the frightened corporal could utter this observation aloud, Nacxit had triggered the portation procedure.

Darius once again reduced the comprehension of reality to his body of knowledge, for everything around him began to dematerialize as in the surreal vision of Tsar's strongest drugs.

6. A Straw Man of Headhunters

Kiret's first thought was that Jamal's estate had been attacked by the nationless persons. He had heard them before, on the way with Jenny across the wastelands, fighting each other in the woods, probably feuding bands. He was more likely to think that Kandrok had found him, but he certainly hadn't expected something like this!

He stood there for a moment, almost dumbstruck, because he had managed to instinctively pull his helmet on.

Out of the cracked ground on Jamal's property was sticking ... a part of a May beetle larvae's body. But hundreds larger than the known original. Estimating by the size of the rust-colored cephalothorax, the grub could have been several meters long. The rest of the body had a dark cream color, covered with hard crocodile-like armor, strong enough that bullets that were being sent from Arab rifles ricocheted off it.

"Fools!" Jamal jumped behind the wall, a couple of bullets bounced off the walls and casing, bit into the trunks of trees. "It's good that we don't have Ramadan now ..."

Necron guessed immediately that it was about curses. He was hit by a ricochet twice, but the armor made of biometal and dhurnsteel elements fully protected his body from the archaic ammunition, so that he felt only knocks, as if a stronger finger touch. The grub reacted in the same way, or to be precise, it didn't react at all. It bent the body into a bow, and with the armored mandibles broke through the dry ground as if through a meringue, destroying white lily flower beds, a manhole trapdoor and a part of a sidewalk.

"Stop it, you can see that it doesn't do anything!" Jamal shouted to the residents of the mansion.

The volley stopped.

Kiret noticed that the women, including Jenny (she had been given a turquoise gown and a blue al-amira, as well as a pair of gold bracelets and beads), peered out of the hallways of the buildings like frightened chicks from their nests.

"Now I understand why you were interested in my weapon and where the damage came from," he muttered.

He raised his helmet cover, looked at Jamal, then nodded at the grub, which was disappearing surprisingly quickly for its size below the surface.

Ibn Yusuf al-Aswani nodded eagerly, comically standing on all fours and peering from behind the wall.

Kiret set the combat plasma thrower's firing mode to the repeating energy ball and fired. It only led to a greater demolition of the area, because the worm had already disappeared in a pit about three meters in diameter, drilled at an angle.

The Kiritian slung the strap of the weapon over his shoulder. He was first to go down, he leaned across, resting his hands on his knees, and frowned. The group of men began to line up in a circle, including Jamal, panting after a short run.

"And it escaped from you," he gasped.

"Is this being dangerous to humans?"

"No, it eats plants, roots and soil, but it destroys everything around. I mean, it can hurt someone if a jinx accidentally gets in its way. The pisser destroys our possessions. In addition, it has settled into the nether regions in this area. We've tried everything from bogies to pouring poison into the tunnels, and nothing. What our weapons do to it, you just saw, brother. And if a larger-caliber bomb was to be used, the entire enclave would be blown up."

"But you have to admit one thing," Kiret said seriously to the Muslim, straightening up. "At least you have free installation tunnels."

Jamal gave him a puzzled look and rolled his eyes. The women came out of hiding when he waved his hand to them encouragingly. Jenny walked over to Necron.

"Where did such a big grub come from, anyway?" The Kiritian asked.

"There! It's his doing! Ask the old man!" Sajid pointed at the exit of the smaller dome, knowing full well who might have come from that side. Biffter spotted blurred, growing human figures behind the canopy. He counted four.

Jamal said a volley of Arab curses under his breath, rolled up his jellabiya like a woman the bottom of her dress, and began to stride towards the exit, tugging the fabric to the rhythm of the steps he took. For Necron, the situation would have been amusing in different circumstances - if the Muslims outside of the homeowner hadn't been armed. Sajid followed his father, as did the rest of the men, ostentatiously keeping the gun in sight.

Jenny touched Kiret's arm.

"What's happening?" She whispered. "I don't understand a word when you speak Arabic."

"There's definitely going to be an argument." He nodded at the silhouettes that stopped between a smaller and a larger barrier. "Nice outfit, by the way." He winked at her.

The girl smiled and pulled the scarf off her hair onto the shoulders.

"Thanks. It is very light and comfortable, but also warm. I was fed up with that itchy sweatshirt and abrasive pants."

"What did you do with them?"

"We exchanged clothes with this Muslim's daughter, she took them to wash. She said that in certain circumstances she would be able to wear them. It's a bit strange."

"That's their tradition."

The arrivals stood in front of the semicircular opening of the dome, which was the entrance to the property. They seemed related, only their ages differed. They all had black hair, a swarthy complexion, short, trimmed beards, and long, spreading noses. Slim and tall, they wore tight, bright uniforms on the border of civilian and military. Kiret couldn't see a weapon, however, unless it was small and well hidden, which he could tell if he had pulled on his helmet and did a scan. On the tops of their heads they wore tiny skullcaps, which were the only element of decoration linking these men with the Jews of the past.

"I've come for a compensation in gold," said the eldest of the newcomers dryly, who looked like a man in his late fifties.

"What a flippancy! You have the nerve to come here, Israelite?" Jamal said as he boldly stood before the taller man. "Next time I will set you in the defense guns as enemies and give you a lesson you will never forget! I don't owe you anything! And get your shabby worm away from here, Aaron!"

"You took my land."

"Are you nuts, man? Your objection is worth refuting with a laugh." The Muslim put his hands on the hips and started to laugh, echoed by his men.

"I bought it. Legally."

"The trade in lands and speculations of Israel don't interest, all the more concern me. This is discretion of your messed-up country, and it has nothing to do with the rest of the world. When you were still under the auspices of the USA, you learned that you get everything and everywhere. But end of story. Europe's glacial lands are no one's! I took what I liked, where lived," Jamal pointed his thumb at his chest," my ancestors ... Legally. You have the place to live, Aaron. Although I must admit that I would prefer someone better to be my neighbor two kilometers away than the country roguery."

"A synagogue was supposed to be built here!" Aaron lost his temper as well.

"No, there will be a mosque nearby!"

"Over my dead body!"

"It can be done! Now get your larva away from here. It's probably chipped and you control its ganglia, or you threw a sonic decoy somewhere under the ground. But don't delude yourself, I won't allow myself to be driven off!"

"I have nothing to do with this. Give me the compensation for the land you specially swiped from me before my arrival in Europe! I have ownership papers regarding it. I know you've gotten gold hidden here somewhere!"

"I'm pissing on your fake property deeds with a straight open pee!"

"So, beautiful is that flippancy of yours, which you yourself imputed to me."

The monothematic scuffle in a similar vein continued for the next minutes, astonishing Kiret, who was looking at the performance with an almost comical expression. Though Jenny didn't understand the words, she also, puzzled, followed the row accompanied by vigorous gestures and frequent fluctuations in the volume of the voice, while the crowd surrounding the feuding parties just waited to, on cue, get at each other's throats.

The Kiritian was about to intervene to reassure them both as a wave of vibrations rolled across the ground.

Aaron and Jamal fell silent.

Out of the ground near Jenny, amidst a rumble and a metallic whine, rushed up the grub, showering her with lumps of dirt and stones. The girl groaned.

The giant was preparing to dive into the ground like a dolphin jumping over the depths into the water when Kiret stood in its way, pushing Sandstorm away.

He fired a ball of energy.

The creature's top splattered in the orange-yellow rain of insides, splashing the women standing nearby, cutting them with fragments of the armor. Screaming and brushing themselves down frantically, they moved briskly towards the houses.

Jenny managed to hide behind Kiret, so the disgusting gore dripped in a small stain onto the bottom of her array. The Kiritian took the biggest blow: the entire front of his armor was smeared with blood, including his face.

The carcass fell to the ground with a crunch and soon went still.

Sandstorm began to laugh discreetly as bedaubed Necron turned to her.

"Yuck. It smells like the opposite of flowers." He wiped the gore off his face with his glove. "I'll have to wash again."

He walked over to Jamal and Aaron who watched the scene.

"Respects." Kiret nodded at the Jewish companions who had previously ignored him, focused on the participants in the quarrel. After his display with the gun, they lost confidence, certain he was Jamal's bodyguard; two withdrew. Necron felt a kind of relief and nostalgic satisfaction: he remembered the old days when, apart from the rebels ostentatiously hating them, everyone felt fear at the sight of Kiritians. He looked at Jamal. "So probably one problem we got over. Now, let me have the skulak."

***

The machine accelerated to nearly four hundred kilometers per hour, then jumped using the anti-gravity thrust and, when it reached an altitude, spread its wings to extend its flight over the Border. Although the ceiling for the skulak was twenty meters, it was possible to cheat the factory-set height sensors in areas with a huge drop that appeared suddenly. In this way, the machine 'felt' as if it had been still moving above the ground, although there could be even a two-kilometer gap below, as in this case.

Through his armor, Kiret felt Jenny clinging to him like a koala to its mother, though she was safe. Before leaving Jamal's mansion, he had meticulously checked the equipment, and had the girl buckle up properly during the trip. The front cover protected them from the blows of the wind.

They managed to fly several hundred meters of the planet's fracture as they began to descend like a landing glider. A good deal of safe terrain passed under the rotors of the engines before the skulak neared the surface and continued its low flight.

"Now you can let go of me and open your eyes!" Kiret exclaimed happily, shouting over the sound of the wind. When the girl hesitantly responded to the suggestion, she looked back at the disappearing Frontier.

"Whew ..."

"Really? You have just committed an unforgivable sacrilege!"

"I have other priorities when it comes to having fun. And it certainly doesn't include a breakneck jump over the precipice, where it is dark as in ..."

Her lungs bit into her throat as the skulak jumped violently over a boulder.

"Could you slow down a bit?"

"Your will." Kiret slowed down; they could talk freely now.

They covered vast areas, once mainly occupied by arable lands. Unlike the areas on the other side of the gulf, these were dry. The only obstacles turned out to be lonely trees or very old, ruined farms. The roads, made hastily and cheaply, of kitschy materials, had long since collapsed or been obscured by a moraine that had been moved along with the ice sheet. In the far east loomed green mountain ranges. The sun was starting to set, giving the surroundings an amber hue.

"How did that grub grow so huge?" Jenny said as a butterfly flashed in the air.

"Probably its origin is similar to that of thousands of other species that were accidentally or consciously introduced into the ecosystem. As advanced genetic engineering developed, it became a natural course of things, in harmony with human nature, to conduct more and bolder experiments. Arrange the wrestling competition with God."

"But why let something like that out into the world?"

"It could have been, for example, about cornering the market. Before the Ice Age, companies and corporations in the world flourished. When one of them was standing out, it started to operate with big money, others tried to extinguish it, for example by arranging a scandal or trying to prove violation of health and safety regulations. For example, someone released such a bug into a forest, and then visually documented its feeding, convincing the world that the creature came from a given laboratory, which had terrible safeguards. Destroying competition was common practice on Earth. And that modificants could pose a threat, it became a matter of secondary importance."

"You think the grub came from CERN?"

"It's a soil organism. Given its size, it is possible that it dug under the Border."

"Sounds threatening to say the least."

Necron had initially wanted Jenny to stay with Jamal until he came back from CERN, maybe came by a ship found (he doubted there would be something serviceable there those looters hadn't taken care of, but it would never hurt to investigate the famous object), however, she had refused, explaining the decision by a lack of trust in strangers. Necron had guessed that she had simply wanted being close to him. She could telepathically scan these Muslims to check their intentions, not to mention that they wouldn't have dared to touch someone else's 'wife', especially the Kiritian's who had made the show with the gun.

"You wanted to go with me yourself," he replied. "So don't loiter now."

They continued their journey in silence. Jenny surveyed the area, and Necron pondered bleak scenarios that might come true if Kandrok was to come to Earth, which he had accidentally pointed out to them.

They soon reached the outskirts of Geneva. The city was close to the mountains from which glaciers might once have flowed down, but it didn't seem to be affected by a natural disaster. Rather bombed long ago and therefore abandoned. The streets covered with birklon[1] were strewn with earth, cracked and littered with rubble. It was guarded by buildings turned into ruin. Trees and shrubs had long since broken through the once solid foundations of the great metropolis.

Kiret stopped in the open and seated the vehicle. With the vision of the helmet, he searched more closely the area in front of him. Apart from the flock of frightened foxes sneaking through an old parking lot and rats wandering under the remnants of the buildings, he could see nothing alive.

"Another ghost town," he muttered. He heard and felt Jenny from the back unfastening the safety lock. "Wait, we're not going anywhere yet. I have to think for a moment."

He was sure she would ignore him and put her feet on the ground, but Sandstorm fell on it like a bundle slipped from a slick seat.

"Jenny?"

Folding his helmet, Kiret spun around sharply. The girl on the birklon road looked unconscious.

"Connor's ass ..."

The moment he saw a metal needle sticking out of her arm, he felt a prick under his jaw. Almost immediately he got so exhausted that he was unable to keep his consciousness with his force of will, and collapsed onto the hard, cold pavement next to Jenny.

***

When he woke up, he saw the dark brown square of the sky, the stars were twinkling atypically only at the edges of the field of view. Orange light was creeping on the side; he heard voices around him. He was lying on hard ground, and as he tried to sit up with his face twisted from a headache, something dry and soft rustled under his body.

Kiret regained full consciousness quickly. He realized that he was stuck in a cage with tightly packed steel bars. The dry material turned out to be hay lining a wooden floor, stuck also to his sweaty, naked back. His armor and weapons, even his boots, were taken away, leaving him only in his pants. A quick inspection in the twilight didn't reveal any wounds on his body, only a stinging spot where he had probably been hit by an arrow with a strong anesthetic. The noises carried by the cloudless night came from the throats of dozens, if not hundreds, of people who, due to their clothes, looked like a happy horde of freaks, runaways, or homeless people; the youngest were teenagers. Many people ostentatiously flaunted firearms common on Earth. They drank, brawled, talked, played, laughed in the flocks, but the main group stood a few dozen paces from Necron's cage, encircling low fires. This was where the most things happened: they shouted, chanted, waved their fists, threw objects as if they had wanted to hound an unpopular agitator on a podium. Kiret was unable to define what was happening there, for the view was obscured by silhouettes of all masses and shapes. Here and there fawning dogs trotted around, sometimes trying to steal something good from the tables.

Necron only established that he had been taken from Geneva. Black hills, bushes and trees loomed beyond the gigantic encampment; still farther hovered mist or lake fumes.

He clung to the bars, trying to find Jenny. He noticed even more cages nearby, all of them occupied by men not much better clothed than he was, with impeccable build and in the prime of life. Two women, more like girls, passed by and started smiling at him, then snickered. One waved goodbye to the new prisoner, the other air-kissed him.

The Kiritian listened for a moment to conversations being held the closest. They all spoke Anglo-American - Earth language, once recognized as global by the world government, to facilitate conversation and synthesis of different cultures. From it evolved Kiritian, which consisted of words similar to the original, also a whole range of new ones, derived from Onkalots' dialects. The persons speaking had a different accent than the one Biffter had used when he had lived on Earth centuries earlier, and there were a lot of neologisms, but he understood the meaning in general. He moved to the other side of the cage.

"Can you explain to me what's going on?" He asked in Anglo-American a hunched prisoner sitting a few meters away, with disheveled red hair. The man was chewing a piece of bread.

"Why, it can't be seen, foreigner?" He snarled and spat in the direction of the mongrels camping out by the bars. The fastest one got and immediately devoured the bitten bread. The redhead waved at the central grouping. "We're gonna have a punch-up."

"We, from these cages?"

"And how the hell do I know how they pick opponents?"

Necron waved his hand towards the rabble.

"Who are these people?"

The redhead deduced that he was not dealing with some earthly fool off base, but with a person from another planet, after Kiret corrupted the language too much and spoke with a decadent note. Just like a relic from another era that had been out of Earth for a long time. The old earthly mentality of being of help to deserving foreigners acted. And the stranger looked like a strong and educated guy, the redhead guessed that he might have even been an androlak or someone awakened from a long hibernation. That was the only reason why he wanted to keep answering.

"This is what Mahrajan Albari looks like, Rite of Spring. All the poor underclass gathers and has fun in their own local way that suits our times. Gladiator fights, as they call it, are the highlight of the show."

"What if I don't want to fight?"

"Then a stab or a bullet," interjected with a smile a fat man from another cage, listening to the conversation.

The redhead went back to chewing the rest of his ration and raising hopes of the dogs that looked at his food with longing, expectant eyes.

"One more thing, have you seen young girls here?" Kiret asked the redhead a few minutes later.

Again, the fat man replied with a rippling laughter.

"Look at him! Your life hangs in the balance, and you've gotten the urge?" He made a vulgar gesture with his hand, followed by such as if he had been smearing paint along the wall with his open palm. "This place is full of pretty ladies, but so what if you won't play the field? You won't live to see the morning one hundred percent."

Rather, he would learn nothing more from these characters. Necron sighed and leaned his back against the bars, their soothing coldness didn't make him feel any better.

Among the primitive, aggressive, unappeased mob, of which only a few people wanted to give him an appraising look, he saw a flash of a familiar face. The young man with an olive complexion glanced at him briefly and moved on, but after a second of enlightenment, he looked again in surprise. He started walking towards his cage.

"Rain?" He asked, frowning. Kiret recognized Sajid, the son of Jamal.

"Hope you have nothing to do with this," he growled in Arabic. They continued to speak that language.

"Of course not! I didn't know myself that Mahrajan was going to happen here and now."

"So, what are you doing here?"

"My friends invited me."

Kiret looked glumly at the cages of prisoners.

"Then you organize lovely parties. Total bestializing."

Sajid seemed genuinely embarrassed.

"Such times. I have no influence on it, I am too petty man to change anything. It is not controlled by any government or service, but the nationless people themselves. But it was even worse, barely a decade ago. Now out of the bloodiest points of the program left the gladiatorial fights. The rest is mostly drinking, games and orgies until the morning."

Kiret tried not to see this as an analogy to *harroweeng*, 'wild parties' once organized by Forkis.

"And of course, I lucked into the highlight of the show? And you coincidentally flew in without problems when Jamal threatened me with the CERN monsters and refused to provide transport?"

"Again, I didn't contribute in any way to your captivity. The father is a carl, but also a prudent man. He spoke the truth about the logistical problems with purchasing vehicles, which is why he almost always refuses to help strangers when it comes to chartering."

The al-Aswani family was indeed not radical if the son shared his facts about the parent so openly. Necron hoped that at least of his old Muslim values, he had left telling the truth.

"How did you get here?" Sajid wanted to know.

"In Geneva, I got a tranquilizer dart as soon as I exposed my head. I don't know how this is possible, as I only spotted animals in the area."

"Sharpshooter. Sometimes they catch people to fight like that. They must have found you dangerous, because easier targets they grab directly with their hands. You probably had the terrain scan set to too little distance."

"I don't know what they did with Jenny. Could you establish it?"

"Of course. I'll see if she's in the pen. I'll be right back." Sajid glanced at something on the edge of the cage ceiling, then walked away.

In his absence, Kiret followed the nuances of the surroundings, with his forehead resting on one of the bars and his left hand hanging over another. The crowd parted for a moment and a dead man was dragged out by the shoulders, so massacred as if he had been thrown into a pit with a starving tiger. Among the tumult of the spectacle, it was possible to distinguish the words of an invisible commentator shouting something about the undefeated player. It seemed to Kiret that he picked up a wolf's whine.

"I don't see it," he muttered under his breath. Two drunks quarreled near his cage. A vodka bottle flew at the bars. Necron was hit harmlessly by the glass shards. This archaic substance was still used to store liquids on Earth, and in space - at least in richer zones - it had long since been replaced by a biodegradable structure produced by a strain of genetically modified bacteria. Such bottles could be torn or deformed, but not broken.

Sajid soon returned.

"There is no tragedy," he announced. "There are women's cages on the other side of the arena. Jenny is sitting in one of them. Fortunately, she didn't go to the pen."

"Did they do something to her?" The Kiritian asked angrily.

"She's safe and sound, no one has touched her. However, this will definitely change if you both lose the fight."

"So, Jenny has to fight too?!"

"Yes, however, you are considered as a team of two, your cages are paired with the same crocodile symbol." The Muslim glanced at the external sign, invisible to the inmate. "This means that you go to the next round if at least one of you wins. The rules are simple. Men fight men, women fight women. The pen is a place for inmates of inferior quality, they squeeze there all those who have not passed the selection. Needless to say, before going to the arena there are often fights, murders, mutilations and suicides there. Cage people are like the elite among the prisoners, the most promising, they are chosen by bettors, they are treated better."

"Ooh, that's for sure." Necron slammed his palm against the grating.

"Every captured is carefully checked by a special committee, even examined with a neuro-mogram to rule out the possibility that someone will suffer a heart stroke or catch an asthma attack during the fight - the audience would be disappointed," the last line, Sajid said bitingly.

"Haven't I mentioned already that you are having a lovely time here?"

"I don't care about fights. The Mahrajan Albari festival is the only occasion for me to have a live chat with my friends. This is the only reason I came here. We live far from each other and we have responsibilities. It will be a long time before a metropolis is built around our property."

"Can you get me out of here somehow?"

"I'm sorry. All you can do is try to win over the crowd during the fight. On rare occasions, they sometimes release someone when they are very pleased or surprised."

Kiret lay down on the hay, put his hands under the head.

"Just great ..."

The Muslim walked over to the adjacent truss so that he could see his face better. The dense circle of silhouettes around the arena parted again, and this time a bloodied gladiator with a torn left-hand stump was hauled out, screaming like being torn to shreds alive.

"No one was particularly surprised that I am a Kiritian." Necron turned his head to Sajid. "That they might be screwed because of it."

"Those who transport the captured are complete noodles, moreover they are not universal persons. They probably recognized you as a soldier from Earth and must have been overjoyed because of it - the high-end armor and equipment for free. Anyone wandering alone in dangerous regions on this planet is asking for trouble. Regardless of social status. That you are a Kiritian only came out during the selection."

"So, on Earth, no one cares about their citizens anymore? Doesn't look for the missing or take revenge for their harm?"

"The nationless persons are excluded from civilization circles. They are deserters, criminals, homeless people, and often persons who voluntarily gave up living in society. They take care of themselves - let's say, because there are often wars between groups - they don't obey the laws of any state. Yes, someone can get pissed, target one of the wild groups and send a military drone or a long-range rocket at it. Coming back to the fight. The rapporteur comments on the duel, as you have probably already heard, the judge announces the winner - the killed or badly wounded loses."

"No shit!" Kiret couldn't refrain from droning these words.

Sajid smiled understandingly.

"If the latter is in poor condition, resources are not wasted on treating them and they are killed. Hyenas clean up and carry away the bodies." He nodded at the men transporting a corpse outside the camp. "As a consolation, let me tell you that only five percent of those caught end up in cages."

"My ego has just jumped five points as well," Necron continued to ironize. "This knowledge will not improve my situation anyway. All I have to do is win this shitty fight."

"Shut up there finally!" A man called towards them, sitting with a bottle under a tree, ostentatiously holding a rifle in his lap. He took a big sip. "Sajid, stop talking to the prisoner at last!"

"The sensitive ranger with a microscopic dick?" The Kiritian asked.

Sajid waved his hand.

"He only uses the gun when there is a holy stink, so don't worry about him. I would be rather worried that they could assign you to a werewolf right away," he said grimly. "The sign on your cage means that these gladiators are fighting the strongest."

Kiret glanced indifferently at the blade-shaped shard of glass. He took it and wrapped half of it in a piece of dirty cloth dug out of the hay, that might have belonged to the previous occupant of the cage, then stuffed it all into a pocket.

Taking out another fighter, this time dead, was announced by a wild, cheering scream coming from hundreds of throats.

"This is the werewolf." The Muslim followed the hyenas moving away.

"And I have a feeling you don't mean the dead man."

Sajid fixed his eyes on one of the bars of the cage, bit his lip. His hazel eyes were absent for a moment.

"Wait, I think I know how I can help you. Well, let's say ... But it will take time."

"They broke the conversation, hearing the guard's next furious roar, closer footsteps, and the screeching of metal. A group of armed men led the redhead and fat man out of the neighboring cages. Looking at all the emptied cages to the right, Necron had no doubt that after the fight the men would have, it would be his turn.

"It probably won't work before the fight," Sajid said conspiratorially, grasping the bars with both hands as if he had felt the urge to free the prisoner by the least effective of possible means. "That person would have to come all the way from the Central Alps. I don't know how the situation will go on. I can only make it worse."

"Wait." Kiret held up his hands. "You know a guy with efficient transportation and you didn't deign to tell me about it before? When Jenny and I were still in Jamal's house?" He didn't like the prospect of having to trust this man. As he had dealt with Earth in the distant past, he associated some Muslims with the Islamic state, which had been part of the army of the European Union, which in turn had been assimilated by the global New Order Army, in which also Kiret had the misfortune to stay forcedly. From the NOA, in turn, came the rebels. He wanted to believe that his associations were stereotypical and incorrect.

"It's complicated. The situation changed just an hour ago. There was a transaction that supposedly was to be canceled."

"What are you talking about, man? Does this have anything to do with your father's anonymous boss?"

The Muslim didn't reply, biting his lip annoyed again as he looked at a dog lying nearby, which immediately waved its tail.

"Alright," Kiret sighed, angrily. "I feel that I will not come to an agreement with you, as with Jamal. But I suppose it is about things you can't tell strangers about because you'd be in trouble." Sajid looked at him gratefully. "But if you can help Jenny, and me along the way, I'll pay you back somehow. If not, save at least Jenny."

"Shut the fuck up!" The guard stood up this time. "Sajid, get your ass away from here or I'll kick you away!"

The Muslim gave the janitor a look that was far from mild.

"Good luck with the werewolf, Kiret."

He bounced off the bars, turned and immediately went away.

A few minutes later, he walked over to a group of Muslims deployed aloof, chatting by the fire, he called one of them aside, and presented the problem. What he didn't mention was that the nationless persons had accidentally caught the former Kiritian emperor himself.

"I hope you know what you are doing," said sharply the accosted, bearded man. "I'm washing my hands of it. I don't want any trouble."

"I take full responsibility," muttered Sajid, staring haughtily in his eyes.

"If it turns out that you are bothering Nelson with trivialities, whereby you will bring his men from afar, you'll pay a heavy price."

"So will you give me this communicator?"

The beardo looked at the man seriously for a moment, then slipped a square, flat object, looking like a precious stone, from a frame mounted on a bracelet, and sent it in an arc to

Sajid. The latter grabbed it while it was flying with his right hand.

"The frequency is set, just connect. Without a password." The bearded man turned and went to his companions to continue participating in the non-alcoholic meeting.

Sajid picked up the connection already after a few seconds, holding the communicator to his mouth.

"I'd like to speak to Jarret Nelson," he said. "He's busy. What do you want? Is it important?" A thick male voice snarled on the other side.

"Perhaps. I found someone who he might be willing to talk to."

"Sajid! We don't need any more foolish Erceses!"

"It's about a Kiritian. They are still hiding well, none of the Headhunters have tracked them ... but luckily, we managed to find one. And not just anybody. Properly pressed may prove useful to our cause."

There was silence on the air, preceded by a short, loud breath.

"Nelson will be here soon," the interlocutor replied calmly, as if scared. "I hope that, as usual, you gave us reliable information."

***

Less than an hour later, the scarred and unconscious redhead was dragged by two men, sort of like medics, to a lazaret barrack, which was located near the cages of the gladiatorial elite. Kiret didn't see the fat man anymore, he guessed what that might have meant. The society occupying the stands of the arena died down and thinned out. It had to mean a break or - hopefully - the end of the fighting for that day. Sajid wasn't coming back, Necron was still worried about Jenny.

It turned out that it was a break between subsequent fights - after a quarter of an hour, three armed thugs came for him.

"Will you be polite, or should I chain and shackle you?" The guard greeted.

The Kiritian calmly raised his open palms upside down in his direction. During his very long life, he had dealt with such people many times, and if he had been to ask them to lead him to their leader, they would have laughed at him or beaten him for his audacity. It was not a reasonable idea to admit he was a Kiritian of the highest rank - he didn't know how these deviants felt about the Immortals, so it might have ended badly for him if it had been revealed who Kiret really was.

The guard who had offered him the bracelets led the way, the two with Necron in their sights closed their little procession.

They reached the crowd around the arena, and Kiret, more and more convinced that Sajid had fooled him, realized that there were many more people there than he had seen from his earlier perspective. The makeshift arena blended in with the natural depression in the shape of a cut funnel with terraces on its gentle slopes. Chairs, benches, trunks had been put there - everything that you could sit on. The fighting area itself was the bottom of a sand-strewn valley; eight pales had been driven on the sides of the circle, and two coils of thick, flexible rope had been pulled on them. Into the arena, you descended along sidewalk lanes, formed among the audience buzzing like a hive. The public's interest in the Kiritian's fight was so great that there were scuffles at the last seats.

There was a fight in the red-tinted arena.

Necron, forced to stop, for a moment forgot to breathe from the impression.

He had been sure the werewolf was the nickname of one of the stronger fighters, some brutal, beefy crowd favorite, but no - it was literally a werewolf. In a sense, not so mythical, changing under the influence of the moon phase or other factors consistent with the canons of fantasy, but a transhumanist who had had to invest a lot of money to take the form of a toothy, shaggy and humped humanoid. Without scanning or injuring the body, it was impossible to determine whether the modification was purely bio or tech plus bio, because the fur covered possible metal elements, but in both forms the fight with such a creature was unequal for an ordinary mortal. The transformed man himself might have belonged to one of the lycan fractions, unless he had altered his appearance for his own satisfaction.

The fight didn't last long and turned out to be colorless for the audience. The beast, weighing over one hundred and fifty kilos, with a blow of a huge, hairy paw, knocked down a man much smaller than himself, who fell to the sand and didn't rise anymore. Dressed in the old Mexican fashion: in a colorful poncho, leather pants and sombrero, the master of ceremonies approached the knocked out, knelt beside him and began the countdown, outstretching another finger.

"Four, five!" Flew from invisible sound amplifiers placed around the arena. "And once again the winner of our play iiiis ... the Werewolf!"

The master of ceremonies raised the beast's paw. The crowd screamed, whistled and clapped, but without much enthusiasm, having received a show not much different from the previous ones. The relentless winner finally becomes boring.

"Maybe a break?" He asked playfully.

The werewolf showed his teeth and growled at him, making onlookers laugh.

"It was definitely more than telling," the master of ceremonies continued in a joking tone. He moved away from the player, began to gesture. "So, ladies and gentlemen, we are about to see another fight, the long-awaited pearl of the night! Because the prodigal son has returned to our postglacial thresholds." The Mexican pointed with both hands to Necron. "A Kiritian in person!"

The crowd laughed, perceiving the announcement as another joke of the swarthy, little man with a curled mustache. Someone not far from the box got up, turned, slipped off his pants, and patted the bare buttocks, bent towards already humiliated Necron. A drunken friend sent the exhibitionist with a kick to the ground between the benches. The falling man knocked drinks from the hands of other companions.

"Admittedly without armor and weapons, but I have heard that he is very dangerous," continued the master with the pitch and expression adequate to the words. "So much that death doesn't take hold of him, because it is not afraid of him. Let's find out about it here and now!"

"At least this one looks like a Kiritian, and not like that thin dick who fought before." Necron heard the words of a bored old woman sitting nearby. "You could be fooled."

"A Kiritian or not, I'd love to fight him personally," added a half-younger neighbor with an alluring sigh. "Oh, I would jerk like a repo man a wall unit ..."

More laughs again.

"Pooh! Forget it, the werewolf won't leave you even a piece of this little body," the old woman knocked out the companion.

"I must admit that the Rooster did his best this time," said someone else. "The guy looks a bit like Kiret Biffter, although he probably left the splendor under the pissed hay in the cage."

"Who?" Asked the boy who, due to the similarity, might have been the son of the man commenting.

"A crawler of Forkis himself, and the latter was the man. Kiret took over from him and quickly smashed his people. Hundreds of years of his predecessor's efforts ... Then he ran away from Kandrok and holed up somewhere, instead of using the Kiritian technology to defend the Zodiac Universum."

"But the Kiritian technology is as effective as putting out a fire in a house with a cup of water," Necron thought automatically.

He closed his eyes, took a deep breath, and slowly counted to five. "This is how Earthlings see my rule," he realized bitterly, without changing the expression on his deceptively calm-looking face. And probably on other planets a similar opinion was held about him. The words of the anonymous onlooker, however, didn't deepen his sadness, on the contrary - when Kiret opened his eyes, he felt anger, which he would have gladly taken out on the werewolf eyeing up his figure, from whose mouths were flowing threads of thick saliva.

"Hey, you, Kiritien!" A youth with a yellow mohawk called out to him. "I've bet you can endure for two minutes, so don't let me down!"

"And I, that you will fall after the first blow to the trap. So don't let me down!" Shouted his long-bearded companion with different betting preferences. "Only that loser Basile bet on your win." The man pointed at the black-clad blonde who was sitting upright, with his hands on his knees, and which with a sigh of irritation looked first at the bearded man, then at Necron. Basile's gaze was more eloquent than the unspoken words - he had considerable doubts about the decision he had made.

Although betting issues were the last thing Kiret should have worried about right now, he felt disappointed that out of hundreds of observers, only one person believed the possibility of his win, but there was also a chance that he had made a choice while drunk, for example. The mob obviously didn't believe he was a Kitirian, but if they had done, the bets wouldn't have been much different. Not against the werewolf. Necron looked around at the primitively assembled stands, rolled his gaze over the savage, poor, prospectless people, who hated anyone who had achieved more than they had done. It's even better that they took him for a normal roundup guy. Even so, the situation didn't look optimistic. Sajid disappeared somewhere, which Necron wasn't particularly surprised by. He was angry with himself that even for a moment he had fallen for an illusory hope of survival. This is how it ended when one had gotten used to living in a truthful nation.

In the first row, he saw Jenny sitting with a guard.

Kiret felt great relief.

Although the girl's head was bowed and she seemed absent, she was still like a flickering light in the darkness of this place. Sad, resigned, tense, but at least safe and sound, in the clean clothes received from Jamal's daughter. She didn't look like a person who had been tortured, beaten or worse. On this point, at least, Sajid had told the truth - both of them were untouchable during the fighting because of some status they had been accorded, sealed with the crocodile symbol. Trying to concentrate, Kiret strained his mind and sent the girl a silent message, highlighted by a questioning expression on his face, hoping that with her abilities inherited from Forkis, there would be a reaction, or at least that he would attract her eyes.

He made it.

Jenny nodded, still looking down at her feet. Somehow, she had endured. Necron bought himself a moment of peace, at least in this plot.

He turned his attention back to the arena. The werewolf staring at him was amused by something because he began to laugh splutteringly, which was like struggling with a partly bitten hunk stuck in a throat. Two cleaners used a rake to pick up bloody amalgams from the previous fight, smoothed the grooves and pits like in ancient sports struggles, preparing the ground for the next long jump competitor. The master of ceremonies known as the Rooster was babbling something with the use of a sound system to the crowd. The latter was buzzing like a herd of wasps waking up in the spring. Jenny was still absent. The ambient sounds in Necron's ears merged into a neurotic whole. He put his fist to his pocket and felt the hardness of a glass dagger, which wouldn't help much against a beast with a thick, black fur, muscles like steel and several centimeters long tusks and claws.

As the cleaners backed up, one of the escorting stabbed him in the back with a rifle barrel. They walked until they were at ropes. The wooden poles around the arena were topped with not white spheres or stones, as Kiret had previously suspected when he had scarcely glanced at one, but human and animal skulls without mandibles. Around the circle stood a cordon of guards, with weapons in hand.

"Any rules?" Necron asked the Rooster carelessly.

The master of ceremonies smiled at him in amusement, showing his yellow teeth.

"I like such specifics. You don't whine for mercy or talk about a misunderstanding like the rest. You fly beyond the ropes - you lose. You spill and don't get up for ten seconds - you lose. You die - you lose. You want a walkover - a bullet to the head."

"Sounds lovely. What if I don't want to fight?"

The rooster chuckled in response.

"No holds barred," he said immediately. "Victory means that the girl won't have to fight anymore tonight. The same goes for you, if you lose and she wins then your duo will have time to recover. If you both lose, bang!" He made a significant movement with his hand shaped like a pistol.

"Are you crazy? She has no chance against this beast!"

"Relax, women fight women and there are no transhumanists there. Your girlfriend was very lucky. Any more questions?"

"So, it was about that," thought Kiret. Probably according to some local standards, they had considered them a pair and therefore made a team out of them. Unless Sajid had contributed to it, eventually thinking Jenny had been his wife. Necron stared coolly in the werewolf's blue eyes.

"Are you getting out, or will you keep staring?" The beast mumbled resoundingly.

"I have no more questions."

He leaned across, took a step, and walked between the ropes. The crowd instantly livened up; some rose up. It unexpectedly flashed through Necron's head that Beliar Drunkenstein must have felt the same when he had faced Forkis in the form of the warlike Onkalot. Except that the rebel had had a powerful ace on the king that Kiritian control had failed to detect - a novel bomb constructed by Dr. Figam. Meanwhile, he went to fight only with the wrapped piece of glass.

The werewolf swung his paws, so strongly that there was a whistle in the air. He was surprisingly quick for his size, Kiret assessed that with such a blow he would surely easily knock the glass out of his hand with his claws.

"How long do I have to wait? Fight, coward, because otherwise we'll grow beards!" The transhumanist growled.

Necron thought frantically about how to get out of this critical situation. Jenny looked at him through the cascade of hair.

"Then I'm starting!" The werewolf announced impatiently.

Hunched, he sprinted towards him, waving his arms. The claws of the lower, mighty paws formed fountains, breaking away from the sand. The wolf transhumanists, like their prototypes, had no retractable claws.

Kiret was still standing by the rope. Out of the corner of his eye, he glanced at a cordon guard who was watching the werewolf's charge with appreciation.

He took the glass out of his pocket and threw it at the opponent, wanting only to make the onlookers focus on it. When the beast easily - as he had supposed - knocked off the gliding projectile with its paw, without harming itself, Kiret swiftly extended his arm and yanked the loosely held rifle out of the guard's hands.

He mentally prayed that it wasn't coded for the user.

It wasn't.

The Kiritian launched the series over the Werewolf, several steps away from him, but in such a way as not to hit the organs.

The beast was hit in his paws and shoulders. He fell and swam over the sand to his feet, losing momentum.

The crowd froze.

The cheerful Rooster got tongue-tied in amazement. Watching the incident with fear, Jenny covered her mouth with her hands, then folded them as if in prayer, and on her lips appeared a cheerful smile.

"End of the party." Kiret tossed the empty rifle beside the squirming and groaning transhumanist. An unexpected thought flashed through his mind, which amused him, whether the bullets of the primitive earthly weapons were not silver.

"Did you hear that? No holds barred!" Necron boomed, scanning the crowd from left to right, with his arms outstretched. "Sorry for disappointing you and that it was so short! Your favorite will live, I just scratched him. So," he looked at the Rooster, "I won?"

"Theoretically yes," replied the latter after a moment. "Nobody had done something like this before ..." With a gaze that promised hell, he glanced at the bemused guard who hadn't secured the gun.

Nearby, another bolt-like shot echoed through the open air among the mountains. At the top of the stands, on the sidewalk leading to the arena, a figure appeared dressed in a black armor suited to the leptosomic body, only the visor of the helmet glistened red. The face was impossible to see through the one-way mirror-class cover reflecting the details of the surroundings. The newcomer had a shotgun in their hands. Kiret's face fell. Indeed, it must have been very bad on Earth that such primitive weapons were used here, as if the planet had had a problem with the electromagnetic field or the weapons had been a relic of such a past.

The onlookers who hadn't lucked into seats and occupied the aisle stepped aside silently and respectfully. Striding, the newcomer soon found themselves next to the Rooster.

"Mr. Nelson wishes that this man be spared. He wants to meet him," announced in a rather thin voice, electronically amplified. It could be human as well as an android or androlak. Kiret thought he heard a gasp of astonishment under the black helmet, as if the stranger had recognized him. There must have been something up, because the yonder leaned back a little in an uncontrolled gesture. Necron was sure he had heard that voice somewhere before, though distorted from the equipment, but with a distinctly piercing natural timbre. Nelson, Nelson... A couple of Kiritians had the name Nelson, but he doubted any of them had anything to do with someone who was clearly an authority among the scumbags around. Though now, for an undefined reason, seemed to be losing confidence.

"Of course, take him with you," replied the Rooster eagerly, glad that someone saved him from the awkward situation.

"I also would be very happy to take this opportunity, but on the condition that the girl comes with me," the Kiritian said firmly. He didn't know if he was getting into an even bigger mess, but he didn't have much choice. Even if he had become the favorite of the crowd, he would still have had to fight stronger and stronger gladiators until he had met his own Kiret.

"Of course." The rooster nodded to the guard sitting beside Jenny. The latter got up, grabbed her arm and led her to Necron.

Without a word, the girl threw herself around his neck, and he hugged her tightly and comfortingly, feeling her tremble. He noticed that Sajid was standing in the distance, watching the unfolding of events with his hands clasped over his chest. Necron nodded gratefully at him, pulling the Sandstorm away from him. He realized he had misjudged him. He couldn't have known what had happened here, or in what kind of collusion these people had been, but since he came under the auspices of someone influential, he wouldn't make a point of taking advantage of the situation.

"Give me back my armor and weapons." Kiret began to boss the show, pointed at Sajid. "And this man, the vehicle you took from me, and is his property."

"Do you understand what the hell has just happened here?" Asked the bearded man from the tribune, who wished Biffter would fall from one Werewolf's blow.

"Yes, you have to pay me now." Satisfied and looking at his friends, Basile was rubbing his fingers together. "And who's a complete loser now?"

"You know what? He's probably really a Kiritian ... Look at his armor with no markings."

Kiret lost interest in the onlookers commenting nearby. The armor was delivered to him surprisingly quickly, he immediately began putting its pieces on himself. They didn't even hesitate to hand the weapon to him, which surprised him greatly. Now he could have smashed everyone in sight with just one plasma gun, and he doubted that the mysterious stranger armed with a shotgun and a handful of hacks with archaic rifles would have been able to stop him, fully secured with dhurnstall and biometal, if he had only slipped on the helmet. Even if everyone had had a weapon here, he would have made a bloody mess before he had been finally rendered harmless. However, he didn't want to kill anyone and arrange shootings in front of Jenny. He felt no resentment towards those people who were victims of their time, the nationless washings of the Ice Age and the global government destroyed by the Kiritians - who then had flown away from Earth and left it on its own.

"They won't hurt us," Jenny whispered to him. "They were ready to kill us sooner, but not after we came under Nelson's protection."

Necron had completely forgotten that his companion was a telepath, getting better and better at her trade.

"Have you managed to find out who he is?" He asked in a whisper as well, nodding discreetly to the man in black.

"I can't read anything from his head. Maybe due to the armor. Or he's an android."

Biffter tried to remember if Forkis had had trouble reading minds if one had had an armored, electronics-laden head that might have acted as an inhibitor. Q'ualel must have mentioned to him that Onkalot psionics hadn't gone hand in hand with the digital technology of humans, at least of those who had grown up on Chulimal and their abilities had been closely related to the environment developed to zero point two on Kardashev's scale. That would be correct, because Forkis had preferred to talk to interlocutors, looking them directly in the eye.

Necron watched as the hyenas carried the wounded werewolf towards the lazaret.

"Let's go." The newcomer in black turned and, much less confidently than before, began walking towards the exit from the stands. Kiret trailed a few meters behind him, hoping to get more information when the company was thinner. Jenny was with him every step of the way, embracing his shoulder with both hands, she glanced anxiously at the people making way for them.

The three quickly left the camp grounds, heading for a wooded hill. The newcomer walked a few meters ahead of

Kiret and sometimes looked around nervously as if he had been afraid of something, not hiding it at all. Though the armor fully protected him, Necron could read his concern flawlessly in his body language. It looked strange in a person who was such an authority among the nationless people or related to someone with immunity. Were they being watched? Did they find themselves in another dangerous area, overrun by some bugs, feral animals or gangs? Because the guy in black couldn't be afraid of him.

They stopped in a small valley surrounded by low rocks. The Kiritian handed the plasma gun to surprised Jenny and passed her by. As the stranger hadn't spoken all the way, he decided to take the initiative:

"Who are you? Can you finally explain what's going on here?" Necron stood in front of the stranger, towering over him, he was amazed when the latter as if shrank in himself. Why would have the armed man feared him, especially since Kiret wasn't carrying a gun?

"Let's wait for Mr. Nelson to arrive," said the stranger sparingly ... in a trembling voice. And that look aside. A total inversion of the behavior previously presented among the taunters.

Something was really wrong here.

He hadn't liked the stranger from the beginning, and this reluctance grew stronger with each passing minute. Kiret had the feeling that the guy had felt hard ground until he had seen him in the arena then, and as they moved away from the safe crowd, he had more and more problems with self-control.

He noticed with an achij's trained eye that the helmet joints weren't tightly attached to the armor body. Trained soldiers didn't make such mistakes, even if they were on a boring patrol, alone in a deserted area.

With a quick movement of his hands, Necron grabbed the black helmet of the latter, twisted it slightly and lifted it. The surprised stranger dropped the weapon like a complete god orphan and also grabbed the head cover, no longer providing him with anonymity.

All three were dumbfounded.

Kiret's astonishment immediately turned to fury.

"YOU?! I can't believe it ... It is a small frigging space!"

Before him stood an Erces named Skelver from the RC Galaxy, paralyzed with fear, a man with fair skin, short dark blond hair, ferrety trap and eyes as yellow as thick urine. A refugee who was Kandrok's crawler, ordered to kill Kiritian's ruling elite, including Jenny in his infancy. He hadn't changed at all since the failed K'otz'ibaja bombing, but Erceses' metabolism was the last thing Kiret cared about now. Skelver had worked for a time clandestinely in his mansion, hired by unaware Jenny. Since Kiret had once saved him from a lynch by achijes on Morascrik, Skelver had, as an honorary compensation, warned him about Kandrok's mercenaries heading for Jenny to Atla.

Then he had vanished like a black planetesimal in a vacuum.

Skelver immediately bolted. On the run, Kiret picked up the dropped shotgun and followed him. Having hardly given up the desire to shoot him in the back, he caught him after several dozen meters of chase, knocked him over and they both collapsed on the grass.

"You shitty fucker! Slippery fucking slow worm!" Kiret stood up, gripping the gun barrel pointed at the other man's head. Skelver lay on his back, with palms open in surrender.

"I didn't know it would be you in the arena!"

When he flipped over, Necron shot where his face had just been, creating two deep holes in the ground.

"What are you raving about?!"

He manually chambered the gun and fired again, feeling a delightful recoil spread through his muscles and bones, reminiscent of old times.

Skelver groaned, jumped, also this time deliberately missed, but grotesquely retreated behind a birch tree as if pellets had hurt his feet.

Jenny watched the bizarre scene with her heart pounding hard. She didn't know Kiret from such an aggressive side, she had seen him as a gentle, sometimes melancholic man who, if forced to use strength, had done it with cold professionalism. And - she liked this other Kiret even more.

"Mr. Nelson sent me a message that I was to commandeer a prisoner from the camp. He said casually it was a Kiritian," the Erces was saying, keeping his back against the trunk. "That much he learned from an informant participating in Mahrajan Albari!"

Kiret was marching toward him like a heavy infantryman in the first line of fire. When Skelver dared to peek out from behind the tree and saw the height at which was the barrel, he heeded the warning of instinct and quickly bent down.

The upper part of the young birch tree, to the accompaniment of the roar of thunder, fell into splinters.

The Erces nervously tripped over a protruding root and fell. He walked a bit like a crayfish, looking at Kiret coming over, keeping his expression gloomy until his back hit another trunk.

"Damn, what a loser ... I even don't want to waste pellets on you, impostor. I think Kandrok hired you for a joke, because surely not out of pity."

"Or they find Kiritians so dumb that they sent the idiot to the task," Kiret liked that thought much less. However, he knew from experience that taking a coward for a spy and executioner, contrary to appearances, made sense. A coward is useless in themselves, but when trained and intimidated by the principal, they arouse pity, not suspicion, and therefore can complete assigned tasks.

"Let's talk like humans, General."

"You're not truly a human. Neither genetically nor behaviorally. You're just imitating a human."

"Please don't shoot anymore!"

Kiret grabbed him by the semicircle of his armor at the nape of his neck and tugged him roughly, bringing him to a vertical position. He tore the shotgun magazines off him, then, slightly tilted, began to lead him to Jenny.

"I'm not going to. I have a better idea: a prison in the nether regions. A cozy cell will surely be found there for you. Oh, it will be best if I place you with Rei'than. Maybe you know each other."

"I don't know the guy. Who is he?"

"A Kandrok member. He's lonely and sad, he will be pleased with the company."

"No ... Everyone but not a Kandrok member!"

"I'm gonna puke ... What a fart, not a man. And someone like that was supposed to kill me?" Necron chuckled, looking at the Erces in disgust.

"First, the girl was going to be killed."

The Kiritian jerked him.

"Shut up, bug!"

They stood by Sandstorm, tightly clenching her fingers on the gun.

"Hello, Jenny," said Skelver, with an expression of a punished dog.

Hearing all the exchange, the girl encompassed him with a despairing look.

"Skelver ... How could you ..." She extended her arms with the plasma gun towards Kiret.

"Keep it, especially since you don't have my pistol anymore," the Kiritian announced. "That's enough for me." He raised the shotgun. "Our new friend won't mind, will he?" He jerked the man again. "Now tell me what's up with this Nelson. Everything, or I'll change my mind and kill you."

"Jarret Nelson. Age forty-seven. He's a new leader of Headhunters ..."

"Is it one of the informal, paramilitary terrorist organizations with a lot of mercenaries?"

"Yes, the same one that comes from Calvary. After the ... incident on Atla, I also decided to escape from avors; I finally dared to do it. I was lucky they hadn't installed a neurocyte in my brain because they could easily track me down. That's why I managed to give them the slip. They probably thought that they had me over a barrel because of the sheer psychological terror and intimidation. Headhunters found me in space and decided to take me in because I knew a lot about Kandrok."

"The Hunters are racists. They hate otherness, especially refugees." Kiret examined Erces' armor more closely, looking for a terrorist emblem - a yellow triangle with three black human skulls without mandibles on it, pointing with their eye sockets at the viewer, slightly to the left and to the right. He didn't notice anything like that. It might be right. The recruits must have earned their stripes to wear the Hunters' logo. However, he preferred to be careful and stick to skepticism. Logic and truth didn't always go hand in hand.

"Yes, but they are now focusing on the greatest threat."

"Kandrok ..."

"Moreover, the enemy of my enemy ... as they said. Now I'm also considered avors' enemy. I could forget about returning to my home planet, I'm not even sure if anybody was left alive there." Skelver sighed. "I managed to join the Hunters as a helper. They sent me back to Earth to protect as a bodyguard those who had interests here."

The universe was ending. Erceses fraternized with Headhunters. Cowardly Skelver became the thugs' bodyguard. Necron looked at Jenny meaningfully.

"I have no idea if he's telling the truth, "She replied in a voice marked by a feeling of guilt. "I can't read anything in his mind."

This was what he had expected. Erceses, although visually looked like humans, shared zero percent of their genes with them. The research carried out on Morascrik showed that their genetic material had developed tens of thousands of years earlier, counting in Terran units of time. And wore no previous evolutionary traces! This clearly meant that Erceses were an artificial creation. This was in line with the account of Aggroteh, who had spoken with Nanawak on Tamasul. Nimja in the past had reportedly created intelligent genres for entertainment and because they just could. Even less than twenty years earlier, all this would have sounded incredible, but then almost simultaneously Erceses, Nimja, previously thought to be the product of Onkalots' imagination, and of course Kandrok - the heaviest caliber, appeared in the consciousness of the Zodiac Universum. Scientific research left no doubt that the new reality was as real and amazing as centuries earlier the first steps on new globes and the discovery of humanoid jaguars on H14.

"Don't blame yourself for that," he said to Jenny. "It looks like your telepathy is associated with the relationship between you and an x-rayed person." He thought at the moment how she would have done with Kandrok, with whom Kiritians and Oderses had as much as eighty-nine percent of their genes in common. Rei'than, who had been captured during the expedition for Dr. Figam, were still held in prison on Cargoo. If they managed to return to the planet, he would gladly test Jenny's telepathy on this avor. "Then we have a problem," he concluded with a sigh. "You're not credible to me, Skelver, and we don't have a way to check you. What is my guarantee that you're not telling me a whopper and waiting for Kandrok's transportation to give us into their hands?"

"No, I guarantee."

"Oh, and these three words are to make me entrust Jenny's and my life to you? Especially after what you did on Atla?"

"I escaped from Kandrok. I have nothing to do with it anymore! Apparently, they killed my family." Skelver got sad, which seemed like a sincere reaction. "There is also no reason for me to keep forced loyalty to them."

Kiret changed the subject, knowing that in that plane, they would agree on nothing:

"Do you know where the entrance to CERN is?"

"Yes, I know this area. But nobody goes there."

"Because?"

"As you know, I come from a distant cosmos and have little knowledge of earthly matters. All I was told was that it was a very dangerous place. Nobody knows what's in there."

"Then we'll find out. Let's go there in a threesome."

Calming down during the conversation, Skelver turned back into a bundle of nerves.

"You must be crazy to go there in a threesome. Anyway, don't count Jenny and me, knowing how to hold and operate a gun doesn't make you a soldier. Mr. Nelson is due here with an army of mercenaries, it's enough strength to explore the research complex."

Kiret looked at him doubtfully.

"It is interesting. CERN is said to have been abandoned for decades, if not hundreds of years. Why does Nelson want to crash into there just when I was planning to do it?"

"The Headhunters haven't been active in the Old Zone so far, because they had no reason. This was not their area of influence. They have learned about the old terrestrial science complex not so long ago by studying the planets - they were looking for anything that might have helped Oderses in their struggle with Kandrok that began to threaten Calvary. And CERN was famous for bold research, also on various weapons. Unfortunately, avors also got to Earth. Therefore, it is necessary to hurry and save everything that is useful and could be left behind by the scientists working here."

"Sounds sensible. You know quite a lot," murmured Kiret. He couldn't confide in a random person, especially the traitor from another galaxy, that the Kiritians had exactly the same problem with Kandrok, which already was an open secret anyway. He also didn't dare to admit that it was because of him that the enemy had appeared on Earth. "We're going," he announced. He absolutely didn't trust this man, and the finale of the meeting with the Headhunters was also unpredictable. But at least Necron now wielded the weapon and could use Skelver as cannon fodder.

"Where?!"

"To CERN. I need to find transportation and get out of Earth as soon as possible, and you will come with us."

"If you must go there, wait for Mr. Nelson. He should be landing in thirty minutes. In a threesome we will die ..."

"Sure, and then you'll hand us over to the Hunters." He motioned to the girl. " Come on, Jenny. You're leading, Skelver. One number and I'll blow your head off."

He pushed the Erces in the back with the shotgun's barrel.

"What am I to do with it?" Sandstorm asked, following Kiret, with the plasma gun in hand.

"What do you think it is for?"

"I'm a little afraid to shoot it."

"You will make it. After all, I taught you to use such a shooter. Wait, one more thing." He stopped, and so did the others. "Jenny, you have a chance to practice with the equipment. Locate the transmitter."

"What transmitter?" Sandstorm and Skelver asked simultaneously.

Kiret turned to the man:

"You are an Erces, the alien. Do you think the Headhunters, who have always been hostile to the refugees who they believe are causing the perturbations of an orderly social system, trusted you just like that? I know them, they are not stupid, though less armed than Kiritians. I don't know what your standards look like in the RC Galaxy, but you don't trust the new ones at the Zodiac Universum. You definitely have a bug. The Headhunters are controlling your every move, they know where you are."

"I don't have any transmitter."

"You probably don't know that yourself. Jenny, scan him for strong signal implants."

Many Kiritian weapons in secondary functions were able to detect radiation or examine the degree of contamination of the environment, in case professional equipment wasn't close at hand. Kiret's plasma gun had such options too. Jenny pushed aside a cover above the fuse on a side of the weapon and switched on the scanner, which, humming at the threshold of audibility, began to x-ray the man with a wide beam coming from below the barrel.

The bug, highlighted in orange on the holographic screen, was detected on the inside of the armor, facing the back.

"Take it off," Biffter ordered.

When Skelver, who had little choice, shed his torso protection, Necron tore out of it a black piece of metal the size and thickness of a small fingernail, very similar to Kiritian celula. Smiling triumphantly, he waved it in front of the Erces' nose, then threw it into the mud and crushed it with the toe of his shoe.

Astonished, Skelver cursed in his native language.

"It was obvious. Put on your armor and let's get out of here," Necron ordered.

***

Thino'pai's eyes glowed with pure, cosmic orange fury, registering such an unimaginable defeat. The diarduk hand of the xepo, which was the rank of squadron or battalion commander, gripped the edge of the lectern with a force of three tons per square centimeter, so that indentations appeared there. If the commander of Kandrok rested it on his enemy's head, he would have crushed its bones to powder.

Another of the seven ships of his little afferis seemed as dead as space. Using his neurocyte as a scanner, Thino'pai found no bioactivity on board and was sure all the organic varoth members must have died there. Before the super virus, brought in by a cursed devokas, had developed into an epidemic, varoth members had contacted each other directly, flying from demo to demo. Unknowingly, they had spread the plague, and then, within a few nirs, they had begun to die in agony. Their lungs had disintegrated like a heroko devoka's tissues treated with chemical weapons.

Only on three demos there was no epidemic, including the flagship unit where Thino'pai stayed, because their crews had had no contact with the infected; no one had left the board since the beginning of the campaign.

Avors and devoka had once been oneness - whatever that meant - or so the present Gerha, the ruler of Kandrok, claimed, which seemed heresy in the minds of the higher-ranking officers. As semi-autonomous individuals, clamped together into a super-collectivity, they afforded such boldness of thought only when far from the gerha, as they were now, during the occupation of the stranger's universe. The mere thought that poor Heroko and Kandrok had once been on a par with each other aroused widespread disgust. Unfortunately, biologically it made sense. The migrating protoplast species had been split by the cosmos, the nations had been created, time had passed, and with-it genes had begun to change. However, the genetic distance had ultimately been not enough to prevent Kandrok from catching the disease from Kiritians, as this damned heroko had been called. The environment in which the cybernetic people had lived had been virus-free. Thus, the enemy had obtained the weapon against avors completely by accident, the only one but perfect. And unfortunately, had started using it. The most grotesque was the fact that the pathogen that had instantly annihilated the organic Kandrok members made Kiritians immortal.

Due to his inexperience, the xepo couldn't have expected that the lonely enemy demo would be a death trap. He was sure that his subordinates had caught and brought aboard the terrified, stray orhada, therefore silent, from whose blood and organs they wouldn't have gotten much kunhikar anyway. The Kiritian, however, hadn't spoken, because he had been keeping a liquid containing pathogens in his mouth all the time. He waited for the opportune moment to spit it on the unshielded face of one of the varoth members.

Thino'pai, being fully Liberated, not even having a piece of organic tissue in himself, didn't have to fear any biological weapon. But the losses in varoth troubled him, also that he would besmear his good name and bring on himself the anger of avors with the troh and lyyh ranks, and even of gerha himself. Not to mention the Lightbringer who might have turned his back on him; the loss of the god's protection, Thino'pai feared most. Despite the failure, however, he was excused by his own ignorance - Kandrok members were punished for mistakes made despite their experience. To blame for everything were anyway, worse than Kandrok, damned heroko, who sacrificed the demo and the crew for the good of its cause.

The enemy's afferis was quite close, but the xepo wasn't ordered to chase the Kiritians across space. Even when you are stronger, you shouldn't throw yourself into the fray when you have become weakened. Therefore, he was assigned a different task.

The only thing he could do now to avoid losing the rank, or even the orhada that fed his electronic body, since so many varoth members had died again because of him, was to get an indifferent form of the Kiritian super virus. Secured, it was not a threat, it became a quick killer only when it penetrated a body and replicated its genetic material at lightning speed.

The capital of the Immortals had once been a repository of ampoules with an indifferent form, which Kandrok hadn't known until the outbreak of the first plague. Not understanding the essence of the new threat, Thino'pai had ordered to kill all the organic and hybrid avors - and unfortunately mostly such had been transferred to Morascrik - by dropping a bomb on the enemy capital. Everything had been annihilated: the metropolis, varoth and precious vials.

And no indifferent form needed to develop an antidote had been obtained so far.

Therefore, any hiding place of the Immortals should have been found as soon as possible.

Thino'pai stopped thinking when he saw that his subordinate wanted to talk to him. To be precise, the xepo, as a machine, didn't have to think, everything for him could be instant, digital interpretation, mathematics and transmission to another neurocyte, but he often allowed himself to use the original possibility from the time of having a biological body he had been left with.

"Gerha could help," discreetly suggested Ka'valha, a red-eyed albino thirty percent cyborgized. A centipede-like leberiks winded around his torso, an electronic pet paired with its owner. Both avors stared through the flagship's porthole at another dead vessel from which biological signals had ceased to come. "He can solve all our problems. Maybe it would be worth consulting him? He is omniscient."

Thino'pai turned slowly, glaring at Ka'valha for a moment, so that the latter swallowed unconsciously. The leberiks moved behind his back and only stuck the head with antennae over his shoulder.

"It won't help," the commander replied gently, however. He glanced at his own leberiks, which was a flying drone with red lamp beads. He stroked its casing with his fingers. "The gerha is the incarnation of the Lightbringer, so it is difficult to see logic in his actions, because we don't understand it as the subtler. However, I'm sure that he rarely helps us because he trusts our creativity. In this way we develop kabo, we become more perfect and powerful in divine opinion. Can you imagine how the gerha might react if we turned to him for help in case of a species inferior to us?" He smiled sardonically, displaying big silver teeth. "Exactly ..."

"Theoretically, we are the same thing, but we were varied by time and the environment ..."

"NO! We are not!" Thino'pai slammed his fist against the support of the cockpit structure, making Ka'valha flinch. Two of the few Kandrok members working at the console shuddered as well, but preferred not to turn, knowing the temperament of their xepo perfectly. "The past doesn't matter. You should watch your mouth, or someone will accuse you of heresy. Remember forever, young: devoka are inferior to Kandrok. We only need them for the production of kunhikar. Maybe once, in ancient times, we really were a bit alike ... But it was us that the Lightbringer chose as his protégés. It is thanks to him that we are invincible."

"Of course. So how are you going to solve, xepo, the Kiritian super virus problem?"

Thino'pai looked at the glowing source of the cockpit light and felt his anger fade away. At the time of Liberation, the orhada had penetrated all of his artificial limbs, and therefore he felt emotions just like the organic Kandrok. However, explosiveness was part of his nature, as was that of many varoth members. This was considered natural and permissible, regardless of rank in the Kandrok hierarchy. Besides, the avor wasn't irritated without reason.

"You'll have to break the link with your leberiks for extra computing power and merge with the last demo on which all varoth died. Since we don't have a Liberated person immune to the plague on that board - I admit I made a mistake while relocating the avors - you'll guide it until we land at base. I will send an order into space to look for the enemy's hideout, because wherever the enemy is, there will also be the super virus. I'll send a signal to all varoth neurocytes within seven circles[2]. Don't worry, it's only for a while," added the xepo with a smile, seeing that his sad subordinate was brushing the leberiks' feelers. "So, get to work."

Kabo Ka'valha nodded, then left the bridge.

Soon he entered the technical center as brightly lit as the rest of the decks and rooms, passed the avors busy with their assignments, and stepped under the plate of one of the reciphertors. He slipped the leberix off his shoulder and placed it on his clasped hands.

"Well, unfortunately, I'll have to turn you off for a while, my dearest friend."

The polychaeta looked at its owner, tilted its head, then curled into a perfectly smooth ball.

Ka'valha activated the reciphertor head. The emitted beam from the invisible range destabilized the signal binding the neurocyte in the man's frontal lobe to the synthetic leberiks' encephalon, to finally extinguish it. After this brief procedure, Kandrok put the ball in the compartment, then moved to another place in the room and took out one of the tens of thousands of rajithar capsules with the appearance of a centimeter-long rod-shaped bacterium. Beneath the transparent casing was a blue liquid containing pico-chips, which performed two functions: when eaten, they became a source of chain released energy for the avor - which was one of several forms of Kandrok's nutrition forms - or they were used to infect the spine or encephalon of a large machine over which the host was taking control.

Ka'valha now had to pair the capsule with his neurocyte, after which he could take control of the ship Thino'pai had pointed out, making it his temporary leberiks. It was easier and more effective for Kandrok to take control of the machine in this way than to control it remotely from the commander's bridge or with the help of an autopilot. Though Kandrok worshiped the Lightbringer, it also silently resented him for not having bestowed upon them in the past the psionic abilities that he had possessed himself. To make up for this, they developed the neurocyte technology to perfection, which became the equivalent of powerful mental faculties.

Kabo went back to the deciphertor and paired the picto-chips of the capsule with his neurocyte. He left the technical center, walked down a brightly lit corridor to a fire post, took a seat behind the gun, and loaded a transport missile with the rajithar. He shot it straight into the armor of a neighboring unit, where the plague had wiped out the crew. The projectile and the capsule burst, releasing picto-chips which, like programmed viruses, immediately penetrated the armor and entered the core.

In less than a minute, the avor could mentally steer the great ship, guiding it safely toward the makeshift base of Kandrok on one of the Zodiac Universum's appropriated moons.

***

Rei'than had already become perfectly familiar with the underground rooms and corridors of sector B, in which his prison was located. If the opportunity had arisen, he could have gotten to the surface with his eyes closed, without hitting the wall even once. A solitary confinement, corridor, laboratories, corridor, corridor, laughable human arsenal, swimming pool and other recreation rooms, server room, elevator, corridor, hangar, corridor ... And even more corridors to rooms that he had never seen but he deduced that there were no barracks in this sector due to too few armed achijes hanging around the facility. That is why he knew a lot about each of them, he had perfectly carved their habits in his memory, which was not a feat if you had a neurocyte in your head, one of the many advantages of which was the immediate, permanent remembering of all kinds of information. He remembered who was carrying a knife and where he kept it, who used the toilet frequently, and who treated disrespectfully his duties. This seemingly trivial knowledge could prove to be extremely valuable in certain circumstances. A celula had been placed preventively only in the corner of the room with its solitary confinement, because all those Kiritian fools seemed to trust each other completely, so they didn't control each other. Rei'than determined that the enemy hadn't installed any more powerful sensors or scanning devices on the surface, not wanting to risk Kandrok tracking the base from space. "And rightly so," he concluded with amusement.

While Rei'than seemed to have an advantage over Kiritians in many respects, he had been held captive by them for six Terran years and never managed to escape or cause even the slightest perturbation. Excluding pissing off the guards, of course, which he loved to do, suffering from a negligible amount of distraction. Although he couldn't say that he was the embodiment of patience, and being in those nether regions tormented him terribly, he tried to wait persistently for the moment when an opportunity to escape appeared. Eventually someone would make a mistake. They were the most advanced devoka members of all at the Zodiac University, but still devoka.

"Oh, my favorite janitors: Mr. Beetroot and Mr. Fart," Rei'than greeted happily the two recently recruited Kiritians whose responsibilities included taking care of him. At least so much good came from being in captivity: he had mastered the art of ridicule. When he had been caught in space, at the time Captain Victor Shane's team was flying to the planet B9 for the scientist, he had pure hatred for Kiritians, dictated by Kandrok racism, but when he became accustomed to the enemy, he often displaced his uploaded antipathy with sarcasm. Many things also began to make him laugh when he noticed the absurdities of his surroundings. For example, the bars of his cell that had just been opened: they were thick and, in addition, made of dhurnstal, which a cyborg or only a Liberated would have handled, and not a fully organic avor, whom Rei'than, cut off from the super-collectivity, unfortunately had to remain. Even if he had kicked the bars from morning to night, he wouldn't have bent them even a millimeter. I guess he really had to be feared.

"Time for the prison yard, scum," said the nineteen-year-old dryly, characterized by the fact that he could be easily unhinged. Often his anger was announced by the flushing on his face, hence Rei'than, already familiar with human standards, coined the nickname Beetroot for him. "And my name is Kogan."

The avor smiled sardonically.

The Kiritians led him out of the cell under arms; he was walking in front of them.

"Why does command even keep the trash, Ryan?" Kogan rumbled to his companion, this time annoyed that the prisoner began to sing to himself. "He's useless. The place of trash is in a landfill or in utilization. He only lives at our expense, damned parasite!"

Rei'than tried to be cautious about his situation, so as not to go crazy like umen Ly due to his separation from Kandrok - and the leberix - but this time he felt offended by further insults of human young 'uns. Specifically those flowing from the mouth of Kogan; Ryan didn't care, he just checked off his assignment on the schedule. An angry expression appeared on the avor's face. He was semi-autonomous, deprived of free will, therefore he had no control over certain behaviors fixed in him. It was tempting for him to turn around in a flash and crush Kogan's larynx in a death grip, but then his twenty-year-old colleague would have come out of the "I don't give a fuck" mode and take him out, or at least injure him decently, ignoring the prisoner's inviolability. Rei'than didn't want to die in these nether regions like his companion.

"Since the prisoner is still alive, the top probably thinks he's still useful, it's logical," Ryan said in a bored tone. He adjusted the cover with the knife he liked to carry with him. "For research, as a hostage for exchange - hell knows. They wouldn't hold him otherwise."

"So, I have an irrecusable offer, gentlemen." Kandrok turned his head slightly towards them. Having swallowed his anger, he resumed his role as the annoying, amused prisoner. "Let me out, here and now, I will go my own way, you will be relieved from the hated job, and we will all be satisfied with life."

"Shut up." Kogan touched his back with the barrel.

"I really don't understand you people," Rei'than continued. The more he irritated the guards, the more satisfaction he got from it. He was in a good mood for the rest of a day afterwards. "Your species feature is that you grumble and groan that it's bad, and when someone gives you a perfect and simple solution, you get pissed off like a beggar who is given food, and not uinals. And where's the logic here?"

"Shut up, you cosmic albino scum."

"But do you realize, Mister Beetroot Hypocrite, that you are also an alien to me?" The avor grew more and more warmed up. "But well, the problem with idiots is that they don't know they are them." He assumed a sad face.

"Hold me back ... Shut up, or I'm going to kick your ass right away and you will fall on your face!" Kogan hummed.

"I think someone hasn't dipped his wick for a long time."

The boy got speechless for a moment before turning to Ryan:

"Damn, have you heard that?! Can I kill him? But I'm seriously asking."

"Such questions ask our batab protector Rudiard Gareth. Blow him off, in the sense of Rei'than." Ryan waved his gun at the prisoner. "Today he is really yapping a lot, he has become quite good in it, son of a bitch, in this prison. But he'll be out of our hair right away."

They walked along the next corridor, Rei'than knew every smallest detail and tiniest speck of patina in it. Two young lab technicians from the science sector F, rarely working in this part of the base, passed them.

"Hello, girls," the avor turned to them with a sly smile.

They didn't give him contemptuous glances or flinch in disgust - quite the contrary. They walked quietly past the men, and as they moved away, they stopped, looked at Rei'than curiously, and began to comment on something in whispers, sometimes chuckling.

Kogan had sufficient reason to dislike the prisoner, so he made a point of bullying him at every opportunity. The reluctance didn't stem from patriotism or experience on a battlefield, as Kiritians had recruited him from a 'quick roundup', trying to fill the gaps in the ranks of those killed in the battles with Kandrok (before that, Kogan had been an ordinary civilian who had wanted to have an exciting job, and at the same time, at a very much young age, he had been suitable for a super virus injection). The reason turned out to be more down-to-earth: Rei'than was liked by women on Cargoo. Kogan bet on his origin - Kandrok had been classified into three and a half degrees on Kardashev's scale, which is almost one more than Kiritian. This supposedly less than inconspicuous one actually made a huge difference when it comes to the level of development of civilization, and therefore technology. The second issue was the exotic appearance of Rei'than, although the word 'unreal' could be more accurate here. Admittedly, he was almost one meter and eighty centimeters tall and had a tendency to slouch his back and keep his head low, but his unusual skin, white as a young bone, a classic phenotype among Kandrok members, compensated for that. The stream of Rei'than's hair, growing only at the top of the head, was also white, and had already reached the ground in those six years. His eyes, with huge irises and tiny pupils, ranged in spectrum from yellow to amber depending on the lighting. The narrow face - usually twisted in sarcasm - with a high forehead and a small number of details looked like the face of a cruel man planning a crime, but apparently to women in the base it was attractive. Each of them checked Rei'than out, sometimes without embarrassment, and other times, for the sake of appearance pretended that they didn't care. They were impressed by the killer, alien, and invader. More human being or humanoid than a man, for the avor had a physiognomy similar to humans, but not the same. So much for the feeling of patriotism among the fair sex; Kogan didn't encompass it. He himself had broken up with a girl some time earlier and so far, he hadn't found anyone, in spite of trying. And Rei'than? Such nothing, total zero, in addition a non-human, and yet he was successful in some matters. It was terribly unfair. That's why Kogan made it a point of honor to baste that damn avor ... But it was he who was always a loser in these confrontations, double-crossed by his young, hot blood and poor self-control - Rei'than provoked him, and he got furious for any reason.

After a few minutes, the three exited through a gate, masked with the pareidolia effect, to the surface. The anemic rays of the K'ajolom red dwarf barely cut through the low-flowing clouds of the gray-brown tones of the rocky surroundings. There was a general excitement, the Kiritians took a chance and poured temporarily into the terrain around the base like ants to welcome General Velkee Warfighter. His ships of several squadrons were already standing on large platforms, which were to bring them to the safe nether regions of the hangars so that their physical or energy signatures couldn't be traced from orbit. The news of Velkee's victory - who had vowed loudly that he was not to be commended - without a single shot fired, over a random small group of Kandrok ships, had spread across the secret Cargoo base long before his arrival. It was the first and only victory over the enemy, irrelevant admittedly, but it improved the morale of the fugitives living in hiding. The warfighter only lost one achij who had voluntarily gotten caught by the avores and infected some, maybe several, with an indifferent form of the super virus before dying - it was impossible to monitor the course of events aboard Kandrok's ship due to their better protective screen. The plan was successful, in any case, because the effects of the rapidly spreading plague in the form of extinct enemy ships could be observed from a safe hiding place in the depths of space. Newly arrived Kandrok's support ignored Velkee's squadrons in an attempt to contain the chaos on its own units, so he managed to escape without a tail.

Now he was greeted with applause and chanting as the one who had planned the successful Operation Trojan Horse and had ensured the soldiers' safe retreat. Some argued in private conversations that Vandringen should have taken over the position of missing Biffter, who deserted and hadn't been heard from again because he had had a mental breakdown.

Kogan and Ryan would have liked to join the celebration, but couldn't because of Rei'than.

"Have a nice prison yard, scum." Kogan spat at his feet.

Ryan ensconced nearby on a wall and lit tumbaku - a popular stimulant among the Immortals. He watched the achijes rejoicing, which wasn't a common sight in these difficult times.

The avor cast an indifferent glance at the newly arrived machines, now being dragged underground, which made no impression on him. He found everything related to Kiritians primitive and pathetic, though not always harmless. "Even the all-powerful gerha shouldn't underestimate the filthy side, a recruit assigned to the worst jobs," was Kandrok's saying. Rei'than himself experienced this sentence in practice when, through his own fault, he had been captured by the pathetic heroko devoka. Years later, he was still furious with himself because of that stupidity, when he had wanted to know something new. Along with the late umen, Ly, he had let himself be caught by Tsar Seymour like animals at the sight of a delicacy attached to a trap, and their ship had been taken over by the enemy. The justification that they had never come into contact with the human drugs that Tsar had fooled them with would have sounded bad in the ergrih's ears, even if it was a new situation for the avors. It was good that, at least, enslaved in the Cargoo dungeons, they avoided punishment by xepo Thino'pai.

The avor became irritated when he heard Kogan's cheerful, biting words:

"The ordinary achij, though already a hero now, just kicked your cybernetic asses, avor. Maybe you are ahead of us technologically, but you are killed by little crap called viruses that we can deal with in minutes. Such teensy as your dicks." He joined his thumb and forefinger. "Though maybe you don't have them at all."

Rei'than kept his face neutral. While he would have liked to know as much as possible about the success of the Kiritian general who had sent his achij to death, it would have been degrading to question the enemy about the condition of his own soldiers. And the last thing he would have liked to see was the sense of triumph and satisfaction visible in the eyes of this rank-and-file janitor.

He turned and began to walk; he might have even jogged or exercised a little - he was within the firing range of at least hundreds of barrels anyway. The armor had been taken from him when he had been captured, on a daily basis he wore a linen sweatshirt and pants intended for patients of medical centers.

And this was what his everyday existence looked like, unless the weather made it impossible to unkink, and on Cargoo it might have been very windy, or snow could fall like small missiles. Rei'than slept, meditated, read human virtual content, or indulged in other modest entertainment that could be done behind the bars of a cell five meters by five. He went to the bathroom, sometimes to laboratories for examination.

His interrogations had long since been abandoned because he had been making fun of such meetings, and there was no intention of torturing him, not to lose the second Avor. The Kiritian sera of truth and other effective methods of interrogating humans didn't work on Kandrok. He ate terrible human food as his rajithar capsules had run out. He would have had a lot more of them if some hadn't been taken for testing, where they had been destroyed. He was left with the last capsule, which he didn't want to swallow due to its 'just in case' status.

The barren, rocky, perhaps too cool Kiritian hideout planet, the secret of which for years he had not been able to tell the super collective, reminded him a little of Asephor 'Cerotis, the mother land of Kandrok, orbiting in a trinary star system. Therefore, he felt quite comfortable here, if you don't count the difficulty of gas exchange when staying in the air for a long time without a breathing apparatus, which he had to use every few hours to saturate the blood with the right amount of carbon dioxide. Kandrok had adapted to life on the globe devoid of flora and fauna, there was only scorched earth there, the pressure was high, and the dense atmosphere was created artificially, so they needed more of this compound to live than humans. Rei'than, like every bio-class avor, was able to hold his breath for a long time, if for some reason he was cut off from the air that was convenient for the body, but so far, he hadn't had to use this skill on Cargoo. Captivity unfortunately had postponed the day he became a Liberated, then all his problems with biological inconvenience would end. He was afraid, however, that this longed-for moment, the most important in any avor's life, might have never come, because he would die on Cargoo, lonely and forgotten, probably presumed dead.

As he sighed sadly, unobserved by the arguing wardens, though closely guarded as always, he unexpectedly picked up a signal with his neurocyte. His pupils narrowed even more, becoming like pinpricks. He felt as if new vital forces had been pumped into his limbs, as if he had been injected with freshly bootlegged kunhikar. It is said that this is how people felt in the spring, on those planets of theirs full of biomaterial, where there were seasons. It was like a gamma-ray burst. Nourishing cosmic energy. The Gift of the Lightbringer and the assurance that he remembered his beloved people. New hope and information: it's time to break free from lethargy, in vain suppressed by harlequinade, and start acting. The only pity is that it was a signal that traveled like a circle in water and it was impossible to send back a message.

Nevertheless, there was finally some contact, by a fortunate coincidence, from xepo Thino'pai to whom umen Rei'than was subordinate. His lips slowly formed into the broad smile he sent over weathered rocks and K'ajolom's star, taking on an intense evening red. He had missed it so much - a moment of happiness, at last some signal from the super-collectivity.

Though no one was looking for him, and only an order was given to all within the range of the seven varoth circles of kabo and below, Rei'than felt a surge of energy and willingness to carry out this task. And it was: "Deliver the inert form of the Kiritian super virus to the nearest ergrih as soon as possible."

It wasn't looking good. It meant that Kandrok hadn't yet neutralized the only but dangerous Kiritian weapon.

The Immortals had these pathogens in their labs on Cargoo, because they constantly recruited new achijes. All Rei'than had to do was get inside, grab a vial with the super virus, kill anyone in his way, steal the best Kiritian ship, and use the last rajithar capsule (luckily, he hadn't eaten it) to take control of it. The last step shouldn't have been problematic as people used the same technology that Kandrok had used much earlier. In addition, avors, unlike humans, had everything older compatible with what was newer. But even as if there was a disagreement, Rei'than would deal with the problem easily. It was like telling a modern Kiritian to use the keys to start a twentieth century car.

Theoretically, the plan was easy, but its implementation by a closely guarded prisoner was a completely different caliber.

7. CERN

The research and development center of the European Organization for Nuclear Research CERN had been rebuilt and developed many times over the centuries. At some stage, it had begun to expand its activities to biological research, work on modern weapons, as well as other branches of many technologies. Already unrelated to Earth, Kiret didn't know what it had looked like at the time of the arrival of Ice Age in 2615, which had officially resulted in the facility being abandoned by personnel. The locals knew all sorts of stories about the place that had sounded like urban legends or conspiracy theories - until Necron saw with his own eyes the postglacial decadence of the former scientific glory.

The first thing that caught the eye in the flashlights of the weapons and the practically negligible starlight was a concrete wall surrounding the complex, once powerful and fulfilling its purpose, now severely devastated, as if it couldn't withstand an artillery fire. Or the pressure of a terminal moraine of glaciers formed in the mountains. A former majestic gate was also in ruins, however, Kiret, Jenny and Skelver entered the facility over the remains of the fence.

Another ruin awaited them there. They found partially or completely pressed objects, overgrown with small vegetation. Internal roads had long ceased to exist, transformed by nature. There was also no question of the existence of a power supply; had it not been for the light of the newcomers, they would have been moving in complete darkness, amidst far from pleasant wind whistling. A distinctive metal sculpture in the shape of a conch, with patterns engraved on it and the names of distinguished scientists and CERN employees, lay tarnished and crumbling on the muddy ground. The semicircular administration building couldn't withstand the test of time and glacial erosion all the more. For now, however, Kiret was only interested in the landing field. Ordering scared Skelver to go in front of him, and Jenny, in the back, he illuminated the disintegrating objects with a long light integrated with the shotgun.

"Ueuhhh!" The Erces flinched as he saw something to a side.

"What are you afraid of, you fool?" The Kiritian directed the beam at the skeleton in the dirty, decaying lab coat sitting on the ground. Having walked a bit with the crunch of debris under his boots, he took ouf of the darkness four more bodies belonging to scientists and technicians, judging by rags. He could feel Jenny pressing against his shoulder.

"Plague?" Skelver asked.

Having freed himself from the girl's hands, Necron bent over the nearest remains.

"It's hard to say. Only clean bones are left." He ran a finger over the ribs and pelvis, where he saw not so old teeth or claw marks of some predators.

The Erces panicked again as the skimpy cacophony of sounds was joined by another one - a spine-chilling, ghastly chuckle.

Kiret examined the surroundings with the help of the helmet's bio-vision device and, apart from the two companions, saw hairy, squat, four-legged figures.

"A European hyena," he said reassuringly. "Nothing I can't handle."

Several curious individuals emerged from the nooks and crannies, their yellow eyes were reflecting Kiret's and Jenny's flashlights, which looked as if they had been light sources themselves. They made sounds like sardonic laughter mixed with the hoots of owls and the screeching of monkeys.

The hyenas froze, perked up their ears, appraised the newcomers, and left, having lost interest in them - especially in this large, healthy male in the armor and with the weapon.

Soon they found the landing field, there was no vehicle on it.

"What have you expected, Kiret?" Jenny got nervous. She quietly hoped that they would find something useful that would allow them to flee this damned planet immediately. "You thought this world was free from looters? Who normal would have abandoned expensive equipment? You said yourself that huge amounts of cash were pumped into CERN."

"But it's always worth checking out. Someone could use the landing site after the glacier retreated."

"So, do we turn back?" Skelver asked hopefully.

"Are you in a hurry? I need to see if there is any connectivity here. From what I remember, there were also hangars in the nether regions."

"Don't tell me you're gonna go in there?!" The Erces looked at the nearest skeleton, then at Necron. He realized something. "Aren't you trying to prove something to yourself, putting us at risk along the way?"

. "Forgive me, but in that I have to give him his due," added the girl. "What are we actually looking for?"

"Skelver, shut up kindly." The Kiritian pushed the man in the back, making him stagger. "Jenny, stay close to me as I instructed you."

Sandstorm needed no encouragement for that. She didn't dwell on the exploration subject, knowing from experience that she wouldn't have gotten anything more out of Necron. His pensive expression and slightly absent gaze alone were eloquent enough.

The main gate leading to the single-story buildings of the center hadn't existed for a long time. After a short search, Skelver noticed a technical hatch with a slammed door, Jenny's plasma gun dealt with it.

Their entry into the area of the collapsed building was announced by a dull thud of metal, which, due to old age, split into several parts, raising clouds of dust. Jenny gritted her teeth and closed her eyes; she had a feeling that the clatter had been heard even in Jamal's house behind the Border. The echo froze for the next seconds, dying in the cavernous bowels of the facility. The slight heat vision in the dark that Sandstorm had inherited from Forkis was of no avail in the cold, dead establishment; it's good that they had lighting.

Walking and lighting their way with the wide beam, Kiret noticed a reception desk and former workplaces arranged on a semicircular plan. There must have been dozens of them in the facility's heyday. Most of the equipment had been either vandalized, stolen, or taken during the evacuation, with only a few computers left that had long since been replaced by capripods, at least outside of Earth. Virtually every step he came across stones, pieces of metal or cables, which crumbled to dust when lightly touched with the foot or barrel. The dry air smelled of dust and dirt. Apart from the prints of the shoes of the three of them, there were no traces on the floor that could indicate that someone had visited the building in the recent past.

Jenny and Skelver got slightly scared when, from the black corridor leading to the deeper part of the complex, rushed bats, to fly out through the created exit.

"There's nothing here," said Sandstorm hurriedly. "We'd better get out of this place, it's not safe here. The facility is old, something may fall on our heads or even collapse."

Kiret didn't listen to her, looking at the ceiling and walls, he tried to find any power source, but in vain. He could have used one of Jenny's six plasma gun generators as a temporary power generator, but he had nothing to connect it to - everything he touched was falling apart and slipping through his gloved fingers. He especially wanted to check logs and a map of the object.

"Look for the plan," he said to the girl.

Once again ignored, Sandstorm sighed ostentatiously and turned away. Lighting her way with the plasma flashlight, she began to look around at poles and other walls.

"I think this is it." She stopped at two pillars interlaced like a helix that were connected to the ceiling. In a steel engraving in the center of the structure there was indeed the plan of the facility.

Pushing Skelver in front of him who tried to sneak away, Necron joined the girl studying the maze of tunnels and corridors.

"It's the official schematic of the facility," he murmured. "It's good. Oh, there are underground hangars. We are going to go there now, but then we have to go ... here." With his index finger, he circled one of the smaller corridors somewhere on the sidelines.

"What is there?" Jenny pointed with her chin.

"Backup control room. I'd love to know what happened here."

"Do you want to check the logs? But there is no power. Is the facility's past so important to us now? Have you ever been here?"

"Yes, long ago. Due to the construction, the use of older but more durable building materials and the location of this level, it is likely that it has been preserved in a better condition. It is located several dozen meters underground and has been well secured. In the past, it wasn't affected even by a strong earthquake that caused cities to fall."

They walked along an oval passage from which bats flew out. The vibrations of spider web curtains indicated that the animals might have gotten in through some ventilation hatch.

Listening to the sounds of the footsteps, they came to an elevator shaft dilapidated like the surroundings, with no cabin. They descended to the underground by stairs made of stone.

After Kiret made sure that the ceiling wouldn't collapse on their heads, they walked for a time along a subway-tunnel-like corridor, branching off into sidings marked with steel engraving symbols, which led to rooms and sectors that had once performed different functions. The main passage turned out to be collapsed and the ramifications eventually led to the blind spots, so they surfaced over a gentle landslide caused by a glacier foot.

They found themselves in an inner square; before the reconstruction, there had been the main entrance to the building there. There was a tattered but still holding up statue of the Hindu deva Nataraja standing on it, around which many myths and conspiracy theories had grown up. It was said that rituals had been carried out there for the success of the experiments conducted at CERN. "Something could be up," Kiret thought glumly, for in front of the god's likeness there was a stone altar - and more human skeletons.

Soon they reached a slammed exit gate of the underground hangar. Then there was nothing more made by human hand - terrestrial objects had been completely swept by the mountain glacier, leaving behind moraines and a swamp.

As it started raining heavily, the three of them went underground again. Using the helmet's navigation and the photographed map, Kiret found the hangar: dark, huge and cool, a haven for echo enthusiasts. No trace of any vehicle had been left there. Apart from garbage, the hall with walls a few meters thick had been stripped of everything, even checkered lamp covers had been removed. Jenny slung the weapon strap over her shoulder and folded her arms into a basket.

"That was easy to predict."

"Let's check also the control room," the Kiritian ordered.

They plunged into the corridors again. The air had changed, was no longer dry and filled with motes of dust as in the administration building, but damp, sticky and smelling of wet soil, even decay. On flat surfaces had infested strange flora in the shape of irregular patches (Sandstorm wanted to believe that it was only plants visible in the infra-vision as animal tissue). The closer they got to the heart of CERN, the more there was of it. Dark liquids ran down the walls, creating thick, as if sugar puddles on the floors.

"Jenny, come on, let me show you something interesting."

Kiret led them through a breach in the wall onto a tarnished platform surrounding the remains of a huge detector with boards. It was possible to go down the warped stairs to a lower level, which they did.

"Look over there."

He directed his arm towards the long, slightly curving tunnel with spans lying on the ground. The flashlights reached all the way to the bend.

"It is round, almost thirty kilometers long," the Kiritian announced. "This is the oldest part of CERN, renovated many times, in the last phase reinforced with dhurnstall, that's why not everything has collapsed yet, although we are several dozen meters below the ground, over which the glacier rolled. These large diameter pipes used to be part of the LHC, or a particle accelerator. In the smaller circle, the elementary particles were accelerated to almost the speed of light, then introduced into the larger one that you are now looking at. They flew at each other from opposite sides, collided and got torn apart. Collisions were monitored, they were to simulate the formation of the universe."

"Universes," corrected the Erces. "According to the knowledge of Kandrok, there are infinitely many of them."

"I've heard it somewhere before, I won't argue," Kiret said amicably. "Anyway, it's a piece of the scientific history of mankind. The device was once the most expensive and advanced on the planet. It is a pity that the center collapsed."

"Since the Ice Age is over and people are resettling the area, there is nothing to prevent the facility from being rebuilt," commented Jenny. "There will always be something new to discover."

They returned to the main corridor of the sector and headed for the control room. Jenny wasn't a fan of underground escapades, she had the impression that her breathing was getting harder and harder, and the space between the walls a few steps away was gradually shrinking. She thought she heard sounds coming from far away. The presence of seemingly fearless Kiret, proudly but cautiously walking forward, encouraged her. Skelver was by nature fearful, he didn't know if he was more concerned about the unpredictability of the Kiritian with the stolen shotgun or the fact that they descended further and further into the dark, unexplored, dangerous areas of the facility. He didn't even want to think about what would have happened if their light had suddenly broken. He forgot which way they had come from the hangar, having showed the next intersections and rooms.

More and more tissue vegetation appeared, as did human skeletons. It was impossible to determine if they belonged to CERN employees, because no IDs were left on the scraps of clothing. Most of the wreckage contained a weapon, and some magazines had a few bullets left. When Skelver, looking imploringly at Kiret, tried to reach for one of the rifles, he pushed him with the barrel, making him stand upright. He allowed Jenny, increasingly afraid, to walk, holding his arm.

Living organisms were enriched with bioluminescent fungi and lichens, quivering curtains of spider webs shone from spores.

There was something else: either a draft raving somewhere in the nooks and crannies - or the systematic breathing of some creature that couldn't be taken out of the darkness with the flashlights.

They entered through a tunnel into what was either a semicircular room with a few small corridors or an overgrown, dirty grotto. Necron didn't find the object on the summoned map.

"Here's the whole ecosystem," Jenny whispered, to whom the surroundings were sparkling with life in infra-vision. She didn't like shells of eggs the size of half a basketball in a bone lair.

Her heart leapt into her throat as a dark brown, massive, rock-like figure with fangs and appearance of a cross between a hippo and a massive dog emerged from a corridor at the end of the room. The growling creature gave off no heat at all, so she hadn't noticed it sooner. It's possible that it had been stuck there, crouching.

"I don't have it on my vision," Necron noted the same.

"What is it, Kiret?"

"This is the first time I see something like this. I think it is its nest."

"Why didn't you let me take that weapon ..." blurted out rapidly breathing Skelver.

The ton beast moved to attack, running surprisingly fast on its grotesque legs.

"Jenny, fire!" Kiret demanded, firing the shotgun himself.

To the first two scattered shots, the creature didn't react, it only stopped when was reached by pellets fired from a short distance - it ran its paw over its mouth as if it had been getting rid of dirt. Its whitish eyes seemed to be a solid glass mass.

The pellets might have turned out to be useless in case of the colossus with skin like a rock, Kiret got worried only when the Kiritian battle plasma didn't hurt it either.

"Impossible ... Run away!"

They rushed into a side corridor. Behind them they heard a bass whine and the thud of heavily taken steps of the accelerating big body. As the beast approached, knowing these tunnels, Necron stopped, turned, and emptied another clip of pellet. The roar of shots in the confined space was carried like thunderbolts. The animal stopped again and, irritated, started to rub its mouth with its paw; Kiret ordered Jenny and Skelver to continue to run.

They reached an intersection where single-track freight little cars had used to go. They descended into the basin of the trackage and began to maneuver between the metal debris.

Jenny tripped and fell, pressed the flashlight cover strongly against the niche wall, fortunately there was not even a scratch on the device. The comrades helped the girl to get up.

"Kiritian job." Necron smiled, knowing what Jenny might have thought. "I can see the control room, there are seventy paces left."

In a shaft that stretched under the ceiling hissed another creature, then slipped through the hole. If it hadn't been for the fur, it could have been considered a monitor lizard. It ignored the human intruders, but jumped on the beast chasing them.

The animals started to fight. Although the furry one was three times smaller than the opponent, it made up for it with aggression and fierceness. More like a feline than a reptile, it was trying to get to the throat of the colossus trying to crush it.

Unexpectedly, another furry monitor lizard joined the fight. Kiret no longer doubted that there was much more life in CERN's nether regions than bioluminescent flora and deep-sea fungi. In the flashlights, eyes flared here and there with orange or yellow, glaring curiously and feistily from nooks and crannies. There was a ghastly chuckle, like those of the hyenas met outside, which in the dark nether regions stretching for tens of kilometers turned out to be much more evocative.

The three found themselves at the control room - a separate room with metal door as well as shields covered with algae that had once been transparent. After helping Jenny climb the wall to the station level, Kiret passed by her and pushed away a skeleton lying before the entrance. In the absence of power to the door, the lock didn't work, it was enough to press the handle and push the long unused dhurnstal with all the strength to create a clearance, which Necron coped with.

As they crossed the control room's threshold, the struggle caused by encroaching on the territory continued; one of the shaggy predators lay crushed on the ground. Instantly, both creatures turned in different directions and fled as if frightened by an extremely powerful stimulus. Jenny noticed that other animals, whose eyes had glittered so eerily when exposed to the light, hid in the nooks and crannies or climbed high, disappearing into total darkness.

Rats of supernatural size began to swarm in the niche of the trackage and in front of the control room - the largest were the size of an adult dachshund. The squeals coming from hundreds of muzzles caused pain in the head and ears. The yammer faded considerably as Kiret and Skelver quickly closed the door. Two rats managed to break through to the control room, the Erces disgustedly kicked them into a corner, and Necron killed them with the shotgun. The others rushed to the control room covers, climbed one on the other, forming an aggressive, lively, mobile wall of matted fur, teeth, claws, whiskers, red to yellow eyes and algae scraped off with the bodies.

"Will they get in?" Frightened Jenny had never seen such a symptom of aggression in any living creature.

"They shouldn't. The shields are of puronax," Kiret said, counting the ammo for his weapons. "It's a material used in the space and defense industries, like dhurnstal. Kiritian materials. Although those from exports are of lower quality, they are still light years ahead of everything developed on Earth. Both don't age as fast as steel or plexiglass. Fortunately, the control room is made of the toughest materials available on the planet, building the nether regions, they weren't idle with subsidies granted from the budgets of various countries."

The equipment in the control room also turned out to be modern and durable. It didn't seem damaged under the thick layer of particulates, cobwebs, and dust that Necron was brushing to the sides with his gloves. Jenny coughed, fanning herself with her hand as the air turned gray with the dirt. The room, thirty paces long, was equipped with capripods, which apparently the looters hadn't gotten to. As the girl stared at the bones of the animal behind the cover, the one crushed during the fight, which had only a minute before had the complete body, she understood with disgust why.

"Give me the weapon." Kiret extended a hand to her. The girl gave him the plasma gun. Skelver sat down in an armchair and contemplated the rats, as mobile as giant vermin.

Necron pulled one of the generators out of the carriage, thanks to which the plasma gun was autonomous and didn't require manual charging. He crouched down and started rummaging through the well-preserved cables under the control panel, having removed the cover from it. Jenny stopped to understand what he was doing when he outthrusted the blades from his bracer and began cutting with them the shotgun capsule projectile into strips, including the cables, but she figured he was trying to put together a hastily working system. In the environment where she had grown up, cables were considered an antique. Any radiation or heat was transferred wirelessly over a distance through intermediaries.

The largest of these were interstellar satellites. CERN's capripods, although once considered the best equipment in the facility, had been equipped with cables like computers. It was no surprise to Jenny that long-lived Necron was familiar with such antiquities.

"Why can't you just connect it to your generator?" She asked, more weary than afraid of the rats.

"Because the principle of compatibility you know doesn't apply to terrestrial devices from several centuries ago. This congruence makes it easy for us to live, but it used to be different. Do you know where this principle came from?" He glanced at Sandstorm, who shook her head. Skelver began to listen to him too. "Due to the fact that there was too much of everything, often within even one brand, there were problems with replacing parts or connecting something. For example, your car engine broke down, it was easy to replace it when the product was launched, but a few years later, when dozens of versions of the same model were released, you would have had a problem with it, because your engine would have become scarce. And there were almost Dantesque scenes, when in one of the production countries, for example China, manufacturers sulked - markets all over the world had a real problem. Due to a small element, let's say a processor, all factory conveyor belts producing cars were stopped. Keep in mind that I'm talking about a time when there were no bots or repair nanites, there were 3D printers, but companies and independent users terribly fought for copyrights to an item they manufactured. As a result, even an ordinary slide in a bathroom closet drawer became irreplaceable, because it was difficult to get a new one. It was the bane of consumerism; it was more profitable to buy a new thing than to repair a damaged one. That's why your father, Forkis, ordered all devices of the same class, and even different types, to be compatible with each other. So, in our reality you will easily connect a generator removed from a gun carriage to your house, and thus you will have an alternative power source. Remember The White, a fighter with AI of your mother's XRS-14 Ghost? If any of its hybrid batteries were damaged, one could be taken from FX-94 Black Panter that the rebels used."

"It's very sensible." Jenny didn't understand much of what Necron was saying to her, but as always, it was nice to listen to.

He tinkered with the old-fashioned console for a long time, making his work more pleasant by telling interesting facts about the ancient Earth. Every now and then he glanced at funnel-shaped lamps under the ceiling. At one point they clicked, and the room was flooded with a dull, yellowish light, too much like the eyes of rats. The capripods also lit up, holographic plates rushed upwards, also the emergency light in the corridors activated, bringing the rodents in the waking state.

A triumphant smile on Necron's lips also appeared on Jenny's face.

"My congratulations," Skelver concluded.

"Mine too, but you broke my gun, Necron."

The Kiritian sat in the other armchair next to the Erces and set about breaking the security features of the capripod's soft.

"I didn't break it. It will only have a limited power supply, but it should be enough to destroy most of the animals that get in our way," he added cautiously, not knowing what else they might have encountered at CERN.

He quickly got into the system. Glancing every now and then at the holograph floating in front of his head, he tapped his fingers on a keyboard plate.

While Skelver poked around the room, stuffing various small items in his pockets, Jenny leaned her forearms on the armrest of Necron's chair.

"What is this language?" She asked. "I can understand some words."

"English." The man continued his work. "It is rarely used in space, but on Earth it is probably still one of the most popular languages, formerly used in computer science. Old times."

"Can you finally enlighten me what you are looking for? What is so important about this CERN that you put us in between murderous rats and other mutants?"

Kiret wanted to glance discreetly at Skelver. The Erces, interested in the question, looked in his direction, so he failed to let Jenny know that he wouldn't say anything in front of the stranger. The girl knew only Kiritian, which she had learned in the traditional way, without the entraser technology, so they couldn't speak another language.

"Tell me finally. I'm sick of this," Jenny pressed.

Necron exhaled with slight frustration.

"All right. Since we found ourselves close to CERN, I thought I'd take a look around here. It had been rumored that - and now it is not known whether the records left by some old advanced civilization had been invented or dug up, but given that we discovered the existence of Nimja a few years ago, the last possibility doesn't sound like heresy at all - at CERN there is only one copy of the blueprints of a very deadly weapon, the most powerful in human history. If it really existed and was so lethal as a small group of insiders claim, we might eventually get a solid whip on Kandrok. You mustn't ignore anything that may help, even if it seems very unbelievable. I didn't want to say anything because of him." He glared at Skelver. "Now you're screwed, buddy. I'll keep an eye on you so that you don't tell your bosses. I should actually kill you now." Kiret made a motion towards him with the shotgun.

"Who would I tell? Kandrok? I have said many times that I have nothing to do with them anymore! Everything I did, I did out of fear!" The Erces said with alleged indignation. He felt a bead of sweat trickle down the back of his head towards his neck.

"You could also report to the Headhunters."

"I don't know what their priorities are or whether they are looking for your weapon at CERN. I'm nobody in their ranks, only a helper."

The girl clasped her hands on her head.

"And you think, Kiret, that the information about the secret weapon will be just like that on top, in the random control room?"

"That's why I need time to bypass safeguards and filter working hard drives wirelessly, because servers have long been gone." He smiled slyly. "Don't worry, baby. Before becoming a Kiritian, and even a soldier in general, I was playing with hacking a bit. Although the current algorithms would find what we need in half a second, in our situation, I only have my brain and hands at my disposal."

"Does this weapon have a name?" Sandstorm skipped asking for details in front of Skelver, though it really interested her.

"Yes. It is called Death Bringer. The Sower of Death."

In the silence that immediately began to linger in the control room, you could clearly hear rats trying to get inside.

"I don't know if I want to know what this weapon can do," Jenny commented in a whisper.

"Perhaps the entire human race will bring bane upon itself if the Death Bringer's plans do exist and get outside CERN," the Kiritian replied grimly.

They stopped talking to each other. Kiret was completely absorbed by the search for information, Jenny watched anxiously at the rodents which, despite Necron's assurances of the place's safety, seemed to had caused several cracks in the cover, which was difficult to affirm due to the dirt - and Skelver again began pacing the room and viewing its equipment.

Another animal appeared outside, drawn by the scent of people and the tumult of battle. It could be described as a forest dog twenty times enlarged, which made it a massive, muscular clog of the corridor, with a huge mouth.

The giant threw itself at the rats like starved and began to eat them alive, plunging its open muzzle into a swirl of the bodies or holding down a few at a time with its paws. The strong, fur-covered body seemed immune to the bites of the confused rodents, which had either begun to attack them or run down the corridors like a carpet of debris into the sewage system.

"Bully-devourer? And where did it come from to Europe?" Biffter thought aloud. "Nice mess this fauna has become."

Jenny moved away from the cover in disgust and anxiety. "How are we getting out of here now?"

"There is a second door!" Skelver called from behind a pillar in a darkened alcove.

Kiret made a face full of disbelief. He activated the multi-meter wall of the holograph, littered with schematics and English inscriptions, then stood up and walked a few paces away, as if he had wanted to have a full view of the perspective of a painting in a museum. The bully-devourer lost interest in the rats; its attention was caught by another light source in the control room.

Jenny stood beside Necron, touching his arm with hers, in anticipation of an explanation.

"The formation of the ice was indeed their fault," he said. "They changed the climate by testing some unearthed device called the Earthworm. They didn't understand its essence because it acted against the law of conservation of mass; the ground treated with it simply disappeared. They blindly conducted an experiment. They created a huge amount of energy that penetrated into the depths of the planet. So, Jamal was partially right: The Border and the Ice Age have their origins in the Haunted Zone. However, it was not about innovative tests in the atmosphere or the earth's core, but about a ready-made weapon, whose authorship is unknown."

"Is that the Death Bringer?" Jenny asked.

"No, something else. Apparently, they indulged themselves completely at CERN." Necron looked at the bully-devourer losing interest in the last remaining rats in sight. "Much information is missing, I cannot read anything more."

A massive thud also drew Jenny and Skelver's attention to the cover of the room. The bully-devourer rested its huge front legs against it, each underside of at least half a meter in diameter. The puronax quickly began to evaporate under the pressure of its wet, moving nose. A pearly sweat appeared on Jenny's forehead.

"Let's get out through the back door," said Skelver.

"I bet it's closed." Kiret moved with the shotgun towards the Erces, who began to press against the door with a grunt, so strongly that he turned red. "Of course! Jenny, give me the plasma gun."

"Can't you just shoot this thing through the cover?" She asked, increasingly panicked.

"You could give that gun to me, not to the baby," Skelver said something in a pretentious tone for the first time.

Necron looked fiercely at the forest dog-mutant, which, like a stegoceras, was hitting the puronax with its head, making the entire control room tremble.

"Neither pellets nor combat plasma can penetrate this."

By the time he finished his sentence, the shield shattered like glass under another impact. The animal lost its balance, fell inside and crashed against the control panel, but began to rise quickly.

"You must have exaggerated the reliability of Kiritian materials," Skelver joked nervously.

"There is no guarantee that it is not a fake bought with less money from a tender," blurted the Kiritian.

Jenny screamed as the beast began to force its way toward them, scrubbing its back against the ceiling, clawing the metal of the floor. The girl with no military training was paralyzed, the plasma gun in her hands became useless.

"Give me that damn weapon!" Skelver boomed, pressing his back and hands against the door. "Kill the dog, I'll try to open it."

Kiret cursed. He took Jenny's plasma gun and tossed it to Skelver.

"Here you are, but try pointing the barrel at me or Jenny, and I'll blow your head off," he warned. "You know how to use it?"

"Kandrok trained me, damn it!"

Frightened, thus aggressive rats began to pour into the control room.

While Kiret, chased against the wall, shot the bully-devourer with the shotgun, injuring, but more annoying it, also kicking rodents, the Erces standing by Jenny was melting the door with battle plasma.

They managed to fall behind it at the last moment - when the bully-devourer was about to grab Sandstorm's head with its jaws.

They moved along a curving, circular tunnel, illuminated at the highest point by a series of blue lamps that drew energy from the generator left at the panel. The lighting, however, faded as they ventured into the complex. Eventually it began to dim, plunging the three of them for seconds into the bioluminescent and flashlight-licked darkness, then there was the crippled brightness again. Human and animal skeletons loomed in it, as well as ubiquitous vegetation with tissues as thick as the skin of an elephant. As if the cuticle-like creature had a lot in common genetically with the covering of the body of the creature Kiret, Jenny and Skelver had met in the grotto.

The bully-devourer knocking around in the nether regions finally caught up with them. Skelver sent a plasma ball at it, much weaker than he had set, but it should have killed the animal on the spot - a traditional animal, made by nature, not the sick imagination of scientists. The bully-devourer broke through the murderous energy like through water splashed with a bucket.

Kiret was shooting at it with the shotgun, banging from the double barrel over and over again, but the effect was that the speeding giant was waving its head as if knocking off nap.

The Kiritian ran out of ammunition when a second bully-devourer, just as massive and huge, joined the animal.

"Quickly, into that little corridor!" He ordered.

Jenny and Skelver led the way, Necron swung his weapon like a pole at the head of the nearer bully-devourer. He ran after his companions as fast as he could in the armor and corridor littered with debris. The animals sniffed with interest at the thrown object, which bought the escapees some precious moments.

They moved through corridors with lower and lower ceilings, and walls located close to each other, sometimes they had to go single line. The light had gone out some time earlier, so they embraced the plasma flashlight, Kiret was using the helmet assist, and Jenny the infra-vision. According to the map of the facility, they were at its eastern, underground end. They could only turn back or take a roundabout path to technical rooms, devastated, covered with earth, in which deep bayous with tiny, transparent creatures had formed here and there.

"Better than rats, mutant dogs and oversized bears." Jenny took a quick two steps back as something scuttled away from under the surface of a puddle she stepped into. She managed to register that it had no eyes.

"At least the dogs aren't torturing us for the time being," added Skelver.

After an hour, they managed to get out of the zone of damp or flooded rooms; in one they had to wade waist-deep in stagnant water.

"Where now?" The Erces looked around the passage, which looked more like a cave corridor strewn with boulders than a fragment of a science complex. They stopped for a short rest. Somewhere far away echoed resounding bark of bully-devourers.

"Look, this part of the wall is red." Jenny pointed to rocky facet.

Kiret shone the flashlight on it, simultaneously surveying it with the vision of the helmet.

"You're not kidding? Here I see an ordinary gray-brown rock. Skelver?"

"I also a common rock." The Erces pressed his boot against the wall and jumped back, pushing himself off.

"I swear it's bright, as if tightly covered in moss with bloody bioluminescence," Sandstorm tried to convince them. "Organic, in a sense. Or on the other side, there is some strong light source."

Kiret pushed the root aside, rested his hand on the hard, glassy, cold surface, ran his fingers over the facet, tapped it with his knuckles. A fragment of the wall didn't stand out from the next sections of the corridor.

"Looks like normal rock. There is nothing here according to the map."

"Will you try to smash it?" The girl suggested. "It doesn't hurt."

"It does. Behind the rock there can be a thermal lake or a storage room for radioactive waste, hence the glow." Kiret himself didn't believe in his assumptions. He would have gotten this information in the vision specification, and he was sure his armor was still operational.

There was a sudden snarl in close surroundings, accompanied by the clunk of digging and the rumble of stones being moved away.

Barely a dozen paces ahead of them appeared the muzzle of a bully-devourer, trying furiously to widen the small corridor with paws and claws as strong as shovels of a mechanical mole. From the opposite pole were coming twin noises.

"Smart beasts," concluded the Kiritian. "They have noiselessly approached us from two sides."

Skelver concentrated the plasma energy and fired at the nearer bully-devourer. The only damage he did was knocking stones off the walls and ceiling.

"Give me that." Unbelieving, Kiret took the gun from him, checked the condition of the other generators. Previously, he hadn't paid attention to the equipment, he had been interested only in the battery. "Great, energy is not renewing itself. Some imbeciles must have been fumbling in the plasma gun when we were taken captive."

The bully-devourer on the north side moved a meter in a minute, trying to push itself furiously into the tunnel like a hamster into a two-centimeter gap. Cornered, Skelver took courage and approached the other beast with the intention of breaking its teeth with a kick, but he backed away three times as fast when the stinking maw gaped at arm's length in front of him. Shreds of bloodied rat fur hung on the lower fang.

Fast-breathing Jenny, who tried to disguise the twitching of her lower jaw with the squeeze of her lips, looked at the section of the wall that glowed in the infra-vision. Skelver and Kiret looked at the same place.

"What do you prefer: to be torn to pieces or to drown in an underground lake or die of radioactive air?" The Kiritian found the nerve to use black humor.

"I'd rather survive," Skelver also tried to joke to curb the mounting anxiety.

Necron ran his look over his companions, saw in their eyes silent permission for what he intended to do. He accumulated all the available energy of the weapon into one hit.

"Against the left wall," he demanded.

Sandstorm and Skelver found themselves behind his back, they clung to rusty pipes, wanting to get as far away from the field of fire as possible. One broke under the pressure of the Erces' body, who lost his balance and fell over.

Kiret stood firm and fired. To his relief, the section of rock pointed out by the girl crumbled like thin ice on the surface of water and fell with a clink of glass being broken. Then there was another barrier of shiny hardened metal - against all logic, gleaming new, as if it had been inserted a day earlier. In the corner loomed a small touch activator with an unusual fractal shape.

The bully-devourer, with its extended paw, almost reached Jenny, who jumped back with a groan and found herself with Skelver close to Kiret.

Not getting his hopes up too much, Necron pressed the activator and, as he had expected, it didn't work.

"Maybe you need harder!" Immediately after him tried Skelver, which was driven only by desperation, so he hit the convex structure with his fist.

A gate as thick as an adult's leg lifted, revealing another silver door that looked like an eight-slice pizza; boards touched by the tips formed an airtight barrier. And these, too, could be opened with the activator, which Skelver also did.

The resulting space wasn't filled with toxins or water. A quick scan with helmet as well as plasma gun indectors[3], in which was left enough energy only for diagnostic activities, didn't indicate any threats to the human body.

They crossed both thresholds immediately. Kiret was relieved when the first barrier automatically started to be slid shut, then the second one interlocked. One of the bully-devourers got into the cave and began to run its claws furiously over the metal; the outer door muffled sounds.

The escapees found themselves in a gray corridor, so huge that medium-class ships could have easily flown through it. It had the shape of an intestine, with alternating narrower and wider segments, and was made of an alloy of an undetermined type, as was the gate. The passage was uniformly lit, though the source of the radiation couldn't be identified, as if every square millimeter of the wall had added an element to the mosaic of blue-white light. The surface visually looked perfectly smooth, likewise slightly slimy. At CERN, every corridor and sector was marked, here the walls weren't decorated even with a badly matched pixel. The temperature, albeit chilly, was soothing after the difficult crossing through the research center.

The astonished three looked at each other, no one had the inspiration to accurately comment on the discovery. Kiret noticed that the plasma gun had been deactivated, and from then on, he could only swing it around like a club. What worried him more, however, was that his helmet, as well as all the electronics supporting the armor, had stopped working. Jenny's Onkalot vision, too, now functioned like in an ordinary human being.

"You think the dogs will come in here?" Sandstorm was the first to speak in the enigmatic tunnel. The echo carried no sound, as if she had been speaking in an open, empty space.

"They are aggressive, but also intelligent, I saw it in their eyes. The question is not whether they will enter, but when they will find out how to open the gate." Necron looked into the tunnel. "According to myths, there were once giants on Earth. The corridor looks as if it was built for them."

"Or by them," Jenny raised the thread.

"What are the giants?" Myths and legends also existed in Skelver's culture, but there was nothing about the giants in them.

"Something that, if it really existed, I wish it had been dead for a long time."

They moved in the only possible direction. They didn't pass embranchments or rooms; the tunnel was constantly uniform. It was the absolutely clean and perfect opposite of the CERN sectors marked on the map - apart from the fact that it was in vain to look for traces of damage, dirt particles like dust or lumps of earth were nowhere to be seen, as if the newcomers had been guests of royal status and someone had cleaned up specially for their arrival. The illumination method didn't change, the light shone off the surface in an eye-pleasing way; visibility was up to a hundred meters, then a slight afterglow could be noticed. It was difficult to determine whether the tunnel was illuminated the same everywhere, or the intensity of the light adjusted to the people passing by.

Eventually the passage branched. They chose the one on the left, soon it forked too. Further it was similar. Kiret estimated that on the map the whole thing could look like side roots extending from the main one.

After a march lasting an indefinite amount of time, they came across another gate. Shaped like a two-dimensional, though rough, shell, they were several stories high, which made them feel like insects. "Perhaps even on Morascrik, where monumentalism dominates architecture, Kiritians don't have such a colossus," Necron thought with appreciation. At least in public buildings that weren't hangars for larger ships and naval craft. As soon as they stood at the gate, it reacted as if it had had a detector and began to open in an unusual way: a metal center spool traveled along the spiral of a lunette, making ever-larger circles, while scooping up material along the way. The phenomenon contradicted the law of conservation of mass.

They found themselves in front of a free space - a conical room so huge that it was logistically and physically impossible to create, as it was as large as a small city. Something like this could have existed only deep underground, and Necron didn't feel that they were coming down a great tunnel. It was occupied by only one object, but extensive - a platform surrounded by heterogeneous structures of pyramids and columns, the function of which couldn't be associated with anything specific. The structures glowed slightly in different areas with azure light, and consisted as if of tiny crystals glued together, filled with liquid metal. From the gate to the center of the platform, led ramp first and then a wide staircase.

"What can it be?" Stunned, Jenny broke the deadness first. Also, here the echo didn't spread. "Landing site? Square? The roof of a building hidden underground? I have never seen anything like this in my life."

"Neither have I," Kiret whispered back, staring at the focal point of the object. Sandstorm looked at him, but hoped that the man who had lived hundreds of years would know something. "Does that remind you of something?" He asked Skelver.

"No." The Erces shook his head.

"Stay here, I'll investigate it." Necron moved cautiously, staring distrustfully at the glassily smooth surface of the ramp, on which, however, the shoes didn't slip.

Taking his time and being vigilant, he climbed onto the platform and looked around at the surrounding structures, some the size of houses. He walked to the center of the plane where there was the most of free space. He delicately examined the lowest cones with his hand, resembling growing stalagmites. The too geometric roughness of one of them contradicted the fact that it was a natural rock. It reminded Necron of a petrified control panel, but certainly not any that mankind had used in its history.

"They built things like that at CERN?" Jenny joined Kiret, who sighed slightly, but made no comment that she had acted rashly with Skelver plodding behind her. The Erces walked away a bit and started to survey another column.

"I doubt it. Rather, they discovered an enigmatic underground complex and sealed it for some reason. I don't know a single metal alloy from here, if it is a metal at all. So, for now there's nothing I ..."

He didn't finish. He felt a wave of gentle vibrations under his shoes, as if a space shuttle had been landing a kilometer away. A humming whistle spread in the air at the threshold of hearing. He glared at Skelver who froze with frightened face and hands raised, like a thief caught stealing in a bazaar.

"I'm sorry ..." he panted. "I've just touched ..."

The vibrations intensified, as if they had been now aboard a machine taking off for a change. Some of the crystals from the closest constructions began to glow a faint red that progressed further and further like a virus infecting the body, dominating the earlier azure. The mosaics under the glass-like surface of the substrate turned a tint of blue. In the center shone a ball of dull white light.

The rest of the city came alive with a two-color blaze, although the whole thing looked fantastic, the encounter with the unknown phenomenon caused anxiety.

"What have you done," the Kiritian said in an accusing tone.

Skelver withdrew his hands, was moving away from the pillar as if from an annoyed, poisonous snake.

The vibrations ceased, and so did the sounds reminiscent of devices being activated. The next moments, they spent, being nervous, but nothing else happened. The immensity of silence could have competed with the size of the facility.

"I think that's it," the Erces finally said with uncertain relief. "Maybe I just accidentally turned on the better lighting?"

No one recorded the moment when a Kiritian medusa-shaped medium transporter appeared in place of the white ball of light, which fit between eight poles bent towards the center. When they looked confused in that direction, it had just already been there. There was no light or sound effect, no blast accompanying it, no smell of ozone or the heat of working machine.

Kiret, Jenny, and Skelver stood like three statues, with mouths ajar and eyes wide open.

The transporter airlock opened; the gangway extended.

A squad sent to Amyrade Anfraktoris began to come out and look around without restraint. They all came back - but there was two Darius Schindlers. They differed only in their hair and eye color, the latter clearly visible from a distance, because they were silver and glistened like in an animal whose muzzle was lit at night.

One group of statues with expressions of extreme astonishment turned into two facing each other. Even assassin Divinus lost his permanent mask of indifference and raised his eyebrows high, barely suppressing a shock that the rest didn't conceal. Only silver-eyed Darius seemed to care about nothing, the disorientation of his companions even amused him.

"Jenny? General Biffter?!" The real Schindler blurted out.

"Captain Avadar?" Kiret asked.

"Yyyy ... eee." In Private Shimizu's throat got stuck what he intended to say.

Aytar looked around the object.

"We're still on Amyrade, right?"

"Come on." Tsar glanced at the barely visible ceiling, put his hands to his head and withdrew them. "I understand that there are strange coincidences, but this is an exaggeration on a cosmic impossibility and scale!" He indicated Kiret, Jenny and Skelver with his arms, then lifted and unfolded them like a guru speaking to the faithful. "Is returning to normalcy such a difficult wish to fulfill?" He looked at Nacxit.

The latter, with a slight smile, moved in front of the group, approached Kiret.

"Who are you?" Biffter sensed that this awe-inspiring person had little to do with Darius. His eyes, with which he stared at him piercingly, bore the hallmarks of one highly intelligent, unimaginably old - and inhuman. For a moment his brain tingled as if there had been a disturbance in the flow of impulses. He felt more uncomfortable than the last hours, though he had fought mutants and discovered the tunnel of the 'giants'.

The Nimja member didn't reply, to Necron's relief he withdrew his gaze and became interested in the two standing beside him.

"Darius? What happened to you?" Jenny asked.

"Oh, the bastard of an Onkalot and a man. Interesting." After another mental surveillance, Nacxit smiled kindly. He brought his face close to Sandstorm's ear and whispered so that only she could hear him. "Which, apart from telepathy and infra-vision, has one more secret."

The girl stiffened, the current of fear that spread along her spine was far from pleasant. Nacxit winked at her, stepped back, then became interested in Skelver, on whose forehead appeared sweat. The Nimja member read the longest in his mind.

"And here is the Erces, as Kiritians appointed you. Unfortunately, I cannot see what I'm looking for in your mind. Sadly, you don't know anything."

"Wh ... what I don't know?"

Nacxit ignored him like had Jenny before.

"Now I understand why the porter activated." He waved his arm towards the transporter. He breathed out loudly. "What a long time I haven't been here! I completely forgot that this place exists."

"And what is it?" Captain Michael Avadar was finally able to speak.

"Tens of thousands of years ago, according to your measure of time, Nimja created conveyors on Earth, connecting it to other planets. Nacxit began to move without looking at anyone, but followed by all pairs of eyes. Darius made an arc with his, knowing from experience that there would be a longer lecture. "It was one of the transfer stations, logistically connected to the mines, where the hordes of imported slaves worked." He pointed to Skelver. "Erceses, I mean. You have always been a people of thralls, only your masters have changed. And so far, it has been like that, but that's how you have been constructed. Now you work for avors. You did better below the surface than terrestrial indigenous people, who in turn served us in Egypt, India, and Mesoamerica, where exoplanets transfer points were also built. Some of your foremen could be trusted, so we added your genetic profile, including its variables over time, to the controls of the porters' mechanisms to improve the transport of resources from Earth without our involvement while we were busy. We haven't reset or changed the settings, so Erceses can still activate them. The porter itself is an object made by Nimja based on the way the nodes work, the same nodes that Perfarius," he glanced at Biffter, "used to get to Tamasul. Therefore, the Earth didn't explode when I set course for it from Amyrade. A porter is such a mini-node, millions of times weaker, but permanent and durable. Nothing is destroyed when using them, but on condition that competent, trained and thinking beings use these devices, because the process is high-energy." The last sentence was addressed especially to Darius, who was afraid of going to Earth, using this method.

Through Kiret's mind flashed a recollection of Q'ualel telling him that when he and Xajb'a Kej had returned to Chulimal shortly after their planet had been taken over by Earthlings, they had smashed half the mountain that had contained the porter of ... Nimja. He suppressed another expression of disbelief only because he thought that it was not proper for the former emperor to display his emotions in such a way.

"Wait. Are you a Nimja member?!"

"General, I present to you, Nacxit," Darius said without enthusiasm, a little bored. "Bone Crusher, Seventh Minister.

Almost a god, who knows many strange things that none of us will understand because they are against the logic and laws of the cosmos known to us. So please don't be surprised that he looks like me. It's a long story anyway. Oh, and he can extract recollections and knowledge from memory, also learn a language by touching someone's head. From here he knows everything."

"Oh ... wow." Schindler absolutely disliked Jenny's considerable interest in the stranger.

"In short," the Nimja member turned to Skelver, "you must have accidentally activated the porter. And I detected it on Amyrade and transferred us easily."

"And that thing was here at CERN the whole time?!" Jelinek raised his voice.

"Yes. This is not the only gate, as I mentioned. Millennia pass, and the objects continue to function, they don't age or deteriorate at all. The rest in your world has been turned off, we haven't needed them for a long time." Nacxit grew serious, his eyes became ice-cold. "I'll do the same with this one. This is not technology for you. Your civilization is too young for it. CERN employees discovered the porter and, without even minimal knowledge of it, tried to activate it, which released a huge amount of energy and triggered Ice Age."

Kiret stroked his chin with a hand. He wondered how the Nimja member might have known this, but remembered that he had abilities like Jenny - but hundreds of times more developed, as befitted more than the five on Kardashev's scale.

"The scientists' reports, including this Earthworm, were also about the porter and the released energy which the eggheads couldn't control," he concluded. "It is not only a mining device, but also the code name for the operation of opening the alien gate."

Everyone's attention was drawn to the drones and the scratching of claws on the floor, coming from the side of the lunette door, which opened.

"So, they found us." Skelver was not so afraid of bully-devourers in large company. One of the giants got carried away by the hunter's instinct. Confident that it was still dealing with weak people with weak weapons, but in greater numbers, it lowered its ears and began to run towards the crowd.

"And what this time?!" Private Shimizu and the rest of the Kiritians from the expedition had already prepared their weapons to fire.

However, they were all paralyzed. Only those from Amyrade who had personally experienced this Naxcit trick remained calm. The over one-ton forest dog was rushing at them on clumsy, strong paws, a bit like a charging crocodile. The closer it got, the wider it opened its mouth, ready to dig its teeth into the closest victim - Jenny. The other bully-devourer waited hesitantly at the entrance and only watched. Darius was already beginning to think that, eager to show off his skills to arouse in the observers more awe and respect, Nacxit would kill the animal with his bare hands. He wasn't worried about the safety of Sandstorm and the rest.

The bully-devourer had left the last few meters to the target.

It jumped.

Keeping the stone face, the Nimja member, however, didn't use his hand, didn't even flinch as he separated the blood from flesh and bones. Three types of biomaterial, after a slight change in their trajectory, flew sideways without bumping into anyone. Moved only by the force of inertia, they fell to the ground with a splash, lap and crunch. The skull rolled several meters towards the transporter. The other animal whined, backed away, and fled into the tunnels. Stunned by the show, the onlookers, especially the Erces, regained power in their limbs.

"And I've thought the drugs has long since stopped working," Seymour said nervously.

"Telekinesis," said the Nimja member. He turned to the transporter, ignoring the pairs of frightened eyes. "I've gotta go now. Those who were on Amyrade don't need to worry about their health - you are not irradiated or require quarantine."

"Where are you going?" Schindler approached him briskly. The rest focused on Kiret and Avadar, a silent discussion was attempted to soften the emotions they had just experienced. "I've thought you will help us with Kandrok."

"There's nothing more I can do for you. You're on your own. As a Nimja member, I'm not allowed to interfere and change a long-established plan. Besides, in my society I'm a private, not a major," he admitted reluctantly.

"You must be kidding." Darius stepped in front of him, blocking his way. "So, you can't do what you want, because you have to follow some rules that were established thousands of years ago? What if they have long since stopped to apply, and those who established them are dead?"

"I'm just going to find out and act very carefully. Our paths will diverge here and perhaps they will not meet again."

Schindler reached into his backpack and took out the artifact.

"What about Forkis?"

"You can handle xik'iri." Nacxit smiled half-arsed. "Maybe someone else will help you soon, it depends how you play it." He patted his shoulder, which looked as if the twin had been encouraging his twin.

"Hold on." Kiret approached the Nimja member. He was followed by the captain and irritated Jelinek, with whom no one wanted to talk. "Thank you for the help shown to us and to the team dispatched to Amyrade. Had it not been for your support, the mission 'Revival' would have ended in a disaster. I heard the conversation with Darius, is there really nothing else that can be done?"

"With your help, we would win the war easily," added Jelinek, folding his arms over his chest. "With our current civilization level, we are without a chance against Kandrok."

"I'm sorry." The Nimja member hadn't even bothered to clarify again things these people couldn't understand, brought up with the idea that everyone's fate was in their own hands. "I'm going to Cargoo now to question Rei'than."

Kiret wondered for a moment if he had misheard.

"You cannot enter the Kiritian hideout without my consent!" He said more sharply. "I forbid you." Nacxit gave him an amused look, like to a suckling bossing around an adult with a rattle.

"Then take us with you as before," Avadar asked. The rest of the group began to gather at the talking.

"If I do it, you will not form another alliance and perhaps hasten your demise," Nacxit replied enigmatically. He took a ball of b'itol from his pocket. "I'll give you an hour to leave the tunnels, then I'll secure them. I can't let anyone else come in after the seal has been broken."

He contemplated the artifact in his open palm for a moment, then the ball rose telekinetically high to the ceiling, where it stuck. They all watched silently as it turned into a glowing blue axis and traveled towards the gate like a rapidly growing root, where it split and wandered into other tunnels.

"Follow the thickest line," Nacxit instructed. "Good luck."

He started walking towards the transporter again, leaving the rest staring at his back.

"Change the look at least!" Darius called after him. "If you cause me trouble, I'll be screwed!"

Nacxit didn't react, he disappeared into the bowels of the machine. Soon also it, without any special effects, disappeared from view as if it had never appeared in the secret, sealed nether regions adjacent to CERN. Tsar shook his head.

"And both of our drops have gone haywire."

"Why is the gun still not working? We're not on Amyrade anymore." Private Bradshaw looked at his drilling machine. Private Shimizu also took an interest in weapons to get distracted from another dose of absurdity at least for a moment.

"These are alien tunnels, they seem to act as an inhibitor to human electronics," Jenny explained, remembering what had happened to Kiret's equipment. She ignored the question of her eyesight. "It's gonna be normal outside."

"About time." Darius smiled at her. "I will take it as a souvenir." This time the attention shifted to Tsar. The man walked over to the head of the bully-devourer half his height and gripped it with both hands like a sack of potatoes, pressing it against his torso. "Then we go, or will you guys keep staring at me?"

***

To travel from one place to another, Nimja used porters merged with a network of connections. The distance between them was losing its importance, because the travel time was constant and a short moment. So, the conveyors could be as well apart from each other by many universes as they could be on the neighboring continents of one planet - it didn't matter. Nimja hoped that in its next stage of evolution they would have the ability to travel only by thoughts, which would require a change of the essence of their material bodies.

Nacxit couldn't use the porter to get to Cargoo, since none had been created there, so he used a node two light-years from the planet and then reached its orbit with an enhanced subspace propulsion. From there, he got to the very hidden Kiritian base, which he had easily located using information read from the Kiritians' brains as well as the transporter's technology.

For the masked Immortals guarding in the open air, the machine appeared out of nowhere. They saw it only after it was stationed on the ground, barely fifty meters from the hidden entrance to the nearest underground sector. They didn't inform the base about the event due to the current electronic silence - someone reported the presence of Kandrok not far away on a cosmic scale. When they saw Corporal Darius Schindler leaving, they were briefly glad that Avadar's crew had managed to return, though they had no idea why they had come by transporter, since they had been sent to Amyrade with two drops.

The achijes found that something was wrong when nobody left from the inside except Darius. The drops also appeared - they found themselves on the ground next to the transporter, like it, materialized as if out of thin air. As one of the Immortals zoomed in on Darius' face, he saw his inhuman silver eyes.

"Corporal Schindler, stop, please," said the guard under a rock offset as the newcomer, bathed in purple-red colors of the west, walked calmly towards the entrance to the nether regions. His shadow was several times longer than the silhouette - K'ajolom's disk almost touched low, rocky mountains.

Nacxit raised his hand slightly, as if to scare away a fly. All the achijes in the vicinity were paralyzed, they could only passively follow bizarre Darius with their eyes, who in an incomprehensible way summoned an elevator to the surface, which was activated only by hand.

Nothing was an obstacle for him as he walked along the corridors of sector B, where Kandrok's prisoner was held. Using only telekinesis, he opened doors, pinned the surprised Kiritians to walls and ceilings, and placed them back on chairs from which they sprang up. A red code was announced, an alarm rattled throughout the area, and an orange one was triggered throughout the rest of the nether regions. Nobody was able to stand up to the lonely Nimja member.

When he entered the cell room, he bolted the solid door behind him, and restored the possibility of free movement to all the people pinned earlier. He knew that nobody would hurt him anyway, at most people gathering in front of the door would shout and pound at the metal. It won't bother him. Unlike primitive psionic species like Onkalots, Nimja didn't need peace and concentration to use its abilities. They came to them as easily as raising a hand. Nacxit had left the Kiritians a working celula, constantly monitoring Rei'than's activities, so they could watch.

Umen Rei'than was sitting on the bunk and playing with a piece of rock that he had been allowed to take from the prison yard behind bars. He ran an indifferent look over the stranger's silhouette, taking him for another young watchman. He smiled sardonically, he was about to make some biting comment, but the words stuck in his throat as he looked into the silver eyes of the strange Kiritian staring at him.

No, it wasn't a Kiritian.

Rei'than had never felt such a specific irrational fear. At least since the standard erasure of his memory, which all avors experienced, so that longings and memories didn't interfere with their military functionality.

He got up from the bunk and stood at the bars, sizing up the stranger with narrowed eyes. He didn't protest when the latter placed a hand on his head, wanting to begin with knowing the current form of Kandrok's language.

Nacxit exhaled softly, feeling disappointment.

"You don't know anything either. I've thought you are someone more important than umen."

"And you, who are you?" Rei'than muttered. After a while he raised his eyebrows high, the tiny pupils dilated despite the bright light in the room. Concerned, he looked down. "You ... Impossible ..."

Although he had never experienced it, he had heard tales of how their monotheistic god, the exteriorization of the cosmic Light itself, sometimes appeared in the body of mortals or in the form of phenomena. He remembered exactly what one ondo had experienced from one of the accounts, and Rei'than now felt the same. Something like an electric shock. Fire burning in the heart. Fear not of danger, but of a great extrasensory power. An awakening. The Experience of Presence. He didn't think the stay in Kiritians' jail had made him so mad, or that he was feeling the effects of poisoning him right now - if he had been to be killed, he would have been executed by firing squad or extinguished in one of the numerous laboratories in Sector B. Apparently, as the ruler of Kandrok, the gerha had the privilege of seeing the Lightbringer more than once, it was even claimed that the god was his incarnation and that he could leave this body at will. Xepo Thino'pai had boasted that the Light had come to him and told him how he should have led his demo to victory over a certain troubling enemy. And indeed, the avors had won then, they had wiped out the enemy's army to every varoth. No one had the right to understand God's will, so visiting less important avors didn't seem unusual.

"The Lightbringer," he whispered. He fell to his knee and bowed his head. "What are you asking of me, Lord?"

"Nothing more. I wanted some information, but you don't have it."

"It is an honor for me to do you a service, at least in this way, and at the same time I am very sorry that you didn't find use in me."

Nacxit couldn't help but smile. Neither time nor technological evolution had blunted Kandrok's religious fanaticism. Though brutal and ruthless, it was also extremely faithful to those it considered worthy and better than itself. But it's no wonder - it was Nimja who had designed them that way.

"Get up, Rei'than. Look at me."

"I understand that you are not here to set me free."

"Unfortunately, not."

The avor made no comment, accepted the Lightbringer's decision with dignity and without objection. He guessed that releasing him would have been detrimental to his destiny.

"I'll go now. Take care, Rei'than."

Nacxit considered whether to actually release him. He didn't like avors or people, but if he had given the ex-prisoner a gun and sent him down the corridors, he would at least have had some entertainment before continuing his search. He had to dispel or confirm his doubts about a certain issue of Nimja, and so far, it seemed that the balance was tilting towards the second possibility.

Meanwhile, the achijes brought the humanoid jaguar to a cell room - who had been on Cargoo with Chimalmat as guests - knowing that the Onkalot with the psionic abilities would know what to do with the dangerous intruder. Nacxit opened the door and stepped out into the corridor, glancing appreciatively at the Kiritians who separated, no longer aiming with their weapons at him - a wise approach since they hadn't achieved anything before with it. Doing the same thing over and over again without getting results was craziness. Aggro, although he had been informed that there was the strange creature in the base with the appearance of Darius Schindler and great mental power, he was still surprised to see him. Remembering the meeting with Nanawak and knowing Nimja's capabilities, he was scared that one of them had taken over the body of Eredal's younger brother and made him his puppet.

Nacxit stared at the humanoid jaguar for a moment, drawing information from his memories.

"Don't worry," he said. "Darius Schindler is safe and sound, it is just a copy of his body that I created from b'itol. He will soon be arriving on Cargoo with General Kiret Biffter, Captain Michael Avadar and the rest of the successful Amyrade team." The words reassured the Kiritians, as they coincided with what the Velkee Warfighter had transmitted to the Cargoo communications center from his ship that was part of the squadrons looking for Kiret on Earth. The general's message was encrypted and covered with the highest security priority, so it couldn't be a forgery.

"You are one of them." Aggro recognized the Nimja member. He didn't cringe before him as Kandrok had recently. When he discovered on Tamasul that Nimja, whom Onkalots took for gods, turned out to be cruel and selfish beings, fond of domination, power, and the humiliation of others, he lost his former pious respect for them. It made him even more lost.

"And I've thought you will call me Nanawak," Nacxit said in Onkalot. The language of humanoid jaguars hadn't changed for millennia, and the species itself had ceased to evolve, the regional dialects were also clear, if you listened to the words properly.

"He had a different look." Q'ualel pointed two fingers at his eyes. "And he despised changing natural form. When the Kitirians came to me and reported what was happening, I was pretty sure a Nimja member had come to visit us. I didn't expect to see any of you again. Nanawak has forbidden to contact them over under the threat of extermination."

"I just popped in. In purely private matters." He spoke Kiritian to everyone. "You don't have to worry, you are not in any danger from Nimja, we are passive towards people like you. I just came to see the prisoner. But it is possible that my affairs will become entangled with yours someday."

He nodded at Aggroteh, then moved back. The Kiritians let him pass, no one harassed or spoke to Nacxit. He soon disappeared with his transporter, and the only evidence of his landing were the two drop spacers left.

***

It took them less than an hour to go outside, Kiret's and Avadar's groups briefly told each other what had happened to them. They didn't encounter a single life form along the way, as if there had been mechanisms to deter flora and fauna in the cool alien tunnels glistening with an unknown wrapper, only two bully-devourers turned out to be the exception to the rule. Nacxit artifact's pointer over the ceiling, which looked like an air train rail, led them to an inner gate on a slope of the Western Alps. Skelver cracked it open with an activator that didn't respond to anyone else's touch. Then he repeated the same with the second and third gate. The outermost one was stylized as a rock that perfectly blended in with the slope on the principle of pareidolia, also in this place Kiritian's equipment still wasn't working. A random passerby in the open air certainly qualified this phenomenon as a strong ferromagnetism of this part of the mountains, and the pre-digital population simply saw rocks unattractive in terms of tourism and economy. Therefore, no one had discovered that thousands of years earlier, aliens had built their base nearby, as it was only shown by the accidental building excavations of expanding CERN.

Once already in the open air, they quickly realized what Nacxit had meant by "allies".

In the moonlight, they fully noticed three men on lookout, who immediately alerted their companions at the sight of the mountain opening and the people leaving the center. More people began to descend from different sides of the jagged slopes, or to come down from them in small ships.

Corporal Aytar, who first noticed that their equipment was working again, zoomed in on the black-and-green armor of the closest figure with the help of her helmet cover.

"Headhunters," she said, having identified the yellow triangle on the chest and the three black human skulls without mandibles.

Skelver twitched as if he had intended to leave the company, but Kiret put a hand hard on his shoulder.

"Where are you going?" He growled.

"Headhunters? Where did they come from?" Tsar felt instantly hot, especially since the number of members of the paramilitary organization was growing rapidly, and in addition they directed their barrels at them like at the pursued after a long hunt. The Immortals took up arms and did the same. Darius moved closer to Jenny and covered her with his body.

Increasing shocks began to run through the ground, everyone's eyes shifted to the tunnel entrance. Kiret didn't have to order his companions to run away from the gate.

The aisle began contracting and at the same time getting sealed with an ice-like substance that eventually filled all the tunnel's light before it began to darken. Finally, part of the visually unremarkable slope was visible again.

For a few nervous moments, there was a deep silence as everyone tried to understand what had actually happened.

"Well, well, saboteurs," said one of the members of the organization. Together with a group of a dozen or so soldiers he approached Kiret, who was ready to give a signal to fire with his hand. Having stood in front of him, he pulled off his helmet, which wasn't strobilized and didn't slide down onto the neck like that of Kiritians. Its tall owner turned out to be a dark-skinned man with black, straight hair longer at the top of the head and cropped over the ears. Aquamarine tattoos depicting abstractions also stood out there. "And at their head, Mr. Kiret Necron Biffter himself." He smiled sardonically. "I never expected you to go in there just to thwart our plans. You made me surprised by the fact that you sided with Kandrok."

"What?! What saboteurs? Who are you?" Necron asked sharply.

"Jarret Nelson, the current leader of the Headhunters." The man looked at Tsar. "Nice skull."

"Yeah. Thanks," Seymour replied confused, still lugging the skull of the bully-devourer.

"How's the earnings, renegade?" A sweet smile lingered on Jarret's face, one of those heralding big trouble. The man felt at ease with nearly a hundred of his men set across the area. Kiritians didn't seem terrible and dangerous to them like a few years ago. "Better than in our place?" He poked something out from between his teeth and flicked it to the ground.

"I'm not complaining." Tsar seemed to be inspired. He put down the skull. "Remember that my father got me into this. I didn't want to!"

"Yeah, yeah. And you didn't have balls to stand up to your daddy, baby."

"I can assure you that my balls and gear are fine."

Nelson pointed his arm behind himself.

"Look at my people. See what we have become and what you have lost."

"Parties with Kiritians were quite good. I'm not complaining."

Kiret couldn't stand it and sighed irritably.

"Can you finish this childish chatter and explain what's going on here?"

"I was with them once, sir." Tsar waved his hand towards the closest Headhunters. "But shortly."

Jarret folded his hands into the basket.

"Skelver, what are you waiting for? Come here."

The Erces looked at Biffter uncertainly. The latter gave him a signal to go to his own people. Behind Kiret, Captain Avadar dulled a loud exhalation from his lungs; the former emperor didn't even stand up, but simply handed over the hostage. Skelver, walking as if aching, joined Nelson's closest people and stood beside him.

"Come for a new transmitter, nerd," the Hunters' leader ordered. Behind the mountain jagged like a bitten slice of cheese, was heard the sound of other landing machines, arriving with full masking, which none of the oderses paid attention to.

"What do you want from us?" Some Headhunters chuckled after hearing Kiret's question.

Jarret watched Jenny for a moment as she leaned out from behind the silhouette of Darius, who was eager to shoot. He frowned as she reminded him of someone.

"Kill you. You no longer have power in both galaxies, you are acting against the Zodiac Universum. Defeated, you deal with the enemy." He pointed to the sealed tunnel with the hand holding the rifle. "You destroyed the only cradle on the planet that could contain loot useful in the fight against cybernetic scum. In the present situation even Wakanda is helpless. You have betrayed your own species."

"I wouldn't sit in judgement without having evidence or knowing the case," Divinus said calmly, glaring at Nelson icily. "Only fools base their knowledge on guesswork."

"We didn't destroy anything." Kiret looked defiantly into Nelson's hazel eyes. "How would have we done that? We were as surprised as you were."

"Matter implosion. I've seen something like that performed by Kandrok. And you probably were trained for such activities."

"You must be crazy, man!" Angry, Darius blurted out.

"Or avors were taught that by someone," replied Necron. "There is no secret weapon at CERN, I was looking for it myself for the same reason you did. It was the Nimja member who sealed the tunnel."

"Who?"

"Stranger."

Another wave of laughter, louder and from more throats. Divinus put a hand to his forehead; Tsar looked up at the sky at constellations that he suddenly found interesting.

"A portable toilet upside down," he murmured.

Jarret moved closer to Necron, as he was shorter, he tilted his head up slightly. The earlier show arrogance disappeared from his face; it became as inaccessible as in Div.

"And to think I used to take you for a role model," he said softly. "You've fallen low, Mr. Biffter."

Nelson turned and walked towards his transporter waiting at the foot of the escarpment, tiny mountain stones were crunching under his boots.

"Destroy everyone except the girl," he ordered. "Take her to the ship."

Dozens of safeties clanged. The Kiritians raised their weapons higher.

"If you attack, we'll do the same," growled Kiret. "We have the better weapons!"

He was pissed off more by his helplessness than the trap whose prelude might have been the abandoned Skelver's transmitter, insufficiently damaged. Though the Headhunters probably encircled the whole stomping ground in precaution, and waited instead of aimlessly run around CERN's mazes. He had screwed it all up again, mindlessly guiding his people outside, nostalgically clinging to the thought that Kiritians were still an intimidating power. And now they would lose not only their lives, but also the artifact with Forkis' atole. The Headhunters who had grown strong weren't excited to have the former First Galactic Dignitary in their hands. But it's no wonder, since Kiret had destroyed his own empire in several years and thus lost his prerogatives, both in real terms and in the collective consciousness of Oderses? The days of martial law came where anyone could punish traitors and subversives without judging.

"Seriously? And there are more of us and we are better set," said Nelson as he walked.

"And these are supposed to be our allies announced by blondie-Darius?" Seymour raised his arms, with palms open. "Nelson, come on. You've gotten something wrong! Let's talk!"

"Traitors have no voice!"

"Take away from here those fools of yours with the guns, or we're gonna blow them to bits!"

An extended line of figures, blackened by the low-hanging moon, emerged from behind the edge of the escarpment. That's why Kiret hadn't recognized them at first, sure they had been another Nelson's people from a fresh transfer. Yet, anywhere, he would have recognized that imperious, stern voice that was used to intimidation and giving orders.

Jenny sighed softly.

"Did we really leave this Amyrade?" Tsar commented. "There is no end to the absurdities."

The arrivals were Kiritians in the number of a few companies, as if they had been going to fight on land in an ancient style. They aimed at the Headhunters, who began to raise their arms along with their rifles or drop them on the ground.

The threatening person was General Velkee Warfighter himself, accompanied by Anna Sandstorm and Captain Wiktor Shane, who had recently returned safe and sound from the end of the Lion Universe, where he had been on duty.

"Now we are more numerous than you. All put the bang-sticks on the ground!" Velkee demanded.

The Headhunters who hadn't done it yet obeyed and threw away their weapons, including Nelson, scowling at Warfighter.

"Jenny ..."

Seeing that the situation was under control and the general would keep them safe, Anna began to walk down the slope briskly, ignoring Nelson and his men watching her. Before reaching her daughter, she stopped and stared in amazement at Captain Avadar's team. Soon she embraced Jenny firmly, at first the girl returned the hug hesitantly, then she hugged her birth mother tightly.

"Mother."

Anna controlled her emotion, stepped back, grasped her face with her hands.

"Are you fine, child?"

"Yes, everything is okay."

"Nice outfit."

"Long story." Jenny managed a slight smile.

"There will be a lot to tell for sure." Anna hugged her daughter again, focused her eyes on Kiret. She greeted him only with her eyes, she was speechless. She didn't want to additionally humiliate him in front of the Kiritians and the Headhunters, and offend him for hiding Skelver's manifesto from her and going to act on Atla on his own, even if he had had good intentions and hadn't wanted to endanger anyone. However, he had done it. He also seemed to get the team from Amyrade into trouble, and worst of all, he had put Jenny in danger. Kiret read the rebuke written in her judgmental but sad look of her green eyes, then focused his eyesight on Nelson, who stood with his hands clasped behind his head beside the two Immortals guarding him.

"Captain." Michael Avadar inclined his head slightly in greeting, Anna nodded at the gesture. She let go of Jenny.

"I'm very happy," said Anna with sincere joy, "that you all managed to come back. Is the mission ..."

"We have it, Captain!" Darius couldn't refrain, interrupted the woman and proudly and smiling lifted up xik'iri. "Together with the atole!"

"Bravo, you idiot," Tsar said to him, glancing at the Headhunters. "Show it off also before Kandrok."

Had it not been for the lieutenant's relaxing joke, Annie's pressure would have increased much more. Though she should have been glad to hear the news, it didn't bring her a relief - she felt uneasy. She felt pulsating in her ears, her legs softened a little. Old memories returned, both nice and nightmarish.

They really had gotten Forkis' atole! It was really happening; it was not a hoax! They brought hope to Kiritians.

Before she stepped into the sea of contemplating what this would mean for her, the nation, and the entire Zodiac Universum, but especially for her, Necron asked a question:

"How did you find us?" He watched the general walk towards him with his hands clasped behind the seat. The Kiritians, led by Shane, had already pacified Nelson's men.

"We searched for your biological signature and armor signals on planets in safe zones, with the help of a cloud of drones." Anna glanced at Warfighter who stood next to her. Avadar's team saluted and the man motioned for them to rest. "After the victorious ... let's call it battle with Kandrok, the general joined me and the search went faster. But we completely didn't expect to find you on Earth, all the more to see the members of the 'Revival' mission. You really owe your salvation to Captain Victor Shane, because it was his idea to search the Earth."

"You won with Kandrok?!" Kiret was surprised.

"One-time win for now," Velkee said. "Our super virus wrecked their ships in a flash, one of the achijes gave it to them in neutral form. We risked a lot. We would have been screwed if Kandrok had picked up any signal from our fleet, unless they did, but for reasons known only to them, they ignored us. The only defense against them was the assumption that the enemy was exposing somewhere far away."

Kiret immediately understood that these words allusive, though spoken in a polite tone, were aimed at him like the barrels of the Headhunters recently - Velkee referred to his decision to save Jenny alone. Even more telling was the look of the general's blue eye - the second, though functional, from birth had been cloudy and resembled a shark's eye covered with a horrible-looking membrane.

"Kandrok has unfortunately arrived on Earth," Avadar said regretfully.

"I'm sorry to hear it." In Velkee's words resounded professional indifference. "I hope we will now have more time and peace to put together all the new facts and come up with an effective plan of action."

"Thank you for saving us all, General Warfighter," said Necron. "There was a misunderstanding with the Headhunters."

"Always at your service."

While Biffter, Warfighter, and the Amyrade teammates engaged in the conversation, Anna and Jenny went aside.

"You're cold, baby. Come on, I'll take you to the vehicle and you will get something warm to drink." Jenny hated being called "baby", especially by her mother who due to kiritianization looked like her a few years older sister, but she didn't feel like arguing about it. It was only when her emotions subsided and she became truly safe that she felt how exhausted she was. She would have preferred to lie down in a warm, comfortable bed, fully clothed, and sleep for several hours.

As they were both walking towards one of the Immortals' transporters, which had crouched in a valley on the other side of the slope after exiting the camouflage field, Anna glanced at the guarded leader of the Headhunters. Instantly she felt a shudder piercing her, which had an outlet somewhere in her brain. A real shock. She stopped. She hadn't heard the man's name. Turned sideways to her, talking to batab Gareth, he reminded her of someone from the past she knew, but not for ten planets she could remember the details.

She accosted Captain Shane nearby.

"Take Jenny to the ship. I want to talk to their leader."

"Of course." Viktor didn't even bother to tell her that the leader of the Headhunters was a dangerous terrorist. He knew that Anna came from a similar background, so she could find a common ground with the detainee, but he had no problem with that. In addition, Gareth and a mass of Kiritians would keep her safe.

Jenny walked away with Viktor, who, with his positive outlook on life and eloquence, quickly engaged her in a conversation. Anna moved towards the prisoner.

Finally, she remembered.

Her eyes widened as if she had seen a ghost. Because in effect it was so.

"Jarret Nelson?" She asked. "Is this some sick joke?!"

Jarret. Born in 2928 on Calvary, where his rebel parents came from. So, the apple didn't fall far from the tree, unless there had been a terrible mistake. Anna had played with him in her childhood on Nephrida, but when the boy had become a teenager, the Kiritians had killed his parents, and he had returned to his home planet. Then contact with him had been cut off. All Anna knew was that he had become a juvenile bandit and had died in some drug scandal or gang war. The man in front of her was about fifty, and like many people in those days who could afford it, he looked much younger thanks to the achievements of medicine. His hairstyle was not marked by a single gray hair. But Anna recognized those eyes, the soft fox gestures were the same, the shape of the jaw also matched, though the face had grown up.

The man smiled slightly at her sight, and his narrow face also reminded of a sly fox. "That's a good sign," she thought, "that he doesn't look at me like at a madwoman."

"Hello, Anna. I didn't expect that we would meet again someday."

And yet they did.

"It's you?! You died!" Her uncontrollably raised voice caught the attention of many people.

"Officially yes. Only a few people knew the truth. I had to hide for a long time, but when I killed all those who threatened me, or they died for many other reasons, I was able to come to the surface. And here I am." He spread his arms.

It wasn't the Nelson she knew. From a calm, mischievous boy he turned into a dangerous killer, as long as he wasn't ostentatiously playing. As a child, no one in their childish gang liked Kiritians, but after the murder of his parents, Nelson even hated the Immortals. And that was probably what he had left, since he treated Kiret and the rest with such contempt, justifying his behavior with their betrayal. He didn't look too friendly at Anna either, rather with mild amusement on his face and a chill in his eyes.

"Well. A lot has changed, we both have our own baggage of experiences," continued Jarret. "And I don't think we should like each other now. You betrayed us. You went so carelessly over to the enemy's side." He glanced at Gareth, who was passively listening to their exchange, ready to act if Nelson did something stupid.

"You probably have an opinion on me, but life is not black and white."

"What are you gonna do with us?" Nelson asked indifferently.

"It is not for me to decide, but my opinion will certainly be taken into account. And what are you doing on Earth if it's not a secret?"

"We are looking for an effective weapon against Kandrok. Sometimes a seemingly innovative project falls into our hands, but so far none has worked. Now, when we were sure of a breakthrough, your friends have buried our last resort under the mountain. You are now working with Kandrok."

"What nonsense did someone tell you?" Anna got mad. "Never ever! They are hunting our dignitaries and they probably want to kill us all."

"What may they want?" The question was directed into the night, Nelson, asking it, wasn't looking at any person.

"This is probably not the place and circumstances for such talks."

"So, let's talk more officially. Prove me wrong," the man said firmly, focusing on Sandstorm.

"What are you getting at?"

A rogue's smile appeared on Nelson's lips.

"And what do you think? It's easy to draw the right conclusions. Come on, say it out loud."

Anna also smiled.

"You're dwelling on the subject, so you suppose you might be wrong, moreover, knowing about the powerlessness of oderses towards Kandrok, you want to form an alliance with a not-so-strong ally."

"Smart as in childhood. Talk to this strict general," he pointed his chin at Warfighter, "or to whoever is in charge of you now?"

"One more thing, Jarret."

"I'm all ears."

"You have my XRS-14 Ghost fighter; I saw it behind the hill. This is the first object that caught our attention when we landed. How did you get it? The White was missing when Kandrok were holding me on Morascrik in the capital."

"Kandrok took it from K'otz'ib'aja, examined it on one of their ugly shuttles and threw it like garbage into space, having considered the machine useless. We found it flying aimlessly around the Libra Universe. The White's AI agreed to work for us because it knew that it couldn't return to Kiritians."

"We have a good hiding place now. I understand you won't mind if I take my property?"

Jarret smiled and shrugged at the rhetorical question as well as seeing every Kiritian with a shooter.

"Take that vehicle of yours. By the way, some tuning would be useful, because it's a bit old technology."

8. The return of the legend

Anna made Nelson's proposal to Biffter and Warfighter. Kiret agreed to the negotiations at once, while Velkee, who had almost six hundred achijes with him, preferred to take Nelson's more important men hostage and hold them until stable cooperation between the Immortals and the Hunters was achieved, where no one would be afraid to turn their back to the other side. Had it not been for the circumstances and the need for allies among oderses, Velkee would have treated the Headhunters much more severely at the outset and would have not even wanted to talk to them. Kiret asked him for a private conversation and told him about Jenny's surveillance abilities that had progressed on Earth thanks to the joint exercise. Anna also agreed to the idea of Nelson's mind probing, believing that Velkee's radical methods could lead to sharp tensions immediately after the alliance was annulled or already during its course.

The land was no longer safe - Kandrok could appear at any moment. Preliminary discussions were therefore planned on Proxima Centauri e, the first terrestrial colonized exoplanet of the Solar System orbiting more than four light-years from the Blue Planet. There were Cosmo politically neutral aging colonies there, the population was not in abundance, and it was unlikely that Kandrok discovered this fifth planet of Proxima Centauri as well. Kiret supposed that the avors pursuing him and Jenny, after mistaking them for the dead, had informed their command about the existence of the Earth and other celestial bodies of the solar system. Returning and scanning the Old Zone within many light years (though the army of Kandrok might already have been flying towards Earth) would take some time, and Proxima e should have been safe by then.

From the Headhunters' ships and Kiritians' naval craft a small fleet was created, protected by heat, radiation and optical vision suppressors. For several years, the Immortals had been building their units based on masking technology similar to that of 'Aurals' used in the mission to retrieve Dr. Figam. They realized that Kandrok would have easily seen through their ruse - 'Aurals' had also been finally detected, and Rei'than and Ly sent out to scout - but such cover was better than none.

Anna Sandstorm flew her White again, nostalgic about the times when she had been a rebel and gone on lonely patrols over Nephrida's mountain ranges. Of course, she didn't regret the decision that had led her to the Kiritians in the end.

Although the fighter had been briefly among Kandrok, its AI with a male, synthetically sounding voice didn't provide any new information about the enemy.

After arriving on the intensely terraformed planet Proxima e, with a gravity seven percent lower than that of Earth, talks took place in a dilapidated, abandoned Christian church. The structure loomed and scared in windswept heathlands, as bleak as a heavy stormy sky, whitening again and again with lightning. Biffter decided to land there because of the uninhabited area and hectares of flat land.

After several hours of talks, it was decided that the Kiritians and the Headhunters would forge a temporary alliance against the common enemy. Supported mainly by Calvary gangsters, the paramilitary organization initially united by anti-immigration ideology and satanic philosophy, had grown steadily and now had over three hundred thousand members. It was agreed that the Kiritians would provide them with equipment in the future, as well as Lacetti's men from Nephrida, provide training, recruit anyone they could, and then the alliance would try to declare war on the enemy. This was not to happen until the Immortals became convinced that the new allies could be trusted. For the most modern equipment, they also had to wait.

The allies also needed a perfect plan, stripped of the weaknesses as much as possible, and time was short. Nobody still knew what Kandrok wanted and what its next step would be.

"Dr. Figam and his assistants are working intensively on the weapons and the rest of the equipment," General Warfighter informed those gathered in the main aisle. "Everything we've had at our disposal so far will prove useless against the avors or not very problematic."

"And we also won't be idle," assured Nelson at the end. "We'll search what we can. Since we've lost CERN, we'll try our luck on other planets."

Kiret glanced at Jenny standing near the porch, by the statue of a crumbled, moss-covered angel. Probing discreetly the minds of the Headhunter delegation, the girl nodded. Already convinced of the mistake with CERN and Biffter, Nelson's people were sincere. They also needed support. For some time, they had started to have serious problems with Kandrok, although they were sure that the plague of cyborgs from distant cosmos would bypass them - they had initially thought that the avors had come to the Zodiac Universum to hunt down the strongest player, the Immortals.

It was agreed that the Hunters would travel to still-safe Mezzo in the Lion Universe, a planet once ruled by the rebels, where more hidden Kiritians now resided, and wait for further instructions. Gradually and obeying the highest security rules, they would transfer their allies from Calvary, which was threatened by Kandrok's attack.

After the meeting, the groups split and each flew in its own direction.

The Kiritians headed for Cargoo.

At the instigation of Aytar, assassin Divinus agreed to fly to the hidden base.

Another serious task awaited the immortals: awakening Forkis, whose body had been transferred to the planet from Tz'aqol's temple on Chulimal.

***

When they landed in the early, cloudless morning and came out to the landing field, they were greeted in a grand and collective manner, it is not known who more: the team from Amyrade, which had survived the most extraordinary mission in human history and captured Forkis' atole, or Warfighter who had brought lost Biffter. Only Darius was stared at with doubts, sometimes fear.

"Let me guess: Nacxit was here and showed me up," he guessed without displaying surprise.

He scared the entire underground base," replied Private Kogan, whose duty was to lead Rei'than out. "We felt completely vulnerable."

"Yes," said his colleague, Private Ryan. "We realized how illusory our security measures were. This alien just entered the nether regions, just like some frigging one-man army! We didn't know how to fight him."

"Don't be so strict for yourselves." Tsar smiled. "These aliens are well above five on Kardashev's scale.

The Kiritians slowly split and went to the nether regions. The landing field staff decontaminated the machines with the help of drones and curtains of disinfectants, then they began to be pulled out of view with the platforms. As Ryan was one of those close to Nacxit, he abstracted to Anna, Gareth, Kiret, and a few more achijes from the group formed, how Nimja's brief visit to Cargoo had gone. They could talk less officially now.

"Don't worry, son," Kiret reassured him when he finished. "Nacxit won't tell anyone we're here, and we'll probably never know what he was looking for in this place. Nimja doesn't interfere in the matters of minor species, which it loves to emphasize."

"Well, the other Darius claimed exactly the same," Kogan said.

"You don't have to be afraid of me, I am the only one, real and unique. Isn't it so?" Schindler smiled slightly as he looked at Jenny, who had been depressed for most of her journey from Proxima e. Although she finally found herself in the safe place, her mood hadn't improved as she looked around the Precambrian barren, rocky environment marked with traces of human presence only underground. Cargoo felt like the opposite of paradise Atla.

"Then now you have to tell us about the entire Amyrade trip." Ryan wasn't giving Darius a break. "We will try to give you a general introductory report today," assured Gareth, who had listened to the story of Amyrade on the Cargoo voyage. "How's our prisoner behaving?"

The batab question caught Jenny's interest. Kiret had mentioned to her that the only one kept at the Cargoo base was an avor. She began to consider what he might look like up close and if she could read his mind.

"No change, sir," reported Kogan. "As for the prisoner, nothing happened in your absence, and he has been behaving the same for a long time."

"He needs to be taken to the yard, by the way, because we forgot yesterday," Ryan added, glancing at the second private.

The group descended by a large-sized elevator, more like a freight platform, to the nether regions marked as main sector A. They stepped out into a bright, clean corridor with a lot of people walking around. They separately came over and greeted Avadar and the rest, everyone wanted to know as much as possible about Amyrade. It was initially agreed that after lunch there would be a meeting in the briefing room, where members of the 'Revival' mission would talk about their expedition, which had lost its implicit status.

Jenny flinched as Captain Shane, who had previously been busy talking to Kiret, unexpectedly touched her on the back. He seemed embarrassed.

"We're going to start ... bringing your father back this evening. Do you feel able, especially mentally, to participate in this process?"

"Yes, I'll be fine." She smiled politely.

"Maybe by then you would like to take a look at the base? Unless you want to sleep or rest."

"Thank you, I got enough sleep on the ship in an orlop." Jenny glanced reluctantly at Necron, who was arguing with Anna. From the moment she left Proxima e, she had had the impression that he had been ignoring her. "Will you get me, Captain, someone to show me around? I don't know almost everyone here," she deliberately said aloud.

"Of course." The last person she wanted to be with now grew up at her.

"That's why I said 'almost'. You are not tired?" She asked Darius. Viktor backed off, went to discuss something with Tsar. "I heard the Amyrade trip was difficult and dangerous."

"Tsar gave me something that effectively warded off the fatigue, anyway just like you, I rested during the flight. I've already recovered from the Amyrade expedition. I'm happy to tell you about it, if you like." He gave her a warm smile.

The girl sighed inwardly. So no could do, she wouldn't get rid of this importuner, moreover, it was she who had provoked the topic for discussion. She had gotten nothing against Darius, he was a pretty good: tall, quite handsome, green-eyed, dark-haired man, brave, perhaps too rough and sometimes explosive - which was probably related to the kiritianization at his young age - but it bothered her that, in his insistence, he took advantage of every opportunity to be close to her. She could have bet that it was Necron who had ordered him to accompany her.

"Okay," she agreed, seeing that Schindler would rather be the only achij willing to dedicate his time for her. She didn't consider herself selfish. She understood that Kandrok's case was a priority and the Kiritians were gearing up to bring Forkis back to life, but she wouldn't have minded if someone other than Shindler had helped her deal with the continuing trauma of her experience on Earth and instructed on how to cope with the change of environment, especially with the gravity and pressure different than those she was used to. The differences were minor, but it would be some time before she settled in.

Darius figured out what she might have been thinking.

"If you feel unwell, let me know and I will bring you medication," he offered. "You can always visit a medic yourself; he can see you at any time of the day; by the way, it lasts twenty-seven hours on Cargoo. I will give you a tour of the nether regions and show you everything, but first let's go to your dwelling, where I will leave you. I need to report to the medical center for a systemic scan, but it will take five minutes - getting into the chamber, scanning, a click and that's it. Then I'll go to wash and get changed. I'll come for you in about two hours. Okay?"

"All right."

"We'll eat at the cafeteria. If you like, we'll go outside and I will show you an atmosphere synthesizer and a hydro station that produces water." Darius remembered something, brightened. "Oh, I have something extra for you. You will surely like it!"

Jenny couldn't not lift the corners of her mouth at his spontaneous, youthful enthusiasm and listening to the chattering. Additionally, she was amused by Seymour, who made silly faces and gestures to Darius until he turned his back to him with a sigh of embarrassment. Contrary to her assumptions, it shouldn't have been sad and boring on Cargoo. She had seen quite a few young achijes along the way, even at her age. At least visually, because a kiritianized 18-year-old biological person might have even been three centuries according to the calendar (the certificate was in force in the Terran time). Darius was thirty years old, and his biological age, including the mental one, remained at twenty-four, but the corporal would probably start to get serious over time, shaped by many events. It was difficult to grasp when you didn't assort with the Immortals. Jenny tried not to worry about their biology, but she wondered more than once about what would happen when she overtook her own mother with age - and then Kiret. In twenty years, Anna would look like her daughter, unless Jenny interfered with the genetics of her body.

Nevertheless, without the super virus, she would eventually die anyway.

The thought of it gave rise to paralyzing anxiety.

She decided to convince Kiret that she wanted to be an Immortal and that she was fit for it. She didn't have to be an achij right away - she could ask for some civilian job.

They got to the social sector by an underground train running between the sectors. Darius showed Jenny her accommodation. It was located in the corridor of the women's section, a few doors further lived Zira Aytar already known to Jenny, so in case of problems she would have had someone to turn to. In the middle of the corridor, a square with a dome had been built, a real tree on an islet, surrounded by a ring of water grew there.

In the room, which you entered after scanning your fingerprints or the outer profile of your hand, there was a small living room connected to a kitchen and bedroom, as well as a bathroom. As the complex was located underground, it was possible to activate a window substitute, and the light was regulated according to the daily cycle. A nice trifle turned out to be the possibility of playing music attuned to the state of mind. In the center there was a column resembling an aquarium, inside, among the bioluminescent coral reef, were swimming fish and small, undefined creatures; on the cylinder wall were feeding snails. On the bedside table was a capripod and a micro-PDA that you could wear like a bracelet.

"You probably know how to handle it?" Said Darius, who was standing in the center of the room with his hands in his pockets.

"Sure, thanks."

"If you need contact with anyone, just connect via PDA or capripod. Rest. I'll see you soon."

As Darius stepped out into the corridor, he found at the corner Seymour with his arms crossed, leaning his back and his booted foot against the wall.

"I'll show you the atmosphere synthesizer and hydro station," he said mockingly. "Congratulations, you won parsley as the main prize in the Embarrassment of the Year competition." He handed him the vegetable.

"Where did you get that weed, Lieutenant? Have you switched to a healthy diet?" he bit back.

"It was lying there on the ground. Someone must have dropped it. Really, man? You go to the chick with such a text? Haven't you learned anything over the years? In addition, you blabbered as if in a competition, like an old-fashioned talking spring-loaded toy. By the way, turn on the communicator, because I had to come here.

"Give me a break. Okay, I panicked a little; Jenny finally paid attention to me. You know I care about her. I've never had a girlfriend. It's not the same as a fleeting affair. And I offered her cats, chicks are after such things."

Seymour stepped away from the corner, chased a butterfly away with his hand, which nearly smacked him in the face, then slapped Schindler hard on the back.

"Go to get examined quickly because Captain Avadar is calling the entire Amyrade team to briefing in the conference room. There will also be General Warfighter and Biffter. And a lot of listeners."

***

Two hours passed, but Darius hadn't come. Jenny assumed that something important must have stopped him, because he hadn't even bothered to use the PDA. Nevertheless, it was good, at least she could rest.

After washing and changing into underwear, pants and a sweatshirt prepared on a cupboard, Sandstorm lied down, prostrated on the bed and lay there for a long time, listening to muffled voices from the corridor and adjacent rooms, watching the lazily moving fauna in an aquarium. Her head finally stopped being haunted by uncomfortable thoughts, her mind turned into a delightful void, which made her fall asleep.

She didn't know how long she had slept like this in her clothes, she hadn't checked the time even once since crossing the threshold of the dwelling. The music coming from an unknown place as well as dark green lighting, effectively blending in with the colors of the aquarium, were still the same. Jenny reached for the PDA and tried to connect to Darius, but his profile was muted. Instead, she found a note apologizing that he had to go to a briefing after a very protracted mission, and he would visit her as soon as possible. Apart from him, no one else was interested in how she was feeling. Neither Kiret nor her mother.

She decided to stretch her legs a little, she took her PDA and went out into the hall. She knocked on Aytar's door, but no one was there. She sat on a casing surrounding an islet with a tree. She didn't know this species with a thick trunk twisted like a towel squeezed out and yellow aquamarine horseshoe leaves; she assumed it was a modificant. From massive branches hung air roots touching the soil and water, flowers grew in the crown, around which a lot of butterflies flew. It was difficult to determine the color of the last two, because in the glow of the ceiling lamps, which stimulated the occurrence of proper tree biological processes, they took on yellow shades. It is possible that also the leaves seen in the daylight of the local star would have had a different color.

Jenny exchanged a few words with Kiritian girls wandering around the floor. Some were with their partners. They all seemed nice, and that was even before she admitted that she was Forkis' daughter. Darius sent her some humorous pictures of the briefing, for example with his tongue sticking out against the back of talking Warfighter or his face simulating sleepiness during Kiret's speech - which was held in the large room. All the seats visible in the freeze frames were taken.

The girl got hungry, a cold store in her room, insurance for such moments, hadn't been equipped yet. She studied the nether regions plan and found a cafeteria in Sector A. She managed to get there after a quarter of an hour. She asked for blueberry dumplings, with which she sat down at a side table, next to the entrance to the kitchen. The mealtime must have already passed, as in the spacious room she counted seventeen people, including young cooks who temporarily had nothing to do and joined her for a chat. Not wanting to feel like a defective projectile detached from a magazine, she asked what she could do for the facility. She willingly agreed to work from the next day as an assistant in the kitchen, where besides humans worked also androids.

She found something on the plan that she had never expected to see in a place like this - an underground palm house. After leaving the cafeteria, she went intrigued to Sector D, where it was located, but mistook her way and reached a platform shuttling to the surface. The elevator was waiting just down, a hangar docker in a gray drill was going onto it in a tracked machine.

"Good morning. Can I go out into the fresh air for a moment?" The girl asked. "Are there any mobility procedures?" Nobody had bothered to inform her about this either.

"Jenny Sandstorm, right?"

"That's correct."

"Nice to meet you." The docker smiled and made a gesture with a cap. "I saw you arrive with the Amyrade team. Don't worry, you can move around freely. If you get to the forbidden places, achijes guarding them will just turn you back. So, are you going?"

"Why not."

The platform moved up a shaft enclosed with dhurnsteel that had once been part of the mine.

"On the surface," the man explained, "the key is the sum of the organic heat signature that can be detected from space and that can be considered, for example, hot springs, not humans. This means that not too many people can go out at one time, but currently the limit is still far away. There is always some risk when machines arrive or depart."

"Heard there are some synthesizers on the surface. They are over a kilometer high. So, what's the point of all these procedures and hiding when they are visible?"

"Visually, yes, you can see colubrins, but their heat and radiation are being suppressed and perceived as zero percent from a certain height. At least with the most sensitive Kiritian receptors, because we have tested it from space. We know, however, that Kandrok is interested in people and less often in installations. It had passed several planets and moons already, where only a blind man wouldn't see the abandoned colonies, without any reaction. As for the Cargoo surface, there is nothing interesting on it, it looks uncolonized and monotonous. You can walk around the square; the base surroundings are completely safe. Nothing lives here."

The platform stopped on the first floor.

"Thanks for the info," Jenny said.

"Have fun, girl. And I wish you that your dad's case tonight was successful. Each of us would like him to come back." He adjusted his cap and drove off, leaving Jenny with thoughts about whether the words could have meant undying love and respect for Forkis, or an allusion to Biffter's inadequate rule. It is possible that the man said that only out of politeness to please her in this gloomy environment.

The K'ajolom star was slowly descending from the zenith, it was the most interesting object in sight. Weathered rock and barren soil stretched along the broken line of the horizon that stood out against the pink-gray sky. It was rare to see a leafless bush waving its branches in the light wind. There was a lower concentration of oxygen in the air than on Earth or Atla, the plant kingdoms, but it was still easy to breathe.

Jenny walked along the empty landing pad. About a hundred meters away, she spotted three figures: a pair of lightly armored young achijes without helmets that she had seen after landing, and a specific man in a loose medical uniform. At first, she thought it was the reflection of K'ajolom's rays on the clothing that covered the entire body, but as she focused on the figure, she realized with a sigh that she was looking not at the fabric, but at the bone-white skin and the same-colored ponytail reaching the ground.

Curious, she moved in that direction. As she was thirty paces away from him, she could see clearly the figure with a rare appearance.

Rare, because it was an avor, not a human. The famous prisoner of Cargoo.

With his back to Kogan and Ryan guarding him, he stared calmly at the sky as if waiting for salvation. The glow of K'ajolom didn't seem to irritate his eyes. Another group of Kiritians was standing nearby in a circle, chatting over smoking stimulants. The guards sitting on the wall were also discussing, probably about something amusing, because they had bright faces and burst out laughing every now and then. Kogan was tearing stones from the wall and throwing them blindly at the prisoner, and he didn't react as the avor turned over and over, giving him a hateful glance.

Then he noticed Jenny. Their eyes met. Kandrok frowned and glanced at her with controlled indifference, while the girl held her breath when she saw the amber of his irises - she had such good eyesight from her father that she could see the color from a considerable distance - covering almost the entire eyes, more like a dog's than a human, and a face full of terror.

When the avor was hit with a stone again, he lost his temper. He bent down abruptly, grabbed a piece of rock and, with clenched teeth, tossed it at Kogan. With an accurate strike, he knocked the moaning private off the wall.

"You bastard!" Ryan, who rarely got angry, raised his rifle, but before he could use a mounted taser, the Kandrok member reached and downed him with inhuman speed.

The group of Kiritians stopped conversating and reacted. They surrounded the prisoner, knocked him down and started basting him with their boots.

"I thought you were in the room." Darius appeared next to Jenny.

"I wanted to take a look around." She looked at his face, then glanced in surprise at Schindler's pocket. "Why is the parsley sticking out of there?"

"Aaah, Lieutenant Seymour decided to take care of my diet." He crushed the parsley and stuffed it deeper. "I'm sorry I was away so long. The party got longer. I had to answer fans' questions."

They both watched as the Kiritians put the bloody but contented avor on his feet and forcefully led him out of the yard. Ryan helped Kogan to his feet and followed him to the medical wing.

Schindler put his hands on his hips.

"I see you've already met our Rei'than. You can see for yourself what a slippery and dangerous scum he is. Let him out of your sight for a second and he will cut your throat."

"It was Kogan who attacked him. Kandrok was only defending himself."

"Whose side are you on?" Darius asked in mock surprise.

"On ours. But the private was throwing stones at him."

"In fact. I'd be mad in his place myself and paste the jester." The corporal grabbed Sandstorm gently by the arm. "Come on, let me show you the palm house, and in it something really cool."

As they made their way back to the platform, Jenny's gaze and Rei'than's being led underground met again.

***

The conference hall was one of the largest rooms in the long-stretched base, its thick puronax portholes, since the renovation, had overlooked the surface, faithful to the principle of pareidolia in case of espionage from space. Similar safeguards were used in the communication center, formerly a control room of one of the mine's embranchments. The huge windows looked like one-way mirrors - if someone had flown over them, they would have seen the smooth section of the rock, and unless they had been an avor, they would haven't caught the signals coming from the nether regions. In turn, an observer from the nether regions could see the surface of the planet through the dusty puronax.

Velkee stood with his hands clasped behind his back, staring at the eroded Cargoo rocks and the tiny sand whirlwinds far on the horizon. K'ajolom was starting to set, it seemed to swell as it approached the gloomy rocks; the color turned red, which reminded many achijes of Betelgeuse from lost Morascrik. When the briefing was over and people began to leave the conference room, the general sat down at the desk and began talking to petitioners. After two hours, the last achij left the room. In the end, remained only Velkee as well as Anna Sandstorm, whom the man with his back to her didn't see at first.

Seeing the desponding of Warfighter, probably thinking he was alone in the room, the captain didn't turn to leave, but stopped. She didn't really feel like talking to him privately, but the reason for this willingness wasn't another fresh wound inflicted by Kandrok. During the briefing, had been discussed the expedition to Amyrade, the participants had been congratulated, then had been raised the subject of Forkis, and the details of his awakening had been arranged, and for the end had been left the topics of the heaviest caliber. As Velkee and his men had recaptured Biffter and Avadar's team from the Headhunters, the enemy had unexpectedly revealed itself and taken over the main Kiritian planet, Eos Endymion, near the Scorpion Universe, where military equipment had been manufactured. The notable transit stations, factories and harbors didn't interest Kandrok at all - it just wanted to weaken Kiritians even more and cut them off from the next planet. The attack on its moon U1 meant the loss of seven thousand refugees from the RC Galaxy, inverted there many years earlier. Admittedly it was a population with whom Kiritians didn't know what to do, but they began to incline to win Erceses over and gain maybe not another ally in the fight against the enemy, but certainly significant strength. Now the fate of the refugees remained unknown.

Velkee heard footsteps as Anna made her way down the final stairs to the lower part of the rostrum. She blocked the door to the room with a switch on the desk, and turned off the hovering holographs of Eos Endymion and U1.

For long breaths, they both stared at the landscape behind the Puronax cover.

"Do you think everything will change today?" Anna broke the silence.

They looked at each other.

"I'll be honest, don't be angry. I'm skeptical about bringing Forkis back to life. Rather, it won't work. Lest there be any understatement: I mean only the possibility of returning a human their life, especially after so long from their death."

"You think Nimja members deceived us all?"

"I haven't seen any so far. I only know them from the stories of the depressed ex-emperor and the team that had gotten overdrunk before the difficult mission. There is also that humanoid cat from the planet Tsar Seymour brings weeds from."

"Nacxit was here at our base. Many saw him. Including a prisoner who doesn't get any drugs. There is also a record from the solitary confinement celula."

"Rei'than? They constantly drug him with sedatives, lately he has freaked out more and more. Today he beat up two privates who were guarding him. The avor is the last person whose account I would agree to believe. Anyway, it doesn't matter. If there really are aliens much stronger than us and Kandrok, then there is no point in doing anything, because everything has already been planned in advance. At any moment, one of them can get in our business without wiping their shoes, and we can't do shit about it."

Although the general's words were saturated with ostentatious contempt, Anna sensed how upset he was, being a man of action, used to solving all sorts of problems by force. She was also furious at their helplessness towards Kandrok, who at any moment could fly out of the void and take over another planet that had been under the auspices of the Immortals for so long.

"Words like that don't suit you at all, Velkee."

"Don't worry, I'm just calculating. The situation absolutely didn't shake the foundations of my personality, nor did it change my approach to belief in human capabilities. I had several centuries to become stable in my worldview. Nothing can change my approach anymore. Even if someone had taken into their head that man has no influence on the future of their own race, I will still do my job. The best I can."

"Those who saw Nimja members agree that the strangers don't want to interfere in our lives. Whatever they do, it only serves their interests."

Velkee looked at her slyly, smiled with the left half of his mouth.

"I suppose you haven't stayed here with me to talk about aliens?"

He was right. There was one problem that definitely needed to be resolved. Anna's doubts and fear oscillated primarily around the approaching inevitable zero hour, as some achijes began to determine the time to bring Forkis back to life. In the history of mankind, there had been no such situation that happened to her. Leaving aside the case of Necron before kiritianization, which for many fell under clinical death, no case of resurrection had been documented so far, especially almost twenty years after death.

Forkis was dead at the moment, and Anna had come in on a long-standing, casual relationship with Velkee.

She still felt something for the former emperor, for all these years she had desired his return, longed for his charisma, power and extravagant animal tenderness. She had tried to find an equivalent of Forkis in Kiret, but when he had brushed her off, she had gotten involved with Warfighter. It was not love, but the need for closeness, satisfying human needs, not to go crazy. Leaving aside the unusualness of the circumstances and long knowing that the former First Galactic Dignitary might have returned to the world of the living, could she be guilty of betrayal? Was it even possible? The closer she got to the moment of resurrection, the more she feared, as if she had been waiting for a serious surgery that would have changed her life, if it had ever worked. She envied Warfighter stone pragmatism, at least in case of Forkis. However, she was inclined to believe that Velkee didn't want to share his real experiences with anyone. She suspected that he might have not wanted the former emperor's return, but it would have been naive and self-centered to think that she was the cause of it.

Velkee leaned his seat against the desk, put his hands on the top, and looked at the first row of armchairs. Anna stood before the general.

"Suppose Forkis wakes up. What will happen then?" She asked.

He shifted his sideways, weary gaze to her. The clipped gray mustache rose.

"And what do you expect? If he still had telekinesis, he would learn everything that happened between us. He is an old being, he will definitely understand our needs. But everything will have to end." The man read everything in her murky, sad look. It amused him. "You don't know your own feelings, do you?"

"He's still dead. I will not pretend to embrace this whole sick situation. Nimja was right on one thing: the things we dabble in are not meant for human minds. At least not at the stage of current human development."

"Don't defend yourself with Nimja. You are afraid that you will not love Forkis with your old girlish love," Velkee spoke with a slight irony. "That an extinct fire won't ignite again, even if you start blowing on it."

"Stop mocking me." She watched him as he wandered around the desk, with his hands tucked into the pockets. "Why do I get the feeling you don't want his return?"

"Of course, I do. A mighty leader will be needed to smarten that whole place of pleasure," he said calmly, but Anna caught a subtle hint of mockery in his voice, like a crystal of salt in a glass of water. Maybe even anger.

"Not that I doubt Forkis' charisma and leadership skills that are part of the cultures of the two species, but how will he stop Kandrok?"

Velkee stopped by Anna. He gave her a sly smile.

"This is a very broad subject that will take weeks to discuss. Perhaps in the evening you will have the opportunity to ask the right person about it."

He pressed her to the desk. She pushed her face away as he tried to kiss her. She saw that the first stars were visible outside.

"Come on," she stammered out.

"Perhaps this is our last meeting. Although, knowing you, I'm sure that you will visit me more than once." He put his fingers to her mouth when she wanted to make a cutting remark. "You should loosen up. And not to think too much, because you're not Dr. Figam and your pretty little head might get overheated. Treat it as your second bachelorette party, although I can bet nothing will happen tonight and you are unnecessarily losing your nerves."

Anna failed to get the information from Velkee about the cause of his frustration, which she had sensed throughout the conversation. It was certainly more than rage at being powerless during the loss of another planet.

She stopped resisting him and allowed herself to be covered with bites and kisses on her face, neck and décolleté. Pumped, she gladly returned his actions.

She was soon lying on the top beneath him, both of them weren't wearing most of their clothes. The stress hadn't gone away, but become bearable. So had remorse.

***

A casual observer from the surface would have had no reason to believe that the Kiritian hideout was vast and extensive. Remembering the magnitude and nature of CERN, Jenny had a different opinion. However, she hadn't expected that the nether regions of the inconspicuous, barren planet could hide such man-made wealth. It was practically a city created from the connection of many mines, self-sufficient on the basic level of existence.

Darius directed her to another sector, marked as D, they reached the place by an underground train, so as not to waste a quarter of an hour wandering.

They found themselves in the ten-hectare palm house, which the Kiritians used to contemplate it in solitude and calm down, spend time there in good company or look for inspiration related to war plans or inventions, as Dr. Maksimus Figam often did. And there were many things to admire. Jenny had stayed briefly on the planet Chulimal so that she could see the body of Forkis hidden in the Onkalot pyramid, but nevertheless she had remembered visually many species of tropical plants there. Many of them, from mini-lichens, which had to be observed through magnifying optics, to multi-story trees covered with vines, decorated the Cargoo underground conservatory. The very warm, humid air was saturated with the aromatic fragrances of the flora. As at a tree in the middle of the floor with living quarters for women, also here were flying a lot of butterflies of all shapes, colors and sizes, as well as other insects that pleased the eye but weren't annoying. On water leaves were slacking off frogs.

"So that's what you wanted to show me." Jenny rested her hands on the rough bark of a tree fern and examined its structure with her fingertips. She turned to Darius, who was standing in the back with his hands in the pockets, watching her.

"I admit, quite an ingenious place. I planned to see it myself, but got lost."

"You should have waited for me." He grinned. "Come on, there will be the best soon."

They walked a short distance along a road lined with crushed mine boulders and surface regolith. On the way, they passed a few walkers.

Jenny stopped short. Darius, smiled behind her back.

At a multi-level cascade, at the foot of a mossy Martian Southern beech, were playing kittens - an exuberant female with turquoise eyes and two brown-eyed males. They looked almost like small, clumsy jaguars with puffy mouths with goofy expressions, but their bodies were also adapted to bipedal gait. The little ones, however, preferred to walk like typical cats, playing with each other. On the branch of a flowering giant Japanese cherry tree was resting Chimalmat.

"They are ..." Smiling more and more, Jenny didn't finish, taken off by the charm of babies. She sighed in delight and shook her fists like a little girl at the sight of a dream toy. "Wow."

"I knew you'd like it."

Indeed, Schindler managed to surprise her. She hadn't expected something like this. Seeing them entering the palm house, she had thought they would end up with some interesting plants, and knowing Darius and his superior - ones that did you good with their volatile substances.

"Can I touch them? Whose kids are they?"

"Go ahead, play," replied Chimalmat.

Jenny approached the kittens, sat cross-legged, and placed the bravest female on her legs, which tilted her head and allowed herself to have her fluffy, white throat stroked. The siblings who watched this also approached Jenny, began to push onto her lap, but the female was pushing them away with all her paws, nervously wagging her tail.

"And what do you think?" Darius crouched down next to her. He broke off a stick ending with leaves and began to scrape the ground with it. The males immediately rushed towards the toy. He smiled endearingly. "Rather, they were not formed by budding."

Jenny stared at Chimalmat in bewilderment.

"Aggro is the father? Really?!"

The Onkalotian woman nodded.

"How cool they are! Lovely litter."

"Yeah. It's good to see some fun in this bunkered place," said Schindler. "I also didn't expect that there would be kittens here."

"Do they have any abilities?"

"Not yet, they're too small," Chimalmat replied, wagging her tail. "They are also before the time of naming, but it will be soon because their character is already visible."

"So, you live here now."

"For some time." Q'ualel emerged from behind the trunk. "We were supposed to go back to Chulimal, but the babies were born in the base. Apparently, it's safer here now. Xajb'a Kej's body has also been moved here, so we don't have to guard anything else."

"I am the Shield-Net, the Keeper of Tz'aqol's House from the People of Ik'ib'akam, the Dark Jaguar," Chimalmat said solemnly, hitting her chest with a paw. "I will return to the land of my ancestors again, to protect it from the hands and hearts of the wicked."

"Certainly," commented Schindler.

"Nice to see you again, Aggro." Jenny put the female aside, stood up and hugged the Onkalot in greeting. "Congratulations."

"Congratulations indeed are deserved," added Darius, changing position as his foot went numb. The little she-cat pushed her brothers away and grabbed the stick with her claws, then flopped over onto her back. "I've heard Onkalots give birth to one or two babies. Three are rarity."

"That's true." Aggro climbed a tree and sat down next to Chimalmat.

Though the raised corners of his lips seemed to indicate that he was pleased, Jenny saw a hint of melancholy in his eyes brown like in the two males. She had heard that Aggro had once been involved with Eredal, the older sister of Darius, and although he had felt sympathy for her, he had brushed the girl off so that she could have a normal life with Anton Rafen from a distant neighborhood on Chulimal. So, it had happened. The memory of his former relationship and his attachment to Eredal must have prevented Aggro from becoming fully free. Jenny gently checked it telepathically, the Onkalot's thoughts followed the same path as hers - and she guessed right. She didn't want to interfere with the privacy of humanoid jaguars, but her ability volunteered regardless of her will. Maybe because Sandstorm was being consumed with curiosity after all. In addition to humans, she could also read the minds of humanoid jaguars, apparently Aggro hadn't learned to block telepathy like Kiret, or he didn't care. She felt sorry for him. Q'ualel had gotten involved with Chimalmat listening to his head, believing it to be right for the endangered species, and was resistant to Kiritian genetic engineering. He had failed to get Eredal out of his heart and memories. She kept coming back to him as if a specter not allowing to fully enjoy his new relationship. Specter of candy, as well as of thorns. He was overjoyed at the decision made, especially the fruit in the form of the beautiful kittens, but he missed the past anyway.

Darius managed to lift all the fidgeting kittens, walked over to Jenny and handed her the female.

"Are you going to participate in the wake-up attempt tonight?" He asked Q'ualel. He struggled with the babies trying to get on his head. The female broke free from the girl and began to climb the tree lopsidedly, spreading her paws as if she had been lying on a large ball.

"I think about it all the time. I don't know if I will be welcomed by Xajb'a Kej if this defiled process is indeed successful."

Schindler understood his resentment towards necro medicine dictated by his religion, so he didn't dwell on the subject.

"Is it about the tragedy in the K'otz'ibaja arena?" He asked gently instead. "I've heard about it ... Are you assuming the complicity of Beliar Drunkenstein's action?"

"It's not about the rebel himself. Xajb'a Kej lost his life by being at odds with me. A long time ago we had an argument on Chulimal and each of us went his own way. And then I destroyed his dreams, even if they were associated with the total annihilation of humanity."

"Maybe you're getting too excited. The achijes said that he wouldn't wake up anyway, because the artifact is a joke of Nanawak and Nacxit."

Chimalmat half sighed, half snarled.

"Stupid warriors! Do you have to talk about death again? Ek Chuah[4] will turn his eyes to us because of it."

The female reached her mother, who, after giving Darius and Aggro an angry look, took her in her arms. The slightly scratched corporal put the other kittens down by the pond.

"So will you be there or not?" He asked Q'ualel.

"I'll see."

***

Forkis' cloned body rested in an airtight cryo-biochamber topped with a transparent puronax carapace. It was located next to a medical sector and laboratories, in a circular room filled with lamps specially prepared for the process. There were no objects nearby, the entire apparatus keeping the organism functional was locked in the cryo-biochamber along with the body. The use of xik'iri didn't require any support anyway. Dr. Figam, remembering the perturbations with the artifacts just before the trip to Amyrade, ordered that no diagnostic or monitoring equipment should be carried to the restoration site, although, like many other observers, he was extremely curious about the chemical, physical and biological processes that would soon take place in the room.

At the cryo-biochamber gathered: Darius, Anna, Jenny, Velkee, Kiret, Figam and his chief assistant Alejandro Cortez.

In the corridor lingered a crowd.

Although Schindler was no longer required to operate xik'iri, it was unanimously agreed to let him continue to use it, having earned the reputation of an expert on Nimja artifacts. The ovoid alien device removed from its wrapper worked in much the same way as it had done on Amyrade - the closer to Nacxit, the more intense it glowed red, but now in the Nimja member's place was the cloned body.

"Come on, boy, get started," Figam announced as no one from the disturbed company broke the void silence with any comment, a word of doubt or a suggestion. For some time now, they had all been standing in a circle around the cry-biochamber, like followers in front of a place of worship that only a priest had a right to approach.

Being a priest fell to Darius.

As he approached the body on the hard surface, the few taps of his military boots almost irritated the eardrums. He looked at Jenny, on whose shoulders Anna was clenching her hands tightly. Staring at the carapace, the girl didn't look scared and tense like her mother, she was just curious. Andro goggled slightly, which made him look like a gopher; on the face of Velkee, standing with his hands clasped into a basket settled cold pragmatism; Figam, with his white hair spiked in all directions and his crumpled smock, looked as if he had come here right out of bed.

As Darius looked at the cloned body of the former Emperor, girded with cloth around his hips, he felt an icy chill. He swallowed hard. A huge responsibility lay with him, it was little consolation that if something had gone wrong - and a million things could have gone wrong - Kiritians would have blamed also Nacxit besides him for screwing the case. But it would have been he who would have been accused of doing something wrong when he had absolutely no idea what he was doing! The scapegoat had to be found, however, since Nacxit, obsessed with the subject of artifacts, had graciously decided to leave them with the problem beyond human comprehension of reality.

"Alright," he muttered under his breath.

According to Nanawak, xik'iri operated on the principle of integrating entraser data with the brain - the merging process was completely non-invasive.

Nacxit, in turn, argued that blood should have been shed for the atole to find a channel to the dead organism.

Go figure.

Cortez, who had a celula attached to his forehead so that the entire base could see everything in real time, slid open the carapace of the cryo-biochamber and raised his thumb to encourage him.

Darius put xik'iri on the edge of the canopy, took a scalpel from Andro, and made a small incision between the ribs on the chilled clone's body. He placed the artifact as instructed by Nimja, with a series of specific marks facing the wound, on the up-down axis.

The process started immediately. Heat and light escaped from the transferer, and the body began to take on the colors of a living person.

Organoleptically, there was no change in the air.

It all happened in less than two minutes and without the expected fireworks.

The alien device turned to dust that covered the clone's chest with silvery flecks.

Darius almost screamed and jumped back as Forkis violently opened his hazel eyes, being brutally roused from sleep. The scalpel fell on the floor with a clatter, splashing droplets of blood across Figam's white coat.

The corporal wasn't mentally ready for this.

He assumed that the awakening process would drag on for hours, extrapolating to the cosmic cryosn. Then vomiting would start, muscles would get flabby, there would be general stiffness, maybe some paresis, weakness, pissing under yourself. If anything worked out.

And here everything happened suddenly. Too fast.

Unnaturally. By inverting one of the main laws of nature.

Darius realized that alien interference had given a tremendous boost to human skills. But this terrible progress could have been just as terrible in consequences.

Behind him he heard various reactions from the people gathered here, but his mind ignored them.

The former First Galactic Dignitary looked at the ajar carapace of the cryo-biochamber, then at the ceiling lights, and at Darius standing with his mouth open, stiff as if he had put his face into the cement. Cortez looked even more interesting, unworthy of being called a Kiritian, because he found himself with his seat on the floor, no less shocked from Schindler. Forkis looked at the stunned people staring at him as they approached him carefully, like a fresh misfire.

Bomb.

Memories suddenly came alive.

"Drunkenstein ..." the clone growled in the same baritone as the real emperor. He was an old emperor now. In his mind and feeling, the fight with the rebel had just ended, Beliar had wounded him fatally, whereby Forkis had been taken to the medical room. The fire that had been lit during the duel hadn't passed, adrenaline rushed through his veins. "Where is he?" He got up freely from the couch, scattering the remains of the artifact around as if his body had been used to physical activity, and began to look soberly at the gathered people frozen in the stupor. He looked at Warfighter. "Did you take me to a medical center? Dr. Maksimus Figam, what are you doing on Morascrik?" He examined his hands, felt the torso. The knife wound inflicted by Drunkenstein had disappeared. "They had to call such an important person as you, to put me back together?"

"Holy shit ... it worked out," gasped out the general, with a jerk of an arm, forcing Andro to get up from the ground. Even Velkee, the biggest skeptic of this process, was very impressed.

"Unheard of," the delighted scientist murmured under his breath and was already starting to formulate theories. "After restoring and reviving the organism, memory is associated with the original DNA, not the one produced artificially, although the latter is an exact copy of the original. So, you don't remember anything about what happened to your cloned body. Unless it is the soul that retains the residual properties of matter and contains a memory record that on Amyrade wasn't transformed into another type of energy. Fascinating!"

"What's going on here?" Now also Forkis was confused, especially since he had failed to telepathically probe anyone's mind. The damned rebel must have done him really hard.

"Forkis ... It's you ..." Anna came up to him and after a moment of hesitation and eyeing up, she fell into his arms. He hugged her, stroked her back, looking at the faces of the rest of them. He stopped his eyesight on Jenny.

"And this girl, who is she? Necron, report. Why are you standing like a pole? Why are you all staring at me?" He began to get irritated. He hoped the extinguished telepathy was a temporary, traumatic effect.

"I can't believe it." Cortez's surprised expression turned to delight. He clenched his fists and raised them. "It really worked!"

Forkis got completely confused when the two cheered scientists hugged and began to pat each other on the back.

"Lieutenant Commander Drunkenstein died, and I killed him," he deduced. He released Anna from his embrace.

There were many voices coming from outside the door, there were scuffles, someone fell and groaned. Forkis noticed achijes staring at him through the porthole as if he had been a ghost, who, after a short tumult, split a little.

The room was entered by Aggroteh, who had decided to accept the invitation and join the small group. He was also dumbfounded, like the rest in the beginning.

"Great gods ..." He fell to his knees, then sat on his hind legs, keeping his eyes on Forkis. "Xajb'a Kej, you are alive!"

"Let someone finally tell me what's going on here," Forkis demanded. "I'm starting to lose my patience."

"One could tell for many hours, and superficially. I propose such a solution, sir." Velkee took a plunger with an entraser from Cortez. "All information is included here, also sedatives, because you will need them. This is a bio and temporary version of a medical chip; it will dissolve in a few days. I propose to sit on the edge of the cryo-biochamber, because even Emperor Kiritian cannot lift the burden of such news."

The general wanted to hand over the plunger to Figam, who would have performed the injection, but Forkis, having a fierce expression, snatched the object from him and immediately stuck a small needle directly into his temple instead of into the back of his head, then injected the contents. He tossed the empty container onto the couch lining where he had previously been resting.

Aggro got up and stood by Kiret, temporarily unable to utter a word.

Nothing happened for a few minutes - the entraser hadn't had enough time to attach itself to the frontal lobe. Once it did so and the transfer of the electrical signal began, which was then being converted to bioelectric one, Forkis decided to follow the advice of Warfighter and sat down.

He wasn't disturbed, they were silent and waited tensely, seeing but still not comprehending on their human and Onkalot level of reasoning what had just happened in the room. But they thought that the most important thing was that it was successful.

Only one person wasn't entirely sure whether to bring Forkis back into the game would prove to be a good solution.

Velkee went out into the corridor and told noisy achijes to shut up, with the positive result.

Meanwhile, Forkis' face took on different shades of emotion, from utter bewilderment to astonishment and anger; even the emperor, toughened in restraint for centuries, couldn't remain indifferent in such circumstances. He clenched his hands on the metal edge of the couch, shook his head, even snarled, though in his new body there was no trace of Onkalot heritage. He brought his fingers to the junction of the jaw with the skull and sighed, irritated. His body hadn't been fully recreated as he could have wished. However, you don't look a gift fighter in the engine.

Having absorbed all the events from 2956 to the present 2975, he managed to calm down, which he did after many long breaths with his face turned to the ceiling. The distant past turned out to be a certain ally - as a humanoid jaguar he had grown up in the culture related to paranormal phenomena, so he was familiar with them. The tranquilizers did their job too.

He sighed deeply and stood up, he looked at his hands closely, examined the rest of his body, glad that those around him were showing patience. With the bitten phalanx of his index finger, he started wandering around the room, thinking. He stopped in front of Jenny. He looked at her for a moment, gave her a warm smile, not because he felt something, not emotionally connected with the child, but because he wanted to encourage tense Sandstorm.

"So, in short: I have this beautiful daughter, our empire has been smashed by the evil aliens, we negotiate with the terrorists, and the dogs rule the universe." There was no mirth in the words. He looked at Velkee. "Should I know anything else?"

A slight smile appeared on the general's face.

"I have the daughter ..." he said softly, tilted his head. He glanced at his wife. "So, you called her with the name I mentioned to you once."

Anna nodded. It was hard to tell right now whether the contracted facial muscles were a symptom of holding back emotion or a smile. Forkis perceived the fact of having the offspring as a pleasant curiosity, a nice surprise. Jenny likewise - that she finally saw her real, living father. She had dreaded this moment for some time, hadn't known how he would react. The two-meter-tall man standing in front of her, with hair as black as hers, and identical hazel eyes, mentally turned out to be someone completely strange. They hadn't had each other when Jenny had been little and then growing up. But one thing she had to admit: she had met her father in the strangest circumstances in human history.

Forkis grabbed the girl's hands. He had a strong, warm touch that gave a sense of security. He looked into her eyes for a moment.

"I can't see anything anymore, Jenny. I'm fully human. I may have to learn to live like this. Now you are the only telepath among Kiritians."

"I'm not a Kiritian woman ... Father." The last word barely passed through the girl's throat. Forkis released her hands, ran a finger over her cheek. Then smiled briefly.

"We'll see what happens next. But I can promise you one thing: I will show you the universe ruled by Kiritians. It will all be ours." He turned to the rest, "Thank you all for the effort you put in bringing me back to life. Together we will recover what has been lost."

Kiret glanced sideways, fixing his eyes on the foundation of the couch. Forkis walked over to Anna and put his arm around her waist.

"Now I have to speak to achijes," he said aloud, "to convince them that I really exist. Let our hideouts on Cargoo, Mezzo and Calcaris know that the former emperor has returned. Tomorrow we will rest, but the next day we will all get to work."

Amazement seemed to have flowed onto Necron's face by itself, but it lasted for a fraction of a moment; his look went to the profile of the animated man. Kiret felt mean. Apart from completely ignoring his presence in this room, Forkis had begun to make plans for the nation as if he had actively participated in the history of the Zodiac Universum for nineteen Terran years. Was he trying to show him with ostentatious disregard that he was blaming him for the current socio-political situation?

"Of course, but careful examination first," Dr. Figam tempered Forkis' enthusiasm. "The war plans will wait, sir."

Warfighter approved with a nod. He was sincerely pleased with the return of such a powerful emperor, like him in action. He had devised his own plans to neutralize Kandrok, preventively without Forkis' involvement, but now they would be able to work together and join forces. He summoned Zira Aytar via the PDA. Soon came the corporal, who after the expedition to Amyrade was again wearing a dyed, lush blue mohawk, and carried into the hall an anti-gravity disk with a uniform and light armor. Forkis thanked her formally for the work she had done on Amyrade - and she tried to come to herself after seeing him alive. When she regained the ability to walk, she stepped stiffly into the corridor, swam across the lake of achijes and, aside, pressed her back and head against the wall. Zira and Forkis had been together for a short time, until an unbelievable incident happened, and from then on, in a silent resolution, they had begun to avoid each other, which had been initiated by Aytar. That chapter was definitively closed. Pretending by Zira that Forkis was exclusively an authoritarian emperor, and she, an achij trained to obey orders, had been going well for many decades, so she hadn't expected that seeing Forkis again would make such an impression on her.

Anna decided that the small nuance in Forkis' behavior, which probably only she noticed when Aytar left the room, should have been forgotten.

Forkis sent Aggroteh to the palm house, promising him that he would call by him later and talk to him in private, he also directed Jenny to the social sector.

Dr. Figam and an assistant finished collecting the artifact dust for research.

"I'll see you at my laboratory for tests right away, Mr. Emperor," said Maksimus, leaving.

As soon as Forkis got out of the padded room, he was greeted by achijes' incredulous looks and a neurotic silence that broke in the clatter of howls, screams and loud applause, amidst the waving of whatever was in hand.

9. Lost hope

Jenny didn't mind that Darius was willing to walk her to her apartment's door. It allowed her to save herself unnecessary thoughts, which could have spoiled her mood, because the corporal constantly entertained her with conversation. Currently, apart from regular exercises, he had no other duties and was willing to offer the girl any help.

When she entered her quarters, on the surface simulating a porthole prevailed a deep night, haunted by ice storms and whirlwinds. Such strong atmospheric phenomena, beautiful nevertheless, in a sense had a calming effect. Sandstorm wasn't hungry, she washed, put on her nightgown and tried to sleep, but lay for a long time staring at the aquarium and thinking about her father. Would they be able to work off at least some of what had been taken from them? Would she still be able to love him? Would they spend at least a few moments together, torn from Forkis' busy days, which would make Jenny finally stop feeling so lonely?

Noises coming from everywhere prevented her from falling asleep; the nether region's priority was to provide refugees a hiding place, so no amenities such as sound isolators had been installed in the walls of social corridors. That night, was discussed vigorously the previous day's event.

What hurt Jenny most was that Kiret had completely lost interest in her. They hadn't spoken to each other since the return, he sometimes greeted her with a polite nod and a blank smile. He treated her as a stranger, someone known only by sight. The girl decided to accost him the next day.

In the morning, as agreed, she went to work in the kitchen. As a temporary shelter, the base was automated in priority areas, with most power and machinery reserved for the medical, manufacturing and research departments as well as the communications center and protective screen, so cleaning and food preparation was the task of humans and androids. Jenny mainly served orders and sorted washed dishes, she often tried to absorb herself in a conversation with her co-workers. Today the entire base was discussing only about Forkis, who had regained power at night without anyone's opposition - every achij wanted him again as First Galactic Dignitary. At least no one had expressed their doubts openly. Corrections to the way of exercising power were to be agreed over the next days, including whether Forkis would rule alone this time or a new Council of Dignitaries would be established.

Jenny learned that Forkis had used to organize wild events for achijes called *harroweeng*, especially when there had been few armed conflicts and people needed to go wild or simply improve their moods. As emperor, Kiret had abolished this primitive according to him ceremony that had reminded him of Chulimal lycans. They both reportedly argued about it in the morning. Necron was exceptionally backed by General Warfighter, who rarely agreed with him on anything. Ultimately, it was agreed that in the evening, in the entire underground base the achijes could have fun on the occasion of Forkis' return from beyond the grave, as well as improve their well-being in general.

There were about three hundred people in the cafeteria.

When Jenny was leading an anti-gravity disk with a special order, she noticed that it was intended for those sitting at a big table: Forkis, Kiret, Anna, Warfighter, Aggroteh, Figam, Shane, Avadar and three other achijes, probably officers.

"Hello, Jenny," Forkis started the ball rolling. "There you go, you are working in the kitchen?"

The girl began to set out the plates, and Kiret and Viktor who were sitting closest to her, rushed to her aid.

"Yeah, I found the activity."

"That's commendable." Necron smiled.

"How are you?"

"Everything's perfectly normal, at least physically. It turned out that the cloning of the body deprived me of my old Onkalot properties, for which none of those who brought me back is responsible. What I once had was the work of q'umaraq, a very powerful artifact. That's why I'll have to ask for your support from time to time."

"I confirm," said the doctor, lifting his fork. "Your dad's fine."

"But why the kitchen, Jenny?" Forkis leaned back in the chair, with his hands clasped over his belly. "I have something better for you: in a few days we will start accepting fresh blood into our reorganized army, I will ask them questions, and you will watch these people from the sidelines and inform me of their intentions. From what Kiret Biffter told me, you have already reached the level to be a perfect spy. That's how I used to recruit achijes, all the selected people were patriotically loyal."

"Thank you, Jenny." Aggro took from her a bottle filled with cactus pulque.

"And this, put it next to me." Figam waved towards a jug of water with lime. "Thanks, sunshine."

"I will think the proposal through," the girl replied culturally. She didn't want to come over as uncouth and rebellious, saying that only she had the right to decide what job she liked and was right for her. Nevertheless, Forkis was right: it would have been a silly waste not to use the unique talent. She remembered about Kandrok's prisoner. If she refused to cooperate with her father - although she felt that she would rather have nothing to say in this matter - she would try to practice her skills on a stranger, since she already did well with people.

She tried to accost Kiret with her eyesight, but he was busy talking to Avadar and the three men. Jenny then decided it might have been better. By the way, she would have had to explain to Anna or Forkis, why she had wanted to talk to the former emperor in private. There were no longer just the two of them on Earth.

As she returned to the kitchen, she noticed Darius sitting with a dozen colleagues cheerfully saying hello to her.

Before the noon she had free time, she immediately went to the palm house to play with the kittens. Darius joined her after training was over. Aggro was absent. Chimalmat walked on the rocky bottom of the pond and watched contented males get better at swimming. She was moving away, and they were swimming to her briskly. Brave and eager to land fights, the female, in turn, was afraid of the water, she disappeared among thick coastal leaves on the other side of the lake.

Chimalmat waved her paw.

"Don't look for her. She does so often when she doesn't feel like something or gets offended. She will come back when she wants to."

Jenny perched on a flat, warm rock away from the shore.

"How is it with this kiritianization?" She asked. "How did you undergo it?"

Reclining, Darius took a blade of grass from his mouth.

"Why, you want to be an Immortal?" He turned to the girl.

"I ask out of curiosity."

"I went with Tsar beyond the base. It was the lieutenant who changed me. At the beginning, I thought that I would undergo the transformation asymptomatically, because that was what it looked like. But when I suddenly came down after some time ... Brrrr." He shuddered, crushed the grass. "Thought I was going to die. The blood as if burned, it seemed to me that the guts were dissolving in me. It hurt terribly. Eventually I couldn't stand it and passed out. But what turned out to be the moments of suffering in exchange for the endless reward? It was worth it; I don't regret my decision. At least at this stage. I'm thirty and feel twenty-four. I have already undergone my first resurrection. Not that I'm scaring you or something like that."

"What is this resurrection?"

"In Kiritians' slang it is - attention, I'm quoting a horse doctor - 'biological regeneration process caused by the activity of the super virus', that is, turning back the biological clock by a few years. In my case it manifested itself so that for a few days I only felt tired and everyone pissed me off. But some people have to lie down as if they were badly sick. Mostly, it works so that kiritianization is the reverse of resurrection. If you undergo one hard, then the other gently."

Jenny remembered Kiret's resurrection on Earth. They must have taken a break while he had been going through this process.

They watched the swimming cats.

"Apparently young people cannot take the super virus because it is deadly for them, hence it is not given to minors. Older persons cope better with kiritianization. Shouldn't it be the other way around, since a young body is strong, healthy and resilient?"

"And this, I'm not able to say." Darius smiled apologetically. He put the new grass in his mouth, began to chew it, and twirled the stem. "I don't know the details."

"This is because in youngsters develops hyper-cytokinemia."

They turned around. Nearby stood Dr. Figam, with his hands clasped behind his back, who had previously walked along an alley between trees with multi-meter, juicy green leaves.

"Good morning, Doctor," Darius said. Figam walked over to a rocky wharf where they had settled.

"Hello, hello. And to you too, Chimalmat. I've already seen Jenny today."

"Hyper... what? Hyperkinesis?"

"A storm of cytokinins, Darius. With some virulent pathogens, paradoxically efficient immune system harms its owner, causes severe discomfort, even self-destruction of organs, while in a child only acquiring immunity, the opposite is true: there is a weak peculiar reaction. Colloquially speaking, in adolescents the super virus can cause havoc because their immune system is too efficient, while in children there is no defense at all. The mentioned cytokine storm can be easily contained, for example with bio nanites, but during an infection with the super virus, it is absolutely not allowed to interfere. Darius can confirm this." The scientist looked at the corporal. The man nodded with an uncertain expression. At least he understood the last sentence. "The super virus was created from a compilation of viruses that were extremely virulent and contagious, and I also added artificial genome sequences to it. So, it has different features, but its strength has been enhanced several dozen times in comparison to any virus that was its progenitor. So that it could infect every cell of the body. Because what would be the point of the immortality it induces if the soft tissues didn't age, but the bones did? Mortality in children and adolescents is on average fifty percent, so they are not kiritianized, even too old people, because they can also die. Your age, Darius, was relatively low, but your body accepted the super virus." The old man smiled jovially. "I hope you've gotten some understanding of this."

"I'm just an ordinary peasant," Darius blurted out.

"Absolutely," Jenny replied. "Thank you for your erudition. What are you doing here, doctor?"

"I'm looking for inspiration." Figam looked at the plants. He sat down next to the interlocutors. "It's a good place. The prettiest and quietest in the entire base. A substitute for lost freedom and normality."

"For what if it's not a secret?"

"Your father wishes Kiritians to completely change their combat and defense equipment. Everything has to be innovative, at worst transformed to more modern standards. Corvettes, ships, shuttles, transporters, ground defenders - everything. That's why I dust off my old, buried projects, try to come up with something new ..."

"It's gonna be a damn high cost!" Schindler interrupted him, jumping up. "Millions of people will have to be trained. In addition, to give Kandrok at least a poke on the nose, we would have to jump one Kardashev's degree forward!"

"Forkis raised a lot of resources over the centuries of space expansion, some of which are still available to us, just enough to rebuild the fleet. There should be no problem in this matter, moreover we'll join forces with our allies. It will be worse with the acceleration of technology development. You are right, skipping a thousand years of natural civilization development in a few years will be quite a challenge, maybe even unattainable in our case. However, history knows cases where humanity faced a problem that threatened its existence and found a solution in a very short time, for example by producing vaccines in a few months that would normally be developed and tested for decades. Every achij who has something interesting can contribute to our current case. Not a single Kandrok can learn about the plans, because everything will be burnt! In the event of a battle, we would have a chance to surprise them, but only during the first attack, before they would get our weapons specification. Hence the Immortals are faced with universal mind-probing; after Forkis' death in K'otz'ib'aja, many achijes joined the nation, so it was impossible to control them telepathically. Unfortunately, baby, it seems that you are going to have a lot of work to do. The First Galactic Dignitary is going to check everyone in this base, then on Mezzo and Calcaris. But I don't know how this is supposed to be done."

Jenny saw a little female emerge from the brush for a moment.

"How many Kiritians are there now?"

"About three million in hiding," replied the doctor. "The fate of many remains unknown."

"And there were eight ..." Darius said grimly. He rubbed his forehead with his hand.

"I could help if I could probe many minds at once, but I can't. It took my father tens of years to build the army, then he checked the next recruits over hundreds of years, so he had everything spread over time."

Figam smiled reassuringly.

"We will cross that bridge when we come to it." He shook her shoulder. "Forkis will certainly not burden you with such a huge responsibility. I'll try to help you somehow. Maybe I will find something that will help strengthen your skills, for example, expand them to many people probed."

"It would be extremely helpful." Schindler spat out the chewed grass. He heard a dialogue being held among trees. "Too bad Chimalmat is not a telepath."

"Oh, I don't think she can be trained to serve Kiritians," Figam said thoughtfully, looking at the Onkalot woman and the kittens. "Her thinking is determined by a completely different culture. Maybe something would come out of it if she had been brought up among people from an early age."

"Get the fuck out of here! How I hate cats!" The three heard the clear aggressive sounding words of some achij.

Guessing what might have been their cause, Jenny got up vigorously and started walking towards the source of the noise. Darius followed her right after, and the doctor began to rise as well. They walked a bit along a regolith path lined with trees, got off it into a tangle of leaves so tall that they had to break through like in a real jungle.

In the square with a fountain shaped into a fish spitting water, stood Kogan and Ryan in summer uniforms. The small Onkalot female clung to the shoe and pants of the first private. The achij waved his leg gently, but the cat didn't let go. She dug her claws into his calf.

"Ow! Go away, you damn reptile! Ryan, why are you laughing yourself silly? Do you know how those little claws hurt? I guess even to the palm house we will have to go armored."

"Stop wagging this stick, I'll try to take her off."

As Ryan leaned across, he almost was hit in a cheek with a paw.

"What a warrior vixen!" commented. "Go away from here! Shoo!"

Kogan began waving his leg harder, as if shaking mud off his pants. And when it didn't help, he stopped caring about finesse, especially after another batch of pain, and made a swing like a footballer scoring a strong goal, almost losing his balance.

The squeaking Onkalot female flew several meters up. If it hadn't been for her light weight and a huge leaf she hit sideways and slid down, she might have gotten broken against trees.

A loud growl pierced the area, too thick and deep for such a small humanoid jaguar. Jenny noticed that the sound came from Chimalmat, tightened on the side of the road in an attack position. The wrinkled muscles of the muzzle obscured her eyes, the fangs whitened in the parted maw. Sandstorm stepped back; she had never seen her so angry.

An attack occurred, but of an unconventional nature.

Moved by tele kinetics, the achijes flew sideways as if fired from a cannon, with a groan they hit bamboo trunks, which they broke in momentum. Kogan additionally took a blow to a shoulder by a coconut knocked off a nearby tree. Everything in the enclave that wasn't too heavy was overturned or moved, including Jenny, Darius, Figam, the little Onkalot female again, water and stones from the fountain, and particles lining the alley. Luckily, nothing serious happened to anyone.

"Kogan, Ryan, what are you guys doing here?" Darius dusted the lime off his hair.

"We have an hour's break, Corporal," said Kogan, who sat down with a grunt.

"Then who's watching the prisoner?"

"The celula. You can always review the recording afterwards. Besides, nothing ever happens there."

"Something always happens," said Schindler. "The prisoner monitoring celula isn't working, at least there is no connection to the capripod."

"Oh yeah, I forgot." Kogan shrugged.

"Get it fixed as soon as possible."

"Of course," Ryan said.

"But for sure, because otherwise batab Gareth will be pissed."

"A kinetic weapon ... Oh yeah, kinetic weapon, kinetic weapon ..." Rubbing his chin, Figam muttered with his seat drenched in the fountain. He got up first. "I guess that's what you need! You raise your equipment and opponent to a critical height, then hit it against the ground."

"It sounds interesting." Darius helped Jenny to her feet and started pulling pieces of leaves out of the hair. "But you have to take into account that Kandrok has dozens of times more durable equipment and armor than we do. And what is the guarantee that there will be fights with them on the surface of some planet?"

"I see that you analyze quickly, you have makings of a strategist. I'm delighted that the Kiritians trained you so. It's just a concept for now. Hopefully I can find solutions to all the problems that come with this. A kinetic attack can also be carried out in outer space, for example using high amplitude waves that would break atomic bonds ..."

The doctor started walking away without saying goodbye, waving his finger and muttering to himself.

"Funny man," Jenny concluded.

"He often acts as if detached from reality, but he's a real genius. Are you fine?"

"All good."

"Figam is irreplaceable, don't let appearances deceive you. Remember that it was he who figured out how to immortalize the body and put into use Alcubierre's drive called subspace. Once he was considered a heretic and truther, he was expelled from the university." Darius grimaced, pulling a long splinter from his hand. "Thanks a lot, Chimalmat!"

The she-cat managed to check her daughter - nothing had happened to her, she was just stunned and amazed that for the first time someone had opposed her. The brothers emerged from the bushes, stood aside and looked at the rest with wide eyes. Unlike their sister, they were afraid to approach the two strangers.

Chimalmat cast a reluctant glance at the mutilated privates who had somehow cleaned themselves up.

"What?" Kogan growled. "It's your baby girl who started it."

When the female roared, baring her fangs and raising her whiskers offensively, the younger achij resisted the temptation to reach for the weapon with his hand, waved it, and together with limping Ryan he moved towards the alley.

"I already know what I will call the baby girl," she told Darius and Jenny proudly. "Tukum, or Tearing."

"It will fit perfectly," Sandstorm said with gentle sarcasm.

"Every cloud has a silver lining," summed up the boy philosophically.

***

They stayed with Chimalmat for another three hours, until Aggro returned from his visit to Forkis and began teaching the kittens Onkalot and Kiritian, having once refused to inject them with entrasers. Jenny decided it was time to pull out and leave the guys alone. Schindler found out that it wasn't known for how long he had had his communicator nonfunctional.

"Where are you at?" Lieutenant Seymour said on the air as Darius moved away from the Onkalots. It was as if something in that place had been interfering with the signals. "Dr. Figam is looking for you. You are to go to the Sector B laboratories."

"I talked to him recently, he was in the conservatory. What does he want from me?"

"I don't know, ask him yourself." Tsar turned off.

"If you like, I can go with you," Jenny suggested. In Sector B, which housed laboratories, a recreation center, a server room and an arsenal, as well as a small prison with avors, she had only been once during the awakening of Forkis. The research laboratories were particularly interesting, so much that Sandstorm would have liked to see them again.

They reached a train station, which ran through the air tunnel from the assembly room to the hangars, and got on it.

"Will you come to the party tonight?" Darius asked as they went down an enormous illuminated tunnel to Main Sector A, the seat of power, administration, and communications center, where Jenny also worked in the cafeteria.

"Honestly, somehow I'm not drawn to it. There will probably be many people there." She had grown up with the Bidwell family and rarely seen larger groups of people. As a child, she had preferred to play alone, running in the nearby, safe forest. She was uncomfortable with the thought that she had been forced to live underground, where so many achijes had been squeezed in a relatively small area. Even now, those fifty people in the car were too many for her. She found she was even glad that extroverted Darius liked to keep her company, even though she had firmly said "no" at first.

"Oh, come on. You will meet a lot of new people." He gave her a sincere smile. "There is nothing to be afraid of. Anyway, I'll be with you."

Jenny also responded with a smile, but nice and small.

They arrived at their destination, left the station soon.

As they walked to the next, which connected the sector B to A with a short track, they noticed four achijes leading Rei'than leaning. Avor had his hands locked behind his back with a dhurnsteel band. Kogan or Ryan weren't among the guards who usually looked after the prisoner.

"Interesting ..." Darius walked over to the nearest achij. "Hey, Vaas. What is the Kandrok member doing in this sector?"

"The boss will question him," the Kiritian replied, as it was not confidential information. Schindler stopped, Jenny beside him; the group was moving away.

"So, the jokes will end now," he said.

"Why?"

"Your old man will take care of him. And it will rather hurt."

"How do you know that? You were not among Kiritians when Forkis was alive."

"But I've heard a lot, and the Immortals are truthful. At least they were such during your father's previous rule. I don't mean to offend you or anything like that, but Forkis didn't belong to people caring about finesse. He punished every enemy of the nation with death, he was famous for his brutalism. General Biffter turned out to be the complete opposite."

Jenny didn't answer. For the next seconds, she stared at the door behind which the prisoner and his guards had disappeared, until she sat up at the sound of Tsar's voice in the communicator, who had a business with Darius again.

***

It turned out that Dr. Figam wanted to question Schindler thoroughly about the devices Nacxit used on Amyrade - generally to grill him on the mission Revival. He presented simulations of device models created at an astonishingly rapid pace, and Darius was to determine if the mode of action was similar to the real state. It bore the mark of a military project, in which a small group of people had been initiated so far, so Jenny was politely asked to leave the room, but Figam's assistant, Alejandro Cortez, declared that he would show her the laboratories.

Back in Sector C, Jenny visited Aytar, until the evening they played cards, till Divinus came for the corporal and they both left. Darius had disappeared somewhere again, his PDA was turned off, though he had asked her himself if she would like to go to the party with him. She also failed to establish contact with her mother. The girl decided that she would start breaking the introverted ice and call by Sector A, where the quintessence of *harroweeng* was to be held in the conference room, whatever was behind that term. Not only had Schindler persuaded her to come and play, but also the kitchen staff.

She quickly regretted not having gotten acquainted with the definition of *harroweeng*, imagining it as a common social event, but for Kiritians.

She didn't recognize the place where, just a few hours earlier, everything had been bright, boring, orderly, and functioning like blood cells in the bloodstream of a healthy body. Now chaos prevailed in the nether regions, as if the body had been fighting the super virus.

The floor and walls of the train in which she traveled, even the ceiling, were puked and smelled like alcohol. She even noticed blood. At first, she thought the cabin was broken, but smoke with a pungent, vegetable aroma was not due to a breakdown. There was a beastly drunk man lying on the floor, a young couple, at least visually young, made love in the corner.

As she left the station as quickly as possible, chants, screams, howls, sounds of a brawl and drunken gibberish could be heard from the depths of the dim sector. She ran away from a group of staggering men intertwined with their arms, who were waving towards her bottles made of a biodegradable, horny structure produced by bacteria, and encouraging her to join.

She passed more pairs making wild love, in one of the offices even collective.

Suddenly, a great weight fell on her shoulder, she was pressed with her back against the wall.

"Why are you walking alone? Are you looking for companionship? Then you're in the right place.

Right next to her face some achij was smiling grossly, he didn't smell like alcohol, but his pupils were dilated and his muscles were trembling. His teeth grinned horribly and sleazily, as if he had been hungry, and here he had gotten a delicious cookie.

"Let me pass." Jenny tilted her head to the side to avoid the Kiritian's mouth, which found itself dangerously close to hers.

"Relax, let's have fun."

The girl's heart was pounding in her chest with an increasingly harder and bigger hammer, like in CERN, when the bully-devourers almost got them. From the layers of her mind surfaced the fear she had felt many years earlier when hooligan Cossack had tried to torture her to death in the wilderness.

Just like then, she swung and left five bloody marks on the attacker's face.

She didn't register how it happened that she found herself within two paces of the groaning man, leaning against the wall and holding his face.

Terrified equally by the fact of the attack of the toasted achij and of the manifestation of the incomprehensible phenomenon, she looked at her hand.

She was gasping for breath. Her heart seemed to have split, and now it was drumming at each of her ears.

She had claws like Tukum and Chimalmat - which suddenly hid in the fingers. It wasn't supposed to happen, not while she was awake. She was reassured by the assumption that she was probably hallucinating from the fear and muck in the train cabin. Yes, she certainly imagined everything, just like she had done with Cossack who wanted to take revenge for humiliating him in front of his friends. Then in the forest she must have grabbed a pointed branch. She had been examined more than once, she had been X-rayed, and her skeleton had looked normal, like of any other person.

She remembered Nacxit's amused gaze, who, thanks to his skill, had easily torn recollections out of her memory, and had probably gotten to know Jenny's body on a subatomic level, having control over matter. For him, the phenomenon of accelerated transmutation, alien to a man, had been something familiar and normal, as a ruthless Nimja member he had derived satisfaction from her confusion and fear. She should have spoken to him in the nether regions of CERN back then ...

To the man, staggering, came over the other.

"Hey, leaff heh alonn. She's Fukriss' daughter. There'll be troubble."

"Look what the monkey did to me."

Jenny stepped back, turned around, and started running away. Although she wasn't chased by the achijes, who would have had a problem catching an exuberant turtle in their present state, she stopped, out of breath, only at the conference room. She had to stand for a moment with her hands on her knees to catch her breath. The door was partially ajar and locked for convenience, above it had been attached a skull baring its fangs and scaring with the emptiness of its eye sockets, which Tsar had taken after Nacxit's intervention at CERN. In the room with dimmed lights had gathered a lot of people. Some of the Kiritians were dancing wildly to loud, sharp, bass music, others were sleeping on tables and floors, and aside still others were shamelessly hugging, kissing, even having sex. The whole thing looked as if everyone had spiked themselves sharply or boozed it up.

The image of Kiritians as an oppressed but organized and serious nation collapsed in the girl's mind. Though they had attained immortality and conquered a great deal of space, being trained for centuries by Forkis to kill everything human in them, they had retained many basic instincts, had mundane needs. They reminded of a bunch of lycans now, but with better equipment. Jenny had no intention of investigating whether these people were externalizing their anxiety, stress and anger, which had been suppressed for years, and Forkis' return allowed them to finally de-stress in full flow. She was already shaky enough after meeting that achij anyway, who probably wouldn't remember anything the next day.

In the prevailing chaos, it was difficult to catch specific words, except maybe "Forkis", which was uttered in various emotional forms, but most often with adoration. Jenny understood fair to middling the dialogues taking place at a table just beyond the threshold, where sat Gareth, Kogan, Ryan, and a dozen other men of the lower rank. She tried to spot someone else she knew, but Darius as if had gone underground, Forkis was absent, as was her mother. She assumed that the parents wanted to take care of themselves and make up for the long separation. She noted with some relief that Kiret also didn't participate in the controversial *harroweeng* attractions.

"... he hit him concretely." Kogan's words reached her ears. She glanced at the men sitting mostly with their backs to her, still standing behind the threshold. "Did you see his bruised face?"

"It would have been better if he had finished him off." Ryan took a sip from his mug. In his other hand he held a dying synth-tube with a drug. "He rather won't say more."

"Probably, he will soon go to the laboratories, like the other before," added another achij.

"Let me tell you, gentlemen," Gareth said, with his hands clasped in front of his chest and his eyes fixed on the sticky floor, "that I don't remember Forkis ever making such a thing to a prisoner. If he had one, he killed them quickly. There were rumors that he sometimes locked himself up with a captive and dissolved their body with acid, but no achij saw it, unless the memory of witnesses was wiped."

"Doesn't it seem to you that he came back from beyond the grave changed?" Ryan asked anxiously. He refrained from commenting that the last thing they needed was a madman in power.

"You'd be pissed off, too, if you had lost a part of yourself," Kogan replied. "Especially such unique traits as Onkalot infra-vision and telepathy. Maybe Forkis wants to make up for this damage with aggression by basting the fake enemy?"

"That's possible. Without telepathy, he must feel like without a hand," Gareth continued. "It was the main link shaping our nation ..."

Jenny had had enough; she stepped back and gave the entrance a wide berth.

She wanted to be in her dwelling as soon as possible and lock herself up there, but choosing the shortest path to Sector C probably meant meeting the achij who had been trying to hurt her. There were a lot of people around, some of them were accosting her with their eyesight. And she wanted to be alone now.

She came to the train station, running on the short route to Sector B, where the laboratories were located. Since areas A and B were close together, it was possible to walk from one to the other through a stile, which Sandstorm did - she wasn't going to enter another filthy cabin, much less be in a closed area with drunken achijes. She decided to sit a little in the quieter sector, calm down, and maybe somehow get back to her dwelling indirectly.

The science facilities were closed. She didn't meet many Kiritians along the way, practically only workaholics trapped in aquariums, including the research team led by Figam.

She misinterpreted the underground plans or saw ones outdated, because she didn't find a small train station in the eastern part of the building, but ended up in a dimly lit corridor with an empty gatehouse glued to it. The hall led to a door, behind which was the last room.

Her pulse jumped once more that evening as she realized where she was.

The door slid open without resistance, the room with cells - and only one occupied - was as dimly lit as the sector's east wing corridor. Jenny stood uncertainly on the threshold for a moment. If anyone was watching the prisoner, ignored the fact that the unauthorized person had gotten inside, believing in the reliability and thickness of the bars, or had contact with reality only through the side of an empty bottle. She thought that the Kiritians really must have trusted each other since there had been such incidents, but either way, the only 'intruders' here were she, the Onkalots, and Rei'than. She remembered Darius mentioning a broken celula, she looked at the corner of the room under the ceiling, and there was indeed a tiny black plate that looked like a ring stone. Since it was damaged, the girl should have gotten out of here as soon as possible, but for some reason she had ceased to feel anxious, and she had no feeling that she was acting inappropriately being in this place. She even turned off her PDA so that no one located her and she didn't have to listen to a reprimand later. It was not her fault that someone ignored the security procedures, the prisoner behind solid bars wouldn't hurt her either, if she looked at him a little, in the worst case he spat in her direction, and then she would pay him back.

At first, she thought Rei'than had fallen asleep curled up on the floor, but as she approached the bars and crouched down, she realized what batab Gareth had meant by interrogation. Though she looked at the enemy whose nation wanted to kill the people of the Zodiac Universum, regret gripped her heart.

Many spots on the avor's body devoid of strength were marked by bruises of dark shades of purple, scarlet, and brown, clearly visible on the white skin. Wounds inflicted with a sharp instrument were also present, some of them were so severe that the blood was still oozing, forming small puddles on the ground. Blood as red as human. Rei'than's eyes were half-closed, his breathing was rapid, wheezing and alarmingly shallow. He must have been thrown like this into the cell after being questioned, no one even cared that he might have needed urgent help.

The avor's hand lay limp between the bars, a small bean-like object rested nearby. Jenny took it carefully and brought it to her face to get a better look at it.

She managed to conclude that he wasn't a biological creation when the avor spoke to her:

"Tanagri devoka. Lumuta. I guess it belongs to me." He had a soft, weak, husky voice. He moved his head and lifted his eyelids with difficulty to look at the newcomer. In the twilight, his eyes with enormous irises looked like illuminated amber, ghastly and beautiful at the same time.

Jenny didn't answer, after a moment's hesitation she placed the 'bean' in his hand, which he closed and pulled back behind the bars.

"It's you," the Kandrok member continued. "I saw you then ... outside. You must be his daughter. You look so much like him." With his bloody mouth, he gave her a sneering, pained smile. He shuddered in a parody of rippling chuckles that ended in a grimace from pain. "He sent you to finish the job?"

He had a coughing fit, which cost him more milliliters of blood.

It was an impulse. The girl got up, she couldn't leave the dying man in such a state, no matter if he was an enemy or a friend.

"Don't move, I'll get you some medication right away."

He didn't protest, although she had expected it. Even if he despised the human race and its help, in his agonized state he must have ceased to care.

In designated areas of each sector, there were cabinets with essential medications to which everyone had access. The closest one was near the empty gatehouse, Jenny took a container from it and threw inside molecular glue, gauze, bandages, disinfectants and remedies to stop bleeding. Returning, she thought of the Kandrok member's clothing that was in tatters, so she set the box on the ground and walked closer to the research department for some clothes. She found a coatroom of the research workers empty and open, she took the two-piece laboratory clothes from the pile in a locker.

When she returned, the Kandrok prisoner was lying in the same position in which she had left him. It would have been most convenient to open the bars and take care of him, but even in his present state it didn't seem like a wise move, moreover, the lock actuator, had one of the guardhouse privates. Since no one had looked into the room so far, they probably didn't know that Jenny was at the cell. She had to deal with the prisoner herself.

"Can you clean yourself up on your own?" She asked.

Rei'than tilted his head back and glanced at the contents of the box.

"Molecular glue doesn't work on me, it is not adapted to my genome. The same for the preparation that causes clotting. Give me some saline, I will wash myself at least."

Jenny poured the liquid generously on the gauze and pulled it under the grate.

The avor tried to sit up, but managed to get a few centimeters up before he fell down with a grunt and clenched teeth. He also moved his hand as if it had weighed a ton.

Sandstorm sighed. The prisoner didn't seem to be the one to pretend to let the victim come close in the oldest trick in the universe and then brutally attack. She grabbed the gauze, settled herself properly on her feet, prepared for a sharp jump.

"I'll help you, but you are to lie down and not move. If you upset me with something, I will go for good."

"Wrigo lumuta," Rei'than replied. "But first, I have a request. Make the light as strong as possible. This darkness is destroying me. They did it on purpose to make me suffer even more."

Jenny got up, walked over to the regulator on the wall, and moved the holo-indicator to the right. The twilight turned to bright halogen light that made her eyes ache.

"Yes ... Perfect. Leave it so," the prisoner announced. His pupils became as small as a pin prick and his irises turned yellow, which made them look even scarier. But at least it was a sign that part of the prisoner's nervous system was functioning flawlessly.

Mentally admonishing herself, "What am I doing?" Jenny returned to her previous place. She crouched down in the 'run away' position again, carefully slipped her hand through the bars, ready to react violently if the stranger really tried to lull her. But Rei'than lay still, only his side was slightly rising.

The Kandrok member's skin felt human to the touch, perhaps a little harder, and - except for the head - hairless, warm with fever. The girl gently wiped the blood from his body wherever she could reach, changed the gauze frequently.

"I wouldn't have let you do that if I hadn't been called," Rei'than began to say at one point. "I have to live. I considered taking the last rajithar capsule, it wouldn't have healed my wounds, but it would have given me strength. Your friends are feeding me plants here, I'm still weak."

"They're not my friends." The image of the young achij who had been trying to get to her appeared again in her mind. "I'm not even an Immortal. You speak Kiritian well. I've heard somewhere that you learn very quickly."

"It's thanks to this." The strong light really had a pro-health effect on him, because he touched his head with his finger without any effort. With a grunt, he flopped over onto his back and got to the bars as close as possible. Jenny pulled up the ragged fabric of his sweatshirt and started washing his chest. She felt abashed when Rei'than looked shamelessly at her.

"Have you been injected with an entraser?"

He chuckled briefly.

"No, I have something much better. This is a neurocyte, our invention. It is applicable in every area of life, from communication to control. It's enough to tell me something, and I will remember it. Years of being with you were enough for me to master your speech to perfection, understand the context of your utterance, learn a lot about your culture, references, and the way of reasoning. Although many things are still incomprehensible to me. The entraser doesn't work on Kandrok, but," he smiled unpleasantly, so that Jenny shivered, "if you injected a devoka member with the neurocyte, they would be completely under our control. It would then be easy to deprive them of not only free will but also personality."

"Neurocyte isn't a word from your language, is it?" This avor even seemed nice to her, although it was probably due to his weakness or deliberate play. In any case, he didn't look like the bloodthirsty fanatical beast she'd heard about every time in relation to Kandrok.

"No, exceptionally it comes from the Lightbringer. It was he who gave us this invention, which is mainly used to control minds."

"Is that a god of yours? Leader? Did you literally translate the title from your language, or so that I could understand it? Because we too have a similar complexity in our culture. *Lux ferre.*" After Rei'than dismissed the comment with silence and piercing her unpleasantly with his eyes, she asked another question: "What is devoka?"

"Our term for your people."

"How many languages do you use in society?" She was really getting into this dialogue, especially since Rei'than, surprisingly, was effusive.

"All Kandrok members as a super-collective say one. It is the same everywhere, there are no vernaculars. This is due to the neurocyte program imposed by the gerha. The neurocyte also allows us to easily master the speeches of other intelligent species."

"Since we are genetically different," the girl was washing his forehead, "how is it possible that the neurocyte affects humans?"

"Although it hardly passes through my throat, a long time ago we were like you, we developed in the same way. Our modern inventions can even be connected to very old ones.

Both those created by Kandrok and every civilization with digital technology."

"The principle of compatibility," she concluded. "Kiret has told me about it. Kiritians has also started to use it, in the past due to the pluralism of devices there were problems with their repair or connecting to each other."

It amazed her that she liked to talk to the prisoner, even when there was a palpable animosity between them.

"I'm done," she announced as the last trace of blood vanished from Rei'than's body. She gave him some saline to rinse the blood off his mouth and teeth.

"Rigab lumut." He managed to sit up on his own.

"What does it mean?"

"Thank you, little star." His every smile looked sarcastic.

She smiled too, but incredulously and involuntarily.

"Why are you talking to me like that?"

"You came like the saving light of a star from darkness. Likum lumuta."

She didn't know how to interpret it - was he mocking her, or was he indeed grateful?

Whatever was his intention, he surprised her with these words, made her feel better. Out of principle, Jenny was annoyed by any terms of endearment addressed to her that sounded like they were turning to a child, but this time she wasn't. She hadn't expected such a response from the mouth of the tortured prisoner, rather insulting, ridiculing or refusing help. However, she knew Kandrok only from stories, mostly ones coming from Kiret.

"So, you don't think anymore that I want to kill you?" She asked haughtily.

"I would do it without hesitation if the bars ceased to be an obstacle. Don't think that your act has changed my approach to devoka."

Though she hadn't divested herself of a serene expression, the words hurt her slightly.

"But I helped you. Doesn't Kandrok's creed, or whatever you have, require you to spare those who may save you from death?"

Rei'than stared indifferently into her eyes for a moment. The girl could be very useful to him, so he didn't want to discourage her too much, and many of the facts from Kandrok's life would have certainly ruined the psyche of this young creature. And so much that without drugs like Kiritian alhedrimucosin, she would have had sleepless nights. But he couldn't be too nice at the same time, because it would have looked suspicious. Backing off with a glance to a side, he changed the subject:

"Can you tell me your name?" He reached under the bunk for a small cylinder with a siphon. Using his thumb, he injected several generous doses of air into his nostrils, then exhaled, content; a sense of relief smoothed his face.

"What are you doing?"

"One of your scientists constructed it for me. From time to time, I have to saturate my blood with a large amount of carbon dioxide. In the Cargoo atmosphere, there not enough of it for me. The lungs of the Unemancipated are adapted to conditions other than human."

Focused on the avor's words, Sandstorm blurted out as if automatically:

"I'm Jenny."

The Kandrok member's eyes flashed angrily. He put down the inhaler.

"That Jenny? Which Skelver was supposed to kill?"

"Apparently something went wrong." The girl moved out of reach of his hands and sat cross-legged. "Then he betrayed you, and recently even helped me and Kiret. Admittedly, he had a barrel put to his back, but he didn't play up, he even turned out to be useful."

Rei'than gripped the bars with his hands.

"As you can see, I'm imprisoned, also cut off from information. The only thing the Kiritians tell me are the accounts of our failures. They have given me one such piece of news over the course of the Terran years."

"I got the hint. Forget it, I won't tell you anything."

He smiled sarcastically, tilted his head.

"Careful, I might run right away and report it to my own."

Jenny looked at him coolly. The earlier sympathy for this avor was displaced by irritation. She could leave him without help, weakened, he would have been more bearable.

"Why did you want to kill me? As well as Kiret and my mother?"

"Now also your father joined this long list."

"I can see that you don't lack human sense of humor."

"When you sit in the blood for a long time, you get soaked with its scent."

"Is that your proverb? Do you take baths in guts?"

"No, I have made that up myself. And your guts are a great, high-energy source of kunhikar."

She found that even when they joshed each other about black humor, she enjoyed talking to him. The earlier anger turned out to be temporary and had already burned out.

Rei'than grew serious.

"I'm just a lousy, semi-autonomous umen, or rather, I was. I follow orders. Questions about assassination orders should be directed to the gerha, whose actions are probably guided by the Lightbringer. But you are not worthy to see or hear any of them."

"Supposedly, when you attack another species, you first kill the authority and anyone who can be in it."

"So, you ask what you already know. That's exactly right, these are even my words that I uttered in one of your cute interrogations." The last point could be replaced with a contemptuous spit. "But I don't know the gerha's will."

"He's some kind of king?"

"You could put it that way in your speech."

Instinctively, Jenny looked at her PDA watch and remembered that she must have turned on the assistant, but sensed she had been with Rei'than for over an hour. And she would have been happy to stay for another, having a lot of questions for him, but at any moment someone could come into the room. It completely slipped her mind that she was going to test her telepathic abilities on the avor. She decided to do it another time. She would officially ask for permission to do the tests.

"I gotta go." She pushed fresh clothes folded into a cube under the bars. " Change these torn and dirty rags. If they ask who helped you, then ... come up with something, but don't reveal that it was me."

"So, you're here illegally, little star." He smiled in amusement.

"I wouldn't put it that way. I wandered here quite by accident. So ... bye."

She scooped up the container, stood up, and left as quickly as possible without looking back. It was strange for her to admit it to herself, but she felt somewhat cleansed by this spontaneous discussion with the person unknown and alien in every sense of the word. She realized that she had long missed something like this. Conversations with Darius tired her, with Kiret she felt awkward, and he ignored her anyway, Aytar had a cold personality, Chimalmat corrupted the speech and talked like a haunted madwoman, while Aggro was constantly serious and worried about something. Her biological parents also completely disregarded her, the prospect of the impending war wasn't an excuse not to find a moment for their own daughter, who had lived in isolation for years, and recently had barely made it out alive and was still traumatized by it. And today this damn achij had been added to the collection ..."

In the gatehouse, she threw the waste into a trash can and hid it under the piles of garbage, carefully rinsed the container and put it back in its place. She checked for any blood stains on her. Who had helped the prisoner would be a problem for Kogan and Ryan, who probably lay under the table now, so it would be easy to bullshit them.

As she sneaked past the labs, she ran on a bend into Kiret, standing and focused on his PDA. The admission of guilt immediately manifested on her face; it reflected in her eyes like in a dog that has stained the carpet.

Biffter, who looked tired and worried, interpreted it, however, in his own way.

"Good evening, Jenny. Don't bother Dr. Figam now because he has a lot of work to do."

"Sure, the door to his studio is locked anyway," she blurted out without thinking. "I've just been on my way back to Sector A. Why are your clothes damp?"

Kiret glanced at his shirt and pants.

"I was swimming in the pool. I didn't feel like drying off thoroughly."

There was indeed a leisure center nearby.

The girl had a certain thought, after which, without thinking it through, she went rogue; talking to Rei'than seemed to give her a boost. Such an occasion that Necron wasn't busy and hadn't a mass of achijes around him might not repeat itself for a long time.

"Kiret, can we talk?" She timidly ran her fingers through her hair.

"What's going on there?" He kept his eyes on the PDA projector.

"But in some more comfortable place, where we can sit down. Not like that in the middle of the corridor."

He sighed, turned off the device.

"Alright, come on. But fast."

They headed for the train station, the route to the adjacent sector was barely two hundred meters long.

"I thought you were with the rest of the dignitaries."

"Forkis, Warfighter, your mother and I had a terrible fight," Biffter replied, rubbing his temple.

"Can I know over what?"

"The division of responsibilities. Forkis is going to recreate the Council, but this time he doesn't want Anna on it."

Jenny realized that Kiret must have trusted her, or what he had just confessed was no secret at all in this base.

"Is he suspecting Anna of having an affair with Warfighter and going to punish her for it without giving any reason?" She wondered. Perhaps Forkis had succumbed to the pressure of what was so secretly said - that Anna, a minor by Immortal standards, had once been on the Council on his whim and only so that he could have an expert on rebels with him? Jenny didn't understand the meanders of politics, though she constantly learned something new by chance, but she was sure that Kiritians and the rebels weren't currently on the warpath.

"And what was it about in your case?" She continued asking after.

"Generally speaking, my views on many things about the future are completely different from those of Forkis. I also have a feeling that Warfighter will support whatever he comes up with."

"It doesn't sound interesting. After all, you and Forkis were friends once."

"Anyway, these aren't matters that you should be concerned about." He smiled artificially, running a hand over her cheek.

Still quite a few people wandered in Sector A, but this time Jenny felt safe having Kiret with her.

Next to the communications center there were former mining anexes, which had been transformed into masked sky observatories, creating small rooms at each. Kiret chose the smallest of them, for private astronomical sessions, semicircular, resembling the inside of an insect's eye and illuminated in blue. They went inside. There were muffled *harroweeng* noises coming from the background, but they didn't disturb the conversation.

Necron rested his seat and hands on a table.

"What did you want to talk about?" In order not to waste time, he turned on holographic reports from the last hours on the activity in the far orbit of this part of the planet.

Jenny felt embarrassed now, even panic. All her earlier verve had vanished. The lighting changed the color of the girl's skin, so blush on her face wasn't visible.

"We have hardly spoken to each other since we arrived on Cargoo." She came up with the relatively safe topic on the spot, from which she should have quickly gotten to the point. As long as intimidation allowed her to continue. "And I would be interested in a serious matter."

"Namely?"

"Am I fit to be a Kiritian?"

The hand with which Necron had been moving the images, he lowered onto his thigh. For the first time since the beginning of this conversation, he glanced more sharply at Sandstorm.

"Unfortunately, no," he wanted to give utter to it more delicately, but for lack of an idea he chose to be direct. "I'm sorry."

"Why?" Jenny defiantly put her hands on her hips.

"You're too young. You could die."

Kogan and Ryan are of a similar age to mine. I mean they were."

"Who are they?"

"The privates who look after the prisoner. I saw them outside. Darius told me they had been kiritianized at nineteen and twenty. Besides, I'm not saying that I want to get infected now. Maybe in a few years."

"Psychologically, you are also unfit. I'm sorry," repeated Kiret. He spoke softly, fully focused on Jenny. "You are too sensitive, the prospect of the passing of anything that isn't related to Kiritians would quickly overwhelm you. And I don't think you wish you were brainwashed. This changes a human's personality, their memories are destroyed, and thus they lose part of their own essence."

"What would overwhelm me?" That wasn't the main topic of conversation she was going to initiate, but Necron's words shocked her. She was as nervous as she had been with Rei'than, who had spoken so openly that he would have killed her without hesitation.

"You want to deprive me of the privilege of everlasting life? Apart from the Bidwells, all my relatives are Immortals. It is rather they whom you will make suffer as they have to watch me grow old and die."

"I haven't expected psychological terror from you." Necron smiled to ease the tension.

"But it won't be up to you anyway. Even if you find yourself on the new Council, others will also have a say."

"Unless Forkis becomes the only decision-maker he once was when the Council of Dignitaries existed merely to support him, relieving him of more trivial matters." He went back to viewing reports. "However, the basis for kiritianization are not sentiments and family ties, but medical and psychological research. So this is your reason why you would like to undergo kiritianization: eternal life? Did you know your father rejected all applicants for that argument?"

Jenny sat down opposite the man to get his attention back to her. The shifting holographs caused the play of green and yellow lights on her silhouette.

"And who did he accept?"

"At the very beginning, the rich people with certain psychological traits, you know - he needed finance to lay the foundations of a military nation. He also established cooperation with sponsors. Then for achijes he looked for fanatics, patriots, faithful to our ideals, devoted to the cause to the last drop of blood. Those for whom the glory and eternity of the nation mattered. Also, people with valuable talents that could be of great service to the community."

"Then I will prove that I am worthy of you."

"I will be rooting for you." Necron put a hand on her shoulder and shook it briefly. "Who knows what the future holds?"

Sandstorm bit her lip. It was high time for the drawing card of this conversation. It was better to say something stupid (though Kiret was not one of those people who would have taken such matters lightly) and make a fool of yourself in front of the single witness than later sweat for not trying out of lack of courage. And it took months for her to collect so much of it that she had in this neurotic moment.

"Kiret." She grabbed his hand and slipped it off her shoulder. She turned off the reports with her other hand. The man looked at Jenny with interest. "I have to say it at last. It has been inside me for many years, it doesn't pass ... so it's not a temporary quirk ... I like you very much," she blurted out stiffly. "This is not a crush because otherwise it would have been over a long time ago. Not a day goes by when I don't think about you for long hours, and the visit to Earth has brought me even closer to you, deepened my feelings. I'd like to be with you. Look." From the pocket of her sweatshirt, she took a blue flower bell embedded in a crystal." She smiled at the beautiful memories. "Do you remember? I ran away from the house, beat Cossack in the woods, and then you had to follow me in armor onto the roof of the house after I sulked. You gave it to me then."

Sandstorm surprised him only slightly. He had supposed that was how the conversation would turn out. He took the crystal from her, turned it with his fingers.

"I remember that flower. You preserved it nicely. I gave it to you because it just fell on my head while climbing vines. I didn't expect you to make a talisman out of it." He smiled at her soothingly. "Jenny, I've known about everything for a long time. I'm glad that you finally brought up this topic openly."

She felt very relieved that the confession didn't end in a total cataclysm, but everything turned out calmly.

"Then why don't you do anything about it? I have the impression that you ignore me ostentatiously."

Kiret hid the girl's hands in his, looked honestly in her eyes.

"You surely know it, Jenny. Mentally, I am many centuries older than you. Even if you take into account my artificially maintained biological age, I am twice as old as you. Your teenage feeling for me is from the category of feelings you have for a mentor, teacher, or someone famous you are infatuated with. It's an ephemeral affect. Although I try to take you seriously, I naturally see you as a child. Look, you're a kid to me, Jenny. I remember when you were so little." He made a gesture with his hands. "I had you in my arms. I wouldn't be able to look at myself in the mirror if I had an affair with someone so young, so trusting, who doesn't know life. I have the same feeling for you as a father has for his daughter."

She pulled her hands out of his warm hold. She was looking at the leg of the table.

"So, you're brushing me off."

"No, I have great respect for you. I'm doing it for your own good. Someday, when you really fall in love, with the right person close to you in age, mentality and interests, you will thank me for everything. I guarantee."

"And that's probably why you're trying to palm Darius off on me." She scowled at him. "You think I don't know it's your doing?"

"He himself is willing to spend time with you, of his own free will. He's a good young achij, although a little quick-tempered."

"He's okay, but not my type. But even if something sparked, we would only have a few years for ourselves, because then I will start to turn into an old woman. It won't work."

She would have extended this conversation, exchanged arguments, but mentally she began to break down. She moved towards the exit before tears welled up in her eyes - she wanted to keep her dignity and not show her sadness at all costs.

Kiret nervously ran his hand over his shaved head.

"Jenny ..." he whispered. The girl stopped. "Know that I like you very much and I always will. Just like you can always turn to me with any problem."

"It is you that I should name my father, but that's not what I've meant for a long time. One more thing: can I practice my skills on the prisoner?"

"Of course, but don't go there alone, but each time with a guard. The Kandrok member is locked up, but who knows what this monster is capable of."

"For example, of dying alone and suffering after these humane interrogations of yours," she wanted to say sarcastically, but abstained and stuck to her resolve to leave the observatory with dignity.

"You should get some monitoring in the sectors, or soon everything will go haywire," she said at the end.

She came across private Shimizu in the corridor, whom she associated from Earth. He was sober, coming back from watch on the surface. Since the barracks were in the same sector as

Jenny's apartment, she asked him to accompany her. She didn't mention out of shame that she was afraid of drunken achijes and that she had almost been abused by one of them, but blamed everything on her lack of orientation in the nether regions.

After locking the door to her apartment, she collapsed with her back on the bed. Mentally, she didn't have the strength to wash or change, she ignored the hunger. In her present state, she was only capable of lying still and staring at the ceiling. She changed into her nightgown with difficulty.

A dream didn't want to come, constantly distracted by unpleasant thoughts. She knew that Kiret had behaved faultlessly and had made the best possible decision, but she was still terribly sorry that her multiannual feeling had reached such an end. But what did she expect? Damp marks appeared on the cheeks. To the notch of the gripe added also the consciousness that just like Jenny had no chance to be with Kiret, she was also deprived of the possibility of being immortal.

***

Kiret had long been sitting in the room since the girl's footsteps died out in the corridor. He noticed that she had left her talisman. He took it, looked at it blankly, turned it a few times, focusing on the reflexes, then hid it in his pants pocket.

10. The prisoner

In the morning she was awakened by a knocking on the metal door, something she had never witnessed in this base. Information was given electronically when there was an intention to meet someone.

Despite yesterday's emotions, she had slept quite well, but she would have rather lied a little longer; she got out of bed reluctantly.

"Jenny, it's me." She recognized Aggroteh's nervous voice at the door. That's true, raised in the Chulimal jungles, the Onkalot had a different concept of manners. She opened, sleepy.

"Is Tukum here?" Clad in a poncho and knee-length maxtlatl covering hips, the humanoid jaguar glanced over her shoulder.

"No, what happened? Come on in, Aggro."

He passed her in the aisle.

"Chimalmat and I have been looking for her for several hours. She never disappeared for that long. We raked the entire palm house."

"But why would she be in this sector? She would have had to travel a few kilometers by train and go through many corridors, unnoticed." Jenny sat down on the bed. "Don't worry. She's probably sitting somewhere among leaves, watching you and having fun that you are looking for her. She was already doing that with me. Ask someone for a bioctovisor or a nuclo-indector, and you will find her in no time."

"That's exactly what I did. Victor Shane himself was helping me look for Tukum when he came back from breakfast. The device broke down."

"Then you could have taken the second."

"Can you believe the next one broke down too? And in the same place."

"Then what? Any diversion?"

The captain joked so too.

Jenny got up.

"If you want, I'll help you search."

"Thank you. I'll take a look at the barracks, maybe Tukum actually got into a car and is rummaging somewhere in the sector."

"Will you wait for me? I'll be ready right away."

Aggro left to wait by a tree in the hallway.

As Jenny was putting on her underwear after taking a shower, the PDA grumbled on the quilt. She accepted the call; a holographic image of Victor Shane was displayed in the air. At first, Sandstorm thought the man had found the little Onkalot girl.

"Good morning, Jenny." The captain smiled perfunctorily. "Today you're off work, General Warfighter has arranged everything. Please come to the gate of the communications center, and I'll pick you up there."

"Did something happen?"

"You'll find out on the spot. See you later." The man turned off.

Jenny became concerned. It had probably come to light that she had seen the Kandrok member without anyone's permission and helped him. The matter was serious, but not so serious as to involve the top itself. So, what could it have been about?

Having put on a black and orange skintight dress reaching beyond things found in the cupboard, black leggings, gray knee-length gaiters as well as boots, she went out into the corridor. She apologized to Aggroteh, explained the situation, and promised to assist with the search once she clarified the matter to Shane.

There were two routes stretching from Sector C to A: a double train ride with a break for passage across Building F, which was devoted to research mainly on weapons, or a direct link to the west. Sandstorm chose the second option, to get there faster and be shut off from the problem.

There were quite a few people in the vast communications center. The girl wasn't given the opportunity to wait long on the appointed spot, because the technician Corporal Darkoris, a pale-faced, freckled achij with red hair trimmed into long rows, came up to her and ordered her to go to one of the rooms on the right. He announced her, then walked away.

Captain Shane answered the door.

"Oh, it's good that you are so soon. Please come in, child."

The small room was simply furnished, suitable for private conversations. Viktor staying in it had, as usual, a pleasant timbre of voice, and in addition he smiled reassuringly, having noticed the uncertainty of the newcomer at first glance of the soldier's eye. He asked her to take a seat in a chair by his desk. He himself sat opposite her, put his hands on the table, and laced his fingers.

"Did I do something wrong?" She asked.

"Of course not. Relax." His broad smile was enough to ease the anxiety to an almost imperceptible level. "Would you like something to drink? Maybe you want a cookie?"

"Thanks, but no. I haven't eaten breakfast yet."

Viktor connected with some achij over the intercom and told him to bring a meal to his office.

"The case is like that." He unclasped his hands and tapped them on the top. "It's been a while since you arrived on Cargoo, but before, we had no way to take care of you. There was always something coming up. Hope you remember the events on Earth in some detail. General Warfighter has requested that you submit a comprehensive report on this. Also tell about everything that have happened since leaving Atla with Mr. Biffter."

Jenny noted that the former emperor hadn't been addressed with any title. She began to consider whether it was possible that all his prerogatives had been taken away so quickly. Maybe this was what he had been worried about a day earlier when she had met him at the sector B labs?

She delicately reached into the captain's mind, and it turned out that he was completely distracted from the dialogue, his thoughts were oscillating around his wife - and child. The couple would have liked to have a descendant, so they had to turn to Forkis, who would officially grant permission to restore fertility to both sides for the duration of the intercourse. Shane wasn't worried about refusal, many Kiritians had lost their lives in recent years and the nation's natality was even required. There was also recruiting involved.

"So, I just have to tell you what has happened?"

"Exactly."

The charm of Viktor's smile and kindness ceased to affect her. It was slowly starting to look like they assigned her Shane, whom she liked for his serenity, to gain her trust and loosen her tongue. She sensed that there was some hidden agenda in the request."

"But what for?"

"Mr. Biffter also made such report. We want to know every detail, especially what you remember about Kandrok and what you saw on the planet. You would describe everything: your emotions, feelings, step by step, what you did, what decisions were made. Everything will be recorded." He pointed to his PDA.

She didn't know much about questioning, but she had the impression that the main problem, which was Kandrok, that Wiktor put as the merits, was a less important matter. So, what did the Kiritians need?

An android came into the office and placed a tray in front of Jenny with slices of bread, a mass of meat and vegetables, chestnut butter, a few fruits, and a glass and a jug of juice.

Viktor encouraged her to have a snack, and he himself left for a few minutes, under the guise of arranging some sort of errand.

Before he returned, Jenny had finished eating alone. After the meal, she felt much better mentally. This time her thoughts didn't go towards the assumption that it could also be a psychological stunt - a full man with a sense of security was sometimes more cooperative.

Sometimes stopped by Viktor's questions, she began telling her adventures from the moment Kiret flew to Atla for her after Skelver had warned him about Kandrok's mercenaries. She described the chase in space, the unintentional flight of the damaged 'Perfarius' to Earth, confusing the avors hunting them, the unequal struggle of the planetary defense of the Earth with the intruders, and then subsequent days of wandering around the uninhabited, postglacial areas of the planet. She ended at the moment the Kiritians left CERN's nether regions and encountered the Headhunters. Reporting took several hours with breaks.

"You did great. Thank you, that's all from me." Getting up, Viktor glanced at the PDA. "I've just gotten the information that you should wait a little longer."

He sat down again; Jenny hadn't had time to move.

To her surprise, the office was entered by General Velkee Warfighter.

"Hi, Jenny." He walked over to the table and put his fists on it. "Thanks, Wiktor, you can go."

"Of course, sir."

Shane left the room.

The general pierced the girl for a moment with the cool blue of his right eye, the opaque left one too, looking like that of a hunting shark. There was no kindness or anger in the man's unusual gaze, but only professional indifference. However, the smile that appeared under the gray mustache didn't mean anything good. Jenny no longer doubted that the Kiritians were trying to get some specific information from her. Something could have gone wrong with Viktor, so they sent the much larger and more dangerous fish.

Velkee looked for similarities in Sandstorm's appearance to that of her parents.

"I'm acting on behalf of your father." He sat in the captain's seat, leaned back in the chair with an adjustable headrest, and crossed his legs. "I wanted to take care of you personally, but something stopped me. Fortunately, Captain Victor Shane did his job well. Don't worry, it'll be short, and I'll let you go. I just want to ask you a few questions."

"Then why won't my father question me himself?"

"Now he has no time, but soon you will be spending many hours a day together. You will help probing achijes' minds," he added, seeing her questioning gaze.

"What if I don't want to do this? Anyone asked for my opinion at all?"

"You have an extraordinary gift, perhaps the only one among all Kiritians and Oderses. You shouldn't be wasting it. This precious link will have a profound effect on the course of the future war with Kandrok, whereby the Immortals will have devoted, righteous achijes. Coming back to the overriding point of our meeting: I am referring specifically to Mr. Biffter.

During your stay on Earth, did you notice anything disturbing about him?"

"I don't understand."

The general leaned forward; his face got closer to the girl's. He was looking into her eyes all the time, studying every reaction. Jenny felt uneasy again. Warfighter was in the fourth calendar century of his life, he was one of the oldest Kiritians, so he could probably spot the hypocrisy on the human face flawlessly, in the slightest twitch of the smallest muscle, in the nervous movement of the eyeball. He didn't need telepathy for that.

So that was what it had all been about from the beginning - Necron. And it probably had to do with his mood a day earlier. What could they have wanted from him?

The riddle was solved by Warfighter himself, making no secret of anything:

"In your opinion, did he make some wrong decisions? Was he nervous? Was he aggressive towards you?"

"I didn't notice anything strange," she replied after a moment of silence and reflection, in no way wanting to harm Necron. "He was behaving properly all the time; I would say perfectly. He defended me against mutants, people and animals."

"Yhymm." The general nodded, still pinning Jenny with his eyes. "Would you like to add something?"

"No."

He leaned back.

"If you remember anything important you didn't mention, report to Captain Shane."

"Of course."

"From today on, you will be working with Dr. Figam. Go see him in the afternoon. You're free now."

She would have gladly reminded the man that she was very far from being an achij, so she was not under his orders, but she preferred not to expose herself and add extra baggage of nerves. She sensed that it would have been best if she had pretended to be naive and submissive.

"Thank you, General. Goodbye." She got up and headed for the door.

"Go finally, girl." He waved his hand. About two minutes after she left, he activated the PDA intercom. "Mr. Emperor, we have everything we need. The girl lied, she defended Biffter."

"Thanks, Velkee." From Forkis' impassive tone on the other hand nothing could be deduced.

***

Aquariums with a variety of small organisms were a frequent element of décor in the nether regions - easy to maintain, improving the mood with their colors and interesting content. They stood in corridors, apartments and places of larger gatherings. Also, in the laboratories of sector A, several tanks were set up to please the eyes and mind.

Dr. Maksimum Figam observed small hydromedusas, barely half a centimeter in diameter, which in the dim lighting of the room emitted the blue of antennae and bells, and contrastively, the orange of gonads. Several polyps were attached to pebbles on the bottom, once they had been adults that regressed in biological development.

"*Turritopsis nutricula*," Figam said, with his nose close to a puronax shield, and hands resting above his knees. "Such a small, simple, inconspicuous thing, and it hides the secret of immortality towards which mankind has been striving for millennia. And to think that this midget laid the foundations for our nation, you might put it that way. There is strength in simplicity. And beauty." He tapped a side of the aquarium. The organisms didn't react.

Forkis, clad in light armor, was standing nearby, with his arms folded over his chest. Anna Sandstorm sat next to him. At the end of the room, in a brighter area, Alejandro Cortez was preparing the equipment for the upcoming tests.

"However, it was only the wise mind that gave Kiritians such a desired and rare gift of nature." Forkis approached the old man. "We are immortal only thanks to you. Too bad you strayed from this path, doctor. History has never had a better scientist. This wisdom should be kept forever."

"Taking again the super virus now at my age would be dangerous."

"Yes, risky, but not impossible. Think it through again, Figam," said the Emperor confidentially as he stood close to him. They both stared at the immortal jellyfish. The door to the lab opened and Jenny entered.

"Hi everyone. Why is it so dark here?"

"Hi." Andro waved his hand, not taking his eyes off the apparatus.

"Good morning, Jenny," Forkis replied. "We've just been watching the hydromedusas. They shine beautifully in twilight and darkness."

"It does look nice. I only have fish in my dwelling." Jenny approached the aquarium.

"Andro, turn up the light," Figam asked after the girl had seen enough.

Cortez restored standard brightness for lab work.

The doctor clapped his hands and rubbed them together.

"What do you say? Are you ready, my dear? Come closer. Andro, get the equipment. So, Jenny, the intensive work related to your telepathy will begin today. General Velkee Warfighter will be recreating the constant Kiritian army, and this cannot be done until we are sure that everyone on Cargoo remains faithful to the First Galactic Dignitary, who, as you probably already know, is Forkis now." The Emperor nodded as Figam and then the others looked in his direction for a moment. "You are very important to us, Jenny. Would you allow me to do research on you? Apart from a few injections, it will be non-invasive and completely painless."

The girl knew that the question was a formality, and she couldn't give an answer other than a confirmatory one. If she had refused, Forkis would have pressured her and even forced her to make a specific decision that would have remained voluntary only in nomenclature. And he could have done it, since there were no family ties forged between them, nay, even on the friend or colleague level. Here she realized that she and her father were simply strangers. She had already seen what he was capable of when Rei'than had objected to him in questioning, especially since Cargoo scientists had failed to produce a truth serum that would have worked on him. Until now, Tsar Seymour had achieved the best effect with his drugs, but they remained dangerous to the prisoner who was evolutionarily unfit for such drugs, and Rei'than was still needed, moreover, speaking while being high didn't go hand in hand with credibility of the testimony.

Jenny suspected Figam was acting on Forkis' orders and had little to say in case of the research," he was bound by the need to be grateful for his rescue from planet B9.

"I agree," she replied.

"Cool. Today's test will be simple. We will check what chemical and physical processes take place in your body, especially in the mind as you probe family members. Overall, the purpose of these tests will be to create a simulator that works based on the properties of your mind. The device will then be duplicated - of course, if we get any results - and thanks to this, entire Cargoo will be quickly examined in terms of loyalty to the nation and the emperor. So, we're acting under time pressure, which has never happened before, because the Immortals were always at the top of the pyramid of power and it was, they who imposed their will on others. Such an invention hasn't been necessary in the history of the nation so far." Figam took from a cupboard a tray with a syringe filled with clear bubble liquid, next to which rested a relay with a needle. "Now you will choose, Jenny, if you want to be injected with bio nanites that will spread over your body and send data on your blood parameters to my capripod, or I'm to drive into your vein a transmitter that plays the same role."

"And how long will I have the bio nanites in my body?"

"You should excrete them all by tomorrow. They are programmed for several hours of operation. You won't feel like having them. You will also not experience any side effects. The data given by them will be slightly more accurate than that from the transmitter, as they will monitor blood in different areas of the body at the same time. However, this doesn't mean that the second method is worse."

"Then I want the nanites."

"So, I will also ask for the little robots," announced Anna, smiling at her daughter.

Andro moved and set up two chairs opposite each other, for Jenny and Anna, then gave both the injection in the arm. Finally, he placed sensors on their bodies to monitor the tiniest biochemical and biophysical parameters.

"Thanks, Andro." Figam also got a chair for himself and sat down beside the women. Forkis was standing next to the aquarium all the time. Jenny, now I'm going to ask Anna questions we had prepared and discussed before you came. Different blocks, depending on the degree of focus on the answers. Your mother will also try to speak so that both in her words and in her mind, a lie looks like the truth. But that doesn't interest you. You don't have to say anything, child, just focus on your telepathy. All clear?"

"Yes."

"The bio nanites and sensors will do all the work for you, the diagrams will keep appearing in my capripod. Well, let's start block one. Anna, say something true."

"I have no wings," replied the older Sandstorm impassively, staring into her daughter's eyes.

"Now a lie."

"I have wings."

"Of course, you do," Forkis joked. "You came on wings once to kill me."

"I wish to remind you, Emperor, that you on Aj wanted to eat me."

"Let's say that I was suffering from a genre dissonance at the time." He ran his tongue over his upper lip.

Jenny felt embarrassed listening to the sense of humor that only seemed to be understandable to her bizarre parents.

"My dear." Figam held up his hands. "You're introducing confusion. Please stick to the arrangements."

"I have wings," repeated Anna.

Jenny couldn't read her mind, it was probably part of the thoughtless, automatic answers that weren't supported by the visualization.

"Good. Then we're starting the second block. Tell the truth, Anna."

"I don't have wings."

This time, Jenny saw an image in her mother's mind. She was standing on a green hill, in the background there was a star illuminating her silhouette with gold. In her imagination, Anna had no wings, in the next, after Figam's command, Jenny saw her with white, majestic wings, like those in the images of angels.

The doctor moved on to the next blocks, more and more complicated questions were asked, without pointing out what was true and what was not. Forkis couldn't refrain and giggled every now and then at Anna, for which he was given pokes. It seemed that both had rebuilt their old relationship, which had been destroyed by the unbelievable, several-year-long separation, over which they had managed to gloze. While Anna could afford to approach the experiment freely, for Jenny it was the most intense mental work in her life. She had practiced telepathy for a long time, wanting to improve herself, but never under duress, in controlled conditions and with such an intensity of mental effort. So far, she had used it out of curiosity, wanting to snatch people's most hidden secrets, which may not have been moral, but intriguing and sometimes funny.

By the end of the second hour of testing, she felt markedly tired and could no longer focus on her mother's thoughts. Anything was distracting her, even the cramps of a tiny jellyfish's bell or Andro rubbing his nose with the sleeve of his smock. And she hadn't even moved to Forkis' blocks.

Figam read all of this from the biochemical parameters.

"It's enough for today," he ordered. "I don't want to overexert you, girl." He put a hand on her shoulder. "You did great. Go to your tasks now, take care of something pleasant, do something nice for yourself. De-stress and rest. Come tomorrow."

Jenny got up, Forkis took her place, opposite Anna.

"Since I'm here, I will be happy to know if we can find in me something surprising after these return to the world of the living."

"As you wish," Figam replied. "I'm also very curious."

***

Jenny considered going and seeing what was going on with Rei'than, since she was now in Sector B. She even moved to the east wing, but resigned, seeing the gatehouse full of achijes, as if there had been a party or a briefing there. She didn't know why she let it go, after all she had gotten the official permission to see the prisoner. She caught herself not feeling like testing her telepathy on him, but just wanted to visit him, see how he felt.

It ended up with her going to the surface to get some air and sitting on a wall in front of an empty, smoothed space designated as the parade square. At this time, Rei'than was taken to the yard, but neither the avor nor his guards showed up. It was a bad sign.

"Jenny Sandstorm, right?" Some achij accosted her.

"That's right."

"I have something of yours. It is waiting in the server room."

"They took an elevator down to the nether regions. After a short walk, the Kiritian opened a door by swiping his PDA, and they entered. There were workplaces between the thin cables of capripod nets, a few people gathered in a semicircle at one of them. They spoke in amusing voices as if they had been entertaining a child.

"Excuse me, ladies and gentlemen." The man walked over to the metal box that was in the spotlight. "I'm sorry, but we have to give the cutie back to the owners."

He took out the little Onkalot girl from inside.

"Tukum!" Jenny had completely forgotten that she was to help Q'ualel search. She took her in the arms. "Thank you. Where was she?"

"She was wandering in the room. If I remember correctly, you are friends with Onkalots."

"Yes, I'll give them the she-cat."

"If she got lost again and found her way to us, nobody would mind," one of the employees said cheerfully. "She's lovely."

"And how quickly she zips on all fours!" Another Kiritian added. "The seven of us had to catch her."

"She broke one of the electronic boxes, though no one has any idea how she did it."

"Sorry for the trouble, see you later."

Jenny stepped out into the hallway, lifted Tukum to her eye level, and looked at her glumly.

"How the hell did you get here? How did you go through several sectors unnoticed?"

The Onkalot girl was too little to say a word, but she understood what was said to her in Kiritian, and sometimes she even reacted with gestures. But now she didn't deign to answer the question in any way, just hung with her hind legs curled up and her tail wrapped around one of them, looking numbly at Sandstorm, moving her nose like a rabbit.

"Someone brought you here? The server room is a closed facility, did you slip through someone's legs unnoticed?"

Tukum covered her eyes with her front paws. Jenny could not smile.

"Sure, now you're pretending you're absent. Your parents are worried. Don't do such numbers anymore." Clutching the kitten to her chest, she moved towards Sector A, from where there was a line to the palm house.

***

Immediately after she gave Tukum back to Chimalmat, she received a PDA announcement. The information was directed to all eight hundred thousand Kiritians hiding on Cargoo: the next day at 10:00 am Forkis was to deliver a virtual message that could be heard on any medium or from loudspeakers located in all sectors.

Jenny had free time this morning, so she went to work in the kitchen. Many Kiritians chose to hear the emperor's words together, which was to be the equivalent of a general assembly in the square on the surface. Even Forkis, famous for his fanatical courage and determination, didn't want to risk the life of his achijes and expose them to the risk of being tracked by Kandrok from space. The Immortals had still not worked out many ways of finding targets by the enemy; Rei'than wasn't helpful in this respect, giving sarcastic, nonsensical answers in interrogations. That's why annoyed, Forkis had beaten him so during their meeting.

Sandstorm entered the dining room a moment before the broadcasting of the message, there were many people everywhere.

"Jenny, come over here to us." Having spotted her, Darius waved his hand. She sat down in a chair beside him, at a table with Seymour, Aytar, Divinus, Bradshaw, and Shimizu.

Forkis' voice sounded shart, and there was silence in the cafeteria as if he had had the power to tighten throats.

"Dear sisters, dear brothers Kiritians," he began in his calm, mesmerizing baritone. "I am very sorry to have to speak to you like this without standing face to face, not looking into your eyes in the general assembly in the open air. That we must hide from the stronger enemy. Yes, the enemy is stronger than us, but its appearance was foreseeable, for even we, though we have achieved so much as humanity, couldn't rule forever, although our bodies have become eternal. I don't want to blame anyone publicly for what happened, because I didn't participate in it, and I only know the accounts of the witnesses. However, we can regain the lost power. And we will do it. I already have a plan. Once again, I will turn for help to our best mind, that of Dr. Maksimus Figam. But before the machine that is to take us back to the top starts, I would like to present a few rules that will apply from now on. You are probably used to the existence of the Council of Dignitaries. There have been discussions among its former surviving members as well as top officers as to whether we should recreate it. After thinking the matter over, I decided that it wouldn't be formed."

Forkis paused. He had correctly predicted that there would be a commotion.

The room buzzed with conversations, some astonished achijes were spinning on their chairs and looking at their colleagues as if searching for an explanation on their faces.

"Then what, authoritarianism or autocracy?" Tsar wouldn't have been himself if he hadn't made a comment.

From her seat, Jenny noticed Warfighter sitting among top officers and other generals, including Necron. She thanked in spirit that when she had met Velkee he hadn't had such a ruthless look and coldness on his face as he did right now.

"Not everyone remembers it, because many of you joined the nation later," continued Forkis, "but that's what governments had used to be like before the Council of Dignitaries was established - there had been just me. I had exercised power alone, had had advisors, taken every opinion into account, and more than once, thanks to their arguments, I had changed a previously made decision. Another issue is widespread surveillance. The nation I know doesn't exist, more than half of the citizens from the time I died in the arena are either dead or missing. The disintegration took place not only because of Kandrok, but also because of too liberal exercise of power, which made the nation incoherent."

"Oho." Tsar took a sip of his strong herbal tea. "Forkis is just hammering Kiret."

"Please, Lieutenant ..." Aytar scolded him.

Jenny focused on Necron, who was staring resignedly at the tabletop. Many people looked sympathetically in his direction.

"Well, he humiliated him solidly," Darius whispered. "I feel sorry. What could it be about ... After all, they were best friends."

"Before we begin to organize an army," continued the First Dignitary, "I must be certain of your faithfulness. No leak can get to our enemies. Therefore, in the near future, each achij will be x-rayed, but don't perceive it as a lack of trust on my part, but a necessary procedure. I'm currently working with Dr. Figam on a method to ensure that the surveillance is carried out quickly and efficiently, because time is not what we have in excess. The enemy's moves are unknown, but it is certain that it seeks our annihilation. I don't want cowards and traitors among the remnants of our nation. Therefore, anyone who cannot bear the burden of immortality, doesn't want to fight against Kandrok, or has something on their conscience that they are not obliged to confess, should give up their right to be a Kiritian and leave Cargoo. The same will be true for Kiritians' hideouts on other planets. This message will be delivered to them in the most secure way possible. Therefore, let each achij make an examination of their own conscience, in the next few days calmly determine their meaning in the nation and what their real goals are in life."

"Thickly, but specifically," Tsar again distracted the attention of the immediate surroundings. He smiled at a nearby group. "So Forkis in all his glory."

"I guarantee such people a safe journey to their homes or other destinations ..."

"Yeah, right." Seymour took another sip of his drink.

"Tsar, shut up kindly," hissed Captain Michael Avadar from the next table.

"The third issue is the introduction of the principles of the law of war after the formation of the army. The same ones that I used after taking power on Earth and then during the recapture of space colonies in the Zodiac Universum area."

"What's with this law of war?" Jenny turned to Darius, who leaned toward her.

"A kind of despotism. To punish the wicked by death, arrest for acting to the detriment of the nation, degrading inept officers, and the like."

"But Kiritians have no other rights apart from the Decalogue. In the sense of limitations. Each case of perturbation is considered individually."

"These are the rules Biffter introduced, you know them from your own lifetime. But it wasn't always like this. Apparently, your father found liberalism to be the wrong way. Remember where he comes from, he grew up in the brutal Onkalot culture, and what youth is used to, age remembers ... Anyway, Forkis doesn't treat anyone with kid gloves." He smiled.

"Kiritians had different laws over the centuries," Aytar said. "The situation forced changes. Our laws softened when we finally had to fight hardly anyone for power in space. So, the present situation is nothing that the nation hasn't already dealt with. The achijes know that it helped them once, so they don't protest." She tilted her chin towards the room.

Jenny considered it carefully - how could such rapid, drastic changes do not cause a wave of protests, but the buzz of discussions among those gathered. Her father must have enjoyed a great deal of attention in the nation.

She still didn't listen to the message, which didn't concern her anyway. She looked regretfully at Necron contemplating a mug of beer.

***

A quarter of an hour after the speech, General Warfighter walked vigorously, with a fierce face, towards Forkis' office.

"Are you crazy?! Did your brain get off-kilter because of that volatile incarnation on Amyrade?!" He rumbled as soon as the door to the room cracked open. As one of the oldest Kiritians, he afforded such direct and obscene behavior with Forkis, and always got away with it. However, he only indulged when they were alone, as now. He stood in front of the First Dignitary's desk and slammed an open hand on it. "Why did you turn away from the Council? It wasn't the deal!"

Forkis was sitting with his legs crossed, his hands clasped over his belly. He looked at the newcomer with calm indifference.

"If you think, Warfighter, that I want to remove you from power, which is exactly what you think, you are misinterpreting my intentions." He spread his arms. "I have given you the opportunity to create an army at your discretion. It will be exactly the same as it used to be, but with no official titles."

The general took his place in the chair.

"So, what do you want? By not appointing the council, you are assigning absolute power to yourself. You are bending the status you received after the lightning-fast referendum among the achijes with the use of PDAs, and our people were hoping for a new council. You are under no obligation to listen to anyone, although you used beautiful social engineering in your message, alluding to your cooperation. However, I heard that even the privates didn't fall for it. Yes, you have the right to establish the chain of governance, after your resurrection, seventy-seven percent of the people again wanted you emperor instead of Kiret. But..." the man got up and put his hands on the table, "you have been alive only a few days, you have been lying dead for two decades, and you only know this turbulent period from the entraser I prepared for you. You know nothing about the new order in space. You don't know the realities. You didn't survive it. You don't have the experience. I do."

Warfighter suspected what could be the reason - no, he was sure - of such a situation that didn't concern only him. The problem of Kiret's removal from his duties was undisputed, there were many offenses and shortcomings oscillating around him. Although he was a model of loyalty and devotion, he wasn't suited to exercising power on such a large scale. He transferred the mass of funds obtained from conquests into the dreams of the return from beyond the grave of the former emperor, and although it turned out that he was right about the existence of the aliens with a high degree on Kardashev's scale, he would have made Kiritians a laughingstock if the crazy journey to Tamasul had not been successful. At least he had enough marbles to keep the mission 'Revival' a secret for a long time. The icing on the cake was the case of Skelver, the would-be bomber whom, according to Jenny's testimony, Kiret had set free on Earth, probably forgiving him only because the Erces at CERN had opened a couple of doors for Kiritians. Velkee and Sandstorm, on the other hand, two former Council members, had had an affair for years that, despite the arrangements, hadn't ended. However, Forkis had no right to find out about it. The general assumed that Jenny might have blurted out for scaring her at the interrogation, and it was more likely that she had done it in revenge for Kiret, whom Forkis and she were going to remove from power. And now Forkis hurt also him. At any moment he could throw him on his ear for just a lapse. The barely discernible smirk on the First Dignitary's face, so easily mistaken for a mask of concentration, confirmed the general's guess.

Forkis busted the people around him because of his own demons.

He took revenge for having wasted so much time.

That Beliar Drunkenstein had defeated him.

That Anna hadn't remained celibate.

That Velkee had seduced his woman.

But Forkis still needed him.

"And if you die again, what will happen then?" Asked the Warfighter. "Who will take command? Should we roll the dice?"

"According to martial law, power will pass to the generals, then to senior officers. Don't worry, Velkee. I'll put people in the right places. Jenny will help me with this."

Warfighter began to walk slowly around the room.

"You want to involve your own daughter in this mess? She's not familiar with anything. In the sense of our matters - I naturally respect your child."

"Doesn't have to. She will only say what she will see in achijes' minds during questioning. Dr. Figam is in the process of developing an interrogation simulator. He is a genius, so he will probably manage to finalize the project. Besides, he already has one that he saved from B9; it is enough for him to remake it. Then even Jenny will no longer be needed, she will be replaced by machines and algorithms. It would take decades to check an entire army with her participation, and we only need a few months at the most."

The general stopped at a liquor cabinet, after a quick inspection, poured himself a glass of Radioactive Supernova vodka. He indicated the other vessel to Forkis, who nodded.

"Did the prisoner say more?" Warfighter put the filled glass next to the emperor, sat down opposite him again, and placed the bottle on the table.

"I pushed him, but for nothing. I was hoping that maybe he would react differently when dealing with authority, but avors only recognize authorities among their own. They spit on strangers. We still don't have enough information about Kandrok. More of its members would be useful for captivity."

"It's easier to find a thirty-year-old virgin in space than to get an avor. To the win." The general raised his glass.

"To Kiritians' victory." Forkis deflected the toast.

"What are you going to do with Kiret? He is no longer that obedient lictor, as in the times of fights with the rebels. Seemingly relieved, he gave you back power, but I could see the anger in his eyes when the referendum results came out - that achijes preferred you."

"Maybe he's just jealous. But I don't care, he'll have to adapt. He missed his chance. Look what he caused."

"I thought you were still friends," Velkee said indifferently. He tilted his glass. Forkis had changed too, and one hundred and eighty degrees. He had created Kiritians only to kill humanity in retaliation for the destruction of Onkalots. However, he had gotten involved and changed his approach when he had felt the burden of responsibility and realized that the millions of people he had shaped under his dictation loved and trusted him. The general, however, preferred not to reproach him for this hypocrisy. There was too much tension in the air, anyway, after the reorganization of power.

"What do you propose in relation to him?" Forkis had a choice: keep either Kiret or Warfighter close. Choose either friendly devotion and ruthless loyalty or high popularity and success. He couldn't have two at the same time, because they would have ended up eating each other. The decision was obvious, though it made him feel guilty. Not friendships, but talent and calculated deeds won wars. Forkis preferred Necron more, he didn't like Warfighter, but he would need the latter the most.

Velkee shrugged.

"I don't know. Maybe a vacation?"

"In fact, good idea. A little rest would be useful for Kiret after taking the enormous weight off his shoulders."

"Like for all of us. Well, maybe not for you, because you were dead when we were being massacred by evil aliens." The general chuckled briefly.

Forkis smiled half-arsed and shook his head.

"We are aliens to them too."

"To defeat the evil aliens." Velkee raised the vessel again.

"And the victory of the good guys."

The glass-like structures produced by bacteria rattled.

***

The following days passed for Jenny in peace and routine. In the morning, she had some time to work in the kitchen, then went to Figam's lab for tests. As announced, she worked on several low-level achijes, also with Darius, who volunteered for research. Curious Tukum escaped from the palm house again, outsmarting her parents, who couldn't be accused of poor care of the kittens.

Jenny longed for Atla's open, bright spaces, full of vegetation and fragrant, warm air. She tried to go out for a walk to the surface every day, and although the sight of the naked, weathered rocks had little to do with the planet of her childhood, at least she could get away from the monotony of the nether regions for a bit.

That day, she saw Rei'than in the yard from a distance, traditionally guarded by Kogan and Ryan. To her amazement, she was pleased to see the avor. At least she knew he wasn't dead, and she assumed that was the cause of her relief. The long distance made it impossible to estimate the condition of the wounds on his body, but Rei'than moved as if he had been fine.

Jenny didn't want to go to the hacks and aroused public interest in her curiosity about the prisoner. She preferred to work with him calmly and alone. So, she waited until Rei'than was taken to the nether regions, and thirty minutes later she made her way to the elevator as well.

She walked through the main corridor past the laboratories, then down the smaller side corridors to the solitary confinement. One was unlit, Sandstorm caught the conversation of two technicians about broken lamps replaced just a week earlier.

She found herself at the gatehouse, in which, judging by the voices, there must have been a dozen achijes having a good time. Among them, she noticed Darius. She assumed that

Kogan and Ryan were his subordinates or colleagues, since Schindler was in this place.

"Jenny, what are you doing here?" He immediately left the cubbyhole and joined the girl.

"I'm going to check the telepathy on the prisoner. I have permission from the top." She didn't mention that only Kiret had given her permission, a person removed from power, but as Forkis' daughter, no one would ask her for details.

"I told you not to go there yourself. I will go with you."

"The gatehouse is, after all, several dozen meters from the solitary confinement. The cellula is already working, you will see everything going on there."

"He's a dangerous man, a trained killer."

"It's more dangerous in other parts of your base," she said without a sneer. "You should deploy monitoring throughout the facility."

Schindler saw a stamp of fear in Jenny's gaze as she spoke the first sentence. He furrowed.

"What are you talking about?"

"About nothing." She glanced to the side so as not to look into his piercing green eyes.

"But I can see that something has happened." He stepped in front of her and gripped her arms reassuringly. "Jenny ... Please."

The girl sighed, looking at the bottom of the wall.

"A few days ago, when everyone got drunk during harroweeng, some achij in the hallway ... was too pushy. Luckily, I ran away easily because he could barely stand on his feet." Jenny skipped the fact that she had hurt this man. She didn't care much about Darius' friendship, but she would have still been sorry if he had brushed her off after learning that she was a freak created out of a fusion of an Onkalot, Kiritian and rebel.

"And you didn't tell me about it?" Schindler grew angry and raised his voice. "Have you reported this to someone? Who was it?"

"I have no idea; I don't know this man. Forgive me, but there are eight hundred thousand people here, and without an entraser in your head you can't remember them all."

"Jenny, for God's sake ... You should have called me! I would have beaten the shit out of the dick-putz so that he'd have been looking for teeth in the corridor for three days. And with one eye."

The corners of her lips rose when she heard such a bizarre curse.

"You had your PDA turned off. I didn't know where you were. What if it was a sergeant or a lieutenant? Achijes are not marked."

"Then I would arrange a blanket party for him." The boy smiled crookedly. He released her. "Status has nothing to do with it."

"Well. It was, it passed, and nothing happened."

"We should do something about it."

"Please, I don't want to go back to this."

Darius sighed nervously, ran his hand over the hair.

"Well, as you please, however, I will investigate the matter on my own. I'll give you a sedative later, because I have it in my apartment. A mini gun with a several arrows load. All you have to do is shoot anywhere in the body and in three seconds you can mow even a 150-kilogram delinquent for several hours."

"Thanks, I will gladly accept it. However, I would prefer not to use such things."

"All the more so now I should go with you to the prisoner."

"And what will he do to me through the bars? Will he throw a bunk at me?"

"I don't know. Spit? Pee on you?"

Jenny collapsed into giggles.

"I can do the same and I can pay him back."

"I would like to see that." Darius winked at her. "Wait."

He returned to the gatehouse for something to sit on and a rifle. The girl rolled her eyes.

As they entered the solitary confinement, Darius set a chair by the entrance and sat down. He looked hard at the prisoner, ostentatiously checked the power supply of the weapon. Sitting on the ground against the wall, Rei'than glanced at him with mild interest, ignoring Jenny. In the first flash of association, he saw the Lightbringer in the body of a Kiritian who had visited him once before in this form. Frightened, he remained silent until he picked up the details of the newcomer's anatomy, especially the quite normal human green eyes and dark brown hair, then he was relieved. So, he could go back to a typical, studied strategy for such meetings. At first, he grinned sarcastically, began snapping the fingers of his right hand that he leaned on his knee.

Jenny noticed that previous bruises that resembled the cool spectra of stars viewed in the holograph, left a few dark spots, while the wounds reduced to three more severe scars. At least so much wasn't covered by clothing.

"Hi Rei'than," she said.

"Hello, little star. Have you brought the gorilla?" The prisoner smiled not exaggeratedly.

"How do you know such an animal?"

The avor nodded toward the bunk where the capripod lay.

"Better shit Kiritian entertainment than none."

"Do you read about nature on our planets?"

"I also listen to music and watch movies." He gave her another sardonic smile.

"Get up."

"No, you sit down here with me." He stuck his hand through the bars and stroked the floor. "Everything still hurts, your father has a heavy paw."

"The Emperor's daughter told you to get up, you pale dog," Darius interjected.

Jenny turned to face him.

"It's okay, I'll be fine."

She sat down on the heated metal out of Rei'than's reach. She began to stare at the piercing pupils framed by yellow irises, looking from above the insolent smile.

"And?" Shindler asked soon. "Have you seen the sea of Kiritian blood and human heads attached to the armor of their ships?"

The Kandrok member chuckled. The girl sighed.

"Enough. You are both worthy of each other. Could you please go, Darius? I can't concentrate. I can't see anything. If you distract me, I won't get anywhere."

"The girl is saying smartly. Go back and play with your buddies while you are still alive."

This time, Darius ignored the teasing.

"Please," Sandstorm added. "If there is such a need, I'll call you, but it probably won't be necessary."

"Yes, go," the prisoner urged him. "I wonder if you'll come running here from the gatehouse in seconds, like a garden dog to the fence, once my hands tighten around that tiny neck of your doll."

The Kiritian gritted his teeth but stood up.

"I will constantly watch you through the cellula."

He left without taking the chair Jenny had shifted for herself.

"Why are you so mean, Rei'than?"

"Because I hate you all. Anyway, it's because of your pretty boy and his friends that I've been languishing in this cell for years."

"Darius is not my boyfriend, first of all. Secondly, if you were romping like that in front of my father, I'm not surprised he got pissed. There's no kidding with him."

"Yes, I had a lot of fun." Another sardonic smile. "If I ever get out of here and go back to collectivity, I will boast that I am the first Kandrok to hit the human emperor in the face."

"You know what I think? You're acting because you're just afraid." Reit'han looked at the girl from under his eye, snorted and glanced to the side. "Theatrically you show contempt and insult everyone so as not to go crazy in captivity. Admittedly, it's better than depression. You are completely alone here, but you're enduring. I have a request," she added when the avor didn't respond. "Can you sit on the cover of the bunk? I would like us to be comfortable and have faces of the same height."

The Kandrok members obeyed. Having grasped his elbows, he leaned towards the bars.

"It won't work, my little star, but try it. It's fun to look at when you strain your head like that."

"Think about something spontaneously."

They looked into each other's eyes for a long time. Rei'than often sneered at her, wanting to upset Jenny, but she tried not to react. She managed to maintain the focused, indifferent face she had seen in Kiret in certain circumstances. The mere sight of the avor's dreadful yellow eyes made it hard for her to concentrate. In addition, he began to drag his tongue over his lip, making disturbing noises at the same time, so that she shivered. She focused hard on Rei'than's forehead, visualized his working brain.

"Can you block yourself from my ability?" She said finally, resigned. Droplets of sweat beaded up on her hot temples, and her head ached slightly from the mental effort.

Rei'than spread his arms helplessly.

"I wasn't doing anything. I was thinking ... about stars as you recommended."

"Aren't you lying to me? Kiret can close his mind to me, and Kandrok, as you often point out, are more advanced than mankind."

"He's probably the exception to the rule. As for the mental faculties, it is more likely that you will be helped by Onkalots than Kandrok."

"You know about them too?"

Rei'than reached for the capripod, stood up, and began wandering around the cell. He could take four steps across.

"Of course, I'm not connected to your central network, but I have been provided with a lot of information for entertainment purposes. Mentioning Onkalots was irresponsible, whoever did it was either a fool or drunk. But don't worry," he tossed the capripod on his prison bed," humanoid jaguars are not attractive to us."

"And we are?"

He stopped in front of her and smiled in a way that made her shudder, as if he had been gazing lustfully at a delicious dish that he could devour soon. Jenny felt as if she had been a horror-struck prisoner, and Rei'than been on the better side of the cell, amused by her consternation.

"Why are you doing this?" She whispered with too big emphasis. "Why are you attacking us? What do you want from us?"

He crouched down in front of her.

"So, it was indeed Forkis who sent you. He failed by force, so he decided to change his strategy and soften me with a dose of girlish sweetness and innocence. But such tricks don't work on avors."

"That's not true. The only thing that keeps me here is my curiosity and willingness to see if telepathy works on Kandrok as well. And it doesn't, at least on you."

"It may have something to do with my neurocyte: digital technology is the enemy of psionic ability. But that's just a theory. It is more likely that our species are poorly compatible. Only eleven percent of our genome differs."

"As many as eleven."

"So, it's possible to talk to you intelligently. Will you answer my question? Unless it's top secret."

"I am telling you nothing more than what Kiritians already know anyway. Besides, I have nothing more to say to them. After all, I am captive," he touched his chest with both hands, "so how am I supposed to have information about the current orders or the deployment of Kandrok's army?" He gave Jenny an enigmatic smile that she disliked like any of his others. "Anyway, even if I had the knowledge of troh or lyyh and I passed everything on to you, you wouldn't be able to do anything about it. You can't defeat us. With the propulsion you stole from us, and which is used to travel only between neighboring galaxies, because it is one of the worst we have, to Asephor' Cerotis you would be flying for some ... ten thousand light years."

Jenny remembered that the journey of Aggroteh, the android Paul and the androlak Kate, from the Zodiac Universum to Tamasul had lasted more than seven Terran years, and the globe was said to be several dozen universes away, according to Nimja's model of the cosmos. For the journey had been used Kandrok's elevator drive (beer for whoever called it that). And now Rei'than claimed that it would take millennia to fly to their Motherland ... From thinking about such distances and time, a human could overheat their brain, and the avor spoke about it completely freely.

"And why do we want to destroy you?" The alien's desired words made her throw physics out of her mind, and she looked at him more sharply. Rei'than chuckled briefly. "That's how we are programmed, star. We are the Lightbringer's program. All our higher choices are the program, not free will. Our every deed, our every thought was once determined, and we have no influence on it. Perhaps differently: we can only have a choice in mundane, personal matters, which don't contradict the principles of super-collectivity, but when an avor goes too far, they encounter an insurmountable blockade, become helpless. Well, unless they are defective, and such need to be repaired or eliminated," he said with conviction and a fanatical twinkle in his eyes. For example, if you had a motive, you could kill your ruler because you have free will, but my hand would drop, I would freeze. The imposed program - which is good because it was created by the Wise One - and the lack of remorse for actions that cannot be committed, are part of true freedom. The less memory load, the less computation, the greater the freedom. Based on this scheme, neurocytes were formed. And here is your answer: the program. Oh, that's not what you wanted to hear." He tilted his head. "You probably expected that I would start talking about the lack of resources in our part of the cosmos, about the search for new living spaces or about space travel for research purposes, which end up rather brutally for the objects under study. No, Jenny, we have everything we need. Well, sorry to let you down, that the cause doesn't sound heroic and contradicts the logic on which your whole human life is based. I said the same to Forkis. He hit me, claiming that I was mocking him." Recalling the memories with a naturally sardonic smile, he pointed to a bruise on his face. "And I gave him back. What it ended with you saw when you first visited me in my cell."

Jenny realized that avors thought of themselves as machines rather than biological beings. She wanted to learn as much as possible about them. Rei'than just like all his kind, seemed intriguing because so different from humans.

"Tell me about your planet."

Kandrok took his inhaler and gave himself the appropriate amount of carbon dioxide, then lay on his back on the bed, spread his arms freely, and took a deep breath.

"Asephor' Cerotis is a bit like Cargoo, so I feel quite good when the achijes take me outside. It is in the optically trinary system of stars, that is, it is illuminated by three suns, but only one provides us with the right amount of energy, even occasionally scorches the planet, but we know how to protect ourselves against it. It's a blue supergiant. The other two stars are yellow giants and orbit much further. From the surface of Cerotis, they look like bright moons. In practice, however, this means that wherever you are on the planet, it will never get dark. Therefore, if necessary, and it is necessary extremely rarely, we artificially create darkness, dispersing ... kragoh grirok."

"What do you disperse?" Jenny even liked Kandrok's language, with its hard accent, where each word resembled the name of some powerful argen[1].

"I guess it can be translated as dark matter in the sky. It's an artificial substance, a slurry that grows and causes darkness, completely blocking any light coming from space. Sedimentation to the ground depends on the material used and can last several hours, days or even months. Asephor' Cerotis itself looks like a light brownish-orange geoid from orbit. Naturally, it had a rare atmosphere, but we concentrated on it according to our needs. As you probably already guessed, because you're a smart girl, we have more carbon dioxide there than human lungs need, and less oxygen. There are no plants or animals there, and the ground is barren, mountainous, sand or rocky. The mountains themselves can be impressive, the highest peaks reach seventy kilometers. There is water, highly mineralized, although you could drink it without harm to your health if you felt thirsty."

Jenny zoned out to Rei'than's amusement, visualizing his descriptions, especially such huge mountains. She listened to him willingly, and in addition the avor began to speak with eloquence. "Probably out of boredom," she guessed.

"Don't you feel sad there without animals and plants?" She asked, getting back to reality.

Rei'than slid his arms under his head.

"No Kandrok member ever feels alone among their own, they are supported by the collective consciousness, moreover, sense the gerha. In addition, we have leberixes."

"Another foreign word. Go ahead."

"Comrades paired with neurocytes. They are machines. If there is a situation that an avor loses the collectivity or is kicked out of it for some offense, they can count on a leberix."

"So where do you have yours?"

"It stayed on Asephor' Cerotis. I chose not to take it on the mission that was supposed to be short." He smiled sadly.

She got thoughtful again.

"It must be wonderful that you never feel lonely in the commonalty," she said, glancing absently at the bars. Kandrok's reality was completely opposite to that of humans, incomprehensible, disturbing, alien, and therefore intriguing. "We have androids and various combinations of them, in the past there was a tendency to buy such a machine and never be alone, for example, depressed or in old age. But it didn't work and wasn't accepted. Everyone had this awareness encoded somewhere, even hypocrites who argued that automating privacy was good, that it was abnormal to replace a real human with an artificial one. However, people had such nature that they felt lonely, even living among the billions, as it was on Earth. Kiritians became closest to the ideal, Forkis introduced Onkalots' customs to the nation, among which tribal communities were important.

"Community is important." Jenny realized that Rei'than was lying on his belly with his hands under the chin and staring at her. "Every avor faithful to the gerha belongs to one, it is called a collectivity." He rose, shifted his clothes and pointed to a black, crossline tattoo on the inside of the arm, near the armpit, which, next to the digital identification in the neurocyte, was a symbolic sign of belonging to the collectivity. "A gathering of collectivities is a super-collective. And you, do you feel lonely, Jen?"

He surprised her. She stared at him, hunting out on the white face marked with the bruises, stamps of deception.

"Tell me why such a beautiful and smart girl hasn't found a partner?" He had a venomously pleasant timbre of voice, as long as you could create such a combination, she had never heard of him before.

"Are you making fun of me now?"

"No, I'm asking honestly."

She looked away. It had all gone too far; it was going too fast. Did she feel so bad that she confided in the killer from space, not having no one else?

"It's complicated."

"Let me guess; you like someone much older, with a high rank, with whom you were related. But he brushed you off when you told him the truth."

In astonishment, Jenny opened her eyes wide.

"Where did this conclusion come from?"

"Deduction, little star. Okay, I lied. There is a rumor among the private achijes who call me that you went for Kiret. Nevertheless, you are clearly harboring a grudge for some reason. You are sorry and you are extinguished. You are behaving differently than at our last meeting. Each avor will notice such nuances, because we are adapted to judging the emotional potential of the enemy, the human eye - not necessarily. Also, it has not escaped my attention that you often say his name in a peculiar way. The first name, not the surname or title."

"I will not elaborate on the topic. These are personal matters."

He smiled warmly.

"If you feel the need to do so, you can tell me anything."

He touched her cheek gently with his warm fingers. He genuinely did it! And she didn't move. She stared at the avor in surprise, as if at least he had stabbed her suddenly in the heart. She was tongue-tied and lost her confidence. After all, Schindler had warned her to stay out of the reach of the stranger!

"Enough of this circus!" No one else burst into the room, but Corporal Darius Schindler. If the door didn't open automatically, he probably would have treated it with a hip or a shoe. He raised the gun. "Get those dirty hands off the Emperor's daughter!"

"Hail, oversensitive," Rei'than replied with amusement, leaning his back against the wall. "Relax, or your veins will break. Why are you all so nervous? A decent, cleansing war would be useful for you. And this I can arrange. And I resent the dirty paws, you give me the opportunity to take a bath every day."

Still stunned, Jenny let herself be led by the arm like a child. She left the solitary confinement with Darius.

The Kandrok member sat down, content, on the bed.

The first part of the plan was slowly coming to an end.

11. The Haunted Sector

"I told you to stay out of his reach," the corporal accused her in the corridor. "Do you want to die? He could have killed you!"

Jenny hadn't had a chance to see a preview of the prison from the cellula in the gatehouse, the picture could be of poor quality or Darius, busy with something, glanced at it just as the avor was holding his hand at her, as he perceived the situation differently than it was. He took her silence as a shock resulting from the danger to life. At least she didn't have to explain what had happened - in Shindler's opinion, the attempted murder by strangulation or throat damage.

"It was my idea," she finally said, coming up with a pretty convincing lie on the spot. "I wanted to check organoleptically if I could read anything in his mind that way. I told him to put his hand out. You probably know that Aggro is a psychometrician, activating his abilities requires touching a body or an object. Nobody understands how I inherited my skill from Forkis, since he was a human and not an Onkalot at the time ... you know. I just wanted to experiment. I thought about Nacxit, he had used the sense of touch on you too." She was surprised she had sold Darius such a gibberish, yet logical fairy tale. Kiret may not have been wrong in his judgment that she was unfit to be a Kiritian woman, since truthfulness was fundamental to the existence of the Immortals.

Sighing and putting his hands on the hips, Schindler gave her a wry look, but at least with an understanding smile.

"Nothing happened, anyway," she said. "I had everything under control. You didn't have to react as if I had been your property."

"I was just worried about you as Jenny, not Forkis' daughter that needed to be guarded." He grabbed her hand and tugged gently. "Come on. The guys in the gatehouse are telling stories. They are okay."

"Oh, Jenny," Kogan said. About ten people were seated in the room. "Come to us. Make yourself comfortable. Sorry for the mess on the table."

Two achijes made space for her, moving over on a bench.

"We're cooler than the pale-faced aliens," Ryan concluded, playing with his knife.

"Said the nigga." Out of all people, Bradshaw being a Negro, fared best with this comment.

"I look like a mulatto next to Rei'than anyway," Ryan noted.

"Okay, let's get back to the story then." Kogan winked at Jenny. "You lucked into the beginning of a good urban legend."

The girl looked back at Darius.

"Stories about the Cargoo nether regions," he explained. "And there are many of them, quite interesting and crazy."

"But start over," suggested the achij named Vaas. Sandstorm had seen him leading Rei'than to the interrogation of Forkis.

"Alright." Ryan rested his arms on the metal surface of the table. He turned to Jenny, moodily lowering his voice and making it solemn, "Have you heard of the haunted bathroom in this sector?"

"What?" She smiled clumsily. "Never."

"Southeast wing. Before Kiritians took over Cargoo, the rebels had stayed here in their makeshift outposts, and even earlier, the colonists from Earth. The situation happened several hundred years ago, probably in the twenty-seventh century. Or rather, for sure, because at the same time there was a scandal with the Liquid 5 android series, the last working specimen of which is Paul helping Aggroteh on his Tamasul expedition. It is not known exactly which group the described situation with the mine concerned, whether the rebels or the land colonists, but probably the latter, as the opposition's property initially came from terror, theft and robbery. The rebels weren't producing anything, so the colonists could set up these mines. The planet has always been windy, barren and dead, it was wanted to keep it like this, because there were no plans to populate it collectively. It would have been too expensive. It was to be in the form of a spaceport, transfer dock or shelter. Hence the Kiritian name

Cargoo, and the Anglo-American name Cargo - from warehouses and temporarily detained goods to transfer ..."

"And then," interjected a bald tipsy achij, "the first restroom on the planet was built, and because it was done wrong, the first cosmic sewage flowed out of it."

Ryan looked at him with pity, laughing to the accompaniment of his friends. Jenny looked with an expression of gladness at Darius, who also smiled and shrugged.

"Stop it ... You're spoiling the climate," Kogan scolded the bald man.

"The mine that we converted into an underground base and hideout," Ryan continued, "was not planned to be built. Once, someone flew over these areas and recorded magnetic anomalies coming from the ground. After examining it, it turned out that there was a huge source of metal ores, including iron, vanadium and titanium. In the following years, there were already mines and a workers' settlement here. Androids weren't used for the works, because, as I mentioned earlier, one of their series, produced by Space Dream, was 'more human than a man', or more precisely, a superman was created, which resulted in trouble. All products of this corporation, as well as androids in general, were branded automatically. For this reason, for a decade or two, many colonies preferred to use physical work, the power of human muscles

or non-AI machines. Maybe it was just about money from the beginning, the lion's share of resources was consumed by building underground complexes anyway, and the cost of buying one android was equal to the annual maintenance of dozens of employees.

And it was the saving that was the cause of the misfortune.

When the mine was already operating at full capacity, an explosion occurred as a result of human error and bad ground checking. One of the injured miners hung from the wreckage of scaffolding over a 200-meter chasm; his companions were thrown to a more stable area. However, there could be another explosion. Saving the unfortunate man became a sad calculation: they would either save him, but more people might die, or leave him, and everyone except him would survive. The guy desperately and tearfully begged for help as the rest of the miners turned their backs to him and began to walk away, condemning him dead. He perceived it so that they just chickened out, and they could do their best and save him. The scaffolding indeed didn't endure; methane gas began to leak from the wall. The miner fell into the increasingly dark tunnel together with the remains of stanchions and rails, he moved away from the dim yellow illumination of the upper parts of the mine. Before he hit the ground, he managed to curse his comrades. He shouted that he would come back to punish them.

The curse worked.

Over the next years, mysterious accidents occurred near this place and, surprisingly, miners who left his companion in need suffered or died in them, as well as their relatives or friends. No one could explain scientifically unfolding anomalies: sinkholes in a well-protected stretch, flooding where there was no water, explosions where only oxygen, nitrogen and carbon dioxide were present, omitting traces of other elements, but completely harmless. There were also screams and groans with no specific source. Even though there is still a lot of ore left to mine, the entire sector was sealed.

Time passed, and the rest of the mines were finally exploited and abandoned. It was taken over by the rebels during the fighting with us. Then we came to Cargoo and turned the mine into the underground facility with metal walls, leaving only solid rock here and there. We merged it with other old mines, bored a lot of new tunnels, eventually creating the shelter for eight hundred thousand Immortals. Even the underground city.

It would seem that evil had awakened again.

Achijes in the south-eastern wing of sector B often hear ghastly whispers and voices, which make the hair on the back of the neck bristle, and the feeling of anxiety is not helped by heavy armor and equally heavy weapons in their hands. When they are looking for a prankster, even with bioctovisors, they obviously find nothing. And that's the worst part of it: misunderstanding, fear of the unknown, a mind that creates unreal things. Sometimes there is a knocking noise carried in the corridor, the lighting is defective, and small items are said to move in the restroom. It is not known where the earth appears on the floor from. The haunted bathroom has long since been abandoned. Some achijes say they have dug to the archives of the area, which show that the worker's skeleton rests behind the bathroom wall, and until he is removed from there and a proper burial is ensured, the anomalies will not cease. BOO!"

Jenny, absorbed in the story, jumped and banged her head against Darius' jaw as Ryan, lowering his voice as the story progressed, raised it abruptly along with his shoulders. The Kiritians laughed heartily. Sandstorm also laughed at her reaction.

"What a story you made up," she concluded. "You must be too bored here."

"It's not fiction, it really happened," Kogan corrected solemnly. He prodded the achij sitting next to him. "Right? Say."

"Right," the latter supported him. "Strange things only happen in this sector. Working lights break down. Clumps of earth appear on the floors, as if someone had brought them in with shoes, although the nearest exit to the surface is a kilometer away. That solitary confinement cellula was probably also broken by the ghost."

"You guys are having me on nicely." Jenny didn't believe a word of the evocative story but had to admit she felt a little uncomfortable when Rei'than's hacks began to connect facts with fiction. "We're in the thirtieth century, who believes in such nonsense now?"

"We've all found out recently that the universe - or the universes - are different from what we thought. The cosmos turned upside down. Besides, our Mr. Corporal," Ryan pointed Darius, "was catching a ghost with aliens' artifact in the afterlife and was directed by the god. Lieutenant Tsar Seymour must have been pissed that he had never even dreamed of getting so high.

Smiling, Schindler just shrugged.

"Exactly, the lieutenant was with them. Probably everybody got drunk!" Vaas said.

"Mr. Seymour is all life in orbit," Ryan added.

The company started cackling.

When Sandstorm lay in her bed two hours later, her peace wasn't disturbed by the wraiths from the east wing of Sector B, but by the memory of Rei'than's warmth and delicacy on her face.

***

Predictably, Tukum was found the next day - she had been poking around again in Sector B. She had followed Jenny secretly and gotten after her unnoticed into the lab where Dr. Figam had been working with the team. Sandstorm tried to get from Tukum the information on how she had entered the building, but the latter stubbornly refused to cooperate non-verbally, as if she had been an ordinary domestic cat. Andro drove her to the palm house.

"Today it should be interesting," Figam informed the girl, as usual walking with tousled hair. For the first time in days, he hadn't connected her to apparatus to monitor the state of her working brain and her entire body, second by second. Sariel Jelinek, one of the doctor's few assistants, the rest of whom worked remotely on a different project, set a device in the center of the table that looked like a carelessly cut, large salt crystal. Sariel assumed a dismissive expression as if he had been there as a punishment.

"What is it?" Jenny asked. She was standing next to Darius, who had also been asked to come to the lab.

"I tentatively called the device a thought exteriorizator," Figam rushed with the answer. "It also works as a zero-one lie detector, which is true or false."

"You built it really fast," the girl said admiringly.

"It's actually my old project that I put away in the proverbial drawer. I made a few minor tweaks. Once I wanted to create a machine that would assist Emperor Forkis in recruiting Kiritians, but he refused to use it. And he was indeed doing great without it. Now, however, the exteriorizator will be very useful, because time is pressing. Kandrok can discover us at any time.

"Supposedly, we communicate with other hideouts and allies in Morse code," Schindler remarked, leaning his lower back against the table. "It's safe? The enemy won't find us?"

"This form of communication is so primitive that Kandrok will at most mistake it for cosmic noise of natural origin, which may have a million sources, but most likely will not detect anything. I don't think it will come to the fact that we are using the form of communication from a thousand years ago, but slightly modified so that the transfer isn't limited to the planet. The muted audio recording is ultimately transmitted via intermediaries, i.e., simply satellites with a portation function. It is a directional signal, not scattered, which makes it even more difficult to detect. Alright, kids." Maksimus clapped his hands. "Sit back, Darius."

Schindler called himself to order in time and didn't ask how the exteriorizator worked, because they would have probably had to listen to the genesis of its creation from the first line circled in the project. Fortunately, Figam limited himself to generalities.

"This time there won't be pricking," he said. Sariel began applying sensors to the corporal's head and wrists in the form of thin, self-adhesive little plates resembling scraps of foil. Figam attached the same to himself. "I will ask questions and the exteriorizator will display your thoughts in a holographic form."

"In the sense that everyone will see it?" Darius didn't like this option very much.

"Indeed."

"Don't fidget like that, man," Sariel grumbled to the corporal.

"Hey, I'm not playing like that. What if I think of something stupid?"

Figam smiled indulgently.

"Ultimately, the recipient will be Forkis, or he will ask for help from dignitaries, i.e. people living even hundreds of years, and I assure you that they will not see anything new. Anyway, the questions will concern the service of the emperor and the nation."

"It may be quite funny." Jenny grinned as she sat down on the table next to the device.

"There are two LEDs at the base, a red and a green one," Figam explained. "On some questions, the green one will light up when telling the truth, and the red one when telling a lie. I made the design as simple as possible."

"I don't think I can survive this," Darius whimpered.

"It'll be all right. Now we'll begin. What color is grass?"

Above the device, the idea of Darius quickly manifested itself - the image of grass in its most classic, green form, often sown along the roads. No lamps came on.

Schindler sighed.

"It doesn't make sense. The grass can be yellow when it is wilted or brown when it is rotting. There are also many species of grass."

"Your thoughts are to be spontaneous, don't weasel. First association. So what color is grass?"

"Green."

A lamp of the same color came on.

"Am I to speak, or is it enough to just think?"

"You say what you think. Now lie to the question asked. What color is grass?"

"White."

The red LED went on and the holograph showed the plant as if smeared with paint.

"It works brilliantly, doctor!" Sandstorm leaned over the machine. Sariel, standing beside him with his arms crossed, followed her gaze. "Maybe I won't be needed for my father at all."

She immediately realized how ambiguous the statement sounded. Thanks to the exteriorizator, Forkis could dismiss her from her responsibilities in recruiting achijes and screening those already in the nation, but he might as well have lost all interest in her as a daughter he wasn't really close to. The invention useful on the one hand would separate them even more from each other on the other.

While Figam kept asking Darius more questions, Sariel was around only to spoil the others' mood with his rudeness. Jenny had heard from Schindler that he was an outstanding scientist, one of the best on Cargoo, but did he have to be such an introverted, antisocial asshole at the same time?

When the tests were over, Schindler breathed a sigh of relief. Not once had he made a mockery of himself, but Figam had prepared simple, yet well-chosen questions, which he had asked at a pace that prevented the cerebral cortex from getting off the track.

An hour later, Jenny was required to report to a 'throne room' as the First Dignitary had named one of the larger, converted rooms of Sector B, adjacent to the conference room. On a landing to which a few steps led, was erected a diorite throne. Forkis had ordered it to be recreated out of respect for tradition and sentiment for the audience hall in K'otz'ib'aja, in which once had stood such a seat. Moreover, a line of columns was copied from the capital; the blue light of the famous Kiritian fire that crept in the antique-styled bowls was the opposite of what Rei'than liked. Jenny realized that the avor appeared unexpectedly in her mind, not for the first time.

Besides Forkis, in the room were: Warfighter, Anna, Necron, Seymour and several other high officers. Sariel brought the equipment from the laboratory on the anti-gravity disk, accompanied by Andro who had managed to return from the palm house. Cortez paled slightly as he caught the Emperor's gaze; from the moment of his resurrection, he had felt like a criminal in his company.

Forkis smiled slightly.

"Come on, come on, boy." He waved his hand encouragingly. "I am absolutely not angry about that incident. If it hadn't been for you, Jenny wouldn't be with us now."

For an outsider, the incomprehensible joke could be considered frivolous. Those gathered knew, however, that the old scuffles between Andro and Sariel, now chased to work together, had ended with Cortez, wanting to make a total mess in Jelinek's laboratory to allegedly show other workers his bungling, inadvertently restoring Forkis' fertility.

The assistants had set up the thought exteriorizator in front of the stairs.

"Sit down, daughter." Forkis indicated the chair to his right.

Jenny obeyed.

There were tests again, but this time more official, though they had nothing to do with the selection of Kiritians. She was ordered to read the minds of the people gathered at the throne, while Forkis asked questions about loyalty to the nation. The event would have taken place in a solemn atmosphere, had Seymour not, as usual, stood out in his cabotism. In a holographic projection with his participation, women's underwear and erotic toys appeared.

"What?" He replied as Forkis encompassed him with a killing glare, Anna flushed, Necron raised his eyebrows, and Andro collapsed into giggles. "I had to test the discrepancy between the subject of the question and the image of the tested object."

When testing Kiret, the device didn't register anything as if it had been turned off. Jenny also failed to read anything from his mind. The man looked indifferently, perhaps with a slight regret, at Forkis, who was eyeing him up intently. The girl guessed that Necron was acting out for it, using his unique property, that he had been removed from power more than good manners would have required.

"As you wish," Forkis muttered to him.

Although the future of overtly rebelling Kiret had become uncertain, Figam had reason to be happy.

"The inactivity of the exteriorizator at work means a mental blockage of the object, a conscious or sick one, for example due to a mental retardation," he said, scratching his chin and bending over the invention. "I was afraid that this aspect wouldn't work. Thank you, Mr. Biffter, for testing it."

"That would be right," Forkis said formally, but anyone familiar with picking up nuances in human behavior would have found a muted note of irritation in his voice. "Mr. Biffter has mastered the control of his own thoughts to perfection."

Kiret's case ceased to interest when the attention was focused on another object - Colonel Robert Milles, a man kiritianized at thirty-one, with blue eyes, fair hair and skin, with whom Forkis had often flown on missions in the past.

Finally, the exteriorizator, out of three hundred questions, made a mistake twice, considering the truth to be a falsehood.

Figam waved his hands.

"Eh, and all the work is for nothing. Well, but this is the first copy after all."

"And what is this Dunning-Kruger effect, doctor? After all, it turned out perfectly. I'm very impressed." Forkis walked over to the machine to take a closer look at its facets. "As always, excellent work on your part. And that's the first time you tried it."

"I wouldn't put it that way. Two mistakes out of three hundred means that we are likely to have a spy or other perturbator in the army. It is also not known whether it is a constant value, or if during the next attempt, with identical values, we would get, for example, a dozen or so incorrect answers. I have to work on the algorithm, automatically and manually dig up everything from scratch. Also run even more tests."

"With the computing power of our capripods, corrections will probably be made quickly and the exteriorizator will no longer make mistakes."

After the test, other issues started to be discussed. When Forkis finished talking to Figam and sat on his throne to drink water, Jenny, seeing Anna busy arguing with Necron and Warfighter, accosted him, whispering:

"Father."

Forkis immediately understood that his daughter cared about discretion. He leaned towards her and said softly:

"Yes, Jen?"

"Am I fit to be a Kiritian woman?"

She surprised him.

"Necron says I don't," she continued. "And what's your opinion?"

"Certainly not at this age. You would have to wait a few years. Psychologically, I don't really see it either."

"Why?"

"First of all, you should ask yourself why you want to be immortal. For your own ambition, or because you want to serve the nation? Because you are afraid of death, or you are going to fight against Kandrok as well as anyone who wants to undermine our power?"

"He already knows everything," she thought. With the rhetorical questions, he reproached her selfishness and the fact that she did fear death, even if it wasn't the final end, as the recent bizarre events involving the Nimja member had proved. She doubted that Necron had reported to Forkis their private conversation at the observatory, probably her father had used his wealth of experience, dealing with millions of recruits over hundreds of years. His atole, who had been in Amyrade for a while, hadn't lost all those memories-information. He didn't treat Jenny lightly just because they were family - but like any other achij.

But Forkis was right. The girl had nothing to do with the nation, she had been forced to grow up far from war and politics. With regret, but also a little shame, she had to ascertain that she was not interested in Kiritians' affairs, although she would have naturally wished with all her heart that they would succeed and defeat Kandrok as soon as possible.

She wanted immortality for herself.

She planned to be kiritianized in a few years, when she was more physically and mentally mature, and then she would get involved with Necron. Then he would no longer have arguments to brush her off.

"Mentally, you are also not very suitable." Forkis interrupted her thoughts. He spoke directly and without any relief, not as gently as Necron so as not to offend her. "You're too sensitive and kind. These are not disadvantages, of course, but obstacles in this case. There is no room for pacifism among Immortals, you have to fight and often kill."

"Thanks for giving me your point of view," she replied. She smiled artificially, disappointed for good this time.

"Don't worry, you don't have to be a Kiritian to live a long and healthy life. Our medicine at Zodiac Universum is second to none. If you have any other problem, contact me," he formally replied. He ran his hand over her black hair, finally brushing the girl's chin and nose with a finger. "And now if you don't mind."

He got up and went over to Milles and the rest.

Tsar and Sariel were arguing about something while standing by the columns. As they walked away from each other like two dogs that barely avoided snapping, Jenny approached the lieutenant.

"Officer."

"You to me?"

"As you can see," she said cheerfully.

Tsar gave her a charming smile.

"I'm not too old for you?"

They laughed softly.

"Okay, enough jokes." The man took out a corn fiber from between his teeth. Then, I'm all ears."

"Is Corporal Darius Schindler still your subordinate? I am asking because now there is going to be some reorganization of the army."

"He indeed is. Did he screw up something? Should I shoot him or throw him alive into the pit with lime at once?"

"No, but I have a big request. Would it be possible for you to give him something to do in the evening, specifically after 5 p.m.?"

"He descends on you, right?" Seymour grinned mischievously. Jenny bit her lip and shrugged. "Can't you just tell him that, instead of changing people's schedule?"

Sandstorm didn't mention that she had few friends here, and that she would have rather not parted company with Darius just in case.

"I don't want to upset him. I mean, I don't mind his company, but I'd rather be alone during these hours."

"Wait, wait." The lieutenant stared at the ground for a moment and waved a raised finger. "The prisoner, yes?"

She nodded, wincing.

"And Darius probably disturbs?" He added, deliberately avoiding the word "jealous". He leaned his back against the column, put his left hand in his pocket, and looked Jenny in the eye. "Maybe something can be done about it."

"Thank you."

"But it is always best to have an honest conversation. One should resolve troubles with the visor raised," he clenched his hand into a fist, "and not avoid them, pretend they are not there and tired. It's best to smash them on the spot."

"I absolutely agree, but there is not enough courage for everything. I understand that you will keep it a secret?"

The lieutenant smiled jauntily, disconcerting the girl before he replied:

"I don't know, sweetie, I've never tried."

"Come on, sir."

"Relax, I'm just teasing you. Have a nice evening, Jenny."

She had nothing else to do here, so she headed for the exit.

Seymour said goodbye to the girl with a cheerful face and raised his eyebrows significantly as she turned her back to him. He rubbed his chin thoughtfully.

"The world belongs to the youth. The old one does, the young one does not," he muttered philosophically. He took a joint out and lit it.

***

As Tukum sneaked out of the conservatory once again, Jenny began to consider whether there was a purpose in her secret escapes. Perhaps the little Onkalot girl wanted access to something unattainable in the palm house, although from Sandstorm's point of view it was the orangery that was the most interesting of all the objects created in the network of old mines.

Though she had doubts about Seymour, the lieutenant agreed to her request and found Schindler something to do for the evenings. Now she could visit the prison without the heavy thought that she was being watched more than the situation required.

The gatehouse was empty that day; Jenny found out about another cellula failure. She considered that since such situations were allowed to happen, they had to be sure that Rei'than was harmless behind bars.

Thoughts immediately went to the urban legend about the miner's revenge. She knew the guys must have made up a story to make fun of her, but she felt far from comfortable walking down the empty corridors towards the prison, accompanied by the whistle of draft and the tapping of pipes. She even flinched when the ceiling lamp hissed behind her. Perhaps this was the genesis of the ghost legend - the constant breakdowns in the Southeast, an insignificant part of the sector that was not worth maintaining due to the lack of important objects. As long as everything stuck together and didn't collapse on your head.

"Hello, little star," Rei'than greeted her as she walked through the door of the solitary confinement. He was lying on the bed, facing her. For the first time, there was no sarcasm in his voice. He even looked somehow different; he didn't smile as if he had imagined her standing in flames.

Jenny felt a strange warmth in the lower abdomen as she remembered the touch of the avor.

What exactly was she here for? Rei'than had sensitized her that she wouldn't get anything out of him that he had not told the Kiritians before. Her telepathy didn't work on him either, maybe it didn't work on Kandrok at all. But ... why not keep trying?

"How are you?" She pulled up a chair to be far out of his reach and sat down.

"If you're asking about health, you're already stable. If it is about the psyche, then rather average." She saw the avor revealed himself to her like to no one else from this base. Although she was scenting the trick all the time.

"What do you need?"

He snorted.

"Guess." This time he managed irony and a standard biting smile."

"Rather, no one will let you out. You would immediately tell your people where Kiritians' hideout is located."

"How? To escape, I'd have to steal one of your shoddy ships. And I'd be flying the best of them to Asephor' Cerotis for a few thousand Terran years."

"You would find contact with yours; they are at the Zodiac Universum."

"Are you going to arrange an escape for me?" He grinned.

"Never ever. Speaking of shoddy ships, let me show you something."

The bracelet PDA generated the mobile holograph of the XRS-14 Ghost fighter. Jenny had seen it during the tunning in the A-sector hangar where Anna had taken her once, then she had downloaded a full pattern of the model from the diagnostic panel, maybe not because it had interested her, but she had wanted to show her mother that she had cared about family history at all. It even came in handy - sometimes in the evenings, when she couldn't sleep, she flew a miniature of Ghost around the room like an autonomous drone. The fighter looked real, except that it could penetrate walls and other obstacles.

Now it was flying under the ceiling, above the floor, around Jenny. It crossed the bars, circled Rei'than, then flew through his body.

The girl found it difficult to understand why she showed Rei'than the toy at all. It is possible that she lacked someone with whom she would have felt at ease, since Kiret, who met this condition, brushed her off. But why was she comfortable with the avor who would have loved to see her dead, as well as everyone else on the base? Out of pity? Because she had nothing else to do? She had hoped that under the dhurnsteel coat of sarcasm, irony, and hatred, there might have been something very different?

"If you want to attack us with something like that, you'd better commit mass suicide at once." The prisoner pretended to grab the fighter as it flew around his cell.

"This one is an old thing. My mother, however, prefers the term classic look, but the equipment of the fighter is modern. Several hundred years ago, there were such planes on Earth."

Sandstorm turned off the holograph. She sat down on the floor, extended her legs, braced her hands at the height of her shoulders, and stretched herself sharply back.

"My back hurts. Today I sat long at Figam, then at my father. How old are you, Rei'than?"

He also sat down on the floor.

"I'm in the third sequence."

"Then you have explained it to me greatly. Can you do otherwise?"

"Seventeen revolutions of Cerotis." He smiled maliciously. "Seventeen Huva. But one huva is loooong."

"Come on, stop it. How old are you, saying it so that I understand?"

"You are probably asking about dikrah which is much shorter than huva. Who cares about that anyway? The life of Kandrok consists of sequences, which are associated with the tasks assigned to the individual and their capabilities. The first is childhood, it lasts an average of forty years."

Nice."

"We live much longer than you. If an avor isn't cyborgized, which is the first step to immortality, they can live seven or eight hundred years in the bio version."

"But what years? Our Terran or yours?"

"Ours, dikrah. The complete revolution of Asephor' Cerotis around one of the stars of the trinary system is huva."

Smiling helplessly, Jenny shook her head.

"I can see we'll get along." She noticed Rei'than was using his neurocyte because he was speaking fast, automatically, switching mindlessly between human and Kandrok's units when she had to analyze to understand something of it.

He laughed.

"You would be at about the end of the second sequence if we converted them into the length of human life. Then there is an early adult one, well below middle age. And this is where I am."

"So, you're like Darius or Seymour. I mean, if they were the normal number of years. Ah ... It's a bit complicated."

"I know what you mean. I'm closer to Seymour."

"You're still young. And how is it with your immortality?"

"As I mentioned, we achieve it by fully cyborgization and gradual synchronization of an orhada with an artificial body. The last organ that is replaced is the brain."

"That sounds horrible."

He looked at her in surprise, not understanding.

"You're talking heresy. It is beautiful! Humanitarian. You gradually get rid of your body, and with age you don't have to watch yourself weaken and wither. Cyborgization is not only a path to immortality, but also a status of respect. The lowest in the hierarchy are those who are fully organic, not counting having neurocytes. So me. Over you." Rei'than assumed an offended expression. "You have made my development impossible. You've disgraced me." On his face appeared again that terrifying smile he had given Jenny. He grabbed the bars. "I would have to commit a wahirka to clear my name."

"Something tells me that I don't want to know what that word means."

"Yes ... You don't want to know."

"And you are here, because you were the first to attack ours."

"I was obeying the order," the prisoner spat. "You have your reasons and your life, we have ours. Is it so hard to understand? This is the simplest space constant."

Jenny sighed. Rei'than withdrew his hands.

"It is rather a vicious circle. We're not getting anywhere so. Tell me about the Lightbringer," she asked after a weary silence. "Is that your religion?"

"We don't have religion; we have the truth. We don't worship as gods as you do, we worship only those whom we have seen with deed and body. The Lightbringer has even visited me." As he spoke, Rei'than looked proudly at the ceiling and raised his hand as if someone had been giving him a valuable item from there.

"You mean that seeing in the cell then? It was Nacxit, not any of your gods."

"HOW DARE YOU!"

Although she was in a reclining position, she somehow managed to leap back as Rei'than attacked the bars like a vicious snake that was stepped on. He slammed his hands on them. The transformation from the sarcastic yet gentle interlocutor to a madman with eyes full of lust for murder took place lightning fast.

At least she found out that it was not a very good idea to ask about religion, whatever the avor called it. In humans, it also turned out badly. If you wanted to throw the proverbial poop at the fan at some boring banquet, you could add politics to it.

Rei'than was holding the bars and staring at the girl angrily for a moment.

"Okay, let's not talk about it," she whispered. "Do you burst like that often?"

"Sometimes. But I wouldn't have hurt you." He looked down. "Sorry."

"We're making progress." Jenny returned to the chair. "So, you wouldn't kill me if the bars suddenly disappeared?"

"I guess not."

"And where does this change come from?"

"I realized that you are a wonderful and valuable girl. In addition, it is unique because of the gift. So the situation changed."

"Are you honest, or do you want to compensate me for the eruption earlier?" she asked indifferently.

"Whatever I answer, you could still consider it a lie."

"I gotta go." Having clapped on her thighs, Sandstorm stood up. The last time Rei'than had touched her cheek, now he was paying compliments that hit her effectively like bullets, wreaking havoc, though of a different kind. It had gone too far. She had to get out of here immediately.

"Haven't you forgotten something?" The avor asked with a chuckle.

"Apart from the PDA, I didn't take anything." She looked around to see if she had left the bracelet.

"We were supposed to practice your telepathy, you were to question me."

She immediately realized that with this allusion he meant to convey to her that they had switched to friendly relations, however it was possible between an avor and a human. The true purpose of her visit had simply evaporated.

"I'd have a request, if I may," he said politely, before Jenny stepped over the threshold. She turned back. "Would you smuggle me some meat? They constantly feed me vegetables in the form of mush or other dirty stuff, which makes me feel weak. Kunhikar it won't be, of course, but the best you have here anyway."

"I'll try to think of something. See you later, Rei'than."

After she left, she rested her forehead against the door and took a deep breath.

***

Jenny had to go rinse her hot face as well as moisten her eyes, dried and red from the intense light of the cell. Someone was in the guard's house but didn't pay attention to her.

It was convenient for her that she hadn't met a soul in the corridor. She tried to sort out the turbulent thoughts of her zero-one dilemma: Rei'than was honest with her, or was he running a game known only to him, which could end fatally for her? Was he playing with her like every achij from the outpost, except that instead of openly mocking and humiliating her, he confused her? Maybe he just missed the company since he had decided to 'descend' to this level to fall in with people?

The bathroom, squeezed into a forgotten part of the sector, hadn't been maintained for a long time. It may have remained completely intact when the Kiritians had been converting the mine complex into the base. Archaic pipes protruding from the walls beaded up with moisture, the floor was covered with old puddles, rust, tar and stone marked many metal surfaces, the doors to the cabins were so thickly covered with scribble that it was impossible to read any inscription.

In addition, there was earth in the middle. Fresh. Jenny noticed it, washing her face. Of course, at that point the lamp must have sizzled and then faded out.

The girl realized that it was the bathroom from that moronic tale.

Concerned, she turned off the water. She had come here unnecessarily. If someone had accosted her now, taken her PDA, she wouldn't have been able to call for help, much less defend herself. Once again, she cursed the lack of monitoring in the complex.

Imagination took its own course in this evocative environment, ignoring the cries of reason. Jenny looked in the mirror, afraid that the reflected toilet stall door would open and something terrible would appear there. For example, the ghost of a miner in the form of a decaying, broken corpse.

She groaned when she actually registered the movement - a long shadow, reaching to her knees, moved over the wall. You could also hear the tread of soft paws.

First thought, it's a rat. How she hated those nasty rodents, after the adventure at CERN, she had probably developed musophobia. Such huge nether regions must have been infested by rats!

She listened for a moment, with her increased pulse. When she registered nothing disturbing, she quietly slipped out of the bathroom, certain that her imagination had carried her away. The corridor branched in two, lumps of clay lay here and there on the floor of the one on the right, like breadcrumbs from some forgotten fairy tale, so the girl moved along the one on the left.

Around the corner, she bumped into Tukum with impetus, who puffed up like a wet hen. The Onkalot girl's pupils grew large like polished black stones, taking up almost the entire space of the irises.

The entire row of lamps under the ceiling went out like from an EMP impulse.

"Tukum? You are here again?"

The she-cat stuck to the ground but allowed herself to be held.

Jenny immediately ascertained facts, including the most important one: about the psionic abilities of humanoid jaguars, and laughed nervously.

"Tukum, you spoiler. So, it was you all along! Then we have our spirit!"

The Onkalot girl, as was her habit, covered her eyes with the paws.

"Because it is you who interferes with the operation of the equipment in this sector, right? Hey, I'm asking you something. Look at me."

Jenny pushed one of her paws away, and the other, the she-cat pulled back by herself. Her large, innocent eyes were so aflame with guilt that you could get emotional.

"You really can break lamps?"

Tukum nodded.

"Will you show me?"

The Onkalot girl slipped from his hands, dropped to the ground and ran on all fours like an ordinary scared cat. The girl joined her under one of the working lamps. Tukum pointed her claw at it, the light immediately dimmed, and after a while it was functioning normally.

"Unheard of." Jenny smiled appreciatively. "So now it is known what your skill is: breaking, turning off or disrupting the work of small devices. There aren't many of them in the conservatory, main lighting, filters and pumps, you preferred not to touch, so you came to practice here in a more secluded place. And it seems to me that only I know about it."

A couple of nods.

"Probably the same happened to Rei'than's cellula," came to Sandstorm's mind immediately. Darius' PDA during his visit to Chimalmat had also failed. One more issue remained unresolved.

"How did you get here in such a short time? In addition, unnoticed?"

Tukum shook her head vigorously, clung to the floor.

The girl glared at her with her left eye, put her hands on the hips.

"Let's make such a deal. You will show me how you get to Sector B, and I'll keep it a secret. Do you understand everything I'm saying?"

Tukum didn't think long, she stood on her two legs and nodded, knowing that if she had been caught in the act, she wouldn't have gotten away with it anymore.

She ran on all fours, leading Jenny back to the bathroom. She pointed to very old tiles in a dim corner behind one of the stalls. She pushed one of them off the bar rack and rested its edge against the floor.

Jenny dropped to her elbows and peered into the hole, old dry air was blowing at her face. She diffused the total darkness with the PDA light.

Before her eyes appeared a mine tunnel that the Kiritians hadn't known about or omitted in their urban plans, considering it insignificant or dangerous. The girl's first impulse was to withdraw and come to examine the passage in different circumstances, better equipped, especially with good lighting and head protection. But she thought that there might not be an opportunity next time, and she didn't want to reveal the tunnel's existence yet. Nor did it look like it would collapse as soon as you stepped inside it.

"I understand this is connected to the palm house?" She looked at sitting Tukum, sweeping the floor with her tail. "This is the way you went? Is it safe there?"

"Yes," she replied indistinctly, in a thin and squeaky voice.

Jenny smiled.

"Here we go, your first word. In addition, in Kiritian."

She stared for a moment at the cavernous tunnel, marked with thick black out of the reach of the light.

"You only die once."

Since the passage had been like that for centuries - as evidenced by the smell - it shouldn't have collapsed right now. If she had moved carefully, made no noise, examined the ground with her shoes, nothing bad would have happened.

She let the Onkalot girl go ahead, after minutes of fighting with the old mortar, she raked over a few tiles, then put them in place fair to middling after entering the corridor. She amplified the PDA light and lifted her wrist as if she had been holding a flashlight. She moved, gently putting her feet down; Tukum, with her low weight, moved freely in front of her. The passage was simple, even Jenny, as a layman, recognized that it had been made cheaply (which in this case was not a bungling), and the builders hadn't been Kiritians. Square in cross-section, it consisted of hardened clay and rock, each section of the excavation ceiling was strengthened by a stanchion of petrified wood, however this process had taken place. In the walls and overhead had been stuck dusty panels of lamps that had long since been cut off from the power supply.

The thrill of emotions slowly subsided as she got used to the monotony of the surroundings, in which warm drafts and whistle turned out to be the most terrible things. Tukum led her carelessly, sometimes she walked away, stood and turned her face towards her, shining her eyes in infravision.

The hallway forked, now Jenny relied only on the she-cat. She was afraid to drill arrows on the walls with the found stone, so as not to loosen something. If she had accidentally caused the rock masses to collapse, it would have taken a long time for the Kiritians to find the body. Tukum didn't think that way - on one of her escapades she had undermined and broken into a shaft connected to an enormous hangar of Sector A. Jenny barely managed to get through, turned off the light and saw through the dense ventilation grid a company of achijes having workout in the center of the hall. There were flying machines stationed closer to the walls, ranging from small one-man to corvettes, she even spotted a shuttle.

She withdrew and followed her guide.

She reached a cave where some mining carts and tools had been preserved, a twisted trackage, completely eaten up by rust, crumbled at the touch of a finger.

There were also dried skeletons in rags.

Jenny held her breath without looking at them as she gave them a wide berth. She preferred not to think what other macabre surprises there were beside the Kiritians unaware of it.

She couldn't tell exactly what distance she had traveled with Tukum, but she supposed it was not less than a kilometer. The corridor ended blindly - it had been buried much earlier, but there was a fresh, oblique collapse in a wall. The soil also changed from dry clay to soft and black. Jenny was a few meters from the light obscured by something.

Tukum went first, stuck her head out like a periscope, then disappeared, having found no one else around. The girl waited a moment and, moving on all fours, followed her out. Shadows were cast by the thick leaves of marsh grasses from the palm house, and when viewed from the other side, they didn't appear to be obscuring any opening, especially since there were a lot of plants around. Well set into the background of the surroundings, it could pass as a stain of bare earth, until someone put a foot there.

As they made their way through the grove of palmettos onto the path, Tukum made the buttery eyes of the devil-innocent.

"Okay, I won't tell your parents," Jenny dusted herself off, "but you know what you do is dangerous? I believe that if you showed Aggro and Chimalmat what you can do, they would start practicing your skill with you. So run along."

Tukum moved away, jumping, she quickly disappeared among the leaves.

If it had been about the humanoid jaguar herself, Jenny would have immediately gone to inform Aggroteh of her antics. However, she intended to use the corridor of the old mine for her purposes, and would have preferred that no one, except Tukum, knew about its existence. A voice of conscience tried to dissuade her from this by whispering about deception and trouble, but she closed her mind to it.

12. Knowledge is a Weapon

In Sector B research and testing on a larger scale weren't carried out, the laboratories located there dealt with biological processes and medicine, and in their lockers the super virus was also stored. The entire sector F, along with its huge caves converted into lighted halls covered with metal, was intended for physical, chemical and technological tests, mainly on propulsion and weapons.

Forkis, Figam and Jelinek accompanying them were walking on a semicircular truss suspended several dozen meters above the ground. Through the railing, on the lower platform, one could observe the team testing the first version of the kinetic weapon, the project of which the doctor had created thanks to Chimalmat's telekinetic show. Using the antigravitational thrust, scientists raised and lowered or moved various objects, from feathers to multi-ton boulders. At least they tried - the larger dimensions meant to symbolize the enemy's heavy equipment didn't even budge.

"I expected it to go faster," Figam openly, though gently, admitted his helplessness. They stopped to observe.

"It promises to be optimistic," praised the emperor, but without tactless delight, knowing that the doctor had set himself the expectation bar extremely high. And such a bar was developing a weapon in a short time that neither humanity nor Kandrok had ever seen before. "When are you supposed to finish?"

"It's really hard to say, but we will do everything we can to get it done as soon as possible. It is thanks to wars that new inventions are made."

"We are not defenseless at present. We have the super virus," Sariel suggested.

"But we need weapons diversification," Forkis replied. "You cannot rely on one weapon during the war. It's only a matter of time before Kandrok finds a way to deal with our pathogen, and it won't be a serum that doesn't work on them anyway."

"At least it doesn't work on umen Ly." Figam shook the mass of unkempt hair as he scratched his head. "It heals us, killed him. And the object didn't have the slightest health flaw." He raised his hand. "So, I invite you to the presentation."

They headed towards a spacious room, shielded from radiation and intense light, where Figam kept his designs.

"I'll show you what we have had so far," he said, dimming the lamps. Sariel wandered between the tables and turned-on holographic designs.

The doctor pointed to the first stand where he and Forkis stopped. An infantry hand weapon hung and rotated above the tabletop, which also came in versions for mounting on land or space machines.

"The working name is a bit of an oxymoron, or hydro-fire," Maksimus began. Sariel joined them. "This is the first weapon to use atopaxial particles as projectiles. However, they don't produce gravity or generate simulations, but, when diluted, they create matter with the properties of fire and water, although they are not them. They work both in the atmosphere and in a vacuum. It seemingly sounds harmless. Destroying the target consists in rapidly heating it to a very high temperature, then treating it with an ultra-icy stream. The temperature difference is nine thousand degrees, which is much more than the thermosphere of Earth-like planets. Research shows that weapons should damage diarduk, common Kandrok's metal, which is to them what dhurnsteel is to us. Problems: invent the metal from which such weapons will be constructed, develop a method of cooling. Dhurnsteel isn't suitable for this because it is not able to withstand such a thermal shock, unless an efficient cooling method alone is developed."

They moved on to the next stand.

"The pressure weapon." Figam pointed to the holograph. "Kiritians already have one, but it has never been used in combat. This version is improved, the firepower has been enhanced. Here, too, I used atoplaxal particles, but with a higher density than in the case of hydro-fire. It only works in the atmosphere because air is required for the reaction to take place. The inside of the projectile consists of unimaginably dense particles, the processor included in the set initiates the reaction, i.e., a centrifugal explosion propagating with a ring. The moment of detonation depends on the operator, if for some reason they cannot initiate it - it occurs automatically. The goal is to sweep enemy units and structures out of the area. I didn't encounter any theoretical problems. The weapon has not yet been printed and tested. The idea came from the Collector's explosion before the start of the Revival mission."

"And here," the doctor pointed to the next table they approached, "the beam directional kinetic weapon we saw in the test hall. This is a reversal of the gravity process, so there are no explosions and missiles, but the force field invisible to the human eye, generated in the barrel generator itself, works. It catches individual objects, it can lift them to considerable heights, i.e., up to three hundred meters vertically, and drop them, simultaneously turning off the stream, which causes their destruction by falling from a height. Horizontally, it flips objects. Recommended for heavy land equipment. Also, an operational weapon in the atmosphere. This time the idea came from Chimalmat."

"Right, telekinesis," Forkis commented.

"Next is the hypersonic weapon." The scientist continued presenting the projects when they moved again. "Gliders that move at tremendous speed. Old school from centuries ago, but still effective, at least in the wars the Immortals waged. However, I have an idea for improving the missiles. It is about an anti-g shield that would create a closed environment with the properties of a different dimension, as in ships and spacecraft, protecting a glider against external forces, especially air friction. This would allow speeds at which a glider powered by an explosive propulsion could fly around a large planet in a minute. Problem: Find a way that would prevent Kandrok from disabling the missile or taking control of it. This applies to all Kiritian weapons in general."

"It would require better technology on our part than that of Kandrok," Forkis grimly muttered. "And we don't have such."

"I'm working on a solution. I have one thing in mind, but don't know how to use it yet."

"I'm all ears."

"Mud. Also fog."

The First Dignitary raised an eyebrow in amazement. Sariel had heard this before, so he didn't react.

"What?"

"Do you remember Jenny and Mr. Biffter's account of Earth? They were in a hazy environment, all covered in mud. Kandrok flew over them. There is a global drought on the mother planet Asephor' Cerotis, it is hot. They don't know mud and fog there, and it is also possible that they didn't encounter them on the globes they attacked, hence they omitted them in military operations. Rather, they wouldn't have ignored such important factors because they are too smart."

"That sounds so ridiculous. Do you want to cover our missiles with mud and create a fog when you release them?" Forkis joked, albeit in a serious tone.

"What I'm saying is guesswork. Without research on this issue, we will not establish the facts. And, as you know, research with the use of Kandrok equipment," the scientist spread his hands apart, "cannot be carried out."

"Do you have anything else?"

"An infantry weapon that turns blood to powder." Sariel indicated the last presentation.

"Sounds at least weird," said Forkis as he approached the table with the virtual invention. "But I like it. Kandrok has rifles that dissolve soft tissue so that only the skeleton remains, so why shouldn't we hit back."

"A short death in agony." The assistant smiled.

"This one wasn't my idea," said Figam. "It was invented quite a long time ago by privates, I developed the method. In the first phase, the projectile acts like that of the drilling machine - it is fired with a controlled, corrected force so that it sticks into the body but does not fly through. It is safer to aim at the body and head than the limbs. The bio nanites present in the projectile rapidly distribute throughout the body substances that cause violent chemical reactions. The temperature drops in the veins. The blood is first frozen and then lyophilized. The problem is diarduk, the metal of Kandrok, which we still can't shoot out. I have tested the armor obtained from Ly and Rei'than, but to no avail."

"So perhaps it would be better to destroy them all with an explosive," the Emperor suggested. "It will be easier and cheaper."

Figam started stroking his chin.

"Let's start with the fact that we would have a better chance of detonation if we used mechanical rather than electronic equipment, because Kandrok wouldn't disable our processors and activators. At our current level of advancement, they would take control of anything, no matter what we would do. Mechanical devices cannot be hacked or shut down from a distance, but only destroyed directly. But that would mean we would have to use methods from a thousand years ago, even before computers were invented. However, the example of Erceses, who have the level of development of people from the First World War, shows that this too can end up poorly. Kandrok swept their civilization away and made the survivors spies or slaves, usually both at the same time."

Forkis put his fists on his hips and stared at the hovering holograph of the hypersonic weapon. He appreciated Figam's work, that he had managed to update old designs in such a short time, even if none of them stood out in particular or caused the delight of "Yes! This is it!" kind. The new weapon was functionally usable, it was enough to print it, but on Kandrok it still proved to be far from sufficient. Unfortunately, even the best scientist in the history of mankind wouldn't have been able to break the barriers of Kardashev's scale that divided two similar but still different species. It was an impassable border for humans.

"So, the main problem in each case is our digital technology," he said.

"Unfortunately, yes. Kandrok members are simply ahead of us in terms of civilization. We would have to think of something to protect our equipment from them. If they turn it off, we might as well fly at them with slingshots and rocks."

"It's good, as long as it's something better than mud." Forkis managed a slight smile.

"If something is stupid, but it works, it's not stupid." Figam wiggled his finger in mock seriousness. Sariel rubbed his face.

"I see everything you have is useless."

The three turned to face the newcomer, who burst silently into the presentation room. Behind him stood batab Gareth, looking like a yelled at dog, which made it difficult to tell if he was more scared or embarrassed by his failure to do his duty.

"Sorry, I was guarding the south gate, but there was nothing I could do ..." he excused himself.

Forkis, however, ignored him, being focused on the stranger who would have looked like Corporal Darius Schindler had it not been for his disturbingly silver eyes and hair the color of a star's crown. In his right hand he held a staff with a head that looked like an amalgam of gems and crystals, which probably had also other functions than an ornament or an insignia of power. Every bone, muscle, and vein of Forkis was penetrated by primal fear he hadn't felt in a very long time - perhaps since he was imprisoned and tortured in the secret facility on Proxima Centauri e^2 where his end had been predicted. Fear of a powerful force that you sometimes heard about but cannot be known organoleptically, because outside the bubble of faith, it is unattainable. He held his breath for a moment. He knew who he was dealing with. All in all, it should have come as no surprise that the stranger had invaded Kiritians' hideout, and no one had stopped him or been able to announce such a solemn visit. This time even the alarm hadn't been turned on - which the newcomer must have taken care of.

"You're back," Forkis said, more softly than he intended. "And I have really wanted to meet you."

Figam froze and just stared, as did Sariel, from whose face vanished all dislike from the previous day. A gang of curious onlookers quickly gathered behind the puronax shield of the room.

"How did you get in here?" Forkis asked.

"Just like last time," said Nacxit. "I came in 'your' transporter. Though it would have been more convenient and faster, using this." Above his gauntlet appeared a ball of b'itol. Those in the room recognized it thanks to the real Darius' account. "But I still have to hide, I am a weak link among Nimja members. By using portation in this way, I would immediately get attention due to a high amplitude unnatural energy disorder. The Observer could spot it."

"So why did you come back?"

"Let's say I want to help you."

"How's that?" Figam managed to speak. He walked over and stood in front of Nacxit. "But you left. You told us to cope ourselves." He almost shed a tear from the impression. He had an almost real divine being before him!

Nacxit tossed him an object that the scientist grabbed with both hands. It was a mini disk the size of a cellula plate.

"These are the plans of the Death Bringer, a bio-radiant weapon; they will be useful to you. You should recreate this medium, doctor. Yes, you are holding in your hand the design of the legendary device from CERN," the alien anticipated the question of the three thinking about the same thing. "I also visited Headhunters, probed their minds. There was the Erces named Skelver, who, secretly from Kiret, but completely by accident, because he didn't know what he was robbing, obtained the Death Bringer's plans in the CERN's nether regions. Then I remembered about this device from our ancient history. The Hunters have much worse knowledge and capabilities than Kiritians, which is why I decided to bring you the project that I had taken away from them. Take care of it,

Dr. Figam. And we," he looked Forkis in the eye, "let's talk. In private."

"Of course." The First Dignitary wouldn't have been able to resist such a powerful mind anyway, though locked in the equivalent of the young Kiritian corporal, which was even a comic composition. He didn't even express his displeasure that the intruder had come from outside and gave him orders, managed his people. He had never felt such respect for anyone in his life. At the same time, he knew that this shouldn't have affected his prestige among achijes, because they themselves were terrified of Nacxit. "Let's go to the throne room."

"Gather some trusted dignitaries."

Figam and Sariel immediately took care of the received disk, they were transferring the data to the doctor's capripod.

On his way to Sector A, Forkis called over communicator all three of the outpost generals: Warfighter, Darf, and Ravage, as well as one new Colonel Robert Milles, whom he had recently promoted, and who had been accepted by the Emperor to his circle of friends before his death. He considered informing Kiret for a moment, but with a slight sense of discomfort he gave up the idea. Aggro, who was now lumbered with Chimalmat and the kittens, he also didn't want to get involved in matters that would probably concern the most modern warfare.

Nacxit, who didn't pay attention to the surroundings, but proudly and with existential boredom looked straight ahead as he walked the corridors or went by the underground train, aroused a real sensation. The achijes were flocking from all over the outpost to watch him.

Anna Sandstorm was just in the throne room when the generals began entering. Forkis and Nacxit were the last to arrive, the Nimja member allowed the woman to stay.

The Emperor was surprised only for a moment when Nacxit sat on his diorite throne, but not in a way as if he had wanted to humiliate Kiritians' ruler and let him know where he belonged, but like someone tired of a journey who had fallen onto a random seat. Forkis shrugged his shoulders barely noticeably and took his place in a chair at the presentation table. Anna and the generals sat next to him. Kiritianized at fifty-six, Darfo looked like an ancient Viking. He had ashen hair reaching the nape of his neck which he braided; two shorter ones adorned his beard. Between a strong jaw, a flat, broad nose and a high forehead, there were small blue eyes, glancing as if the man had been constantly alert and dissatisfied. He spoke little, and when he did, it was usually to give orders sharply. Black-haired, with a crew cut, Ravage, in turn, was a cheerful extrovert. He had set himself the goal of easing all disputes, but when there was a fight, he had no mercy for the enemy, exceeding even Forkis in cruelty.

"Shall I order something to drink or eat?" Anna suggested.

"There's no such need. Hope it will be short," Nacxit decided for everyone. He turned to Forkis, "They are your trusted people, that's good." He embraced everyone. "You are probably wondering why I came back. You will only partially understand my reasons, so I will approximate. Also, I will partially tell you about the reason for my decision, so that you can logically solve the problem. I didn't port to you, but came in a transporter, I didn't take on my true form, because I'm still hiding, as I recently mentioned to your emperor." He pointed to Forkis. "I wanted to establish in confidence what relations there were between Nimja members, and if I could find a place for myself somewhere. I learned that a very old oath had been broken, which was to remain in force forever after the fratricidal war. In short: neither of us was to put themselves above the other, because indulging in the case of such powerful beings as we are always ends in a catastrophe on a cosmic scale. Tepew, called the Off-kilter Fang by Onkalots, and the Sovereign among earthly Indians, seems to want to seize power again, at least that's what his moves look like. Ultimate power has always been his ambition, he even dreamed of defeating Kzan Mukata, or at least becoming like it, which would be the height of madness. Nevertheless, the purpose remains unclear. The fact is that Tepew is acting secretly, none of us knows where he is, not even the Observer. All I have been able to do is establish that it is he who controls Kandrok."

"What?!" Warfighter blurted out. He looked confusedly at the rest. "So, it's all your fault?!"

"Wait, something is wrong here," Forkis interjected. "You said you had to hide, because you were in danger of dying at the hands of your countrymen. And now you are saying you spoke to them?"

"I didn't talk, only secretly figured out some facts," Nacxit continued as the murmur of comments died down. He smiled. "I'm really good at hiding. I warned you may not understand many things. Tepew had to deceive the gerha, which is not difficult with our mind control skills."

"Do you have any proof of that?" Velkee asked.

"Yes, I do. What avors do in space is not natural. They are stronger than they should be, therefore they have no competition, they are only successful. Their power stretches too fast and too far. In short: they've been improved. If they are not stopped, apart from Nimja, they will wipe out all in ... kala duwan," Nacxit couldn't find a word in the human equivalent, "in a thousand, maybe two thousand of your years. In this kala duwan they had already defeated Erceses and other lesser species. You are next as well as last."

"What is kala duwan?" General Milles asked.

"A cluster of universes that qualifies for a certain group. This is the entity known to Nimja. As if you had a lot of buckets of stones. Assuming the stone is the universe, kala duwan will be the bucket of them."

"Tepew is going to take power," Anna began to analyze. "For this he uses Kandrok who wants to destroy almost all life in this divan?"

"Kala duwan."

"Why? Who would Tepew rule then? Kandrok, who is his tool? What for? I don't understand ..."

The dry, distant gaze of 'Darius' made it clear that to this question the Kiritians couldn't get an answer. They assumed that this knowledge would be too frightening or beyond their understanding, maybe Nacxit couldn't provide such information, but he certainly didn't want to make their lives difficult by concealing important facts.

"Then you can't stop this madman?" Warfighter said belligerently after a long silence, as everyone tried to digest what they heard.

"First of all: Nimja members are not herd creatures like humans, we cannot cooperate with each other, although such situations have happened in the past. But now it will not succeed; in the event of an emergency, everyone will act on their own. Second: Tepew is the oldest and most powerful of us, not because of his skill, but his cleverness, charisma, splendor and cruelty. If compared to wolves in terms of power rather than hierarchy, he would be an alpha. Only Nanawak could equal him and even defeat him, but he holed up on Tamasul, from where he watches the development of events, treating them as good entertainment." Nacxit sighed. "So as always. Other Nimja members pretend not to see anything, they don't want to interfere, since they are not related to the kala duwan area in which Tepew acts. Some are limited by tradition and respect for the law."

"The law is supposed to have been broken after all," Ravage remarked, pressing the braids against his chin with his fingers. "Shouldn't that make the rest of Nimja members react?"

"You would have to understand who we are and how we operate. I am Prometheus among them, I decided to bring you fire on my own responsibility, guessing what the real threat might look like."

"It's probably what you've just chosen to pave over," said Milles, knowing there would be no answer.

"But you have to remember that it is not I who created you," Nacxit added colder, to remind the Kiritians that there would always be distance between them.

"Maybe I will ask for a treat." Without waiting for acceptance, Anna placed the order in the kitchen via the PDA.

"You guys are pretty crazy," Velkee said fearlessly, addressing the words to Nacxit. Darfo reacted to it with muttering, leaving it for free interpretation whether he did it approvingly or disliked Warfighter's audacity. Forkis had been staring at the table for some time, tapping his finger on it almost silently and thinking. Aggroteh, Paul, and Kate all agreed that Nanawak had gone crazy in his old age. Tepew, apparently, even more so.

"Nanawak is still young," said Nacxit, "he's a million Earth years old. Tepew, in turn, is seven million."

"Fuck, what numbers ..." Ravage rubbed his hands over his face near his mouth.

The mention of Nimja's age couldn't do without reflection and asking each other questions. Every human in the room thought of themselves as being kiritianized. Would they too go crazy, if they lived a thousand years, two, three? What would their thinking and well-being be like if they lived longer? Maybe Kardashev's scale was not about the development and the ability to process energy collected from the environment, but was in fact a measure of madness? It concerned all intelligent species? The Kiritians usually tried not to look that far into the future because the thoughts were both frightening and pointless. "Immortality is not for man," said many who might have been kiritianized, but had rejected the tempting possibility. Figam also claimed so, although he had created the super virus at Forkis' request and then helped build the army of the Immortals.

Anna opened for a moment the door blocked for the duration of the talks. Staff brought food and drinks, then withdrew. Nacxit reached for the wine, which had been set on a table next to the throne. He took a sip from the goblet, muttered appreciatively, and continued to drink. In his new body, he ate more comfortably and drank the same things as humans.

"If he is so powerful, why is he hiding?" Anna said, eating fruit that was grown in the economic part of the orangery. "If he works alone, you can easily stop him with some organized group, since you don't want to or cannot fight yourself. How many Nimja members are there anyway?"

"I can't answer any of these questions," Nacxit admitted. "Kandrok's super-collective, who is also a super army, is not without significance. Neither Nimja member can cope with it on their own. If they put their own minor strength of a minor species against it, they will also lose. The only hope is in you Kiritians."

"Explain." Forkis took his eyes off the table.

"You are most like Kandrok, you are following the same evolutionary path. Plus, you are a military nation like it. And second only to it in development in your kala duwan." Nacxit got up and started walking near the audience. He twirled the glass, setting the remains of the drink lingering at the bottom in motion. "There may be beings more powerful than avors, maybe even us, but we've never met them. We must therefore use the resources at our disposal and not waste our energy looking for better solutions."

"I guess you mean Kzan Mukata, whom you mentioned earlier in the conversation." Forkis got up, walked over to his table on the other side, and began helping himself to specialties.

"Yes, Forkis. Kzan Mukata is allegedly the strongest species ever created. Not recognized by many Nimja members. Some have theorized that it is they who created the q'umaraq artifact. However, this is not an issue that interests us."

"I fully agree. Coming back to Kandrok. If we meet it in battle, it will destroy us. To the last achij. Our only sure weapon is the super virus but infecting any enemy with it ... can be problematic. First, we would have to break through to them."

"We miraculously managed to infect the avors on their ships," Warfighter confirmed, sipping his vodka. "That stunt won't fly a second time. Kandrok is not stupid. It learns from mistakes quickly."

"That's right. If you attack, it will sweep you away. Annihilate." The Nimja member smiled slightly and looked towards the entrance. "Unless I open a few forbidden doors for you."

He waved his hand lightly, as if shooing away a fruit fly flying in his face.

The door to the throne room, though locked again, slid open. Ryan and Kogan flew over the threshold and collapsed to the floor. The achijes standing behind them quickly fled from sight, only two remained.

"Oh, oh! I said it would end this way!" Darius grabbed Kogan by a T-shirt and lifted him upright.

"We apologize." Ryan stood up immediately, as if he had fallen on hot coals of a bonfire.

Tsar pointed with both hands to the three Kiritians.

"Ladies and gentlemen, this is the elite of humanity's defenders! And even of the whole kala duwan, or whatever this set of universes is called."

Anna hid her face in the hands, but quickly came to her senses and ran her fingers through her hair as if she had intended to correct her hairstyle from the beginning.

"I just wanted to see if you still looked like me," Darius explained, glancing at Nacxit. "Because some said you didn't anymore." He shifted his look to the privates. "Hope you didn't cause me trouble throughout half the space."

"But we didn't hear anything!" Ryan added too eagerly.

"On the contrary, you heard a lot." Nacxit smiled again. "Well, Mr. Forkis, there is probably a slight downfall among your people."

The Emperor dismissed his remark with a forced smile. He immediately thought of Kiret, who might have wanted to do good, but the effect had been counterproductive. The centuries-old order had collapsed and the Kiritians began to lie during his reign, and the recruits hadn't known the old good manners at all.

"Since you are here, I invite you to the meeting." Nacxit traditionally decided for everyone. "Maybe your uncomplicated minds will bring something fresh to the discussion."

"There really are many universes?" Kogan couldn't resist and asked before he sat down.

"There are," the Nimja member confirmed.

"They look like this one here?" Darfo made no comment as the private scooped up a cookie beside him, just frowned on him.

"They could be compared to a living cell. Each is made up of structures ranging from small ones like planetesimal to black holes the size of several galaxies. A universe naturally tends to be spherical, but like everything in space, forces act on it too, the sphere undergoes distortion, for example into a geoid. The space between the universes is filled with the cosmic matrix. I'm sorry, but I will not explain to you, given your level of knowledge, what it consists of. However, if you were there, no exact sciences knowledge would be useful for you."

"Are all universes the same? I mean space, planets and so on?"

Forkis didn't silence Kogan, especially since the private asked interesting questions. In addition, the bursting of the low-ranking achij into the room slightly relaxed the dense atmosphere of the meeting.

"There are different, but the ones you and Kandrok come from are the same in terms of type."

"And they flew to us using elevator drives?" This time it was Ryan who asked a question.

"They use this propulsion to jump when inside the universe, usually between galaxies."

"So where did they come from?" Darius interrupted.

"Inmates Ly and Rei'than refused to answer that question," muttered Forkis, glad that the achievements arrived achijes come down to the key topic of the trip.

"You could easily get it out of the prisoner." Darius turned to Nacxit.

Tsar sighed.

"Do you think at all, man? Nimja knows it well, after all."

"That's right." Nacxit nodded to Seymour. "Kandrok has the drive that enables it to travel rapidly between the universes, but you won't need it because ..." He paused smiling, "I'll teach you portation. Two hours and you will be on Asephor' Cerotis."

"Oh shit ..." only Ravage said anything, because the rest either held its breath, froze, or looked at the neighbors, trying to make sure it hadn't misheard.

Forkis immediately remembered the porter at Toniatuh's temple on Chulimal, with the use of which, he had accidentally traveled with Q'ualel to the planet Aj. This had saved their lives when human colonists had been exterminating the tribes of humanoid jaguars on Chulimal with drones. He wondered if Nacxit was referring to the same technology.

"Yes, it's the same method," the alien confirmed. "Nimja's technology. Kiret's group and the team returning from Amyrade also had to deal with it in the nether regions of CERN."

"And you want to share some of your knowledge with us?" Velkee doubted.

"I've already calculated everything. I will reveal nothing that could harm Nimja as a species. Anyway, after the war with Kandrok, I could easily clear your minds. As well as undo the changes I intend to make."

"I'm summarizing how I envision your plan." Forkis began to move. "You give us guidelines and a few toys, we have to fight and die in the name of rules we don't understand, and you hide somewhere and watch the situation through binoculars? Am I right?" He stopped in front of the stranger.

"More or less," the Nimja member concluded with a cheerful smile.

"And if we don't agree?" The Kiritian raised his eyebrows.

"I mentioned what will happen. What Kandrok members will do to you. You must go to Asephor' Cerotis."

"Can't we just clean our yard? If Kandrok sees us kick their asses, they'll let us go."

"They will attack again, better prepared. They will harass you until you fall." The Nimja member lowered his voice. "I will give you some new information about them, everything that will be useful in the war. You will use entrasers, necessarily soluble, to assimilate new knowledge. Those who go to war and have older generations of entrasers in their heads - insoluble and embedded in the brain - will have to remove them without whining. The porter will not break through Kandrok's neurosphere that Tepew ordered to modify. It's a barrier I can't deal with, it almost overlaps with its planet's ionosphere. Your fleet will have to land in front of it, then break through to the surface. It will work on androids, androlaks, and entrasers, so you can't have any of these things during an attack. The sphere, in principle, is intended to exterminate unstable avors, irreparable, who try to escape from Asephor' Cerotis, which happens rarely - neurocytes are burned there together with the brain, and the rebel dies, but it also affects the electronics of aliens from outside, whom Kandrok doesn't have in the system."

"What about the rest of our equipment? Ships, naval craft, orbs?"

"The neurosphere is related to mind control, it was created with local application in mind. So, the entrasers and brains of artificial people are at risk. Androids, androlaks or robots could be redirected by Kandrok against you. The signal from the neurosphere will pass through even the thickest armor of your ships, which will not act like Faraday's cage. For Kandrok, dhurnsteel is what paper is for you."

"Why would we attack only this planet?"

"Since it is the seat of the gerha, there is no reason to leave it at the moment. Remember, Forkis, Kandrok members are semi-autonomous, they function a bit like bees: if you kill the most important one, the rest will be scattered, confused. Then you just need to catch and hit. The avors will no longer be dangerous."

"It sounds like a serious mistake in such an advanced civilization. Quite unimaginable. It's enough to just kill the leader?"

Nacxit's smile widened slowly.

"Not 'just' Forkis, not 'just'. This is doing 'as much as'. The thing that is practically impossible. It has never happened. However, you will have an ace up your sleeve: Kandrok will not expect an attack on Cerotis because no one has attacked it before."

Forkis looked at the steps leading to the throne landing.

"He'll probably be heavily guarded."

"On the contrary, as long as it is dealt with quickly. I have already said that Kandrok members don't attack anyone, so they focus on the offensive of other worlds, not on defending their resources. You will meet resistance, yes, but it can be overcome with my help." The Nimja member returned to the throne and leaned his back against the headrest.

"Then much learning awaits us all," said the Emperor.

"No." Nacxit smiled good-naturedly. "I will use my most powerful skill on several of your scientists: I will accelerate the evolution of the human mind by tens of thousands of years. In this way, it is easier for people of your own kind to impart to you the knowledge, albeit more of a clue, than if I were to do it."

Forkis realized that there must have been a flawless silence in the room for some time. Everyone had been listening to their exchange of sentences, the last two of which astonished the achijes.

The standstill must have been disturbed by Tsar, of course.

"And I've thought I won't experience anything stranger today than seeing two Darius at once," he said. "Well, and what does a man need drugs for? It is enough to have a Nimja member close by."

***

Kiret sat in the canteen connected to the cafeteria in Sector A, staring sadly at the fourth mug of beer, half empty. He had asked for the largest vessels available in the service. There was a murmur of conversations coming from other regulars everywhere, and to Necron's delight he was left alone, skirted off into a corner. He didn't object, however, when Captain Avadar entered the room, walked over to him and sat down at the table.

"Sorry, sir, but you shouldn't flaunt yourself with the alcohol like that," he said quietly.

"I'm not flaunting myself." Kiret stared at the golden liquid. "I just came to have a drink. And you shouldn't call me that. Let's be casual."

"Forkis, right?"

"The plus is, at least, that I can do whatever I want. Have a drink with me while you're already here."

Michael went to the bar where he got a cup of coffee from Jenny working in the canteen on the afternoon shift.

"I completely don't understand how you could fall out with him so much," he thought aloud as he returned.

"I talked to him. Do you know what he invented?" Kiret glanced at the captain. His head swayed slightly, and his eyesight seemed absent, which made it difficult for him to focus on it. "That I had been conspiring all the time. That I had maintained contact with the enemy and therefore I hadn't died on Earth." He chuckled sadly. "That I had knowingly let spies into the Zodiac Universum. As I resisted the thought exteriorizator test, he decided to remove me from the throne, even stripped me of the rank of general. And Warfighter and I were to reorganize the army."

Avadar shook his head. Jenny, staring in their direction, puzzled, caught his eye. She turned immediately, pretending to wipe a shelf with a cloth.

"You are such a traitor as avors are pacifists. Where did these conclusions come from? You couldn't prove him wrong? Anyway, now's a great opportunity to clear things up - Nacxit is in the base."

Necron, as if not listening to him, was looking into the corner. He drank again.

"Forkis didn't even summon me to the convention, he replaced me with Darf and Ravage. He even appointed Milles from a colonel to general to have an extra person to help! If someone is unlucky, even a brick will kill them in a wooden building. This isn't the Forkis I used to know anymore. Amyrade changed him. I see it. We shouldn't rummage through things we have no idea about ..."

"Enough. Alcohol seems to loosen your tongue too much." Avadar slid the handle of the mug from between his fingers. "Come on, let's go to your room, you'll sleep."

He helped the man to his feet and led him to the exit, taking care of his legs getting tangled.

"I think I'll talk to this Naxcit," Kiret muttered. "I am also interested in my blockade of psionic abilities, and now it turned out that also Figam's machine doesn't work on me. They thought that I was doing it on purpose, with this exteriotor ... Exteriaror ..."

"Sure, ask him about it. But later."

They left the small room.

Jenny had watched Kiret the entire time he had been in the cafeteria, served him, but he had completely ignored her, as if she had been one of the androids working here. The old, sincere conversation with him, though with a painful ending, nevertheless turned out to be cleansing and salutary, which the girl ascertained after many days. Indeed, it happened exactly as Necron had announced. He was her first love, and this one had a right to be specific, and although it might have seemed that it would never go away, it slowly began to weaken. The textbook example worked for her as well. But the feeling didn't pass by itself - the equivalent had appeared that had replaced the predecessor. And he had turned out to be ten times weirder than in the case of the former emperor.

The girl went to clear the table. She found Kiret's PDA in the chair. She put it in her pocket. She decided to give it back to him later.

***

After a brief consultation with the Kiritians and a joint selection of the most suitable candidates, Nacxit ordered Figam, Sariel and Andro to be brought to the throne room. Although it was suggested that scientists could be visited at their workplace, the Nimja member laughed and said that galleries located at high altitudes could prove disastrous for them. Of course, no one understood him.

"The plan is like that," Forkis began to explain before the three arrived. In the room were also the same people who had previously attended the conference with Nacxit, now silent, limiting themselves to the role of observers. "As you know, the ways of reasoning of Nimja and people is separated by the colossal space of Kardashev's scale. So, we won't understand much if Nacxit starts explaining something to us." Darius, sitting on the throne, nodded. "The idea arose therefore to accelerate the evolution of several scientists, so that they were able to produce a weapon suitable for the fight against Kandrok. I will tell you immediately what the risk is: a few are to be selected carefully, because such a significant interference in the nervous system can be fatal."

The scientists looked at the First Galactic Dignitary as if he had lost his mind.

"What do you mean by accelerating our evolution?" Andro was the first to stutter out something. "Will our heads get bigger, and our arms and legs shrink? Will the core muscles decline?"

"Physically, you won't change much," the Nimja member replied as Forkis took his place in the chair. "Only your brains will change, but not in terms of volume."

"How are you going to do this, my friend?" Figam asked politely. Nacxit raised his hand.

"As I read in people's minds, except that I will touch your heads, and not do it remotely. Shaping the brain of an intelligent being, that is, changing their tissue and program, is the most difficult form of telekinesis, but I have mastered it to perfection. If the transformation is successful, there is minimal likelihood of suffering physical harm such as concussion, vomiting, or visual disturbance. I would be more worried about the psyche. The weaker the mind before transformation, the greater the chance of going mad. After all, we are talking about the evolution of the most important organ that would naturally take tens of thousands of years. Do you voluntarily agree to me to change you? Perhaps it will only be for the duration of the war with Kandrok, and then I will bring your brains back to normal."

Scientists turned faces towards each other in lightning-fast, silent consultation.

"Tens of thousands of years ..." Andro couldn't shut his mouth from the impression. "Such possibilities! We can do so much! Change the face of the entire Zodiac Universum!"

"Don't rush like that," Sariel slapped him down with a snarl, folding his arms over his chest. "Do you trust him?" He nodded vigorously to Nacxit. "Anyway, you've heard that it's only temporarily. In addition, we can die!"

"After what you saw on Amyrade, you should have a more open mind," Cortez retorted. Oh yeah, I forgot: You pretended to be dead most of the mission."

"What are you raving about, man? What open mind? The guy jumps out of the blue with the proposal to change our brains! We may not survive it!"

"If you were to perform such a treatment on me, I wouldn't accept the offer even for a trillion uinals. But this is Nimja! It is like gods! What could go wrong?"

"Have mercy. Stop arguing again," Figam chided them. "Nacxit takes care of his business anyway, it has already been settled, but along the way, we too can benefit. He hides nothing, he warned us of the consequences. The probability of failure is low."

"Correction: Likelihood of complications if the treatment is successful. Nimja members need slaves like all of them. This is how this species works. And Nacxit is a low-ranking coward in their society. It is as if our fate was to be decided by Darius Schindler." The corporal sitting at the table frowned as he caught his name in the whispering conversation.

"Easy, buddy!" he commented.

"Maybe we shouldn't get along with him?" Sariel finished.

"Why are we standing on the sidelines like clods, anyway? It can be heard what we are talking about anyhow," Andro announced.

Figam rubbed the forehead with his hand.

"Unfortunately, we have to make a decision now. When Forkis got in touch with me and told us to come here, he announced that Nacxit would be departuring soon. Jelinek, if you don't want to participate in it, you can go back to the research center," he said seriously. "I understand that you are afraid and have doubts, because it fell on us like a bolt from the blue, and in addition, we were not given time to consider the matter. We'll find another scientist."

"And we can die." Andro smiled mockingly at him. "However, it is worth taking such a risk. For which man in history has been offered to make a leap in development by tens of thousands of years in a moment?"

"So, I understand, Cortez, that you agree?" Maximus asked after.

Alejandro nodded. He was also terrified, probably more than Sariel, but he tried to hide it from his eternal professional-matrimonial competitor, turning his fears into mockery. He made a point of using even such a solemn cause to increase his self-esteem and feel better than the latter.

"Then, me too," Sariel hissed, looking at Cortez defiantly.

"Guys, are you sure?" Figam asked. "This is not some kind of a juvenile bet, who will walk alone, without light or weapons, through a forest at night."

Andro glanced at Forkis, staring seriously at their group.

"For sure."

Sariel's response was a hard, unapproachable stare.

"So, it's settled. We agree." Figam turned to Nacxit, who had approached them in the meantime. The rest of the crowd were still watching everything in silence.

Only Forkis got up and walked over to the scientists.

"Figam, think it again." From the beginning, he hadn't liked the idea of getting the old doctor involved in the brain evolution treatment. "If we lose you, we'll be screwed."

"But if we do nothing, reject the Nimja member's proposal, we will lose one hundred percent," Maximus replied with a sigh.

"Let these two undergo the treatment." The Emperor indicated Sariel and Andro with his arm, openly demonstrating that he put Figam ahead of other scientists. It was a time of calculation and honesty - not of soothing the consternation hanging densely in the air.

"Mr. Maksimus' mind will be the best in this case," Nacxit said. "He will beget the best inventions. I will explain briefly and simply how the evolution of the mind works. Let's compare three brains to trees, one meter, two and three meters high, respectively, which is related to the knowledge we have today."

"So, a meter tree will be Sariel's," Andro couldn't refrain from making the biting comment.

"Don't assign a tree to a specific person, I want to present the problem to you in general, and the given values can be easily distinguished from each other. After the brain evolves, the meter tree will be thirty meters high, another thirty-five, and the last forty. So the tallest tree before the transformation will continue to be the tallest, but many times more powerful. That's how it works. Time for an official decision. So, gentlemen, do you agree to my interference?"

The three looked at each other. After a minute, everyone finally agreed. Forkis, pondering why Nacxit couldn't just help them, returned to his seat between Anna and Warfighter. The rest of the Kiritians sitting in the room waited tensely for the spectacular finale.

But the spectacle itself was not there.

Having rested his staff on the edge of the table, the Nimja member placed his hands on the heads of Figam and nervous Jelinek, and ordered them to keep their eyes closed.

The transformation took place only in the bodies of both men, it reminded the rest of a spiritualist session or some lycan ritual.

At first, Sariel and Figam thought they were dreaming. They followed their own dreams, which began to accelerate, changing more and more rapidly. Visions created by brains turned into facts and authentic scenes from life. They took form like dying delusions of someone who would die any minute.

Quickly, sometimes chaotic, other times chronologically.

Memories of several hundred years of Figam's life condensed into three seconds. With Jelinek it took as long as the blink of an eye. The personal experiences of both men collapsed, now they followed historical events concerning the exact sciences, although it began with harnessing fire and the invention of the wheel. They saw former celebrities and Nobel Prize winners, the most important discoveries. It was as if they had participated in a holographic session closing them with a hemisphere of bright images.

They reached the present.

From that moment on, a pandemonium of incomprehensible knowledge began, frightening even those who had acquired immortality and built Alcubierre's drive. But the two evolving scientists began to understand it all. They learned about phenomena that were yet to be discovered; still unknown forces of nature. They saw souls as carriers of bioenergy in organic forms. The laws of conservation of mass had been abolished, thanks to which Kandrok had created a rajithar capsule long ago that could rebuild enemy machines, and a million years earlier Nimja had obtained b'itol. They learned about the elasticity of the universe's matter, about forms of radiation unknown to the Kiritians in the 30th century. They understood what the matrix between universes was. Their human minds began to resist. They both felt panic fear, wanted to stop this stream of changes, break out of the dream-non-existence state, shouted and raved, but the journey continued. They find themselves in a mental trap.

Finally, everything stopped.

There was such a deep silence in the throne room as if everyone there had died or turned into statues.

Sariel lifted his eyelids, began to look around as if he had lost his memory. Suddenly he screamed in panic and, not stopping his scream, sprinted towards the wall. He crashed against it with force, bounced a little off it, and measured his length, with the bleeding nose.

Velkee, Anna and the others, unable to sit any longer, approached the young scientist. Tsar leaned over him first.

"Are you sure you have evolved him in the right direction?" He turned to him. "Can he at least start a fire by rubbing stones?"

"It's good. I've already seen more strange things." Nacxit propped himself up on his staff, placing his hands on its head.

"So it worked?" Darius checked the scientist's breathing and pulse with his hands. "He's unconscious."

"Take him to the medical center, let them revive him," the Nimja member ordered. "Do what he's saying," Forkis ordered, wondering why the alien couldn't handle such a trivial thing.

"I'm exhausted," Nacxit explained promptly. "But I have enough strength to take care of Cortez. I want to focus only on him."

Kogan and Ryan carried Jelinek out of the throne room.

Figam was also looking around unconsciously, he raised his hands in different directions as if he had been trying to catch beautiful butterflies seen only by him. Out of his mouth were constantly slipping: "oh!", "gosh!", "whoa!" and similar vocatives. These were not, however, symptoms of cerebral palsy or regression, but a reaction to the boom of inhuman knowledge, receiving answers to the most existential questions. Along with the knowledge in the scientist's head, amazing ideas began to be born. Now he could easily refine and finish started projects!

He grabbed the Nimja member by the shoulders and shook him enthusiastically.

"Thank you, Mr. Nacxit! I know how to create and use b'itol! But first, I will construct a semicircular barrier above our hideout on Cargoo, Kandrok won't see us anymore! We will be able to freely go to the surface, gather equipment there and train the army!"

"Perhaps you would first tell us all, doctor, how you feel, instead of thinking about work and inventions?" Forkis spoke.

Figam looked around the room and saw the shocked, waiting faces directed towards him, especially Andro's, who had lost confidence after Sariel's stunt.

"Thank you, I feel very well," he reassured with a smile. "Physically even better than before the metamorphosis."

"I'm glad that the transformation has been successful. You probably didn't put a lot of effort into the process, but from the point of view of us humans, it's an amazing feat." The emperor nodded appreciatively towards Nacxit, overwhelmingly relieved they hadn't lost Figam. The Nimja member returned the gesture.

The Kiritians approached Maksimus, rejoiced with him, patted him, asked questions. They thanked Nacxit.

As the exchanges subsided and the doctor convinced the rest that he was fine, Forkis continued:

"So let's see where we're at: could you, doctor, create a protective screen also for our ships and naval craft? So that the enemy doesn't see us when we move through space?"

"Of course. That's easy!" Figam's eagerness seemed to intensify. "I can't wait to see what I can do! Now, in just one day, we will be able to create several shuttles, or modify the ones we have. Now, please calculate it for the days of the next months ..."

The rest of the Kiritians, except Darius, wondered if it understood well for sure.

"A shuttle in a day?" Ravage was surprised. "It takes months of work."

"It will grow by itself." Figam cleared his throat as he saw that there was even more consternation. "I think in this case the explanations will turn out to be unnecessary. It is important that you can handle what I create for you. As the old saying goes: a pilot is to fly, they don't have to be able to build their machine from scratch. I will also be happy to deal with the issue of breakdowns and repairs."

"I've already seen something like this on Amyrade," Darius said. "Naxcit created his carrier from a ball of b'itol. And with the help of thoughts."

"But you humans are not fit for mind control of matter," said Nacxit. "That's why you have robots, programs, and algorithms in the make up. It's your turn now," he turned to Andro, who hadn't snapped out of shock yet. Only for a brief moment had he wanted to laugh at Sariel when he had sped up and hit the wall.

The process of his transformation took about the same as his predecessors', a few minutes, which Alejandro felt stretched into exhausting hours. Even before it, he had asked Tsar to catch him if he started making strange locomotive movements.

When the Nimja member finished, Cortez reacted similarly to Figam, that is, he looked around, but stunned, not delighted. He felt as if he had moved here in an undefined way from a distant future and hadn't known his surroundings, which in a sense was true. Now he knew so much, understood so much. His smile widened more and more.

Ravage grabbed Nacxit by his arm, who staggered and might have fallen if he hadn't rested on the cane.

"I have a few more pieces of b'itol with me, I'll make an amplifier and I'll be fine soon," he said, rubbing his forehead. "If I did these things on Amyrade, drawing energy from the specific surroundings there, I wouldn't even feel tired," he added as if to excuse himself.

"And I suggest you rest normally in bed." Anna stopped his hand reaching into his pocket, grasped his other arm.

'Darius' smiled at her and thanked her with a nod. In this respect, he differed from other Nimja members, who equated showing weakness with hurting their ego, and accepting the help of inferior species, considered blasphemy.

"I, in turn, will make you some more balls of b'itol," Andro immediately suggested. He recovered the fastest of the three transformed.

"It won't be the same b'itol used by Nimja," corrected Nacxit, "but inferior in quality, yet still powerful and very valuable. I couldn't put in your hands exactly what we use. But thank you for your help."

When Andro took Nacxit from Anna and Ravage and helped him out, Forkis formally addressed the others in the room:

"It's time to act. Captain Anna Sandstorm." He gave the woman an indifferent look. "I will put you under the command of one of the colonels, who will select people and send you to Nephrida, where you will theoretically train the rebels in our strategy. Not on machines, because we will create new ones from scratch and rebuild the ones we have, as you heard before. In addition, for now, let's treat Nephridians like the Headhunters, as dubious coercive allies who are not allowed to give equipment in the first stage of joint action. I hope Dr. Figam will now easily find a way to check all our allies with our mind exteriorizators. Lieutenant Seymour, you too will be assigned to Mezzo, where the Headhunters are currently stationed. You will receive the same task as the team with Captain Sandstorm. I'm sending you," added the Emperor firmly, seeing that Anna was slightly confused, and Tsar was standing with his raised left eyebrow, "because you know best the nations you are associated with, and you have a chance to end your old private conflicts. I don't want a situation to occur in which we stick knives in each other's back before we even get to Kandrok. You will depart as soon as the research team has built and installed new protective screens on our machines in the hangar. You'll also get planetary shields for on-site installation." Forkis took a sip of water from the mug, then rested his fists on the tabletop. "What is the condition of our army, General Warfighter?"

"Thirty percent of the achijes from this facility is checked, sir," Velkee reported.

Once Figam had managed to create the final and perfect version of the thought exteriorizator, Jenny's help became unnecessary. More than a dozen such devices had been built in sector F, and more were on the way. Work on achijes' selection under the supervision of Warfighter lasted from morning to night. No traitors had been found yet, but seventy-four people had proved unable to continue working together for a variety of reasons. Once they were given antiviral serum, they would be able to fly back to their homes when interstellar travel was safe.

"Among those thirty percent are there achijes of enough rank to train the rebels and Headhunters?"

"There are, sir. But we don't have permanent divisions yet, for a sure reason."

"Okay. For now, what we have is enough. You gentlemen," he looked at Warfighter, Milles, Darf, and Ravage in turn, will take care of our troops at base ... or no. We'll do so. You, General Darfo, will fly to Mezzo with Lieutenant Seymour and you will immediately take care of the local Kiritians and the Headhunters."

"Yes, sir." Darfo nodded.

"General Warfighter will be working on Cargoo because we have the most Kiritians here. In creating the army, instead of Biffter, the appointed general Robert Milles will support you."

"Yes, Emperor," both men replied simultaneously.

"Now, after the carrying-on with scientists, the creation of a trusted army should go very quickly. There is also the question of our people on Calcaris in the Libra Universe. General Ravage, this will be your job."

"I am happy to introduce them to the new standards of warfare."

"Could I go to Calcaris as well, when my role on Nephrida ends?" Anna asked somehow wistfully and in private, as the generals engaged in talking to each other. Forkis guessed immediately why she was asking for it. Calcaris was her first home, she had been born there. Her father, Krystian Sandstorm, after the Kiritian-Rebel War, when Anna had joined the Immortals, had quit serving as a pilot in the opposition, returned to his planet and founded a transportation company that had provided services within that planetary system. He had broken off contact with his daughter. Fearing his reaction, Anna hadn't gotten in his way, but decided to close all her affairs before the next war. She was ashamed that it was only in such circumstances that she decided to reconcile with her father, since she could meet him at any moment, for many years. She hoped that maybe she would improve relations with former friends also on Nephrida.

"If you want, I can go with you." Forkis didn't add to the problems. He smiled. "It will be some time before you leave Nephrida, then I could check how our people and allies are doing after training on these three planets. It would be nice to find the rest of the missing Kiritians who might be out there somewhere." The emperor gestured with his chin toward the ceiling.

"We can pitch another idea to the doctors regarding it," suggested Seymour, who ensconced himself on the table.

"As long as we don't overload them," added Anna.

13. The human fighter

Nacxit quickly recovered and was soon able to leave the Kiritian hideout. As might have been expected, he didn't tell anyone what he was going to do next or what his plans were. He neither confirmed nor denied that they would meet again.

Necron caught him shortly before departure, and they managed to chat on the surface near the transporter. They witnessed the Sector F research team spread an inhibitory shield against Kandrok over a patch of the planet. It wasn't just the cover itself that made a colossal impression, but more the fact that Figam had created something like this only two days after his brain had been transformed. Spreading the shield consisted in the fact that in its center, i.e., on the edge of the parade square where Rei'than was taken for walks, a small metal cylinder-launcher was set, from which a programmed ball of pat-b'itol was fired to the height of half of the stratosphere. Admittedly, it differed from the one used by Nimja because it was more primitive and suited to human digital technology, but sufficient to compete with Kandrok technologically. Its prefix came from the word 'pathological', as one of the achijes had named jokingly the invention, but as the name had spread like wildfire throughout the base, it had been decided to keep it. After reaching the height, the ball exploded and began to spread radially an ever-larger energy barrier in the shape of an umbrella, until its edges touched the ground. Seen from below, it looked like a transparent, orange-blue semicircular net tens of kilometers in diameter, made of hexagonal mesh like in honeycombs, but when two pilots were sent under the ionosphere, they found they could see the very surface of the planet. For observers from outer space, the cloak selectively covered everything except rocks and dead earth, so if the achij regiment appeared on the square, they would remain invisible. Keeping machines in the underground hangars also became unnecessary, but Forkis ordered this to remain unchanged for the time being.

"I'd like to ask you something." Necron couldn't take his eyes off the unusual barrier. Holding a staff, Nacxit let the man finish, though he had already known what he wanted to say. "I used to think that being around Forkis had allowed me to train my mind, learn to block my thoughts from him. It was similar with Jenny, although in her case I was better able to control it. But when Figam created the exteriorizator, it turned out that it didn't work for me. What is this about? Why do I have full control over this blockage once, another time partially, and in your case not at all?" He shifted his gaze to the Nimja member.

"It is not related to psionic skills, because people don't have them. Your nickname comes from the fact that you were practically dead for a while. Forkis killed you in front of the crowd in London so that Figam could administer to you the super virus, and the nascent emperor lent credence to his power. This condition causes permanent changes in the brain. You could correct it medically with your level of development, but you've never been interested in it."

"So, the point is, have there been some changes to my brain?"

"Yes, but it's nothing serious. You didn't even notice anything. Therefore, psionics, on an evolutionary level close to yours, don't have full or partial access to you. And the machine is not the human mind. Figam's thought exteriorizator is based on an algorithm inspired by Jenny's mind. Biological language has been rewritten into digital. When you worked with the girl in the lab, you probably blocked yourself from her. Hence this entry in the algorithm. If you were thinking of extending this constant to other combinations, you would have to sit down in front of Figam and Jenny again, and the scientist would have to recreate the algorithm, also take into account chaotic and random trials, because that's how your brain works. It is possible that this would also be effectless during the creation of the next version of the invention. The exteriorizator doesn't work on Forkis either," added Nacxit. "He also has a non-standard brain because he was dead."

Kiret was confused.

"But Forkis is a clone. His body never died. Or it had been dead before taking the atole." He shook his head. "I don't understand. Everything has gotten so messed up. I'm sorry."

"Don't worry about it." Nacxit tapped him on the shoulder. "Maybe Figam, Andro or Sariel will explain it better to you if you feel like learning more."

"Thanks."

Nacxit moved towards approaching Forkis and the generals who had been present at the opening of the barrier. Kiret sighed silently. Initially he wanted to ask the Nimja member to confirm that he had nothing to do with treason or espionage (where did the derogatory rumors about him even come from?) but rejected the idea. He realized that Nacxit hadn't come to Cargoo to resolve individual disputes. Had he asked him for help, he would have compromised himself even more, had tainted his broken reputation more. No, he should have tried to rebuild relations with Forkis so that they were like before Beliar Drunkenstein's assassination. He preferred the old, secret name of a sidekick to the idea that he was hiding his dealings with the enemy.

He put his hand in his pocket and found he didn't have his PDA. He had probably left it in his apartment. He had received very little messages lately, so he rather didn't miss anything important.

***

Achijes kept their fitness by training in the barracks, and when the workout required platoons or even several companies, they went to a vast air tunnel connecting the factory and assembly room of Sector D with the hangars. In the area of over three kilometers, there was a lot of space and room for maneuver. There could even practice pilots on small machines. However, now everything was to be more comfortable - thanks to the barrier, the surface would become available.

Darius was in a good mood when he finished training, not only because of his adrenaline surplus. Everything slowly became clear and orderly, and finally some sensible ideas for saving the nation appeared. Forkis' return and the meeting of Nacxit propelled this nightmarish, long-standing stagnation. Having simplified the organizational units of the military[1], Warfighter and Milles divided all Cargoo achijes into permanent tactical associations, divisions and sub-units. The newly formed teams got used to working with their assigned colleagues, but during the reorganization it was considered who had previously collaborated with whom. Thus, the refreshed Company D of the Third Battalion of the Second Regiment of the First Cargoo Infantry Division was to be commanded by Captain Michael Avadar, who was replaced by Lieutenant Tsar Seymour. The First Platoon subservient to them was assigned to Rudyard Gareth, who was appointed senior sergeant, since a city guard no longer existed on Cargoo. To it, in turn, reported three teams named after - like all the others in the army - stars. Proxima Centauri was to be led by Corporal Darius Schindler, and it included among others Kogan, Ryan as well as Divinus who was also decided to be included in Kiritians' army, although he had become neither an achij nor Immortal. Relagard agreed to lightning-fast training with a brain-soluble entraser. He didn't have to exercise physically anyway, as it turned out that, being a Karikon assassin, he was one of the most capable people in the base. Zira Aytar became the commander in the Antares team, while the technician corporal Rasmus Darkoris in the Sadr team, which included also his former subordinates, Bradshaw and Shimizu. This whole company reported to Warfighter. As Nacxit had suggested, no androids were placed in the army, at least not in the units that were to fight Kandrok.

In terms of assimilating the theory related to working with new equipment and vehicles being developed in sector F, Warfighter enjoyed the use of soluble entrasers as transmitters.

Darius was following his colleagues towards the bathroom as Tsar grabbed his arm and dragged him aside.

"What?" He protested.

"Are you planning to go see Jenny tonight?"

"I've had such an intention; I've rarely seen her lately. I have more responsibilities."

"I'd give up on this chick in your place."

Schindler wondered if he got it right. Rarely did the lieutenant have a serious expression, and he also looked weary.

"After all, you persuaded me that I should walked up to her."

"Yeah, but that was before. There is something wrong with her." Darius summed up the lieutenant's words with an urgent and surprised look. "Sometimes I watch her when she is around. In the cafeteria, I just stare at her even intrusively. Deliberately. She is nervous, she avoids my eyesight."

Darius snorted.

"And that is all your reasoning? Oh cool. You stare at her, so she's afraid. She had an adventure with drunkards in the corridor once, and the trauma remained. Don't scare her, Tsar."

He smiled crookedly.

"I'm one hundred percent sure she's conspiring. Hides a secret. She takes advantage of the confusion at the base. She doesn't want to see anyone, not even you."

"How do you know that?" Tsar had promised, so he didn't tell his subordinate that Jenny had asked him to restrict Darius' access to her.

"I feel that she will grow into a second mom," he said vaguely. "The apple doesn't fall far from the tree. You'll see there will be trouble because of Jenny."

"I don't see anything wrong there."

"Because you're involved and therefore blind."

Darius might have argued on the last point, but he knew Tsar did know a lot about people, and he had never been wrong in judging them since they worked together. Since he wanted to tell him about his observations, something must have been going on. Schindler had hardly seen the girl lately, so he was unable to draw any suspicions. All he knew was that she was often in the palm house and played with the cats when she wasn't working in the kitchen.

"Act wisely," only Seymour warned.

"Of course. See you, lieutenant."

The boy walked away past him.

Tsar sat down on lowered forks of a loader and began to watch other teams practicing, which he brightened with a joint.

***

Jenny no longer needed to go to Figam for tests and simulations. Simply put - she ceased to be needed. The doctor had created many copies of the exteriorizators that made her job, and after Nacxit intervened, he devised a method to check all the Cargoo Kiritians in a week. Eight hundred thousand people. On the one hand, the girl was relieved that she no longer had to fulfill her father's requests and work for the nation that she would never become a part of, but on the other hand, she felt even more rejected. Insignificant, irrelevant. After asking Tsar to find Darius something to do for the evenings, she realized that she had even liked the company of this energetic, uncouth corporal. She had gotten used to him. Unless she became a living example of the principle that you should enjoy what you have. Forkis and Anna seem to have forgotten about her. Everyone was nice to her (she avoided drunks), but also strange. She felt lonely. She didn't belong here at all.

There was only one person who understood her, listened to her and had time for her (to be precise - she was never short of time).

Rei'than.

Stranger.

Enemy.

"Worm, scum and slowworm," others said.

Only she saw in him a lonely, aggrieved soldier whose companion was killed, and who was being kept in prison for years, it was not even known for what purpose. A soldier armed with a dhurnsteel armor of mockery, contempt and hatred, but what else was he to do in his position? He probably adopted the best strategy, because he didn't break down or end his life.

Sandstorm found a clever way to see him almost every day. Tukum helped her in this, treating the secret precedent as an adventure and an escape from her parents. Jenny was a bit embarrassed every time she used the little Onkalot girl - and for trysts with Rei'than! But Tukum's mind was too young and simple for Aggro to psychometrically test it, and he preferred to forge family ties on mutual trust - so Sandstorm's secret had remained safe for the time being.

It started with Jenny coming to play with Tukum in a miniature jungle. She sometimes took her for a few hours away from the wooden house made available to the Onkalots, which had once served as a resting point for visitors - into the overgrown meanders of a huge hall, which was a substitute for the unspoiled nature of Chulimal. Aggro often went to Figam for various tests, so he didn't keep an eye on them, he had full confidence in Jenny, and Chimalmat was grateful to her, because thanks to her, the siblings avoided many fights, scratched eyes and torn fur coats. Tukum was not very fond of her brothers, who envied her that she had developed the psionic skill very early, and quite a specific one. Onkalots' talents were as a rule related to the environment in which a kitten grew up, and Tukum had been born in Kiritians' base, among machines and the ubiquitous metal. So, Jenny couldn't have found a better person. She started taking her to the secret tunnel, making sure no one was looking for them, then, as they made their way through the 'haunted' bathroom to the east wing of Sector B, asked the Onkalot girl to spoil the cellula in solitary confinement. The guards got used to the fact that there were frequent breakdowns in the area, and as Rei'than turned out to be extremely polite in recent times, sometimes for many days no one felt like repairing the damage. The entrance to the prison wasn't visible from the gatehouse due to the arched shape of the corridor; the only known way to the inmate was from the center of the sector and meant passing the guards. The watchmen themselves were often absent from their posts - they were called in for training and exercises related to the inventions of the team of scientists and the reorganization of the army.

So, you could say that Jenny was free to go. The interest in them both ceased. It even happened that no one came to the avor for several days and if it hadn't been for her, he would have weakened from hunger and thirst. And he still hadn't decided to eat his last rajithar capsule. To Sandstorm it looked a bit as if he had been waiting for something and hadn't wanted to waste it unnecessarily in advance.

"Here you are." Today she brought him a sausage stolen from the kitchen, made of artificially produced meat.

"You, too, help oneself." Rei'than handed her a piece from a fresh, fragrant chain. Jenny was no longer afraid of sitting down or crouching next to the bars itself - and of having physical contact with the prisoner more than once.

"What filth," the avor made a fuss. "You feel at once that this is not real meat, but laboratory-grown."

"Hey, don't look a gift skulak in the engine."

They ate in silence for a while, looking at each other until they started laughing.

"Give her too, she has deserved." The avor pointed to the Onkalot girl, squinting at the sausage with her eyes glittering above the mournful face. The girl handed her a piece, immediately improving Tukum's mood. "Thanks, Jen, for coming."

She smiled gently, though her mind was a repository of extreme emotions. It happened every time she called by the solitary confinement.

Kiret was right - she had lost interest in him, though not entirely. Apparently, the first love didn't rust.

But how did it happen that she began to feel something for Rei'than?! Did Cargoo offered few better catches, even if the first days of her stay here had started with nerve-wracking situations? Healthy, immortal, fit, wise, and in addition of the same species?

At first, she had come to the cell for a thrill. The fact that she had been doing something forbidden that no one had known about except Tukum had made her feel alive again like in her childhood on Atla. Finally, she had had some entertainment heated with a pinch of fear of detection.

She had long ceased to care if she could read the enemy's mind. Rei'than told her interesting facts about his mother planet, as well as other ones that had been conquered by avors. One after another. He spoke with a mocking vein about the bestialities and possibilities of his super-collectivity, Jenny should have hated him more and more for his aggressive nature - but it fascinated her. In a sense, not the crimes, but the person talking about them. The prisoner began to appear to her as a hero staying far from his cradle, with which he was connected by a bond which she didn't understand. As someone strong and invincible. He fascinated her as the complete opposite of her fragility and impermanence. Did she need the feeling that there could be an uninterrupted continuity, since she had heard more than once throughout her short life as the Kiritian nation fell apart? In general, something was constantly changing in people's existence, something that you loved for a long time disappeared. It was the other way around with Kandrok members. They were constantly growing in strength. Using strength, they also took over those who met the standards of their army, were physiognomically fit for it. She listened with bated breath - though she understood little because of cultural distances - about the Lightbringer, the devotion to the gerha, the collectivities, the world of machines, the neurocytes, the immortality obtained through the complete loss of the biological body, which was a dream of every Kandrok member. From somewhere she remembered the theory that the matter of the cosmos tended to become immaterial, become thought. Something similar she had heard from Nimja whose goal in an undefined future was to get rid of bodies and become pure energy. Perhaps at the stage of development of Kandrok there had been stirrings of the same aspirations? As she wondered, hadn't the Kiritians been beginning to show similar tastes? Immortality first, and what would happen next?

"It's freedom, not monstrosity," Rei'than whispered in her ear; their faces were close to the bars. "The highest form of respect."

"What?" Thoughtful, she lost the thread.

"You just asked how we can mutilate ourselves. Strive in life for cyborgization and then complete robotization. I don't think we will understand each other. What will remain macabre, monstrosity and madness to you, is for me the most beautiful, most intelligent form of freedom. The path indicated by the Lightbringer." He raised his hand to the ceiling, staring passionately at the lamp. "Permanent awareness. Beating the entropy of nature."

She didn't feel comfortable talking about topics on which they had conflicting views. Rei'than had turned out to be angry a few times already, and she had been only nervous.

She decided to take a chance and finally ask him about something she had been hiding from everyone. She had been trying to hold this conversation for a long time. She found herself trusting Rei'than more than her parents and the few friends she found here, including Aggroteh. At least Rei'than wouldn't make a research object out of her and subject her to these hideous experiments. He wouldn't consider her a freak, as in her childhood Cossack and his gang - he was too intelligent for that.

"I'd like to tell you something. But be warned, it will be strong."

As usual, it gave her chills when she saw his amused, belligerent gaze.

"You've intrigued me. I'm all ears."

She didn't have to bother to feel anxiety that favored the change. During the sleepless nights, she had exercised a lot with her paternal ailment, and had gotten better and better at controlling.

At the site of the nails, claws appeared. Tukum approached and meowed, surprised.

Jenny feared a misjudgment - that Rei'than would react with disgust or shock, but he only stared at her hand as if she had shown him a new kind of flower. He grabbed it in his and looked at it with passing interest.

"The aftermath of an accelerated transmutation, I think I can put it so linguistically," he said. "Species conglomerate. Nothing out of the ordinary."

Sandstorm breathed a sigh of relief. The super collectivity with three and a half degrees on Kardashev's scale, however evil and cruel, eventually had to keep a certain level.

"Will you explain it so I can understand? Somehow straight."

"In our community, cyborgization is a crowning process, thanks to it we perfectly understand the changes taking place in a body so that we can make connections with metals. Sometimes we accelerate cell regeneration even many thousands of times so that a newly created warrior is immediately ready for action. More than once cells have to be changed from one form to another. The process takes place in no time, of course it is artificial. This is just accelerated transmutation. The Lightbringer taught us this skill."

He must have been talking about Nimja, Sandstorm had realized that already some time earlier. Rei'than's community had once dealt with them, just like Onkalots, people or the inhabitants of Karikon. Everyone called them different. But she wasn't going to raise that question again, remembering what it had ended with the previous time.

"However, we rarely use it, although we know the essence of accelerated transmutation," the prisoner continued. "Our methods of improving a body or returning to full functionality are more ... radical." He laughed wholeheartedly at his thoughts. "You probably wouldn't like them. We like contrasts, not smooth boundaries."

"Could it be hereditary?" The girl asked quickly, who didn't quite like some of the spine-chilling, loose disquisitions of the stranger.

"In the sense of transmuted parental traits? This can happen. After all, you are an example of this."

"I know, but if it can go further. How does this transmutation even work?"

"I won't explain this matter to you, because you won't understand it."

"At least try it. Approximate."

"Each matter is a form of cosmic record. A code. An information carrier that can be reprogrammed into an infinite number of combinations. When it happens by itself - or due to some factor - for example, with a biological being, mutation occurs. The process is very slow, low-energy, so it cannot take place in a minute. Something different, new or known for a long time, is created. For example, someone gets an ugly skin cancer. Artificial change of information, on the other hand, is limited only by the imagination of the creator. In this way, an Onkalot can be transformed into a human, without interfering with the orhada, or the water into stone. In your case, or rather your father, who used a living artifact, a genome change took place abruptly in a high-energy process. It was an artificial process, biotechnologically advanced. Transmutation is a sudden change of information in the genome that immediately manifests itself, but at the same time the old, original record is encoded, and therefore it is hereditary. You were born as a result of the intercourse of the two human beings, one of whom, Forkis, had a double-coded genome. In addition ... contaminated with the b'itol of the living artifact, which also passed into your body. That's why you look human, but you have some Onkalotian features from your father. I would have to explain to you how the living artifact works, but you won't understand it at all."

"Damn," she thought, a simple soldier, but the higher rank of Kardashev was doing its job. Kandrok's morons may have had Figam levels in humans - not that she thought Rei'than was such, he was an umen after all.

She indeed didn't understand much, but overall, she realized what it was about.

"Is it possible to get rid of it somehow, I mean the Onkalot qualities? At least this one, because telepathy is useful."

"Making changes to the transmuted genome?" Rei'than lifted the corners of his mouth. "It's very easy for us."

Jenny grimaced shyly.

"Does it hurt?"

"No. Just a few injections. And the little claws won't show up anymore." He watched as the girl restored her nails with relief after the third try. "If I had the opportunity to take you to Asephor' Cerotis, I would quickly relieve you of your problem." He gave her a cunning smile. "And everyone else. You would be a great avor if you would choose to live like us," he added after mock consideration. She shared the same values.

Absorbed as ever in his words - and more person - Jenny had completely forgotten about the existence of Tukum. She didn't notice when she came to a corner of the cell and easily squeezed through the bars. The sigh died down in her tightened throat. Sandstorm looked anxiously at the prisoner she still feared. To a very small extent, but still.

Rei'than sat calmly on the ground, allowed Tukum to get on his legs, then squeezed herself between his hands. The Onkalot girl stuck out her mouth and they touched their noses.

"No more pain, no more suffering that only a body can feel, no more destruction." He started gently stroking her head. Tukum pressed against his chest. "No more fear. And the beginning of power. It's like a new life. New possibilities."

Jenny breathed a sigh of relief once again.

"I won't get it anyway."

"I'm not asking you for it." He smiled grimly. "I'm not forcing you to do anything."

He lifted the humanoid jaguar girl and moved her to the bars for Jenny to take over.

He gently grabbed the girl's hand as she released Tukum onto the floor. Their eyes met and Jenny began to breathe faster.

"We've known each other for quite a long time. Have you gained your trust in me during this time?" he asked gently.

She only managed to nod; words refused to squeeze themselves through her throat as he ran his finger over her skin. She sensed that he would surprise her with something right away.

"Are you absolutely sure about this?"

"Yes," she finally said.

He grasped her other hand.

"So, you will let me out for a while? You mentioned there was a bathroom nearby. I'd like to empty and clean the little bucket, including myself."

Surprised, she withdrew her hands. Unable to bear his disturbing and at the same time attractive gaze, she looked at the Onkalot girl, making flips and playing with her own tail.

"I'm scared," she said through her teeth.

"Of me or the consequences?"

"Both. But I don't know of what more."

"Nobody will do anything to you, including me. Besides, no one is here, and they don't care what is going on in the cell."

"Then no witnesses when you want to kill me. I don't count Tukum."

Rei'than became sad and sighed theatrically.

"So, you don't trust me."

Jenny was at a loss. She was really scared. Was the avor playing, or was he honest? She had a fifty percent chance that her decision would be fatal if she made a mistake.

"It's not like that ..."

"And how? You must be afraid of something other than the thing you mentioned." He smiled wickedly.

She was aware that she acted terribly recklessly to come here without anyone's knowledge, even if she had only intended to stand with a weapon in hand, many meters from the bars. The most knackering was the uncertainty. Did she trust Rei'than? Was she afraid of him? Did he really only want a break from those few square meters of sad, monotonous cell? What if she let him out and he would lung at her, kill her on the spot, as she had just joked recklessly? The avor had seemed to feel better since she started bringing him meat. He had the strength to practice in the cell, as much as the spatial limitations allowed it, since he was no longer walking.

So, was he playing or not?

Would he kill her or not?

"Jen, let me out," he said softly, pleadingly. So that she felt guilty. A soulless monster that allowed a lost, lonely, jaded creature to suffer. "Please."

Rei'than held the inhaler to his nose and drew a massive dose of carbon dioxide. Breathing deeply, he looked up contentedly.

Sandstorm looked at Tukum and decided to seek her support. However, the Onkalot girl was what she had been all along - still a silly kitten for whom their entire present universum is the slobbery tail, crumpled fur and tongue-cleaned claws.

Maybe she had a hint right under her nose: it was enough to follow Tukum's behavior. She had trusted Rei'than, allowed herself to be stroked and taken in his arms. But how was it to be interpreted: as an animal instinct or as the prudence of a rational being? What fallen stars were exactly little Onkalots?

Jenny closed partly her eyes.

She would regret it most.

Regret very briefly, because in a minute she would be cooling down against the wall with her twisted neck and broken head.

Or she would receive a well-deserved reward for her courage, which after all, she had desired so much for some time ...

She was unable to unlock because she didn't have a deactivator. The achijes didn't leave it in the gatehouse but carried it with them.

She picked up the she-cat.

"Tukum, I'll bring you a whole bunch of sausage, if you unlock this door for a while."

The Onkalot girl looked into her eyes, pressed her paw against Jenny's collarbone, then glanced at the lock of the cell.

It yielded almost immediately with a click of a complicated mechanism; Tukum jumped to the ground.

The well-preserved bars opened soundlessly as Reit'han pushed them gently with his hand.

The girl's heart seemed to be pounding in many parts of her body at once, evenly in her chest, temples and ears. Her legs trembled.

The avor left, for the first time in many years, without the company of guards. He took a deep breath, closing his eyes contentedly as if there had been better air outside the cell, the breath of the planet Asephor' Cerotis itself. He stood in front of the girl, smiled half boldly, half tenderly.

"You see? It hasn't been that bad. Rigaba lumuta."

He slowly hugged Jenny, who was so scared and stiff as if he had been going to swallow her. Fortunately, the state of paralysis was short-lived.

She hugged him too, but first she examined with her hands his chest and shoulders like an unknown area on a map. In a split second, they clung to each other like lovers separated for a decade, except that Rei'than with the face like a mask, contorted by mockery behind her back. Jenny rejoiced at his closeness, which she had needed so much and hadn't had for a long time, he, as a Kandrok member, in whom sterility and asexuality were high, and sex drive was very low - such a mechanism had been developed by nature when avors had learned to prolong their lives and finally immortalize - didn't feel this kind of emotion so intensely. In addition, Jenny was still human, a terrible heroko devoka. Surprised, Tukum looked at them with her head tilted, meowed.

"I didn't notice what time it is?" Rei'than's casually asked question didn't reach her at first, she needed time in which she blinked several times before she realized its meaning.

The avor smiled at her confusion, he was about to go back to his cell to check the time on his PDA.

"A few minutes past 7 pm," she replied, glancing at her assistant. She had completely forgotten that the second copy she had left in her room, she was to return to Kiret.

Rei'than cursed silently. He often returned from the yard at this time, and always passed laboratories full of scientists, but now that Figam's, Sariel's, and Andro's projects that Jenny had so eagerly told him about were being realized, the rooms were certainly overcrowded, and the work was beaming. In both sectors. It was a pity, he let it go for now. He had been stuck here for years, so what difference would a day, two, or even a week more make? His plan had been crystallized for a long time and he had been patiently implementing it. But how do you get this naive girl to let him out at a certain hour next time?

"And why are you asking?" She asked. Thanks to the closeness he had favored her with, her fear had almost completely disappeared.

"I'm afraid someone will catch us. I remember clearly the times at which the achijes were around," his words sounded plausible.

"There is no one in the nearest corridors. I myself am terribly afraid of being caught." She felt shivers running down her spine as she imagined that she was caught red-handed by such General Warfighter. She didn't even want to think how the case would have turned out if Forkis himself had found out about the incident ...

Rei'than put his hand to her cheek and ran his fingers over it. The girl stared at him as if at an unusual painting. Good.

"Will you lead me to the bathroom?"

"Of course." She smiled. She grabbed his hand. "Come on. Tukum, you too. You are to be quiet and not move away. I mean, I've talked to the Onkalot girl."

"Wrigo lumuta," said the avor cheerfully.

They looked out into the corridor to experience the relaxing silence. Jenny pulled Rei'than with her, Tukum was trotting on all fours next to her legs.

In the bathroom, the avor stripped off his two-piece medical suit, showered, then dried his body in a stall, where warm air was blowing from all sides. Sandstorm was waiting in front of the mirror in the next room, staring at the slightly steamy surface, smiling and once again neatening her hair with her hands.

"That's better." She saw Rei'than's reflection on the right. He put his hands on her shoulders and turned the girl towards him. "Thank you again for these few moments of freedom."

He moved closer - and kissed her gently on the lips. He didn't have to bend down because they were almost the same height - they were only two centimeters apart in favor of the avor.

Surprised, the girl lost the ability to speak and move, she felt the strong pulsation of blood again in various parts of her body, she tried in vain to breathe quietly, looking into his amber eyes. For many sleepless nights she had fantasized about kissing Rei'than, everything had looked beautiful in her imaginations when she had arranged the smallest details conveniently, but now she was scared to death. That she had let the enemy out, that she was doing something terrible, that her feeling was misdirected, she also considered herself a traitor in a way.

It had already happened.

Her mother had once acted similarly!

Sandstorm had broken too many rules, but she didn't feel particularly bad about it.

She put her arms around his neck, he pressed Jenny against him, enfolding her waist. She pecked him on his lips with the same delicacy he had just pecked her on hers. He kissed her back.

For the first time in her life, she kissed a boyfriend. She considered herself a bit old for her debut, because according to the Terran calendar she had turned eighteen, but fate seemed to compensate her for this neglect, making the first time forbidden and extravagant. Because what girl took the enemy as her first partner, and in addition from another species?

Her face crimsoned as it flashed through her mind, whether bastardizing people and avors would be possible.

They kissed each other more and more vigorously, caresses were added to it, but still within decency.

"Wow, I think it is I who should fear you." Rei'than chuckled as if it was Sandstorm who set the pace.

When they stopped, they huddled silently as before in the cell, enjoying the warmth of each other's body. Rei'than couldn't deny that he was quite enjoying it. In Kandrok, asexuality grew with a higher degree of cyborgization, which was related to the electronization and mechanization of the body, and he, apart from the neurocyte, was still fully tissue.

"I think I should go back," he said. "Someone can come at any time."

"You're right. I'll just show you the tunnel I was talking about."

They walked to the corner of the shower and toilet room, Jenny deflected the tiles and shone her PDA light into the mine corridor.

"Nice." The avor smiled, standing on all fours. "So, this is how you come."

"It leads to the orangery, thanks to Tukum I also found the entrance to the hangar, through the ventilation. There are probably more secret passages, but you would need the right equipment to discover them."

Rei'than stood up, trying hard not to show his interest in the information about the hangar.

"Be careful," he said with concern. "When they find out what you do ... I wouldn't like to be in your shoes then." He added sadly. "Mine are already lost anyway."

"Don't say that."

"You think they will let me live here forever?" He said more sharply. "My days are numbered. There is no more hope for me." He hugged Jenny. "But I'm glad that the Lightbringer has brought me such a wonderful creature to strengthen my orhada before my imminent death."

Worried, she slipped out of his hug.

"I'll figure something out."

She amused him with her promise.

"It's time to go back."

After a few minutes they were already at the cell. Rei'than stepped inside and Tukum slammed the bars lock back shut.

"Maybe see you later." He brushed Jenny's chin, winked at her, walked away and lay down on the bed.

The girl took Tukum in her arms and quietly left the prison.

Looking towards the wall, Rei'than couldn't suppress the sense of wild satisfaction twisting his face as he recalled that guilt mixed with helplessness in Jenny's eyes when he began to catch her out saying about his end. This stupid, young devoka really fell in love with him madly!

***

Having ambivalent feelings all the way, because on the one hand she was enjoying what she had experienced with Rei'than, and on the other hand, she worried about his position, Jenny returned through the tunnel to the palm house. She led Tukum to Chimalmat; Aggroteh was absent. Telekinetically, she sensed that the girl was struggling with an internal conflict, tried to talk to her about it, but she smiled stiltedly and politely refused. With humanoid jaguars having a higher emotional perception than humans, she should have been careful.

She took a train to Sector C and returned to her apartment. She found Kiret's PDA on the table and gritted her teeth. In general, she respected someone else's privacy and property, but this time curiosity won over her irritating voice screaming "no!" in her head. At least she'll finally get her mind off what had happened between her and the avor.

The PDA turned out to be completely unsecured, as if Necron had ceased to care about the protection of his data. Jenny lay back on the bed and looked through the messages in the air, in the form of handwriting, images or videos.

"What a colorless man," she thought after a quarter of an hour. Kiret hardly contacted anyone, he didn't conduct private correspondence with his friends, when someone wrote to him, it was in professional matters: he received reports, orders, requests and questions. From the moment Forkis came back to life and took power, it was scarce anyway. As if Necron had suddenly become unnecessary.

Jenny sighed. She hugged the PDA against her like a miniature portrait of a loved one.

Darn it, she still had a lot of affection for him. What if it was solely due to Necron's rejection that she had gotten near Rei'than to make up for the loss?

With these thoughts, she fell asleep.

The next day in the morning, when she finished working for several hours, she was going to return the PDA to the owner. She couldn't find Kiret in Sector A, where he usually stayed, and no one knew where to find him. She had seen him in the canteen sometimes, but not today. A lot of achijes had moved into an air tunnel as part of the new tests and validations. She decided to look there, maybe see something interesting at the same time.

Also, here Sandstorm didn't find the former emperor, but witnessed an interesting scene; she perched on one of the side terraced parking pockets for little devemers, from where she had a perfect view, like from a hill to the valley. A circle of people had gathered around an empty take-off platform. Closest to the center was Cargoo flower itself, including Dr. Figam. The space, limited on all sides by metal, additionally amplified the sounds, even in the distance one could hear decently.

"Come on, I invite you." The doctor showed Darius, who had an expression and look of a person that doesn't quite encompass what is going on around, the center of the platform. "Stand here."

Schindler obeyed.

"But I don't know what to do," he emphasized.

"And that's what the experiment is all about." Figam smiled heartily. "You are to act spontaneously, intuitively."

He tossed him a small ball that easily fit in hand, which Schindler grabbed without any problem. He looked at it. As announced by the Nimja member, Figam had created an inferior version of b'itol, but sufficient to compete with the equivalent used by Kandrok, thanks to which they could implode matter or construct bombs that decomposed to subatomic sizes, penetrated walls and regained structure on the other side.

"Now, please, everyone steps back," the scientist ordered, waving his hands. "There, behind the yellow circle. And preferably even further. Mr. Emperor, this applies to you too."

Darius wanted to make sure that he hadn't been handed a grenade.

"Now imagine your favorite little fighter, sir," said the doctor suddenly.

Schindler was completely baffled by the order. He was sure that he had been selected to test some form of weapon that he would use in simulating anti-aircraft combat.

How wrong he was.

He was very fond of small but deadly fighters with a classic pre-colonial appearance, that is, unlike the biological structures often used in Kiritian constructions, so he thought of one of this class, a 20-meter-long Parabellum 2820. Among oderses and Kiritians, a technological standard had developed that if something worked, and moreover was unrivaled and ergonomic, didn't go by the wayside, but it lasted as a series for centuries. That is why many devices looked exactly like their ancestors from centuries earlier (the shape of a machine in space didn't matter anyway), only internal components evolved. This was also the case with the Parabellum series, where only the numbers, often related to the year of production, were changed along with the type of drives, covers and weapons, or letters were added after them. The fighters could operate in and out of the atmosphere, had a triangular shape, four drives behind the tail, weapons that retracted from many niches, and an autonomous AI that didn't conflict with the pilot's will. The names of intelligent machines didn't include quotation as was the case with 'Perfarius'.

So, Schindler thought spontaneously about the P-2820.

A ball of pat-b'itol slid out of his hand, rose and got stuck to his chest like a slobbery candy. It disintegrated into many luminous pixels that began to ... multiply!

Schindler sighed and raised his arms, sensing that he was in no danger. Digital luminosity, neither virtual nor material, covered first his chest, then other parts of his body. It quickly devoured him completely. When the particles multiplied enough, they tilted him to the level. A material fuselage formed around his body, out of it grew wings, tail, nose and undercarriage.

Everyone who watched the phenomenon was speechless, even the scientists who had known what to expect.

Jenny stared at this unusual transformation with her eyes wide open, and breathless.

The structure changed completely; Darius became the Parabellum 2820 fighter, or more precisely - its core closed in a bio-cocoon, i.e., an operator. He could easily satisfy all his physiological needs; the wrapper also regulated any abnormalities of the body and performed a protective function. In addition to air, it was able to supply the produced nutrients and liquids, as well as remove metabolic products, thus creating an independent environment for the operator.

The AI of the machine was the self of Darius.

Satisfied as never before, Schindler was charmed by the new toy. From somewhere he knew how to direct it, it was enough for him to imagine the movements of the fighter, and the pat-b'itol particles rewrote the bio-pulses into their own language and transmitted them to all parts of the machine in a lightning-fast manner, as if the operator had been giving orders to his own limbs. The practice was not about controlling thoughts - if Schindler remembered it correctly, Nacxit had argued that supposedly humans had been able to influence matter in this way - but about receiving stimuli from the body and the brain.

He was integrated with the machine. He had no idea how it might have worked, with matter swathing him, but he could see the image in front of him, as if he had been viewing it on a HUD or directly through the canopy above the nose. Figam had programmed the comrade-enemy recognition in the most mill runway possible: friends green, the latter red, indefinite orange. Now only green dots were moving around Darius.

The Parabellum rose to a height that allowed for a trial execution of a barrel roll, made a loop, flying to the very ceiling, and finally began to circle at a controlled speed in the entire air tunnel.

Darius had never had such a great time.

He spotted Jenny - though he had rather tracked her down and recognized her.

He settled upright next to her on the terrace and opened the cockpit cover.

"Do you want to fly?" He exclaimed happily. His voice came from the cabin as if it had been Parabellum's AI speaking. Jenny remembered that the White XRS-14 Ghost had spoken to Anna in the same way.

She nodded as she managed to break her astonishment and focus her thoughts. She was also consumed by curiosity about how it all might have worked. She climbed into the cabin; the cover closed as she sat in the chair.

"Is that puronaks?" She asked.

Darius took off, headed for the vertical exit of the hangar that swung open, displaying the stars in the sky.

"I doubt it," he replied. "The doc wouldn't have invented a novel piece of equipment that Kandrok could smash. I have no idea what this fighter consists of. Or how the hell it's all powered up!"

"And how you feel?"

"I am in a position as if I were flying a wingsuit. And I feel ... quite normal." He laughed. "Besides, it's crazy fun. You must also try!"

She smiled.

"I will pass. But you, don't be embarrassed."

They left the area protected by Figam's semicircular cover. Darius imagined himself and Jenny, as well as all the gear and hull, becoming invisible, and it indeed worked. As they flew over ice fields among rocky hills, in the sheets, in the glow of the three moons visible at the time, there was no reflection of the fighter.

"Did they even let you fly out of base like that, Darius?"

"Nobody is complaining yet. Do you have any wishes regarding the route?"

"Let me surprise you. If you are to have fun, then fully. Just don't kill me."

"Okay! But speak if you feel any discomfort."

"I'm a little scared. This is your first time wearing this toy and you probably don't know how to use it."

"On the contrary: I know exactly what I am doing!" Schindler's excitement didn't subside. "Maybe the pat-b'itol particles delivered something like an entraser to my brain."

"Hello, Corporal," Figam said over a comm module located in front of Jenny's lap. "Can you hear me?"

"Perfect," Darius confirmed.

"Test the equipment, use it in many ways, within reason, of course. I will collect all the data."

"Right away! Can Kandrok see me?"

"I doubt it."

Darius wouldn't have been a purebred man if he hadn't started by checking to what speed he could accelerate. He chose to circle Cargoo, which was nine percent larger in circumference than Earth. He flew around it at the height of half the stratosphere in a minute but bearing in mind that he was carrying the fragile passenger without any suit. Neither he nor Jenny felt they were moving at all, just as when Darius and Seymour had been returning from the B9 in hijacked Kandrok's ship, escorting Dr. Figam. The girl didn't even have time to get sick from the rapidly moving area behind the cover.

During the flight, of course, shooting couldn't be missing.

Sandstorm had a hard time guessing what was leading in this farce: Darius was showing off to her, or he forgot about her existence and was testing the possibilities of his deadly mascot. She tried to telepathically reach his mind, but couldn't - the hull, maybe the biocon, was probably blocking her abilities.

The corporal was moderately pleased with the armament, even disappointed in them. He had at his disposal retractable energy cannons (although he didn't recognize what powered them, but he had seen this type of weapon a million times), a limited number of rockets which, after a short break in firing, somehow regenerated, and a beam of several seconds rooting deep pits in the ground.

"Eh, kind of a bit of poverty," he summed up. Figam heard everything that was happening in the cockpit.

"I admit it looks archaic, but it will break through Kandrok's diarduk," he answered immediately. "We have tested it on pieces of Rei'than's and Ly's armor. You can destroy everything with this weapon. With the beam, you will cut through the walls of buildings, as long as the avors on Certoris use similar materials that we captured from them at the Zodiac Universum. The rockets are renewing themselves against the law of conservation of mass ..."

"Can I fly out of the atmosphere?" Darius asked quickly, knowing that Maksimus was about to start accelerating with his erudition.

It was audible through the module that the doctor was consulting with someone.

"I was counting on it," he said shortly. "Jenny, how about you?"

"It's okay," she said brightly, relaxed.

The fighter raised its nose sharply and began flying towards space. With the last, upper atmosphere far below them, it hung like a satellite. Darius positioned the machine so that Jenny had a good view of Cargoo.

"Mr. Figam was right about that cover," she said. "You can't see that people live here."

"You better check it out."

Darius zoomed in so that they seemed to hang a hundred meters above the secret base.

"Not bad."

"The cover works. When we left the hangar, there were a few platoons outside and a couple of flying machines. And here, for human eyes, purges, apparently dead, weathered soil. Hey, are we going around the K'ajolom star?!"

Jenny snorted with laughter. Even if she had preferred to turn back, she would have sacrificed herself, not wanting to spoil Schindler's promising entertainment. She had to admit that the young corporal's carelessness greatly cheered her up.

It was winter on Cargoo, the planet was at perihelion to its star, and the two celestial bodies were separated by two AU.

The growing red dwarf made an electrifying impression, the sight was terrifying, but it was impossible to take your eyes moist with joy off it. It was like standing by a sea on a fragile bridge in a huge storm, when a ten-meter wave is approaching, but you are still staring at it with sick fascination. But now, before the face of K'ajolom, the experience was magnified several dozen times.

The operator and passenger lacked words expressing relevant emotions as they circled the orange and red spherical hell. Darius kept the distance, he wasn't going to test the maximum strength of his armor, especially since he was responsible for Jenny. He put filters on the cabin so that the girl could freely see the star.

Jenny had a small orlop behind the cabin where she could eat, refresh and sleep. Another of the many things they both failed to grasp was the illusory gravity aboard such a small vessel. Kiritians were able to create the gravity needed to move around space shuttles thanks to the dense atoplaxal particles. Separated by an extra-dimensional environmental bubble to reset the ship's 'moon mass' effect, the ball was so dense for its volume that a planetary gravity was created. Somehow, Figam made it possible that like in Kandrok's machines, on the P-2820 you could function as if you had been standing on an Earth-like globe. Jenny still couldn't feel the flight, no matter what speed Darius was developing.

They returned to Cargoo four days later. Darius couldn't help but take one more lap around the globe.

When they had a dozen or so kilometers to the base, they noticed a group of human figures below. The Kiritians didn't see them - the fighter was in full camouflage.

Darius hovered in the air, zoomed in. Sandstorm covered her mouth with her hands as she realized they had stumbled upon an execution.

"Sorry, Jenny, I haven't known." The corporal turned off the image immediately.

She managed, however, to register that the firing squad was led by Kiret, who was nowise pleased with what he was doing. He kept a grave, resigned face, as if it had been he who was to be executed. On his command, seven people were killed with impulse rifles; the girl guessed that it was probably the result of subsequent batches of collective interrogations.

"It's not your fault," she said softly. "Can you turn off the audio? So that no one eavesdropped on us?"

"Of course." Darius cut himself off from the base. After all, no orders had been given to him to be constantly tapped.

"My father ... He lied. He said he would let go those who would no longer wish to be part of the nation. That's the only reason I agreed to help Figam create the exteriorizator. They deceived me. People are dying now because of me."

"You can't think that way. Perhaps Forkis' message didn't apply to traitors. If these people were released, they could have taken us out. Tell the enemies the location of the hideout."

"They could have done it all the time."

"The Communications Center was constantly under strict control, and so was the off-planet flights."

"So, what's the problem with wiping traitors' memories, as Forkis once did partially with Figam when he decided to leave Kiritians? Why kill at once?" And not so long ago she had wanted to become a part of this nation. But she had to admit that she had always lived apart from the affairs of the Immortals. Sometimes she had heard that they had used cruel methods, but it was the kind of information that is caught with one ear and released with the other, since it doesn't concern the existence of a given person.

Darius sighed. He didn't understand her way of thinking, but he was far from speaking out loud, how simple-hearted she was.

"Jenny, I really don't know. I'm too small to understand the motives of the emperor and the staff."

She shook her head sadly.

"And also, this Necron. After everything he's been through ... Forkis made him do something like that." She found it easier for her to use his first name instead of 'father'. "In addition, he sent the former Galactic First Dignitary to do such degrading work. It is an officer who should deal with executions."

"Since we are at the stage of sincere confessions. With all due respect to your father, but for my taste, he punishes Biffter for bringing Kiritians down. He mentally abuses him. It is also an allusion to let him know how the traitors end."

Darius' words barely reached Sandstorm's ears, focused on her thoughts.

"Necron hates to kill, and if he does it, it is as a last resort. He prefers peaceful solutions, punishes with imprisonment at worst. Now I understand why he started drinking."

"Well, in our nation a big heart is an easy target. We'd better go back."

Schindler fired up one of the drivers and began the flight at a drifting pace.

"I will talk to him." The girl felt complicit that some achijes were sentenced. What if the exteriorizator didn't work properly? Could the scientists changed by Nacxit still make mistakes? She was also puzzled by the behavior of Forkis, in whom a dissonant between the promise and the deed occurred. Didn't the former Kiritians' community rely on sincerity and truthfulness, which was a point of their code, thanks to which they had gained an advantage over all mankind? Would Forkis have acted this way if he hadn't died? Is it possible that his atole may have been transformed on Amyrade? Jenny didn't know Forkis from before the resurrection, but had heard rumors that he had returned changed, more offensive. She also had to take steps regarding Kiret. Regardless of what had happened between them, it was he who had practically raised her and provided her with every amenity, so she should have repaid him. "I'll see what he has to say about destroying his own resources," she said ironically.

"I don't know if that's a good idea. I feel so sorry for these people, too, whatever they did, but neither I nor you have any idea what is going on in the higher echelons. Especially you. Maybe it's better to keep our heads down?"

"A father should listen to what his own daughter has to say."

Darius didn't answer. After a while they reached the landing field. When Jenny left the cockpit and moved away from the machine, it began to shrink quickly, disappearing particle by particle, so that in the finale there was the kneeling operator and the ball of pat-b'itol lying on the ground next to it. Satisfied, Schindler kissed it hard and put it in his pocket.

The girl withdrew discreetly as more achijes came up to the corporal to talk enthusiastically about his machine and journey.

She was going to have it out with her father right away. As she descended underground, she made her way quickly and confidently to the communications center of Sector A. After the selected people had departed for Calcaris, Nephrida, and Mezzo, Forkis stayed mostly in this crowded room. Information was exchanged no longer with Morse code, but by standard amplification of signals jumping on intermediaries placed in universes. Figam, Andro, and Sariel set out their stalls in this area by securing Kiritians' signals against avors.

The girl wondered how to play it all out. It would have been mature to approach her father and ask him to talk face to face. However, when she visualized the face of broken Kiret and the convicts falling on the icy sand as a result of the false message, she changed her mind - she decided to attack big. She would make a screaming hysteric out of herself who didn't care about the emperor's reputation.

She ignored a sergeant at the entrance telling her something and burst inside.

"Father, why did you have the achijes executed in the dunes? I've seen everything on board the Parabellum."

After those sentences were uttered out loud in the communications center, where several dozen people stayed, there was silence, as if with Jenny, vacuum had broken inside. Forkis, Warfighter, Milles, senior officers, communications officers, technicians, scientists, and the rest of the staff looked at her as if at Nacxit appearing unexpectedly. The achijes shifted their gaze to the emperor, who closed his eyes in frustration and mumbled a curse.

It was too late to walk the girl aside.

"It's true, Jenny. Every collaborator pays death for treason," he replied loudly and grandly. "We have the law of war. This is normal procedure. Everyone in the base knows what the punishment for dealing with Kandrok currently is. Now go back to your room, child. Don't try to get involved in things you don't understand."

"Jenny ..." Darius entered the room. Embarrassed, he gritted his teeth.

"You lied to me," Sandstorm continued dryly. "You didn't say you were going to kill when Dr. Figam was creating his invention. I would never allow my telepathy to be of service to someone's death."

"Jenny, please calm down." Schindler was trying to do something by moving his lips rather than whispering.

Forkis put his hands on his hips.

"What did you expect?" Under his severe gaze, the employees of the center began to return to their activities. "Great, my daughter grew up to be a haunted pacifist."

Sandstorm realized that she owed her views to Kiret. Something she considered an advantage her own father regarded as a fault. But what could she expect from the person who had had to deal with death, violence and suffering from an early age?

She walked closer to him; Darius waited at the door.

"Why are you humiliating Kiret?"

"I'm not humiliating him. I want to make him aware of what can happen if he also turns out to be a traitor."

"So, Schindler deduced well on the surface then," she thought.

"Are you crazy? Why would Necron be a traitor? I spent a long time in his company, especially on this unfortunate Earth - he is faithful to Kiritians."

"He raised you, you like him, so your words aren't credible. We currently have too few witnesses for his crimes. Even Figam can't prove it. For now, I'm watching him."

"Then check me out on my own exteriorizator."

"You're a telepath. Your memories are also unreliable."

Jenny sighed rebelliously.

"Sure ... And this is how you treat your friends who have always served you faithfully, with whom you were on good terms? What did this Kiret do to you?"

"I'll give you some advice," Forkis droned, growing weary of this exchange. "Stay away from politics."

"You won't tell me what to do, especially since I don't report to you."

"And you wanted to be a Kiritian. Just look at you. Listen to yourself."

"You know what? I wish you are taken down by Kandrok, you fall over, and you are kicked in the butt by your loved ones," she couldn't stand it.

"I don't have time for crap."

Forkis grabbed the girl's arm, so tightly that she groaned in pain, and, dragging her behind him, he moved toward the door.

"I will escort her to her room, sir," Darius offered hurriedly.

"You are to let no one else in," Forkis ordered the sergeant at the door. The man confirmed and saluted.

Jenny and Schindler found themselves in the corridor.

"Didn't I tell you it would be like that? Just goody ... to wish the old man death." The corporal tried to make his words sound neutral and cheerful. He didn't want Jenny to perceive it so, that he, too, was scolding her. "Currently on Cargoo, probably only you and Rei'than have enough courage to tell Forkis directly what you think."

"You aren't helping. I have the father despot."

Darius looked around to see if anyone else might have witnessed this conversation. The guard sergeant for sure, but his face expressed purely professional impassion. Schindler, who had dealt with combat more than once, didn't agree with Jenny, but he didn't want to explain to her that the situation in which Kiritians found themselves could only be improved by brutalism and despotism - he didn't want to upset her more. Nevertheless, he liked the attitude of the girl that she dared to defend her point and tried to change something, even if it was because of her immaturity and emotions.

"You're probably his first child. Maybe he has been living for several centuries, but he has absolutely no experience of paternity."

"What are you talking about? Don't try to change the subject. It's about Kiret and the death achijes. They deceived me. I feel complicit in what I saw."

"Don't worry about Kiret, he'll be fine. Come on, I'll escort you to the room. Can be mine."

She frowned on him.

"Okay, yours." He smiled.

They started walking towards the station of the train running to a welfare section.

"By the way, couldn't you probe the right people before you started creating this exteriorizator?"

"I don't like doing this when you can talk. I also have a resistance to getting into people's minds. Besides, who thought about it then?"

He patted her friendly on the back.

"Well, I can see that you are a decent girl. Damn, Forkis had such an expression when he caught you that I thought he was going to kick you out that door."

Sandstorm snorted with laughter. Darius cheered her up. A bit. When sometime later she found herself in her apartment, she realized that she had forgotten to return the PDA to Kiret again.

14. Escape

She went to bed late at night, staring at the released holographs of planets and stars circling under the ceiling. Sleep didn't want to come as during the last few nights.

When, after four hours of struggling with her thoughts and fidgeting around the bed, her eyelids finally started to stick together, she was awakened by the clink of Kiret's PDA. Curiosity tempted the girl to open the message. It was short, from Forkis:

"Come to the Communications Center. Bring the prisoner."

The seeds of sleep withered instantly. Jenny sat upright in bed like a private after hearing a red-code alarm. She was also worried, just like the theoretical achij, because she could only guess what it was about. Certainly, the news delivered in the middle of the night didn't bode well.

In her mind's eye, she could see the gloomy face of Forkis sending that laconic message. She had noticed more than once that when he was angry, he used short, dry sentences. The thought of her father was immediately superseded by another.

"Rei'than ..." she whispered. "Oh no."

She didn't have to sense - she knew that something bad was going to happen. It was a blessing in disguise that Necron didn't receive this message, whatever he had to do with the avor. Jenny had to get to him first. But what then?

The answer came spontaneously.

She was chilled to the core by fear, as if the air conditioning in the room had broken.

If they caught her, she would be finished. She might even end up like those achijes she had seen from the fighter board - she knew too little of the Emperor to predict his moves. The fact that she is his daughter was unlikely to be a discount tariff.

But she had no choice. She had already lost Necron, but she wouldn't let fate tear Rei'than away from her. Where she would hide him and what the consequences of this mad act would be, she would worry about later. It was necessary to act quickly, even if she still felt irritated after the previous day's incident with Forkis, and therefore didn't think entirely rationally. But paradoxically, anger and fear could be a powerful catalyst, pushing her to act without thinking too much.

She put on hastily a tightened dress, leggings, and flat shoes so that she could move more comfortably. She pocketed Darius' tranquilizer gun.

She looked out into the corridor. It was quiet, dim and empty. Having passed the living area, she trotted toward the station of the train running to Sector D with the palm house. She had already made a preliminary plan to take Tukum with her to unlock the cell. If it failed, there would be a problem, because the guards always had the bars activator with them. Then they would have to improvise.

She thanked Kiret again for choosing not to install surveillance in the nether regions, which Forkis hadn't changed so far.

Unfortunately, there were some people around the car. The machinery factory and assembly room in front of the conservatory had recently been working at full capacity, around the clock. One of the operators Sandstorm was taking the car with asked where she was going so late, so she lied that Aggro had asked her via PDA to bring Tukum a drug for poisoning. She had come up with nothing more credible. The man obviously didn't believe her and smiled understandingly, thinking that she was going on a secret tryst.

In Sector D, she avoided the main corridors filled with people, only once glanced from behind a high-hanging technical bridge at the production hall, where sizable ships and vessels were being shaped from pat-b'itol, and the old ones were being rebuilt. The view was really impressive. She spotted Darius turned into a fighter with a group of people wandering around and taking measurements. In order to gain time, Jenny flew up to the palm house in a skulak taken without question. Her pulse was constantly elevated, which seemed to resonate with the sounds from the assembly room, her sweaty palms trembled. She might have already been late, and Rei'than taken.

She placed the skulak on the ground and entered the conservatory through a stone gate. The night lights were on at this time, only at the gazebos there was a brighter yellow light, but for Sandstorm using soft infusion, both were unnecessary. She took a shortcut, scattering leaves larger than herself.

She had traversed this micro jungle many times, so she had no trouble finding the humanoid jaguars' house. In the glare of the glowing crystals mounted at the entrance, she could see all five through the open door. Tukum slept on the bed, cuddled to Aggroteh's head, while the other kittens lay next to their mother a few steps away.

So, the worst-case scenario had realized.

Jenny hoped to find Tukum wandering outside the cottage at night, which she often did, unaccustomed to the daytime cycle imposed by artificial lighting, or at least not sleeping, cuddled to one of her parents. Then it would have been enough to call her out with gestures or silently 'borrow' for a while. Then the arrows would have turned out to be unnecessary. Did they work on Onkalots at all? Stupid, she didn't think ...

But the bombs went away.

Aware that humanoid jaguars were more organoleptically sensitive than humans, she tried to tread the soil in front of the porch. Jenny could still outmaneuver Q'ualel, whose senses had gotten blunt during the centuries of being with people, but Chimalmat who was the guardian of the temple on H14, had only recently entered the world of 'demons from the stars', completely alien to her.

No wonder then that she woke up without losing her vigilance even in her sleep.

She turned her head and saw Jenny. They both froze for a second.

The Onkalot woman saw the gun in her hand. She knew it - the Kiritians had injected her with an entraser in a similar way. Jenny's eyes expressing remorse completed the well-assessed threat.

"You!" Chimalmat growled, waking Aggroteh and the kittens.

Before she used telekinesis and sent her back, the girl fired, slightly losing control of her hand. The dart stuck to the base of the tail, though Sandstorm aimed at a thigh.

Chimalmat dozed off after a few seconds; Jenny got breathless as she hit the ground with her back.

"Jenny, what are you doing?!" Aggro jumped to his paws.

"Sorry, but I have to," she muttered and fired a second time. She missed, because the Onkalot jumped back and abruptly retracted an arm in the line of fire.

"We trusted you!"

He was hit just outside the door, two paces from Sandstorm, hoping to catch her before she could take aim and shoot a third time. He staggered and fell with his mouth on her shoes.

Jenny's mind was tossed by a colossal sense of guilt as she realized what she had just done.

Tukum's brothers hoofed it into the bushes on all fours outside the building. Surprised, the Onkalot woman was stuck in place, not comprehending what had just happened and unable to judge if Jenny was still her friend or an enemy. The turquoise irises were almost completely covered by the black saucers of her pupils.

Seeing these signs of fear, Jenny ostentatiously threw the gun aside, stood up, grimacing and rubbing her back. As she neared the entrance, the spitting humanoid jaguar girl retreated to the farthest wall.

"Tukum, I'm so sorry." Sandstorm dropped to her knees in front of her, shook her head. Her face expressed genuine sadness. The two brothers emerged from the bushes, then cautiously approached Aggro who was lying on his belly. "I didn't do anything to your parents, they just went to sleep for a while."

The Onkalot girl kept her eyes on Jenny as she gave her a wide berth. She approached Chimalmat, stood on two legs and began to stroke her mother's head.

"Wrong," she managed to say in Kiritian.

"Tukum, I did it because I needed your help. Aggro and Chimalmat wouldn't have been convinced, and I didn't have time. They'll be fine, they will just sleep for a while, I swear. You can see for yourself that your mother is sleeping and breathing."

"She's sleeping," confirmed Tukum. One of the brothers, after examining Aggro, looked at her and lifted a thumb, which he had learned from Darius.

"Only you can help me, you can save Rei'than. They want to hurt him, but you can save him. You, no one else," Jenny tried to influence the Onkalot girl's ego.

And it probably worked. Tukum looked at her with interest.

"You like Rei'than, don't you?"

The she-cat nodded, dropped on four limbs and approached Jenny.

"I just want you to do what you always do. We'll go down the tunnel and you'll open the door to his cell. Then you will go back to the palm house, and I'll hide Rei'than somewhere. Please." The girl folded her hands as if in prayer. "Do you agree?"

To her great relief, Tukum nodded briefly. She let herself be held. Having gotten up, Jenny kissed her between the ears and hugged her tightly.

"Thank you. And now there is no time. Let's go."

The Onkalot girl jumped down on the boards, left the house and started running on all fours towards the well-known hideout. The brothers hesitated for a moment, then followed her.

"You're staying."

They stopped and looked searchingly at the girl in the eye. Sandstorm sighed, capitulated. By chasing the kittens away, she would have wasted another precious minute.

The four were covering a short section of the mini jungle.

They circled the gazebo where the man and the woman were talking and smoking tumbaku, taking a break during the night shift in the assembly room. They glanced toward the trees as they heard noises. Tukum and her brothers deliberately showed themselves in plain sight to make the Kiritians think they were playing, thereby they lost interest in the rustling sounds.

Jenny flashed, unnoticed.

Once inside the cave, the girl turned on the PDA light, which in case of a rush was a better option than infra-vision.

Reaching sector B took place rather dynamically - sometimes the males had to be rushed when they stopped, scared by the change of surroundings. Tukum entered the bathroom first, followed by Jenny. The brothers hesitated, unsure of another place devoid of vegetation and space, but after a few encouraging meows, the Onkalot girl passed through a hole in the wall. The girl didn't even bother to draw the tiles.

They traveled through an extinct corridor.

With her heart beating wildly, Sandstorm peered into the prison. She felt as if she had lost half her weight when she saw Rei'than sleeping on the bed.

The avor awoke to her footsteps and a clang of the lock being opened by Tukum, who then softly jumped onto his chest.

***

Sergeant Major Gareth woke Kiret in the middle of the night. Rudyard had been ordered to bring him to Forkis' office without delay, and as he was of a minor rank, he was unable to answer the question of the reason for the summoning. Nevertheless, it had to be serious - you rarely wake a man at night to give them good ne

Kiret dressed hastily and walked with Gareth to the train that ran directly to Sector A.

Soon they found themselves outside the office of the First Galactic Dignitary.

As Kiret stepped inside, he saw that besides Forkis, also Warfighter was in the room.

"Thank you, Sergeant Major, you can go." The emperor with a fierce expression dismissed the former batab without even looking at him. Gareth saluted and immediately left the room, then walked away.

"How many times do I have to call you?" Forkis turned sharply to Kiret. "And what about this prisoner?"

"What prisoner?" Necron didn't associate, only after a moment he remembered that he didn't have that damn PDA with him. He didn't bother looking for it or getting a new one from the warehouse.

"You got the message an hour ago," Forkis confirmed his suspicions. "Never mind. I invite you here."

Biffter glanced at the general at the presentation table, who was looking at him not very eagerly. He kept an almost contemptuous, serious face; Forkis' expression was no better anyway.

"Here is a video," said the emperor, "from a week ago, captured in close-up shot by one of the few surviving intermediaries near Mars. It wasn't delivered to us in real time, because the transfer activity at the time of sending would have led the enemy to Cargoo as if it had followed a thread to the hank. They waited for the enemy to fly away, which luckily happened. Our intelligence from the Old Zone also included a report."

They both watched the arrival's reaction as a holograph was displayed above the table. Forkis accelerated the playback without receiving losses, as the recording lasted two Terran days.

With growing horror, Kiret watched the offensive - Kandrok's attack on Earth. Several of their ugly, shapeless war shuttles anchored in orbit, out of which, small ships began pouring. These immediately stuck into the atmosphere.

Biffter bit his lower lip to blood. So, they did come back. Though many achijes had told him it hadn't been his fault, but an unfortunate twist of fate that of all possible colonized planets, he had landed with Jenny on Earth, he felt like someone caught committing a crime whose evidence was being presented to them.

"It is still the same." Forkis stopped playing. "Only Wakanda resisted with surface-to-air artillery, the rest of the world didn't have the equipment to counter such a technological might. Figam's communication improvements have not yet arrived on Earth, so we are not in touch with it. It may have been lost for good. I received the recording and the report shortly before I wrote to you. So far, Gareth, me, Velkee and now you know about the attack."

"What were they looking for on Earth?" Kiret asked, with a movement of his lips rather than the voice.

"Only people. They were doing a roundup. Part of the population has retreated into space. They were not pursued, because what for, since avors got what they wanted," the emperor concluded emphatically.

Kiret felt pinned by their gaze. He preferred not to get into what these poor people Kandrok needed for. Besides, he probably knew as much as Forkis and Velkee.

"Will we attack? We'd have a chance now."

"Whom and where?" Replied the general. "Avors flew, it is not known where, they probably ported themselves to a node at a garrison set up on some planet in the Milky Way. They left no thermal trace of themselves, not even the tiniest flux of particles. We might as well toss a coin."

Necron could have sworn his interlocutors shared his dilemmas. Their cold faces seemed to say, "It's your fault, it is you who brought them there."

"So, what are you going to do?" He asked the emperor.

"There were agents on Earth who knew we had the Cargoo hideout. Part of the planet would be able to name and show all our colonies in the Zodiac Universum on a space map. It is only a matter of time, probably a very short time, when avors find out everything they want from the captured. It is enough for them to give them neurocytes and take control of their minds, although they probably have hundreds of other ways to get information. Now we have no choice but to attack their gerha as soon as possible, as instructed by Nimja. This is the only way out. A preemptive attack, by surprise. A suicidal maneuver they don't expect."

Kiret bridled.

"You want to attack Asephor' Cerotis?! We are not ready! We know nothing about this planet and the forces stationed there, or how to find it!"

"We already know where it lies, to within two kilometers," said Velkee. "Cortez extended the formula of Baks' equation, which before, as it turned out, we could only apply to our universe. Now it allows unlimited mathematical exploration of the cosmos, assuming it is infinite. The result is consistent with the data provided by Nacxit. We won't be any more ready, but we can give ourselves two more weeks to prepare, although it is risky. Each day brings Kandrok closer to the discovery of our hideout, and then we are screwed. End. We lie down."

"Then how are we supposed to attack their main planet in another universe, probably guarded as hell, when we can fall over about a tenth of the force, they threw into the Zodiac Universum?"

"According to the Nimja's member's words, they have more troops in the attacked zones," the general continued. "Their planet is practically unguarded because they are not expecting an attack. Nobody has ever attacked them. They believe that there is no greater force in the cosmos than them, excluding the Lightbringer. And as we already know, that's what they called the Nimja member. They built the foundations of their fanatical religion around one of them."

Forkis picked up a figurine of the new devemer model from a shelf and began tapping it against his finger as he walked around the room.

"Before your arrival, General and I discussed an initial strategy. We will not train anymore Kiritians from outside Cargoo, mercenaries and our allies, everyone will get a dissolved entraser, which was not necessary before, because time was our ally. We will therefore shorten the weeks of learning to a few hours. Pat-b'itol technology will also enable us to create new combat machines in two weeks instead of several years. Perhaps it will even be possible to reduce this time to the necessary minimum. The shorter the time, the greater the chances for us. For the attack on Asephor' Cerotis, whole Cargoo would certainly fly out, and we would have to evacuate anyway. There will also be divisions formed, whose task will be to simulate a misleading attack on Kandrok within the Zodiac Universum - although it will probably end in a real fight. This will increase our chances of reaching the main target, which is the gerha."

"What if oderses-allies refuse to accept the entraser?"

"When they see what happened on Earth, they will certainly want to," replied Warfighter. "If this doesn't help, psychological terror will apply, and we will scare them with Kandrok. They will get the enemy into which they can lace."

After these words, Necron fully understood that Kiritians had returned to the old regime.

"How do we get to the site of the main attack?" he grilled.

Velkee rested his hands on the table. Looking at Biffter, he smiled with the left side of his mouth.

"We already know the Nimjan portation technology. Without any intermediary nodes. Directly from A to B. In a version that we can move entire vehicles."

"Doesn't it require an active destination? There would have to be one on the enemy planet."

"It was just the first thing scientists took to debate. I don't know exactly what this is about, you'd have to talk to our Big Three of Eggheads, I understood that porter B doesn't need to be set on the opposite pole before traveling. As the fleet enters Porter A, the pat-b'itol molecules fly many light years ahead to a mathematically calculated destination and produce a second porter in advance. On a planet or in outer space. In the second case, it will look as if we were ending the journey with Alcubierre's drives. We'll appear out of nowhere. Kandrok on Cerotis will fail to react. Of course, the journey doesn't take place in real time. There is some time dilation between the port tunnel and the classic space," the general waved his hand, "regardless of the distance traveled, the perceived travel time will be constant, but I don't encompass it at all. For an ordinary achij it is irrelevant anyway."

"It's an opening comment," announced the Emperor, putting the figurine back. "We have to discuss everything with the created staff and plan carefully. Consider as many possible scenarios as possible, and under time pressure."

From a small amount of sleep, an excess of alcohol, which he hadn't gotten rid of with blood specifics, the executions carried out, and the overwhelming amount of information that was beyond human understanding, Necron collapsed. He had to sit in the chair. Having sighed, he rested his forehead on his hand.

"God." He bent it into a fist and brought it to his mouth. "Things have gotten so weird."

He stared down at the hemisphere of the holographic display, feeling his companion's burning glares at him. He knew that they carefully appraised his every single movement, looking for characteristic textbook signals. They checked how he had received information about the attack on Earth and how he would react when he heard the plans of the blitzkrieg. They really thought he was working with Kandrok, and that he went to the Blue Planet only to do some reconnaissance for an enemy attack later! That was the only reason why he was summoned to the orderly room. Forkis had no remorse for being done out of key matters, and he hadn't decided to keep him close again, as in the good old days.

"Go get the prisoner now and take him to the lab," Forkis was still looking for nuances in his body language as he said it.

"What for?"

"We'll get out of him where the units that attacked Earth are stationed."

"He's been questioned many times before, even by you. I don't think he'll say anything else. He's just a minor soldier, he doesn't know such things. And he certainly knows Kandrok's current tactics and strategy."

Kiret wanted to bite his tongue. He had just made the speech as if he had been defending the prisoner, even if it was facts.

Forkis was irritated.

"We have developed a new, effective method of filtration. It should act on the representative of Kandrok. Bring him without question."

Amazed, Kiret got up and stood before the emperor. Though he was tall and strong himself, he had to look up to meet his eyes. He begged his body in spirit not to show signs of weakness. Over the centuries, they had argued with Forkis more than once, but it had always been innocent arguments. Never dictated by pure anger and coldness like on the last planet of any star system, especially present in gaze. Forkis wouldn't have been angry with him by himself. Did he really believe he was a traitor? What could this be about?

"I'm not your errand boy," growled Necron. "Send Gareth or call a sergeant."

The Emperor raised his eyebrows slightly. He had expected more submission from jaded Kiret.

"Fulfill your emperor's request," he said softly in a toxically polite manner.

Biffter gave him a hard look, turned, and calmly left the room. Psychosis continued. Now those two probably thought they would lower his morale even further if they told him to bring Rei'than, with whom he allegedly kept in touch. He would keep his dignity and wouldn't explain that it is nonsense, but he would also not kill the prisoner if they told him to do so.

He wouldn't allow himself to be a pawn in the game incomprehensible to him.

***

"Jenny?" The surprise awakened the avor more effectively than the icy water splashed on a naked body.

"We have to escape," she said. "They're coming for you."

He didn't ask questions, because it was obvious who was going to take him and what for. There was only one enemy.

"How do you know that?"

"Kiret had lost the PDA I found and that's where I saw the order. Tukum, unlock."

The Onkalot child, sitting at the girl's leg, looked at the lock and turned it off immediately.

Jenny threw herself in Rei'than's arms, and he hugged her uncertainly. He could feel the intense pounding of the young heart against his chest, and his was not weaker, but for different reasons. He smiled slyly, which the girl didn't see.

At last! He had been waiting for this moment for so long!

"Rei, it hurts," he heard the whisper. Thinking about his regained freedom, he squeezed Sandstorm too tight.

"Sorry." He stepped back. He noticed that two more kittens were shyly entering the room.

"Is this your army?"

The girl turned away.

"They have followed me themselves. I didn't have time to do anything with them. I'm compromised at this base. While walking for Tukum, I had to put her parents to sleep, who saw everything. I can't explain it away. But it doesn't matter. We must hide you somewhere," she said anxiously. "Forkis will kill you this time. The scientists have new ways to get all the necessary information out of you, then they won't need you alive anymore."

"Wait." He didn't move as she tugged his hand toward the exit. She looked at him questioningly, and he at her. His eyes with tiny pupils seemed scarier than usual, like a portent of doom. "Don't hide me at the base, they'll find me sooner or later anyway. I have to get out of here." He didn't let her gather her thoughts, explicitly asking right away, "Are you with me? Will you help me?"

"Yes," she replied after a brief moment of silence. She wasn't decisive, hesitated, something seemed wrong to her, like a tiny cactus thorn stinging irritatingly somewhere in a pad, which, however, couldn't be seen with the naked eye. She was terribly afraid, but she had no choice but to act spontaneously. Now only she could help Rei'than, and *vice versa*.

They went to the door, looked out into the plunged in twilight, silent corridor. The un-cyborgized avor could barely see in such a dim night light.

"I need to get to the lab. This is important."

"What for?" Sandstorm had more doubts.

"Also, to get some weapons, there's an arsenal nearby. My armor in which I flew to Cargoo, I will certainly not get back."

He spoke quickly on purpose, not letting her collect her thoughts. The last thing he needed now - in the moment for which he had been waiting for years - was that the scared girl would withdraw from the offered support and ruin his plans. He tugged her arm and as he walked, he was using the specks of the meager light of the lamps as landmarks. It would take a while for him to get used to the twilight, but he would still see twice as bad as humans in such conditions. He wished he had a vision booster integrated with the brain.

Escorted by the kittens, they headed towards the gatehouse empty at this time.

They stopped dead as they heard the voices of young Kiritians coming from down the curved corridor. The two people were walking towards them, judging by the laughter and dialogue.

"Gahreka!" Rei'than cursed. From what he had observed many times, achijes carried statutory basic armament, usually X17A4 pistols. Civilians not necessarily, but in this part of the sector stayed mostly soldiers who frequently used a leisure center. If they only saw their duo, they would paralyze them at best; Jenny would also be punished for acquaintance with the enemy. Rei'than couldn't back down and demanded that the girl led him to the mine tunnel she had told him about. He wouldn't have been able to give up and not comply with xepo Thino'pai's order sent into the air - the neurocyte was blocking his free will in the case concerning the super-collectivity. Besides, he would have rather let himself be killed than to be disgraced, and perhaps miss the unique chance of taking over the only human weapon capable of slaying avors.

Jenny wanted to suggest that they could stand behind a bend and put the Kiritians to sleep by surprise, but she remembered that she had lost Darius' pistol somewhere in front of Onkalots' house. She also cursed.

From the problem, they were saved by Tukum, quickly assessing the situation and showing amazing wisdom. She threw out a series of meows from her throat, to which her brothers reacted almost immediately, hesitating only for a moment. They replied something to which the she-cat responded with even more insistence.

"You, stop," she stuttered out towards Jenny and Rei'than as the two Onkalots started running like in a short-distance race.

They were noticed by achijes who was unconsciously heading towards the fugitives.

"Look, the kittens."

"Hey, these are probably the kids from the palm house. Apparently, someone put the big ones to sleep."

Jenny, clearly hearing the exchange, was not surprised. Probably half the base knew about the incident. Sleeping Aggro and Chimalmat must have been noticed by that couple by the gazebo.

"So, what do we do?" The young Kiritian asked his companion.

"Chase and catch them!" The clatter of claws on the metal floor was joined by a stompy sound of footsteps and calls. The sounds grew softer.

Jenny breathed a sigh of relief; the tense avor relaxed his muscles a bit.

"Great idea, Tukum," she said.

They moved towards the arsenal located closer than the laboratories. The door to it was always open, which Rei'than had learned during one of the guards' casual confabulations. Achijes was very good at handling a weapon, there was no theft, no taking it out covertly, or other forms of conspiracy, so there was no point in keeping the object under lock and key. No one, even in a drunken state of consciousness, would have taken seriously the scenario that the prisoner could get out of prison and his obvious first goal would be to get a gun. But they had no idea of Tukum's abilities - and that someone infatuated could free Rei'than.

They both heard the sounds of the pursuit with the Onkalots in the distance. It didn't last long, because after a disagreement over how to stop the little ones without hurting them, one of the Kiritians fired a stun gun. Unconscious Tukum's brothers were taken to a train station.

Rei'than and Jenny managed to hide from a few achijes - in cubbyholes or turning into another corridor - whom the unarmed avor didn't dare to attack.

Unexpectedly, another obstacle appeared in their way, this time unavoidable.

Behind the corner was standing Ryan, leaning his back against the wall and devoutly looking through something interesting on his PDA, thanks to which he wasn't heard. Rei'than, walking in the front, almost collided with him.

In the first second, the three stared at each other, only Jenny inhaled loudly.

In another, the achij reached for a knife at his belt.

The avor was faster than him.

He yanked the tool from his casing and stabbed Ryan hard in the side of his underbelly. He kicked far away the PDA that slipped from his hands.

Scream of Jenny holding the she-cat in her arms, died in the throat.

Grimacing, Ryan grasped the hilt protruding from his body, curled up, propped his arm on the ground, then fell heavily on the metal. Apart from hissing and moaning, he couldn't make any other sound.

Rei'than ruthlessly yanked the blade from his wound, which began to bleed even more. It turned out that the private dressed in civilian clothes had no other weapon with him.

"Killed him," Sandstorm whispered hoarsely in shock. "You killed him ..."

"What have you expected?" The avor said dismissively. "Either I killed him or he me. Besides, I didn't kill, but neutralized him. He will be fine, there are a lot of devoka members hanging around here, someone will find him in a moment, and they will quickly repair his wound. And that's what I wanted," he added in his mind. He would have liked to get rid of this achij, as he had programmed in the neurocyte, but the dead wouldn't have been looked after, and the wounded would always delay the pursuit for a certain time. So Rei'than didn't in any way disturb the imposed scheme, according to which he operated - he didn't betray the super-collectivity, sparing the enemy. Killing was no longer a priority when a living Kiritian could be used ingeniously.

"Come on."

He had to yank the dazed girl. Only now did she realize what she had done, freeing the dangerous prisoner. However, she couldn't run away or start screaming, as she was too afraid of the bloody knife Rei'than was holding in his right hand. Anyway, she chose such a fate herself and had to bear the consequences of her decision - after all, the avor had asked her if she would want to help him voluntarily.

They managed to run and reach the arsenal unhindered. And then an alarm sounded that took over all the corridors of the sector. The dim night light turned to rotating crimson.

Code red.

This meant the slamming of all doors and bulkheads in the area that no one would open without authorization from the top.

The gates to the arsenal slid shut in front of their noses.

"Tukum, could you open it?" Rei'than said politely. The she-cat who liked him, interpreted wounding Ryan conversely than Jenny - that the avor had attacked the achijes, whom she associated with violence and inflicting pain on Onkalots, so she helped him right away.

The door yielded, Rei'than moved it easily with his hand. Tukum slipped out of Sandstorm's embrace and entered the room through the gap.

"Keep nit," he said to Jenny, still unable to snap out of daze.

He didn't have time to rummage around the huge room, so amid the monotonous sounds of the alarm and the rotating red that irritated his eyes, he grabbed from the nearest open closet an energy mitrailleuse with the possibility of spreading a defensive shield. Tukum's help turned out to be unnecessary - as the weapon wasn't of high priority, it wasn't in the blocked part. It hadn't been personalized and could operate in any hands. Rei'than also donned unmarked Kiritian armor; he didn't find a helmet. "It's always better protection than running in medical gear," he thought. He would get over it and endure this filth until he got out of base. The bloodied knife slipped behind his belt.

When he left the arsenal and saw depressed Jenny peering nervously at both ends of the corridor, he sighed and came to his senses. He clasped her to him with his free hand and kissed her tenderly on the lips.

"Don't worry, it'll be okay." Hugging the girl, he stroked her head. She looked at him sadly in the eye, but nothing else could be read from them. It was a good sign that she didn't want to step back. "Now the lab."

She nodded.

They moved, trotting, with Tukum running ahead of them.

Ryan managed to crawl to his PDA and informed the headquarters of the prisoner's escape; got the closest achijes.

On call, came those in the recreation center. They quickly found the intruder. They were surprised to see Jenny with him. Forkis had already given the order: to hurt him, put him to sleep, overpower him - anything, but not killing him yet. The achijes hesitated, not wanting to accidentally harm the girl behind him.

Rei'than took advantage of their uncertainty in a second. He grasped the several-kilogram, eight-barreled mitrailleuse with both hands and began to fire energy puncturing walls.

The achijes threw themselves behind the toughest shields, two of them were hit slightly, the third got shot in the shoulder, so strongly that he was pushed away with impetus. Everyone had the X17A4 pistol, but they couldn't use them against such densely rushing energy. They had come here directly on call, with what they had had at hand, confident that they would easily deal with the problem - they hadn't known that the prisoner had obtained the weapon. The avor cut them off from the arsenal and going to a different sector for equipment had also been problematic in such circumstances.

"Put your weapon down, the sector is secured!" One of the newcomers exclaimed. "We'll finally get you anyway!"

Rei'than switched the weapon's mode before the heated beam barrel finished spinning, a rocket was fired from the small launcher, aimed at the ceiling in front of defenders. The structure didn't endure it, a metal wrapper fell from the ceiling, and after it, tons of rock and earth from the old mine, effectively cutting off the side corridor.

With a jerk of his hand, the avor forced Jenny to run further. The alarm continued.

They passed the first laboratory of no interest to them; at the sight of the mitrailleuse in the hands of the prisoner, the workers raised their arms. They found a blocked door in the vestibule of the second one, the lock turned out to be too complicated for Tukum. Rei'than tried to pry it with a kick, and sideways with momentum, and when that didn't help, he smashed it with hundreds of energy shots.

"Stay here." He showed Jenny an area in front of the devastated door.

"What exactly are you looking for?"

He ignored the girl and started walking.

In this lab stayed more daring scientists responsible for key experiments who had either ignored orders to keep the enemy alive or had been given no instructions. They pulled their guns and, hidden behind tanks, shelves, experimental equipment - anything they could, in general - started firing at Rei'than. Several items flew at him as well. Someone grazed harmlessly his exposed cheek before he produced an oval energy shield in front of him, almost his height, returning projectiles from the X17A4. He couldn't, however, exchange fire in such a position. Cringing behind the cover, he headed for a locker containing hundreds of capsules filled with blue liquid.

There was a Kiritian super virus in it.

An indifferent form.

At last, this memorable moment came.

His time!

He scooped up the metal-puronax object with his free right hand, brought it closer to his face, and looked thoughtfully at the liquid inside. Invisible death. Possible destruction of the organic part of the super-collectivity. However, this time avors, after unknowingly gaining experience in K'otz'ib'aja on Morascrik, would already know how to handle this inconspicuous bioweapon.

Rei'than, who was bombarded in the cover, wanted to withdraw, but after a quick calculation, he took two more capsules. He slipped them into a compartment next to his thigh.

The impact of the stray ricochet damaged a pipe, from which thick, green, acrid smoke began to emerge.

Coughing, Rei'than managed to withdraw to Jenny. He heard the curses of scientists whose priority became now decontamination of the room. One broke through the thick, milk-like vapor, thinking the avor had run away, and fell unconscious on the head, after being hit with the mitrailleuse's butt.

Footsteps and voices of approaching achijes sounded nearby.

"We're running away." Blood from the wound formed trickles on Rei'than's face, flowing down behind the collar of his armor.

"Wait, this way." The girl directed him to another corridor.

Now all that mattered was speed.

The Kiritians who knew the sector were sure that they would eventually chase the fugitive into a dead end like a rabid animal - which they would have definitely preferred to do as soon as possible.

Someone lurked in the alley and as they both trotted, thinking the way was clear in that section, that person jumped out and hit Rei'than in the face with a bracer of the armor. Blood started to trickle from his nose as well, which only increased his rage.

Jenny was frozen for a moment.

It was Kiret.

Just as pissed off as the avor. He managed to snatch the mitrailleuse from him and throw it far behind himself. Rei'than, in turn, grabbed the wrist of the hand holding the gun. Necron did the same with his hand reaching for the knife.

They both started struggling, each holding his weapon. They fell to the ground, one didn't let go of the other, knowing that whoever would gain even a slight advantage, would shoot at the other or stick the blade into him.

Frightened by the fight, Tukum who hadn't been scared off by shooting or toxic smoke before, now did a fade towards the bathroom.

Jenny had no idea what to do. The two men fought each other for whom she had a certain affection. There was no point in yelling to them because they would have ignored her pleas anyway. Separating them by force seemed an even worse idea.

"Give up, you have no chance," Kiret droned, trying to crush the avor's chest with his knee. "The achijes will be here in a minute."

"Are you so afraid of me?" Rei'than satiated the words with a huge dose of sarcasm. Only by successfully provoking Biffter could he dispose him to make a mistake. He was shorter and slighter than the Kiritian, and with prolonged struggle he would surely lose, especially since he had been in the cell for many years and hadn't moved much. "A platoon for one avor? Or maybe a battalion at once?"

Necron didn't succumb to his provocation.

The prisoner used his own blood flowing into his mouth, and with a spit in his eyes dazed his opponent for a moment. Kiret pushed him strongly with his shoe so as not to be wounded in the organ with the knife - unlike Rei'than, he was wearing civilian clothes. He would never have thought that such an episode would happen at night; he was on his way to his cell when the alarm sounded. Like the rest of the achijes, he carried the statutory pistol that had hardly ever been needed in the Cargoo nether regions.

Rei'than rolled beyond the reach of the Kiritian's arms, stood up - and grabbed startled Jenny from behind, holding the knife to her throat.

"Drop the gun or I'll kill her," he growled, looking at Necron with hateful eyes. The effect was heightened by the gore on his face and the red eyes in the glare of the alarm lamps.

He mentally begged the girl not to speak. She must have shared his fears because she was silent, although Rei'than suspected that it was more likely that it was panic which made her speechless. If she had said in a surprised voice something like, "Rei, what are you doing?", she would have been totally finished on Cargoo. Continuing so, at least, once Rei'than had already abandoned Sandstorm before getting into the vehicle, the Kiritians would be convinced that he had forced her to compulsorily help. As a telepath, she would probably resist Figam's probing methods and Aggroteh's psychometry, so she may avoid revealing the truth.

"Stop swinging this boomstick, throw it away! Kick it! Step back! Hands up! Stand like this!" He burbled instructions.

"Let go of the girl," Kiret muttered. He obediently followed the orders, except for raising his arms. He clenched his hands in helpless rage.

The avor, clutching Jenny to his chest, was retreating towards the bathroom. The confused girl lost her understanding of whether her companion was playing or acting seriously, so she preferred in the style of Necron, to execute his will and be silent.

As the men were several paces apart, Kogan, Gareth, Shimizu, Darkoris, Shane, and a few other achijes, already solidly armed with their arsenals, ran out of the parallel corridor. The officers and their subordinates.

Rei'than panicked only for a short breath as nine sights pointed at him.

His mind worked automatically, as if it had been controlled by the neurocyte, though this time he was guided entirely by his free will.

"Kiret, you said nobody would come here!" Rei'than feigned surprise and fear. "How could you deceive me, brother?!"

"What?!" Necron stared at the avor in amazement, unsure if he'd heard well. He turned to the Kiritians who were no less surprised than he was. "Don't listen to him, he's talking nonsense!"

"No, it is he who's talking nonsense!" Rei'than kept going back with the hostage. "He's been in league with me for a long time. He let me out. We had a little argument, there was a fight between us. And now he wants to save his own skin and rejects everything he has done!"

Rei'than achieved the intended effect. Confused, the achijes looked now at their former emperor, not at him.

"I hope you don't believe him!" Necron shouted. "Get him!" He looked pleadingly at Jenny. The avor held her head so tightly that, with her larynx constricted, she could only stare at the ceiling. More drops of blood bloomed on her quivering neck. The only hope for confirming Biffter's words was effectively excluded from this sick game. The girl would have died instantly if she had made even a sound from her mouth.

When Rei'than locked himself in the bathroom, the achijes broke into a run, as if their fossilized bodies had regained the full properties of a living organism.

"What a moron!" Kogan boomed. "He won't get away from here, it's a dead end."

"He did it out of desperation," Darkoris replied, trying to open the door ajar.

"We have to get Jenny back." Kiret leaned over to grab his gun.

"Stop, Mr. Biffter," Shane said with obvious resignation. He didn't like what he was going to have to do. "Withdraw your hands. Don't move."

Necron slowly straightened and looked at the captain in amazement.

"Victor ... Are you crazy?"

More Kiritians were coming up the corridor, also already awake Aggroteh showed up, as well as Forkis himself.

"Where's Tukum?" The Onkalot asked Necron. His sons had been delivered to the conservatory earlier, but they in a stated omertà[2] didn't reveal which way they had gotten to sector B, while Aggro had no desire or time to question them using psychometry.

"Mr. Forkis, we have a problem ..." Shane was about to report back when the Emperor made a sudden gesture with his hand, ordering silence.

"I heard it all over Sergeant Gareth's comm," he said firmly. "Kiret, you're under arrest."

"Are you all crazy?" Necron took a step back as Gareth and Shane approached him, with their weapons raised. "I didn't do anything! You judge the situation, being influenced by only one party's words. It is not the way to act. Rei'than has messed up with your heads!"

"No, Kiret. He has messed with your head," Forkis replied with calmness evoking anxiety. "More than one person has already testified that you cooperate with the enemy. Did they all collude against you too? Now we have living proof that they were telling the truth."

In front of the bathroom, the achijes tried to negotiate with the avor, but their questions and demands were answered by a silence that heralded a not very favorable scenario. They would have smashed the door with their guns without any problem, but they didn't want to hurt Jenny.

A wave of anger flooded Necron.

"Who is spreading such nonsense?! I am faithful only to Kiritians! Stop raving, Forkis! You didn't see the whole incident! There were no witnesses! I mean Jenny can confirm I'm innocent!"

"Jenny's not a credible witness. I have heard that you have a close relationship." The Emperor, unmoved by Necron's obscene behavior, waved his hand towards the achijes. "Lock him in the cell."

"I'm sorry. Gareth positioned himself by regulations behind Kiret's back and aimed the gun at his back.

"This way, Mr. Biffter." Shane showed the direction to Rei'than's prison.

Kiret took control of his nerves, wanted to cooperate and clear up the misunderstanding as soon as possible, so he obediently let himself be led.

From the bathroom side came the crash of a fallen metal door. Everyone looked that way, even Kiret, Shane, and Gareth stopped. Three achijes from the team went inside.

After a few moments, first from the room, emerged Kogan.

"Emperor, no one is here," he reported, knocking the lime and sand off his gloves. "I think they escaped through some tunnel we had no idea existed. The entrance to it is buried."

"Catch him at all costs," Forkis ordered. "The avor stole our super virus. Secure all vehicles. Place people in strategic points. The prisoner can't get out of the base. Kiret," he turned to Biffter as the achij immediately began to obey orders. "If Rei'than escapes, you will be punished with death under the laws of war."

A daze bloomed on Necron's face, he stood wide-eyed, unable to say even syllables in response.

He didn't move until Shane nudged him in the back with his gun.

***

Rei'than was angry with himself for losing the mitrailleuse in such a foolish way, for with it he could have collapsed the beginning of the mine tunnel as effectively as previously the corridor in the sector. After appraising the ceiling, he found that it wouldn't pose a risk of a chain collapse of the rest of the mine.

After he walked with Jenny from the bathroom to the tunnel, he dug up the tiles a bit, destabilized all loose material from the walls and ceiling with knife blows to create a makeshift barricade. He even managed to loosen some boulders and larger rock blocks. Muffled cries of the achijes were heard behind the wall; someone managed to deal with the blocked door.

Jenny watched in silence as Rei'than worked, and when he approached her moments later, she still didn't muster a word from her larynx. The little wound on her neck was already sealed with a clot.

"I'm sorry for the blood and all the fear I evoked in you," the avor said humbly, lowering his head while piercing Jenny with his ghostly eyes. Tukum stood at his feet and curiously peered alternately at them. "But that was the only way I could authenticate the whole show. I had everything under control, I couldn't hurt you."

"I thought it was serious," she said softly in a breaking voice. "I still have doubts ..."

"Well, I don't think I seem as cool to you as I did when I was behind bars." He smiled impudently to ease the tension in his own way. The girl allowed herself to be stroked on her cheek. "Since you're afraid of me, just show me how to get to the hangar. And we will part there, forever. I'll try to deal with it myself, but we have to hurry," he emphasized as the achijes' voices grew louder.

"This way."

The girl overcame fear (now she was more afraid of her father's reaction than the avor), grabbed Rei'than's hand and led him through a straight tunnel at first. After alternately marching fast and trotting several hundred meters, they reached a fork.

"Tukum, but you come back," Sandstorm, gasping for breath, turned to the Onkalot girl, who was still with them, instead of taking the wider path leading to the palm house.

The she-cat just leered at her, then walked into her trench leading to a shaft at the eastern wall of the Sector A hangar.

"Is it this place?" Rei'than asked.

"Yes." Jenny nodded.

He embraced her with an affectionate look.

"Thanks for everything. I can handle it already."

"I'll escort you to the end." Ignoring his reaction, Sandstorm squeezed herself rigidly after Tukum into the claustrophobic oval aisle with clay walls.

Rei'than followed her. As he wore the armor that gave him volume, he was breaking through with considerable difficulty. At one point he even thought he was going to be stuck for good, but he managed to twist the arm and loosen a few tunnel spots with the knife, while his armor, acting a bit like a mine mole, took care of the rest. Louder and louder sounds and echoes came from the corridor - the Kiritians were pacing the mine. The avor calculated that he had at most two minutes of advantage over them.

In the square metal shaft, they advanced single file on all fours until they reached the nearest truss with a net consisting of fine, dense meshes. The light and sound alarm was broadcasting also in the hangar, pouring red layers on them regularly. They saw only a few achijes near the north adit, which meant the pursuit still had to be focused on Sector B - no one expected the fugitive to get into the hangar through the secret passage.

"Remember that fighter you showed me in the cell?" Rei'than whispered in Jenny's ear.

"The White? It's there behind that transporter." She pointed to one of the large ships. "As long as they haven't moved it."

"You mentioned that it was recently modified."

"Yes, definitely the elevator drive and the latest shields invented by Dr. Figam's team were added to it. What else, I don't know. I'm not really interested in this."

"It is enough for me."

The avor, without effort and noise - which was favored by the sound of the alarm - took the grate out of its frame and set it down beside him. He jumped from a height of almost four meters, landing in a crouch. The armor support cushioned the fall somewhat. None of the achijes far ahead turned their head.

When he wanted to wave goodbye briefly to the girl, he realized to his annoyance that she was jumping right after him, so he had no choice but to catch her. Tukum, in turn, jumped out of the opening straight into the girl's arms.

Using supports, machines, crates and loaders as covers, they quickly made their way to the XRS-14 Ghost fighter.

"That's the hardest part right now," Rei'than said. "Better run along now, kid, because after what I do, everyone in the hangar will see us."

He didn't like that Jenny decided to stay. Well, it was her business.

He happily took his last rajithar capsule from the armor compartment. He contemplated it seriously for a short moment - then with a mighty blow of his hand, he smashed it against the rear part of the White's hull.

From the site of impact, a shockwave began to propagate, similar to that present during the collision of a great meteorite with a planet. Gradually, it inevitably covered larger and larger parts of the fighter with the luminous tarpaulin. The pixelated light lasted a few seconds in the area and then faded out. The process, incomprehensible to Jenny, she associated with the production of fighter matter around Darius, but she sensed that it might have been a technology completely different from that of Kandrok.

"What's happening?" She asked.

"Picto-chip infection. This is the second use of a rajithar capsule in practice. It serves us either as a source of food or, in cooperation with the neurocyte, it reprograms a selected unit, adapting it to the operator's requirements on a digital and partially material level. Simply put, I'll take over this fighter from Kiritians."

One of the achij noticed the play of light. He immediately called his colleagues, and the armor-plated, armed group ran towards the White.

The industrial infection process was complete.

"Stop!"

Rei'than hadn't had time to come aboard - he was still standing on the ground when the order was given.

Tukum cringed behind his legs.

Jenny did the only thing which came to her mind to save her friend who was only armed with the knife, or at least she wanted to make a fuss and buy them some time. She stared ostentatiously at the covers of the achijes' helmets, then threw her arms around Rei'than's neck and kissed him passionately on the lips.

"What the ... Jenny?!" One blurted out.

The avor was surprised no less than them. The girl burned her last bridge in this place. The event was witnessed not only by the Kiritians in the semicircle in front of them, aiming at them with their barrels, but also by the mass of others, who began to pour into the hangar from the side of a passage connecting the sectors.

"This is the only way I can save Kiret, whom you falsely accused of treason," she whispered to Rei'than, putting her hand to his face.

He really didn't have time to discuss it now.

"The white, can you hear me now?" The avor silently asked with the help of a neurocyte.

"Of course, sir."

"Diagnosis."

"All systems are operational."

Rei'than breathed a sigh of relief in spirit, at least in relation to that part of the plan. His salvation and the success regarding xepo Thino'pai's order now depended entirely on that enemy fighter. But as always, the machine couldn't be unreliable, at least in the reality known to Kandrok. Nevertheless, the XRS-14 had just become part of that side, the better one, so it couldn't go haywire.

"Kill them all and clear my way. Spare the girl."

Originally, the White, back in the days when it had belonged to the rebels, had been equipped with missiles hidden in the hull, under-wing retractable tamari cannons, rear plasma rifles and an energy cannon that fired from under the nose after a short accumulation of a projectile. This weapon had been preserved, although recently improved to be able to resist diarduk - Kandrok's metal. In addition, Figam, following an idea suggested by Chimalmat, had included in the fighter's armament a defensive kinetic shock wave that could make a mess within a hundred meters, especially protect the pilot from being dragged out, as well as an offensive wave, acting as an improved EMP, which could penetrate the barriers.

The fighter's AI calculated that defense would be better to move the enemies away from their new operator. After a dozen or so warheads slid out of the fuselage, which created the field, an explosion took place. The achijes and lighter environmental items were centrally scattered throughout the hangar. Smaller machines that could fit up to a few passengers also moved. Jenny, who was standing hugged Rei'than, the wave didn't reach.

Sandstorm was horrified by Kandrok's technological possibilities. Was it enough to break the small capsule for the machine endowed with artificial intelligence to change the front in seconds? Without any resistance, without any 'remorse'? Zero and one. Either I belong to them or to the others - what's the difference? So much for the reliability of the Immortals' machines to be sent to the war with Kandrok. It was forbidden to take androids to it, but what about the rest of the equipment using AI? The girl hadn't yet thought about the power of the enemy. In Rei'than, she saw only a wronged creature, a lonely prisoner held by aliens, over whom the specter of death hung every day. Now she realized, as the avor had easily seized the Kiritians' fighter, that she had fraternized with a formidable enemy. Yes, she was afraid of him - but that was probably why he was even more attractive to her. She loved his patience, courage and strength, even his relentless irony.

"Thank you for everything, I gotta go." The girl's thoughts were interrupted by Rei'than, who kissed her forehead and immediately moved towards the invitingly open cabin of the White.

Sandstorm had just realized that she had been his puppet all the time, whom he hadn't intended to take with him from the beginning - she thought that after what she had just presented to the achijes, Rei'than would free her from vegetating in this base, at least drop her somewhere else. She hadn't counted on an effusive goodbye, given the circumstances, but she didn't register any emotions on the avor's part. She felt betrayed and crummy.

Rei'than didn't love her, although he had to admit that this reckless, naive girl aroused his sympathy and he genuinely liked her, as well as her company. All right - he liked her even very much. This fact alone seemed unusual, considering that Jenny belonged to the human species, nevertheless it was inconsistent with a neurocyte program that rejected anything that could harm Kandrok. Rei'than had heard of a case where a woman had saved an avor-castaway, there had even been affection between them, he had even taken her to Asephor' Cerotis - but it hadn't ended favorably for them. Most of all, Sandstorm was Rei'than's pass. Ticket for a one-way journey from here. Bargaining chip. He could have used more of these comparisons after learning them from humans.

Nevertheless, something had inspired him when he already had his foot in the cabin. The girl had after all helped him, and many times. She had taken his time talking to him, visited him without condemning him to loneliness, fed him with stolen better-quality food. Putting her life on the line, she had dared to open the door for him. If it hadn't been for her, he would have been dead by now. The ethics of Kandrok dictated paying debts, though it concerned only its own kind. However, if he did leave her, Kiritians were unlikely to show mercy to her. Maybe they wouldn't kill Sandstorm, since she wasn't an achij and no war law applied to her, but it would surely end up for her with long-lasting suffering.

He looked down at her, holding Tukum to her chest, pathetic, silent, into her sad eyes expressing fear, disappointment and disbelief.

He snorted and shook his head. He slipped onto the fighter's wing.

"Come on." He leaned down and extended his arm with the open palm. "However, I honestly warn you that if I take you to my own, there will be no turning back. I am giving you no guarantee that I will be able to defend you against people more powerful than me."

Scattered around the hangar, the achijes had already bounced back. Not being informed about the last modification of the White, they opened fire in its direction. The newly arrived support also started firing. The fighter activated shields that absorbed the energy of the missiles, which could then be used as power after collecting and processing it. It also protected Rei'than and Jenny.

With no time for common sense and logical thinking, Jenny followed the impulse and accepted the outstretched hand.

The avor helped her into the cabin, it was immediately sealed by a hermetic cover of ultra-puronax, which was also one of the last inventions made to fight Kandrok.

"Leave the planet Cargoo, find the nearest node and use it, but within this galaxy," Rei'than gave the fighter a command using the neurocyte. He was sure that Kandrok members were still numerous in the area of the Milky Way. The strategy from a few huvas earlier, of seeking, enslaving, talking over or exterminating Kiritians should have still applied, unless there had been a sharp change in this direction.

The XRS-14 took off, rose vertically above the floor, then headed towards the exit adit. Before that, the achijes stopped the senseless fire.

***

Though it was almost the middle of the night, Darius wasn't exhausted at all, for he was still accompanied by the emotions regarding turning into the fighter. For the umpteenth time, he recreated in his imagination the space flight as the operator of Parabellum, as well as other possibilities related to the pat-b'itol technology. After a diagnosis that concerned the operation of the machine, its interaction with the operator and Schindler's biofunction while in the 'armor', Darius could finally afford a little privacy. He was leaning his arms on the railing of one of the galleries above the assembly hall of Sector D, sipping water from a cup, and watching the technical staff modifying old Kiritian machines. Also creating brand new ones that literally grew before the eyes, like Parabellum before. The pat-b'itol ball rested safely in his pocket.

Someone sent a message to him. Darius glanced at the PDA and saw that it was Corporal Technician Darkoris, one of his colleagues.

"Hello, Rasmus."

"I've been right thinking that you are awake." The man's accelerated breathing indicated that he was running or doing other intense physical work. There were many voices in the background. "Is Jenny with you?"

"Not at this time. Is something happening?"

"A lot, ignoramus," in other circumstances, Darkoris would have said it in the form of a joke, not unrest. "Forkis ordered to arrest Kiret, apparently he had been in dealings with the enemy for a long time. He helped Rei'than escape, but their plan failed, and they were caught. Jenny was with them as a hostage."

If the PDA had been made of brittle metal, it is possible that shocked Darius would have unknowingly crushed it in his hand. Indeed, alarms rotated in the hall for a while, but Schindler thought it was a recently approved technical signal related to a situation that resembled the red code. However, the hall remained closed, and the staff behaved normally.

"Holy shit, what a hat trick ..."

"Wait, there are new orders." Darkoris went silent for the time of listening to the announcement. "The runaway is in Sector A hangar. He kidnapped Jenny and took over the fighter. I'm supposed to pursue him."

Schindler didn't even manage to drone a curse, but blurted out:

"I'll do it faster."

He made his decision immediately, influenced by emotions just like Jenny a few moments before, when she had decided to shake Rei'than's hand. Holding his PDA in hand, he started to sprint over the truss parallel to the wall of the assembly room. Without apologizing, he pushed aside those who stood in his way.

"Schindler, don't do anything stupid," he heard the corporal technician's voice, which in turn heard his boots clattering against metal.

Darius tucked the activated PDA into his pocket and pulled out the ball of pat-b'itol from the other. During the diagnosis, he had been told to activate and assemble the Parabellum armor many times, thanks to which he had mastered the ability to do it in no time. A few people from below turned their heads towards him or choked on air as he jumped down into a small chasm, having bounced off the gallery railing. He spread his arms.

"Dar, you don't have any orders!" Darkoris' voice was still audible.

A few meters above the ground, Schindler began the flight as the Parabellum, treating the person standing around to a powerful blast.

Through a large air tunnel, which he opened electronically, he got to the hangar of Sector A, and from there he set off in pursuit of the White, which had previously smashed the airlock of the adit stretching vertically through a rocky hill. Desperate, with a firm resolution to save Jenny, he ignored any announcements ordering him to turn back - an organized pursuit was to begin soon, when the best pilots were roused.

"I'll bring her back," he only informed Forkis, who had contacted him from the air traffic control center.

TO BE CONTINUED